P9-AZX-907

Praise for the novels of *New York Times* bestselling author Beth Kery, recipient of the *All About Romance* Reader Poll for Best Erotica

"One of the sexiest, most erotic love stories that I have read in a long time."
—*Affaire de Coeur*

"A sleek, sexy thrill ride."
—Jo Davis

"One of the best erotic romances I've ever read."
—*All About Romance*

"Nearly singed my eyebrows."
—*Dear Author*

"Fabulous, sizzling hot . . . You'll be addicted."
—Julie James, *New York Times* bestselling author

"Action and sex and plenty of spins and twists."
—*Genre Go Round Reviews*

"Intoxicating and exhilarating."
—*Fresh Fiction*

"The heat between Kery's main characters is molten."
—*RT Book Reviews*

"Some of the sexiest love scenes I have read this year."
—*Romance Junkies*

"Scorching hot! I was held spellbound."
—*Wild on Books*

"Nuclear-grade hot."
—*USA Today*

Because We Belong

Beth Kery

BERKLEY BOOKS, NEW YORK

THE BERKLEY PUBLISHING GROUP
Published by the Penguin Group
Penguin Group (USA) LLC
375 Hudson Street, New York, New York 10014

USA • Canada • UK • Ireland • Australia • New Zealand • India • South Africa • China

penguin.com

A Penguin Random House Company

This book is an original publication of The Berkley Publishing Group.

Library of Congress Cataloging-in-Publication Data

Kery, Beth.
Because we belong / Beth Kery.
pages cm
ISBN 978-0-425-26612-0
I. Title.
PS3611.E79B45 2013
813'.6—dc23
2013017133

PUBLISHING HISTORY
Berkley trade paperback edition / November 2013

PRINTED IN THE UNITED STATES OF AMERICA

10 9 8 7 6 5 4 3 2 1

Cover photograph of Pearl Necklace © Tammy Hanratti / Corbis.
Cover design by Sarah Oberrender.

*My heartfelt thanks go out to Leis Pederson for her patience,
guidance, and support as we traveled along this new territory together.
Mahlet, as always, I appreciate your honest, constructive feedback.
A special note of gratitude and admiration to the Berkley art department
for the elegant, sensual covers for the Because You Are Mine series.
And as always, my deepest gratitude to my husband. You are my rock.*

Prologue

Francesca walked out of the dressing room carrying a blouse, jeans, and underwear, pausing when she saw Ian enter the suite. Her fiancé met her gaze, somber as a judge, and locked the door. A smile pulled at her lips.

"I was about to shower," she said.

His eyebrows went up, his bland expression conveying wry disbelief. *You're doing no such thing,* she could just imagine him thinking. Francesca chuckled. She knew what he intended every time he locked that door. His actions would have made her smile—not to mention her heart begin to pound faster—at any time, but today, it made her uncommonly happy. He'd been so preoccupied and worried about his mother's health, tortured that he'd made a wrong decision in regard to her medication and care, convinced there was something else he *should* be doing but wasn't. The care and protection of his mother had been ground deeply into his very bones since he was a child too young to be forced to consider such matters. He couldn't escape the heavy responsibility as a man. Sadly, Helen Noble was making little-to-no improvements. Ian had been making frequent trips to London, crowding his already packed work schedule.

"Lucien and Elise are coming for dinner. We don't have time," Francesca reminded him.

He walked toward her. She wondered how long it would last—that shiver of anticipation she experienced—every time she saw that hungry gleam in his blue eyes and that predatory stalk. They'd been together now for over half a year, and her excitement had only grown. His recent preoccupation and worry only made that need to join with him sharper and more imperative.

"I called Lucien and asked them to come an hour later," he said calmly as he removed the garments from her hands and set them on an upholstered chair.

"And Mrs. Hanson? She's busy making roast beef and Yorkshire pudding."

"She's turning down the temperature in the oven. I told her I needed a nap."

She studied him as he came toward her again. His "lie" to Mrs. Hanson, the housekeeper, was a true one. He looked as arrestingly handsome as usual, wearing a white-and-blue-striped dress shirt open at the collar and dark blue trousers—casual wear, for Ian—but the months of worry over Helen Noble had taken their toll. His facial muscles were drawn tight from tension and there were shadows beneath his eyes. He swore he hadn't lost weight, and his clothes hung on his tall, fit frame as appealingly as ever, but Mrs. Hanson and Francesca agreed that he looked thinner. He'd been trying to diminish his anguish through his already rigorous exercise routines, the result being a leaner, harder . . . impossibly more intense man. She reached up and touched his jaw as his arms encircled her waist.

"Maybe you really should rest. It would do you good," she said as he pulled her against him. A jolt of arousal awakened her body at the sensation of his masculine contours fitting against her so perfectly.

"It would do me much, much more good to watch your beautiful face while you're tied up and helpless," he said quietly before he leaned down and kissed her.

She opened her heavy eyelids a moment later, drugged by his potent kiss and the sensation of his body hardening against her.

"Helpless against what?" she murmured next to his plucking lips.

"Helpless to resist me."

"But I . . . don't . . . want to . . . resist you. You know . . . that," she managed between kisses, her body melting against him as he leaned over her, demanding every existing modicum of her attention. He lifted his head and his hand slid down her arm. He grasped her hand and led her toward the bed.

"The ropes will just reassure me," he replied.

"Ropes?" Francesca asked, dazed. He'd used cuffs to bind her during foreplay and sex, and padded restraints and whatever else he might improvise with on the spur of the moment, including his own hands. But *ropes*?

"Don't worry," he said once he'd led her to the edge of the bed and encouraged her to sit. He leaned down and nibbled at her lips fleetingly . . . but convincingly, Francesca decided. "The ropes are made of silk. Do you think I'd ever put anything next to your beautiful skin that would mar it?" he asked near her ear a moment later, his low, rough voice causing goose bumps to rise along her nape.

She just stared up at him, enraptured by his small Ian-smile.

Less than ten minutes later, she lay completely nude horizontally at the foot of the large, luxurious four-poster bed, her hips at the corner and her torso along the bottom edge. She'd watched in amazement and growing arousal as Ian had meticulously—and knowingly—bound her wrists to her calves in an elaborate, precise design of black silk rope twists and knots. She lay on her back, her knees bent toward her chest, her thighs spread wide. He'd instructed her initially to hold her calves, the pressure of her gripping hands pressing her folded legs into her body. Then he'd begun to bind her, forearms to calves and then calves to thighs.

She was trussed up good and tight, although she was not uncomfortable. Unless the erratic pounding of her heart and the mounting need for friction on her exposed, naked sex counted as discomfort.

She watched Ian anxiously as he returned from the room at the right side of the suite, their private sanctuary—the room that was typically kept locked and contained all manner of instruments for bondage, punishment, and pleasure.

"What have you gotten from your room to torture me with?" she asked teasingly, her head twisted to see what he held in his hands. She saw little, however, with his body blocking what he set on the top of a bureau. He turned toward her, still completely dressed. Her nipples prickled beneath his hot stare as he examined her, as ever his gaze striking her as cool and assessing and blazingly possessive at once.

"*My* room?" he repeated as he came toward her. Her clit twanged in conditioned excitement when she saw the small pot of cream he held in his hand. It was the clitoral stimulant that he always rubbed on her when he was doing something new to her . . . something challenging. Francesca had dubbed it a "wicked cream" because it was known to make her want in ways she'd never before imagined. It was known to make her beg.

"Yes. Who else would the room belong to?" she asked distractedly.

"You, of course," he said, holding her stare and untwisting the cap of the cream. She watched his every move with tight concentration as he dipped a thick finger into the little pot, a dull ache mounting in her by the second.

"You are the only one who has a key," she said as he withdrew his finger and a dollop of white cream. He placed a knee on the trunk at the foot of the bed and leaned over her supine, bound form. "Therefore it is yours."

"I control the room, yes," he said, reaching. She lifted her head off the mattress, holding her breath as he neared her spread pussy, her mouth watering uncontrollably, her nipples tightening into almost painfully hard points. He'd conditioned her body so exquisitely. "But the room exists for your pleasure," he continued. She gasped, and her head fell back as he knowingly massaged the cool cream between her labia and onto her clit. "Therefore, it is fair to say it is both of our domain, wouldn't you say?" he growled softly as he rubbed.

"Oh . . . *yes*," she moaned. Already the cream warmed beneath the hard, agitating ridge of his forefinger. Soon, very soon, it would make the nerves tingle and burn. It would make it so that she did just about anything to climax. Despite her growing arousal, what Ian meant was not lost on her.

Before they'd met, that room had been for Ian alone, the ecstasy he gave other women a mere by-product of his personal pleasurable aims. He still was the master of that room, but for him to say the room was *theirs* was special, and she was touched.

He straightened and stood, screwing the lid on the pot as he looked down at her with a hooded gaze, his expression hot but also vaguely frustrated.

"Why do you look at me like that?" Francesca whispered.

His nostrils flared slightly and he turned away. "I was thinking there is nothing more beautiful than you on the face of the earth," he replied, his back still turned to her. "And that . . ."

"What?" she prompted when he faded off as he picked up some items on the bureau.

He turned and walked toward her, and for once she was so preoccupied by his intensity and what he was telling her, she didn't immediately try to ascertain what was in his hand or determine what he planned to do to her, like she normally would.

"Ian?"

"I wish I could . . ." He paused, his gaze once again trailing over her from face to bound legs and arms. "Keep you with me always," he said after a moment. He came toward her.

"I am with you always," she said. Sensing his dark mood, however, she strained to lighten the moment. "Just try to get rid of me, and you'll discover how hard it is to escape."

He gave her a swift smile. "It would be an utter impossibility for me to escape you." She opened her mouth to continue the conversation—she sensed it was important—but he sidetracked her by setting the items he carried on the bed and reaching between her thighs. He rubbed her clit with a quick, expert touch. She gasped. She'd always wondered at the fact that he touched her even more knowingly than she touched herself, as if he were inside her head and could feel what she did.

"Is the cream starting to work?" he murmured.

"You know it is," she accused between gritted teeth. He met her eyes and she felt his smile all the way in the pit of her stomach. God, she loved him so much. Sometimes she worried he didn't realize how much . . .

"I'm going to put something into your ass," he said quietly, still rubbing her clitoris.

"Okay," she said, sensing the pointedness of his comment, but not the significance. He didn't use plugs on her all the time, but it was certainly one aspect of their sex play with which she was familiar. He must have noticed her slight confusion, because he pulled his hand away—making her whimper in protest at his absence—and reached for something on the bed.

"This," he said, holding up a four-inch plug with a base. It wasn't that different than ones he'd used on her before, with one exception. The base and the plug itself were completely transparent.

"Is it all right?" he prompted.

"Yes," she replied without hesitation, even though she blushed.

Something leapt into his blue eyes . . . something she cherished. He quickly lubricated the clear plug. He watched her face as he carefully inserted it. She moaned softly and bit her lip. The stimulation of her anus seemed to make the clit cream go into full action. She tingled and burned. He pressed until the base came into contact with her skin. She felt beads of sweat pop onto her upper lip.

She jumped when Ian abruptly shoved the heavy wooden trunk away from the foot of the bed and leaned down over her. The tip of his tongue flicked over the top of her lip, gathering her sweat, before he kissed her with barely restrained passion.

"I have never loved anything or anyone the way I do you," he said gruffly when he sealed their kiss.

"I love you, too," she whispered feelingly. A shudder of pleasure went through her as his fingertips found their way beneath her bent knee and he began to finesse a nipple. He put his hand on her shin, gently pushing her knee toward the other one, exposing her breast. His dark head lowered. She stared up blindly at the elaborate crystal chandelier over the bed as he kissed the nipple with warm, firm lips before he took it into his mouth and sucked, sometimes gently . . . sometimes not. Her ass muscles tightened reflexively around the plug and her clit pinched in achy pleasure. By the time he lifted his head, both of her nipples stood at attention, reddened and hard. He gave the left nipple one last gentle pinch. She whimpered in mounting pleasure and he released her.

"Have I ever told you that you have the most beautiful breasts in existence?"

"Once or ten thousand times," she replied.

"They deserve even greater praise."

The air between her spread thighs seemed to lick at the moisture gathering there. She watched, her breath coming erratically, as he straightened. Her heart lurched in excitement when he began to unbuckle his belt. When he'd lowered the zipper, he reached into his white boxer briefs and removed his cock, releasing the long, thick, veined shaft so that the base fell against the waistband of the briefs. His penis bobbed before settling, the heavy, swollen head causing it to fall at a slightly downward angle as it protruded from his body. Her mouth watered instinctively. Her pussy became even damper.

The sight of his cock had once both intimidated and aroused her. After months of making love with Ian, however, only excitement remained.

As if he knew precisely the reaction he was giving her, he stepped closer to her face and pressed his thighs against the bed. She turned her cheek against the edge of the mattress and opened her lips. He leaned closer and delved his fingers into her hair. She no longer needed him to direct her to meet his need. Not in this, she didn't.

She strained her head, bathing his warm, rigid length with her tongue. He tightened his hold in her hair and she took the fleshy, firm crown into her mouth, her lips stretching around it, squeezing him. She gave the slit a firm polish with her tongue, making his fingers tighten in her hair, before she slid the shaft into her mouth and sucked.

"Jesus, that's good," she heard him say roughly from above her as he pulsed his cock in and out of her mouth. "You always seem so hungry for it . . . as hungry for me as I am for you."

Her increased fervor was an assurance that what he said was true. After a moment, she closed her eyes and let him have control, trusting in him completely. Her attention narrowed to a concentrated channel, every sense pinpointed on him—his familiar, delicious taste and scent, the arousing texture of his cock, how his flesh became even more rigid and swollen with every thrust and draw of her clamping mouth. She loved the way his fist tightened in her hair, his unspoken demands not harsh, necessarily, but as always, unapologetically firm. Ian relished in pleasure, and she'd come to adore giving it to him without reservation.

The cream had gone into full action on her clit, making nerves sizzle and burn. The pressure of the plug in her ass added a primal, dark edge to her arousal. She was bound and couldn't relieve the swelling ache in her, and that made her pleasuring of Ian more desperate and wild. He'd become a part of her in the past months, his pleasure her own.

Her excitement mounted as his thrusts into her mouth came faster and his cock swelled. She strove to take him deeper and succeeded, her reward his rough, slightly stunned groan of pleasure.

"No," she protested, her voice roughened from his cock when he swung back his hips and his cock slid out of her mouth with a wet sucking sound. His cock was like a drug; his pleasure addictive to her. He loosened his grip on her hair, his fingertips lightly massaging her scalp before he backed away.

"Yes," he said simply, and she didn't argue. She wasn't surprised. He occasionally spent himself quickly, taking her in a greedy rush that she loved because it betrayed the depths of the desire of a man whose self-control was legend. Typically, however, he drew things out, drowning her in pleasure and excitement, making their need mount to unbearable levels, building the fire so that when climax came, it was explosive. This evening, she sensed his need to hold on to her for as long as he could, to mingle their essences and prolong the sharp intimacy.

She swallowed thickly when she saw him pick up a red rubber vibrator from the bed. It was new, one he'd never used on her before. The rubber was shaped into an oval loop at the tip, its circumference about the size of a penny. She saw his thumb move, and the tool began to vibrate almost silently. He held her stare as he pressed the rigid, pulsing ring against her mouth, both soothing and exciting the sensitive flesh. Her lips felt feverish and swollen from his earlier strident thrusting between them. She willingly opened them as he moved the vibrator, his actions striking her as more intimate and arousing than she would have expected. She moaned softly as he pressed the vibrator deeper, sliding it against the moist flesh just inside her mouth. Her vagina tightened as she stared up at him in helpless arousal and granted him full, undeniable right over her body.

"So beautiful," he murmured, and she knew he'd seen her submission as clearly as he'd seen her face. "I could look at you forever when you're giving yourself to me."

He removed the vibrator from her damp lips and caressed her cheek tenderly. She turned her face into his palm and kissed the center of it. He made a rough sound in his throat and removed his hand. He once again pushed one of her knees toward the other one, exposing her naked breast, using the wand of the vibrator to stimulate the curving flesh. She bit her lip, trapping her soft cry when he inserted a taut nipple into the vibrating loop and pressed softly.

"Feel good?" he murmured, his gaze returning to her face.

"Yes," she whispered.

And it did. Her nipple was surrounded by the pulsing loop. The mysterious pathway of nerves connecting her nipples to her clit flared to life. She twisted her head on the mattress and moaned, her need growing sharp and untenable.

"*Shhh,*" Ian soothed gently.

She cried out when he parted her labia matter-of-factly and encircled her clit with the vibrating loop. Her cry segued to a groan of ecstatic misery when he turned up the power on the vibrator. She closed her eyes and shuddered at the intense, concise stimulation, her hips twisting on the bed. He placed his hands on the coil of rope at her calf and kept her in place. She had no choice but to accept the distilled pleasure full on.

"Come," Ian said a moment later.

She followed his command to the letter, her bound body shaking in the onslaught of release. After the first, most powerful waves of climax had passed, he removed the vibrator. Her head came off the bed and she bit off a scream when he pressed his cock to her pussy, grabbed her thighs and impaled her with one stroke.

"Oh God . . . *Ian,*" she gasped as she continued to climax around his penis. The sudden intrusion overwhelmed her. It primarily felt wonderful, but it also hurt a little, overfilled as she suddenly was with Ian's large cock in her pussy and the plug in her ass.

"That's right," he rasped as he began to thrust, his handsome face rigid with restrained pleasure. "That's what I wanted to feel. So hot.

So wet," he grated out as he fucked her, and her vagina clamped around him as she continued to come.

"No," she muttered desperately a minute later when he again withdrew from her. She lifted her head, staring at the erotic sight of his heavy, glistening cock poking out from his opened fly and lowered briefs. He often didn't remove his pants completely as he played with her while she was bound. It drove her wild with thwarted longing. It drove her a step away from madness to watch, bound and helpless, as he ran his large hand over his moist, rigid shaft. Her vagina and ass muscles clenched tight. He gave a harsh moan.

She realized he stared fixedly between her parted thighs at her spread pussy and the inserted plug. Her cheeks heated. She experienced an overwhelming desire to cover herself. She'd never felt so exposed to him as she was at that moment. Was she foolish for opening herself to another human being so wholly . . . for allowing herself to become so vulnerable?

His facial muscles convulsed slightly as he stared, the expression somehow speaking of longing so intense, it bordered on pain for him. All of her doubts about her vulnerability faded to mist. In many ways, Ian laid himself as bare during their lovemaking as she did for him.

"Ian," she murmured. He looked up, meeting her stare, and she knew her heart was in her eyes.

"You shouldn't look at me like that. You know what it does to me."

"I'm sorry," she replied.

"No you're not," he said grimly, moving toward her head and unbuttoning his shirt fleetly as he did so. He whipped the shirt over his shoulders. Her stare lowered covetously over bulging, lean muscle. She'd learned over the past several months that when she was bound, her eyes had to take the place of her greedy fingers, making her a keener observer. Since Ian also blindfolded her at times, her nerves, too, had become exquisitely sensitive to his every move and touch. "And I'm not, either, to be honest," he continued. "If I could bottle that look in your eyes, I would."

She was in such a powerful, strangely combined state of both satiation and sustained arousal, it took her a moment to notice his rigid, and yet somehow hesitant expression as he stroked her neck, the sides of her breasts and ribs, making her quiver with pleasure.

"What is it?" she asked quietly, puzzled by his mood.

He didn't speak for a moment, just continued to caress her with his large, warm hand.

"I would like to video you while we continue. Just your face," he added quickly when she didn't immediately speak.

"Why?" she asked, even though she thought she knew the answer.

His expression grew unreadable, but she sensed his turmoil nonetheless. "Like I said, I would bottle your sweetness if I could," he admitted. "Carry you with me everywhere."

Her heart seemed to swell two sizes in her breast. He'd known so much pain in his life . . . been so fearful of abrupt rejection, been primed for unexpected fearful, and even violent, reactions from a schizophrenic mother.

"All that I am is always here for you, Ian," she said softly. "But of course you can video me, if you think it will help . . . somehow."

His averted gaze zoomed to her face. "You're sure? Of course you know it will only be for me. I will guard it assiduously."

She smiled. "I know that. Do you think I'd allow it otherwise?"

His nostrils flared slightly as he studied her. "You think it's an odd request, don't you?"

"No. I don't share your need, but I understand it, Ian. I do," she added pointedly.

He leaned down and kissed the diamonds on her bound hand— the engagement ring he'd given her weeks ago.

"Thank you," he said.

His solemn manner made her eyes moisten. She was glad when he moved away. When he returned to her field of vision, he carried a small video camera. He set it on the bureau and quickly focused it, the lens aimed toward her head.

"It's trained on your face," he said as he approached her again a moment later. She noticed that far from diminishing during the brief absence from her, his erection appeared every bit as firm, heavy, and flagrant. Her love and trust in him made her glory in the evidence that it aroused him to tape her during sex. It was merely another level of intimacy for them to explore. She wasn't put off by his request.

"You know I love seeing you give yourself to me," he said, stroking her hips and then her lower belly, his long fingers inching toward her mons and spread pussy. "This way, I will have the vision always available to me."

"Wouldn't you rather have me in person?" she asked, her cheeks flushing as he teased her, his long, talented fingers tickling skin just inches away from where she burned. She whimpered when he caressed her humid inner thighs.

"I would prefer to have you in person a million times over," he assured, his mouth twitching into a small smile. "What sane man wouldn't want this . . ." he paused, plunging a thick, long finger into her slit, making her inhale sharply. "Exquisite flesh?" he finished.

She was so aroused, she could hear him as he moved in her wet pussy, finger-fucking her. He withdrew and immediately transferred his lubricated finger to her clit, rubbing her so accurately her eyes rolled back in her head and she clamped her lids shut. His innate talent in combination with the clitoral stimulant was almost unbearably potent and precise.

"No, lovely. Open your eyes. Look at me."

She strove to do what he demanded, focusing on his much-loved face. He continued to stimulate her clit bull's-eye fashion. Her lips trembled. He was going to bring her off again very, very soon.

"What do you enjoy better?" he asked unsmilingly. "A vibrator or my hand?"

"Your hand," she said without hesitation, pressing her hips against the divine pressure. "Always your hand. Your touch," she added shakily.

"The video will be the same for me. I allow you to use a vibrator in my absence, don't I?"

"Yes," she mouthed, too overwhelmed with growing arousal to speak audibly.

"But you would rather have me?" he asked, and despite his typical palpable confidence, she heard the thread of uncertainty in his voice . . . of naked need.

"A *million* times over," she repeated his words brokenly, looking into his scoring blue eyes. Emotion overcame her. She clamped her eyes shut, a tear shooting down her cheek, and came against his hand.

She returned from the realms of bliss at the sensation of the plug sliding out of her ass. He was almost immediately there—a fuller, throbbing replacement. He held her stare as he slowly entered her, his eyes a brilliant contrast to his rigid features. The raw intensity of the moment overwhelmed her. There wasn't a spot in her body or soul she wouldn't willingly give him.

"Don't look away," he said harshly when he pressed his testicles against her buttocks and she gasped for air that didn't seem to adequately expand her lungs. He must have sensed how powerful the moment was for her. He spread his hands on her hips and began to fuck her, his pelvis slapping rhythmically against her ass. "Don't ever look away, Francesca."

He sounded almost angry, but she knew he wasn't. It was the intensity of the moment that strained his voice. She merely shook her head, too inundated by the sensation of his cock plunging in and out of such an intimate place, too saturated with love and desire to do anything but surrender. The clitoral cream in combination with Ian's primal possession made her burn yet again. Even the soles of her feet heated and prickled. He spread his hand over her lower belly, continuing to thrust his cock in and out of her. She cried out sharply, her back arching slightly off the bed, when he slid his thumb between her labia and rubbed her clit.

"Oh no," she gasped, hardly aware of what she was saying.

"Yes," he corrected between clenched teeth. "Open your eyes."

She did as he demanded, not realizing she'd closed them as ecstasy mounted. The sounds of their bodies smacking together faster and faster seemed to match the pounding of her heart in her ears. His thumb moved, creating a delicious friction. She was about to ignite like the tip of a struck match. She focused on him with effort, biting off a moan. Sweat sheened his face, chest, and ridged abdomen.

"Tell me you love me," he rasped.

"I love you so much."

"Always."

"*Yes*. Always," she said, her lips trembling as she crested. She felt him swell inside her, the slight pain of discomfort only fueling her desire, providing the edge she needed to come. Her sharp cry was silenced by Ian's roar of release.

A moment later, he fell between her bound legs, holding himself off her with his arms braced on the mattress, both of them still quaking and panting in the aftermath of the sheering storm of climax. A drop of sweat fell in her eyes. It burned, but she didn't blink; the image of him was too beautiful.

"I'll call Lucien and Elise and cancel for tonight," Ian said, his gaze running over her face.

"It'll be too late. They'll already be on their way. Besides, you could use an evening with friends. You always seem to relax and enjoy yourself around Lucien. He has a good effect on you."

His mouth twitched. "I enjoy myself much more around you. And you wouldn't believe how relaxed I am at the moment."

"You know what I mean. You've been under so much stress lately, with your mother being ill." Her grin faded. After a moment of studying him, she reconsidered. "Do you really want to cancel?"

He straightened and slowly withdrew from her, grimacing as he did so. "Yes," he answered honestly as he began to unbind her arms and legs. "I'd rather spend the night with you right here," he said after a moment. He shot her a darkly amused glance as he whipped the rope from around her limbs, releasing her restraints with as much methodical precision as he'd made them. "But I suppose I shouldn't be so selfish. A couple hours spent with friends isn't going to make a big difference in the scheme of things. I'll be back in bed with you soon enough, right?"

"Absolutely."

An inexplicable chill passed over her heated flesh like an invisible shadow, and was gone in an instant. She sighed with relief as she straightened her freed legs and stretched like a content cat.

She hardly thought about her automatic, certain reply until later. Naturally she and Ian would be here together later.

They would be in each other's arms, where they belonged.

Chapter One

SIX MONTHS LATER

"Nothing is certain, is it? Nothing," Francesca said bleakly as she set down the investment and finance section of the morning paper, the headlines exclaiming over the faltering Japanese economy. Her gaze lingered on one headline: *Japanese Conglomerate Hires Investment Banking Firm to Sell*. She bit her lip nervously, jumping slightly when her housemate, Davie Feinstein, touched her shoulder.

"Some things are certain," Davie said with a significant look she endeavored to ignore. She accepted the steaming cup of tea he offered her and gave him a smile as he sat. He started doling steaming pancakes onto their plates.

"Like taxes and your weekend breakfasts. Like your friendship?" Francesca asked, forcing her voice into an airy tone because they were skimming a sensitive topic, and she refused to go there on this bright December morning. *The* sensitive topic: Ian's abandonment of her a half a year ago following his mother's death. But not just his mother's unexpected death, also the discovery of the poison truth about his biological father . . . a truth that had been revealed by Lucien Lenault after Francesca and Ian had made love so intimately that summer evening. One moment, their future had been secure and bright. All of that changed in a matter of seconds by the slashing knives of truth.

And doubt.

She knew Ian had been fearful his entire life that his unknown father had at the very least taken advantage of his mentally ill mother, at worst, raped her. The identity of his biological father had remained a mystery to him, however, until that evening six months ago. That fateful night when Lucien and Elise had come to dinner, Lucien had known he'd been providing a shock by telling Ian they were half brothers, but that wasn't the worst of it. He'd also revealed that their common parent, Trevor Gaines, had been a rapist and serial reproductionist—a man who got a sick fascination from impregnating as many women as he could. The impact of that revelation, along with his mother's sudden worsening condition and death, had had a decimating effect on Ian.

Francesca didn't like to think of that other issue that she'd suspected had been yet another crack in Ian's well-being, the bizarre coincidence that Ian had asked to videotape her during sex the very night he found out his criminal father got his kicks out of taping his conquests and victims. She suspected Ian had made some self-condemning judgments after that, but he'd never given her the opportunity to assure him he was a far, far cry from being remotely similar to Trevor Gaines.

She'd wanted nothing more than to comfort and ease his suffering, but he'd left . . . disappeared without a word to her or a personal message. Gone. The man she had meant to marry, whom she loved more than life itself.

As had become the custom, she and Davie were avoiding the fact that the man she'd been the most certain about in the world had disappeared off the face of the earth, and was determinedly refusing to be found.

"Taxes and my friendship are definitely certain. As for my weekend breakfasts, I'll make them as long as somebody comes to eat them," Davie was telling her, passing the syrup.

"I miss Caden and Justin the most during weekend breakfasts," Francesca said.

"Actually, Justin said he'd try to stop by after going to the gym this morning."

"Really?" Francesca asked hopefully. Davie nodded.

Why did everything have to change? Davie, Justin, Caden, and she had been tight friends and roommates for years. But then she'd met Ian, and her life had taken a course she'd never imagined. She'd spent more and more time in Ian's luxurious downtown penthouse and planned to move there permanently when they married. As one of the wealthiest, most influential men in the world, Ian had taken her to places she'd only dreamed about before and exposed her to movers and shakers not only in the art world—*her* world— but from all walks of life, from business leaders to politicians and celebrities. He'd introduced her to challenging lovemaking, taught her the power of submission . . . turned her body into a honed instrument for experiencing distilled pleasure. He'd transformed her into a more confident woman who was sublimely comfortable in her own body, a woman who fully owned and took pride in her accomplishments and sexuality.

But then tragedy had struck. Ian had willfully vanished. Justin and Caden had both prospered at their jobs and moved into their own homes. When she'd returned to live with Davie full-time in his Wicker Park townhome, so much had changed. She herself had altered; the free-spirited, gauche young woman she'd once been had disappeared, and a more sober, contained, sad and bitter woman had taken her place. Davie had always been there, though, a solid, reassuring pillar in her life. He'd been there to help her stanch her wounds, encouraged her to focus all her energy on finishing her master's program and her painting. Thanks to Ian's prestige and patronage, her reputation had grown in the art community. She was at no shortage of commissions for her work, and had even turned down a few lucrative ones.

Still, sometimes it felt like her life had come to a shrieking halt. She was still disoriented, her brain quivering from the jarring impact of abrupt loss.

She poured the syrup on her pancakes, her attention once again drawn to the newspaper and the news about Tyake Inc. selling because of the Japanese financial crisis. Davie noticed her preoccupation when she began to drown her pancakes. He touched her hand. She blinked and lifted the syrup bottle.

"Is there something in the paper about Noble Enterprises?" Davie asked cautiously, referring to Ian's multibillion-dollar company.

"No, not that I see," Francesca said evenly before she set down the bottle and picked up her fork. She was once again highly aware they'd come very close to the topic of Ian. Ian was synonymous with his hugely successful company, after all. Or at least he had been, before he'd forsaken his position at its head.

She heard a knock at the front door and set down her fork, glad for the distraction.

"Why is Justin knocking?" she asked as she stood, perplexed. Justin, Caden, Davie, and she were practically family, after all.

"I don't think I unlocked it yet this morning," she heard Davie say as she left the kitchen and walked down the hallway. Francesca twisted the lock and whipped open the front door.

"You're just in time—" She halted midsentence when she realized it wasn't her friend Justin standing on the front steps.

"Lucien," she said, shock ringing in her voice at the unexpected sight of Ian's half brother. Just looking at his classically handsome face and dark, tousled hair made her flash back to that horrible night. She vividly saw Lucien's rigid, concerned expression and heard Ian's hollow tone as he'd stared at the photo of his biological father.

My mother. That's why she sometimes acted afraid of me—all my

*life, she'd wince and cower at times at the very sight of me . . . because
I looked so much like him. Because I had the face of the man who took
advantage of her. I had the face of her rapist.*

She forced the excruciatingly painful memory of Ian's words
from her brain and tried to focus on Lucien. She'd been avoiding
him, just like she'd been avoiding everything associated with
reminders of Ian. It was nothing against Lucien, or his new wife,
Elise. In fact, she cared deeply about the couple. It was just a survival instinct. Reminders of Ian cut too deep.

Lucien's nostrils flared slightly as he studied her somberly, his
sharp, assessing gray-eyed stare reminding her uncomfortably of a
blue-eyed one.

"I'm sorry to invade your privacy," he said quietly in his rich,
French-accented voice. "But it's very important that we speak."

Her heart sunk sickeningly. "Is it Ian? Is he all right?" she asked,
shivers of dread crawling across her skin.

"I still haven't heard from him. From what I understand from his
infrequent communications with Lin, he's fine. Alive and function-
ing anyway," Lucien added under his breath, referring to Ian's talented executive assistant, Lin Soong. His mouth pulled tight in
what Francesca thought was concern . . . or was it anger? She knew
Lucien didn't agree with his brother's self-imposed exile. According
to Lucien, he didn't have any more of an idea where Ian was than
did Ian's grandparents or Francesca. Lin insisted she didn't know
where Ian was, either, but Francesca wouldn't be surprised if Lin was
lying at Ian's request. Lin was unfailingly loyal to him.

She became aware that Davie had approached and stood near her
elbow.

"David," Lucien said, nodding his head in a sober greeting.

"Lucien, come in. It's cold out," Davie said, urging the other man
into the entryway. Francesca backed up, vague embarrassment striking her when she realized she'd left Lucien standing outside in the
cold. "What's going on?" Davie asked, shutting the door.

Lucien spoke directly to Francesca. "It's Noble Enterprises. We need you Francesca. You know the arrangement Ian made. A unique set of circumstances has arisen. We need to make some crucial decisions."

It felt like the blood rushed out of her head. Dizziness assailed her. She became uncomfortably aware of Davie's perplexed glance of query in her direction.

"What's he talking about?" Davie wondered.

Francesca swallowed uneasily, avoiding both men's stare.

"You and the others can make the decision," she said shortly under her breath to Lucien, as if she thought she could still hide the truth from Davie. From herself.

"We need you to make a decision this large. That's the arrangement Ian made before he left. And you, out of all the members of his ad hoc board, have the majority powers for liquidating assets and making major acquisitions. Noble Enterprises needs you. Ian needs you."

"Is this about Tyake?" Francesca asked, glancing into Lucien's face hesitantly.

"You know that Ian has wanted to purchase that company for a long time?" he asked.

Francesca nodded. Davie and she were usually careful to avoid using Ian's name. Hearing it not once, but several times this morning, felt like tiny missiles piercing her flesh.

"What's this about? Francesca?" Davie demanded.

Francesca's desperation mounted when she saw Davie's bewilderment. "I'm sorry. I didn't tell you because . . . because it seemed ridiculous. Ian walked out on me. He left me—"

"He left you access to a vast fortune, use of all of his properties, and a senior position on the temporary board of directors that he named to manage his company in his absence. I understand why you've refused to acknowledge those things, Francesca. I do," Lucien added more softly, his compassionate gaze paining her more than an impatient or disdainful one would have. "But that doesn't negate the reality. Thousands of people's livelihoods depend upon the health and prosperity of Noble Enterprises. The same could be said of Tyake. You and Ian may not be together, but you, perhaps more than anyone, understood his personal feelings and goals for his company. I believe that's why he left you with unique powers of attorney the rest of us don't have. Ian's grandparents are here in Chicago, as is Gerard Sinoit, Ian's cousin. The only person we don't have available on the board is you, and we're hamstrung without you. I understand your saying you feel ill equipped for this, but Gerard, James, Anne, and myself can provide you a large resource of business knowledge. We'll guide you. Ian's vice presidents and executives have been managing day-to-day operations, with our casual guidance and instruction. But among the five board members, your vote carries the most weight in matters of major acquisitions and liquidations. The time has come when we can't proceed without your involvement."

"If I don't have a place in Ian's life, how can I take a place in his damn company?" Francesca hissed, her anger breaking through her brittle emotional armor. Lucien's face remained impassive, his enigmatic stare trained on her. He didn't say out loud she was being selfish by clutching her resentment, but Francesca imagined that's what he was thinking. Lucien had his own marriage and business concerns to look out for, after all, but he'd made time in his busy schedule to do his part in helping to oversee Ian's company.

She gave Davie a wild glance, all the while knowing her good friend couldn't help her in this. *Damn, Ian.* How could he have walked away from her at the same time he stitched her into the very fabric of his life, into the company he'd poured his blood and sweat into, where he'd given the very essence of himself?

She'd never felt so cornered.

Screw him. He'd forsaken both of them—his company and her, the two things he professed to care most about in the world. She was a wreck he'd left behind. Let his company be another travesty, it was nothing to her. It had once felt like she was burning alive to know he was in pain, and that he'd denied her the opportunity to offer solace. Her grief and hurt at his absence had been so great, her anxiety for his well-being so immense, it'd made a husk of her. Surely she had nothing left to give.

Despite her thoughts, a poignant memory of the last time she and Ian made love sliced into her consciousness.

Tell me you love me.

I love you so much.

Always.

Yes. Always.

"As I said, I understand why you've been determined to stay uninvolved," Lucien said, bringing her back to the tense present moment. "People tend to hunker down when they're in pain in order to nurse their wounds. It's only natural . . . a healing instinct. But I'm still asking you to do this, Francesca, and not for myself."

She barely controlled a shudder of grief. She winced and looked away from Lucien's steady stare. He was speaking of her pain and reaction to it, of course, but he was referring to Ian's as well. Isn't that what he was doing? Holing up and licking his wounds?

"I'll meet with all of you and see what you have to say, but I'm not promising anything," she told him stiffly.

He nodded once. "That's all I ask."

The first heavy blow was seeing Ian's large office, the very picture of masculine, austere luxury, and the familiar corner view of the river and skyline. Her thrumming heart leapt extra hard upon seeing the eager, concerned faces of Ian's grandparents, Anne and James Noble.

She loved Anne and James. Confronting the harsh reality head on that she was no longer destined to be part of their family made breathing, let alone talking, a challenge for several seconds. She just nodded her head politely when Lucien introduced her to Ian's cousin, Gerard Sinoit.

The only spot left at the gleaming cherrywood conference table was at the head. Francesca was forced to take the seat. "Thank you," she said quietly once she'd sat, briefly meeting Lin Soong's gaze as Ian's executive assistant set a club soda with lime in front of her. Lin abruptly reached and squeezed her hand, as always, her genuine compassion and warmth a striking contrast to her cool beauty and polished professional elegance. Francesca turned her hand and squeezed back, thankful for the subtle show of support in these difficult circumstances.

"Lin, you're welcome to stay for the meeting if you like. No one knows more about Noble Enterprises on the face of the earth, save Ian himself," Gerard said kindly.

"This is a matter for the board to decide," Lin said with a smile. "I'm right outside the door if I can be of any help."

Gerard looked at Francesca in the silence following Lin's departure. "We recognize this must be very difficult for you—"

Francesca shook her head once, and he halted. She gave him a weak apologetic smile at her abrupt gesture. "Can we please just get to the issue at hand? What's happening with Tyake?"

Gerard cleared his throat, glancing from James to Lucien. Lucien just lifted his eyebrows expectantly, and Gerard launched into a description of Noble Enterprises' bid for the gaming and technology conglomerate. Francesca listened carefully, studying him as he spoke. His presentation was eloquent, confident, and knowledgeable. She'd never met Ian's cousin before, but knew Ian had called him "uncle" as a child, despite the fact that Gerard was only eight years older than Ian. Ian had only been ten when his grandparents had found him and his missing mother in northern France. When he'd returned with them to Britain, withdrawn and distrustful, Gerard had helped Anne and James to bring him out of himself and know security for the first time in his life.

Gerard looked younger than his thirty-nine years, the white dress shirt he wore along with a herringbone blazer highlighting his fit, muscular build. His hair was a chestnut brown that matched the color of his eyes, but she definitely could make out the slight nuances of a family resemblance. A flicker of annoyance went through her at the automatic thought as she searched Gerard's face.

Would there ever come a time when she didn't compare a man to Ian?

She knew that Gerard was an attorney, although he'd primarily used his legal education to help him manage his investments and properties, which were considerable. He was the owner of a hugely successful electronics firm that boasted lucrative private and government customers. She knew that Sinoit Electronics was one of Noble Enterprises' suppliers, just as Ian provided Sinoit with certain patented computer technology. Ian had told her in the past Gerard possessed a brilliant business mind and had easily quadrupled his parents' inheritance when they had died, passing it on to him at the tender age of eighteen. Gerard was also the heir to James Noble's title of Earl of Stratham, although Ian would inherit his grandfather's properties and fortune. As an illegitimate child, Ian could not inherit the title by law. As a result, the title would fall to James's considerably younger sister Simone's son, Gerard, who was the next male, legitimate descendent of James. Francesca recalled that Gerard was divorced and childless. He was also rich and quite handsome. All of those things had combined to make him one of the most eligible bachelors in Britain. Ian used to occasionally allude, with wry amusement, to that fact that Gerard was an expert at eluding the greedy grasp of a majority of women, while effortlessly seducing the select minority that pleased him. Now, Francesca understood firsthand what he'd meant.

"So as you can see," Gerard was saying in summation, "we are poised to make the necessary move to purchase Tyake. Fast action is required, though. Given the Japanese financial crisis, the owner is desperate to sell. He values quick cash even more than a good deal at this point. I understand from Lucien that you're aware of how much Ian wanted Tyake?" he asked, brown eyes focusing on Francesca.

She nodded. "He made several offers, but they refused him every time. He was always envious of their programming talent. He said Tyake had contracted the most exceptional men and women on the planet before the business community in the West even understood the market. I assume the employment contracts will transfer to Noble Enterprises in the deal?"

"Absolutely," Lucien said, leaning forward, his elbows on the table. "That was a crucial element of the proposed deal."

She transferred her attention to him. Lucien had the benefit of knowledge of his adoptive father's hotel and entertainment conglomerate, and had made his own mark in the hospitality and restaurant industry.

"What do you think, Lucien?" she asked.

"I think we should do whatever we can to acquire Tyake. I think it's what Ian would want. But I'd advise against getting the capital for the purchase through this acquisition loan fund. Their contracts can be trickier than banks, and if Noble should default on the smallest item, there could be a risk of—"

"Noble Enterprises is enjoying robust financial health," Gerard said. "There's no reason it should default on anything." He turned his attention to Francesca. "Time is of the essence here. It could be weeks, even months, before we get enough money by liquidating assets. This acquisition loan fund is willing and ready to give us the capital to buy Tyake now. As soon as we have your word, that is, Francesca." Gerard added with a polite nod and a warm smile. She attempted to smile back, but her lips felt stiff and frozen.

"And I suppose no one sitting here will admit to being in contact with Ian?" she asked, her voice sounding stronger than she'd expected saying Ian's name. She examined each face at the table in turn. "Because that would be the simplest solution: to merely ascertain from Ian what he'd like us to do."

"Francesca—" Anne Noble began, a wretched expression on her lined, but still lovely face.

"We're telling the truth when we say we have no idea where Ian is," James finished for her. He covered his wife's hand with his own in a comforting gesture. "We haven't heard a word from him. Gerard and Lucien are as much in the dark as us. We're all—each and every once of us—both ignorant of his location and well-being, and sick about it."

She sensed the truth of what they'd said, intuiting the couple's misery. With a sharp pain, she realized this was the second time in the couple's lives that a loved one had vanished. Helen, Ian's mother, had gone missing for over a decade before they finally discovered her, weak and psychotic, being cared for by a boy with the manner of an adult, a child forced to grow up far before his time.

"I'm sorry," Francesca said, recognizing she'd lashed out on the undeserving in her anguish. Perhaps she'd even been hopeful someone would confess to speaking with Ian. She looked away from Anne's eyes because the pain she saw there was too much of a reflection of her own. "What do you two think of the purchase proposal?" she asked, valuing not only James's long lifetime of experience managing his own extensive holdings, but also Anne's acute business understanding that came from wisely managing some of the richest charity funds in the world.

"I know how much Ian coveted Tyake, and I agree time is of the essence," James said.

"As do I," Anne seconded.

"Even you would have to agree that quick action is necessary, isn't that right, Lucien?" James asked.

"Yes, but prudence is always just as crucial," Lucien replied quietly.

"We've used this acquisition loan fund before when we needed to make a quick purchase in our own ventures," Anne told Francesca. "They have always been dependable. Gerard has been working nonstop for the past four days to hammer out this deal."

"Thank you for all the hard work," Francesca told Gerard.

"It was nothing. I was more than glad to do it for Ian."

James gave a half smile and glanced at his nephew. "Gerard has always been willing to sacrifice his valuable time for Ian. Remember that motorcycle the three of us put together when Ian first came to us as a boy? You were right about that. It really did help us to bond with Ian . . . make him a little more comfortable in a strange land with strange people," James mused, his expression faraway and a little sad.

Gerard smiled. "If only we could do something as simple now to connect with him. He needs his family now more than ever," he said, nodding in Lucien's direction as if to include him. It confirmed Francesca's suspicion that Gerard knew Lucien and Ian were half brothers. How much else he knew about their father, Trevor Gaines, and Gaines's unsavory history, she didn't know. Anne and James knew the entire truth, but she wasn't sure where they would stand as far as telling Gerard.

Lucien shifted in his chair at Gerard's words. Was he as uncomfortable with all this talk of Ian's family as Francesca was? She was the biggest outsider here, but perhaps Lucien was a close second. True, the Nobles had accepted the painful fate that linked Lucien and Ian as blood relatives, but neither Lucien nor she could claim the intimate bonds of family history that only years of experience and love provided.

"So you're uncomfortable with all this, Lucien?" Francesca prodded gently.

"I'd like to examine our options. As I said, these contracts with acquisition loan companies can be extremely delicate and convoluted. Ian didn't tend to use acquisition loan companies, unless it was in the most extreme circumstances."

"Ian has used them in the past when he wanted to jump on a deal," Gerard said. "I asked Lin earlier, and she assured me it was true on two other occasions when Ian recognized timing was crucial."

"He chose not to use them on dozens of other occasions, and always did what he could to avoid it," Lucien said.

"And there are other options, aren't there?" Francesca asked. "We could liquidate some assets for the purchase?"

"No," Lucien corrected, moving his stare from Gerard to Francesca. "*You* could, Francesca. Ian left the power of attorney for such large liquidations and acquisitions only with you."

Francesca nodded, hoping she adequately disguised how overwhelmed she felt as she studied the four other faces at the table. She tried to imagine what Ian would want. A voice in her head urged caution.

She didn't like that the voice was Ian's in the slightest.

"I agree with Lucien," she said at last. "At the very least, I'd like the opportunity to read over the deal in detail before I decide. Of course, I'll need all of your advice. As you all know, I'm an artist, not a businesswoman."

"We'd be happy to give whatever clarification we can," Gerard assured. He gave James a knowing sideways glance. "Besides, Ian once told James and I that he'd been regularly coaching you on business matters and that you had more innate understanding of financial intricacies than some of his top executives."

Perhaps Gerard had thought she'd be flattered by Ian's compliment, because his smile faltered when he saw her expression. She stood abruptly.

"May I take a copy of the proposal with me?"

"Of course, Lin has one prepared for you," Gerard said, standing as well. He was nearly as tall as Ian. "But we—that is, James, Anne and I—were going to suggest that you stay with us for the next few days. It'll be easier than having you try to get us by phone every time you have a question. We can put in some late nights and plow through the deal together."

"Can you take off a few days from your painting?" Anne asked. Francesca hesitated as she looked into the elderly woman's cobalt-blue eyes. Ian had inherited his grandmother's eyes. "We'd so like to spend some time with you. James and I miss you."

"I miss you, too," Francesca said honestly before she could stop herself. She examined the polished grain of the wood table, waiting for her composure to return.

"I can manage a few days, I think," she said after a moment. "I just finished a piece that was meant as a Christmas gift for the buyer's wife. I was planning on taking some time off until the New Year."

"You'll have to tell me all about your work, and how your final project went for school. I look forward to hearing about everything in your life. We have so much to catch up on, aside from this business deal," Anne said warmly, coming toward her and taking her hand. Impulsively, Francesca gave her a hug, smiling at the familiar scent of Anne's perfume.

"I'd like that," Francesca said.

"Good. Well, that's all settled then. Why don't we get everything we need from Lin and head over to the penthouse? We can have dinner together," Gerard said.

"The penthouse?" Francesca asked numbly.

"That's where we're all staying while here in Chicago. I hope it's all right," James said in a conciliatory manner. "I know that Ian bequeathed the use of his properties to you, but we realized you weren't in residence. And Anne said . . . that is . . . well, that she hadn't been able to get ahold of you to tell you our plans," James said awkwardly. Francesca felt her cheeks warm at his delicate handling of the fact that she'd been ignoring phone calls and deleting e-mails from Ian's grandparents. "Eleanor begged us to stay there instead of a hotel," James continued, referring to Ian's housekeeper, Mrs. Hanson, a longtime Noble family retainer and loyal friend. "Poor lady. She's been quite lonely rambling around that big old place by herself. She misses family. She misses you."

Francesca's throat swelled uncomfortably. How horrible she was, not to have visited Mrs. Hanson or even called. She knew how much the housekeeper doted on Ian. She must be so lonely.

"I look forward to seeing her then," Francesca said, her heart beating very fast. When she noticed Lucien's gaze on her, she knew her anxiety hadn't escaped him.

"Will you be there, too, Lucien?" she asked hopefully.

"I'm afraid not. Elise is returning from Paris this evening after a visit to her parents."

"Please give her my love," Francesca said regretfully, thinking of all the concerned e-mails and texts she'd trashed from Lucien's vibrant, beautiful wife. Francesca's friend. Pain rushed through her as if a floodgate had been opened. She'd even missed Elise and Lucien's wedding.

"I will do that," Lucien said, his brow furrowing. He clearly saw her sudden distress. He quickly strode toward her and took her hand.

"Lucien, I'm sorry—" she began, her voice cracking when he pulled her to the far side of the sprawling office.

"Don't be. I understand. We all do," he interrupted quietly. He glanced at the others, who were chatting in subdued tones several feet away. She swallowed down her sudden swell of emotion with effort.

"It just struck me all of the sudden that I've never asked you about your mother," she said in a thick voice, searching his face. When Lucien had broken his life-altering news that he and Ian were half brothers, one result had been Ian's plunge into darkness. The other, much happier one, was that Helen Noble, who had been Lucien's mother's employer for a period of time, had been able to tell Lucien his biological mother's name and the location of the city where her family resided in Morocco. "Have you found her, Lucien?"

His sudden smile was a familiar flash of brilliance that made her chest ache, but heartened her as well. "Yes. Elise and I located her together last summer. Not only her. My grandmother, my grand-father, an aunt and uncle who both have huge families. My mother never married, so I don't have any brothers and sisters in Morocco, but I have more cousins than I can count. My mother is well. It was a very . . . special moment, meeting her for the first time. She's been to visit Elise and me twice already, and we've made several trips back."

She drank in his exultant expression like a much-needed medicine. Yes, she'd been avoiding the pain by shutting herself off from those she cared about, but she'd missed out on some wonderful things in the process as well.

"I'm so happy for you," she said feelingly. "An entire family—all in one fell swoop."

"It is pretty amazing," he agreed.

"You deserve it, Lucien."

His focus narrowed on her. "Francesca, listen," he continued in a pressured tone. "I'm at your disposal in regard to this deal. In regard to anything," he said pointedly, eyebrows arched. "All you have to do is call, and I'll come by or do whatever you need to make sure you're comfortable making this decision."

"Thank you," she said gratefully. "I definitely will call you after I've read over the proposal and contract. I want to hear about these potential risks you spoke of." She went up on her tiptoes and kissed his cheek. Lucien cupped her shoulder with his hand.

"Are you sure you want to go to Ian's penthouse?" he murmured, for her ears only.

"No," she said. "But if I keep running from my past, I'll never have a future."

Lucien said nothing, his gray eyes looking concerned in his otherwise somber face.

Francesca accepted a cup of tea from Mrs. Hanson with a smile and shoved back a mound of papers.

"It's chamomile. It'll help you sleep. You look like you could use it. I've never seen you so thin, and you look tired," Mrs. Hanson said, her gaze moving concernedly over her face.

"Thank you. You take such good care of me," Francesca said, taking a sip of the soothing, hot liquid, hoping to make light of Mrs. Hanson's maternal worry.

The four of them—Gerard, James, Anne, and she had convened in Ian's large library-office following dinner in order to get down to work. Anne sat near the fireplace, reading portions of the proposal through a pair of stylish glasses, a knitted afghan spread across her knees. James and Gerard sat at the oval table with Francesca, perusing different portions of the contract and pausing frequently to answer Francesca's queries. They never once grew impatient with what she suspected were very novicelike questions. Their kind support humbled her.

"We've been at it for hours," Gerard said, leaning his long body back in the chair and accepting the tea from Mrs. Hanson with a gracious thank-you. He checked his watch. "It's two in the morning. You do look dead on your feet, Francesca. You should rest. We can resume picking this apart in the morning."

"I am a little sleepy," Francesca said, rubbing her eyes and feeling the burn. Mrs. Hanson glanced at her hesitantly.

"I had originally thought to put you in the blue room," the housekeeper said, referring to a guest room with which Francesca was familiar. "But Gerard thought—"

"You're the rightful mistress of this home, so the master suite is yours," Gerard interrupted. "I had been staying in it, but I moved everything out earlier, and Mrs. Hanson has readied it for you."

Anne's head came around sharply. "I hadn't realized that," she called across the room, sounding mildly alarmed. "Gerard, I don't think that's a very good idea."

"No?" Gerard asked, bewildered. He looked at Francesca, realization dawning. "It will only take us a moment to switch. I was only thinking of your comfort. Many of your things are still in there . . ." he faded off.

"Of course you were. Thank you," Francesca said, giving both Gerard and Anne a reassuring smile. "I'm not that fragile. But I am tired. I'll say good night." She stood and went to Anne, kissing her cheek.

She was proud of herself for walking so calmly out of the room.

* * *

She paused in front of the elaborately carved wood door of Ian's suite, memories assailing her. She could see Ian's arresting face as he looked down at her, desire gleaming in his eyes, speaking in a hushed tone.

"You've never done anything like this before, have you?" he'd asked.

"No," she replied, equally as anxious as she was excited. *"Is that all right with you?"*

His mouth had twisted slightly in an expression she'd since identified as irritation at something he considered a personal weakness. *"It wasn't at first. I want you so much, I've had to come to terms with your innocence, however."*

She'd taken that step across the threshold that night into a world of untold emotional challenges and sensual delights . . . into a realm of indescribable love. Her life had changed forever.

And here she stood again, now as empty and bereft as the rooms where Ian had once lived and breathed and loved.

He *had* loved, hadn't he?

Finding the question unbearable, she inhaled for courage and twisted the knob. The door swung open.

It looked much as it ever had: the luxurious seating area before the fireplace, the rare paintings, the decadently rich four-poster bed, the lush fresh flower arrangement behind the couch, this one of white hydrangeas and purple lilies. She couldn't imagine how it all could look so familiar and unchanged, when she felt so different.

Five minutes later, she walked out of the bathroom, hesitating by a gleaming, antique writing desk. Moving quickly, as if she knew she must endure the pain but wanted to get it over with, she opened a narrow drawer. She flipped back a folded square of black silk and stared, her breath lodged in her lungs, at the exquisite platinum and diamond ring. She recalled perfectly how cool the metal felt as

Ian had slipped it on her finger, the sound of his low, rough voice uttering those precious words forever burned into her memory.

Yes, she'd replied simply, the vision of Ian blurring through a veil of tears.

I'm afraid I'm being selfish, he'd said starkly.

She blinked and his image came into focus. *Loving is never selfish. You're taking a risk. Don't think I don't know it. Personally, I think it's the least selfish thing you've ever done,* she'd whispered, touching his hard jaw, wishing she could soften him . . . make it so that he was just a little gentler on himself.

The drawer slammed shut.

She sat on the edge of the bed wearing nothing but the tank top she'd had on under her blouse and a pair of panties. She had night-gowns in the dressing room, but she was too weary to go in there tonight, too fragile to inhale Ian's scent. The smell that lingered there was one she always associated most with him—his spicy, unique cologne, the fresh-laundered fragrance of his dress shirts, the leather from the rows upon rows of shoes, the cedar scent from the hangers and shoe trees.

She'd dare the closet tomorrow. Tonight, she used all her resources just to perch on the bed where they'd slept in each other's arms, whispered endearments, and made love countless times.

It hurt so much, but for some reason, she craved that pain tonight.

She shut out the bedside lamp and hurried beneath the covers before she could second-guess herself. This was *good* for her, she told herself. Therapeutic to confront her memories head on. Maybe after she'd stayed here for another night or two while they hashed out the details of the Tyake acquisition, she'd gain some perspective . . . some freedom for herself. It wasn't unlike visiting a grave, was it? She needed to accept the emptiness of this suite, of this bed.

She needed to let Ian go, once and for all.

Instead of plunging the room into complete darkness, as it usually did when she shut off the light, a luminescence remained. She realized a lamp was on in the distant seating area, turned to a dim setting. She considered getting up to turn it off, but something seemed to weigh her to the mattress. It'd been hard enough getting into this bed once tonight. She'd rather not do it again.

She clamped her eyelids shut, trying to avoid the sweeping memories of sharing the bed with Ian, of his touch, his quiet, commanding voice . . . his mastery over her body. Her skin prickled with remembered sensual memories. Even though she knew the sheets were freshly laundered, she imagined she smelled his scent when she pressed her nose to the pillowcase. She inhaled deeply and made a choking sound, not because she despised the fragrance.

Because she couldn't bear living without it.

He heard the distant moan of misery, saw the movement beneath the bedclothes. He watched, rigid with attention, willing her with all his might to throw back the bedding. She did so with a muffled, frustrated cry.

His gaze traveled hungrily over long, smooth, gleaming limbs, breasts straining against clinging white cotton, pale, frantically moving hands. Dark gold hair tinted with red spilled across the white pillow in a lush, wanton display. Shapely thighs parted. His body quickened in an instant, arousal stabbing at him when her fingers slipped beneath her panties and rubbed. He didn't hear it, but imagined the sigh through dark pink, beckoning lips: a silent siren call. She seemed eerily focused, wild in her mission, straining for release like she might a denied breath. She had tried this before, he sensed—again and again—never to be fulfilled.

Wretched, stunning woman.

The hand that wasn't busy between her thighs moved feverishly over her body, cupping hip, ribs, and breast. She almost angrily shoved aside the fabric. He silently cursed the dim light, wishing to see the pale, firm flesh and large, mouthwatering pink crests more clearly, wanting to feel the soft skin slipping into his mouth, craving to draw on her until her cries filled his ears.

His hand now moved just as avidly as hers between his thighs. Was it his imagination, or had the hue of her cheeks deepened, the color of them a pale echo of her lush mouth and plump nipples? And was that the dampness of tears he saw glistening on the smooth surface? It was so hard to discern with the inadequate eye of technology.

So wild. So desperate. So beautiful.

She jerked down her panties in an inpatient gesture. He paused with his hand wrapped around his swollen cock at midstaff.

Jesus. What a pussy. The color of the hair between her thighs was a shade darker than that on her head. She spread her legs, and he hissed as he inhaled. He focused the camera in closer on the delicate, flushed folds of flesh, his anticipation sharpening. Her fingers burrowed between the sex lips. She parted her thighs wider, revealing pink, wet, succulent flesh. He moaned roughly when she pinched strenuously at a nipple, her clenched white teeth flashing in the dim light as she twisted her head on the pillow. She cried out, and this time, he heard the name.

He jerked in his chair, muttering a blistering curse.

She hated herself for what she was doing, but she couldn't seem to stop it. She needed it—the sharp edge of arousal—even knowing how empty she would feel following the rush of pleasure, even knowing she would have to endure the inevitable emptiness.

"Ian," she called, seeing clearly with her mind's eye his handsome face rigid with lust as he looked down at her writhing beneath his hand. He stilled her for the pleasure, forcing her to take the stimulation in full, undiluted form, never allowing her to squirm in avoidance. He was always so ruthless in extracting bliss from her, always watching so hungrily as she relented to his hand and mouth and cock, seeming to drink in her bliss, as if her pleasure sustained his very existence.

Francesca muffled her cry of surprise, starting in shock when the brisk knock penetrated her thick arousal. Without thinking, she tossed the covers over the wanton display she made upon the bed. Had she locked the door?

"Francesca?" someone called.

Dazed by the interruption—by the fact that she'd so easily succumbed to desperate desire in Ian's bed—she scurried out from under the covers, rushing across the suite like a guilty fugitive.

"Just a moment!" she called.

She had a confused image of herself in the mirror as she quickly washed her hands and donned a robe—rose-gold hair strewn everywhere, her cheeks pink, whether from embarrassment or arousal, she didn't know. She tried to smooth the long, mussed tendrils before she hastened from the bathroom.

Gerard looked very tall standing in the shadowed hallway when she flung back the door. He was wearing nightwear—cotton pants, leather slippers, and a luxurious dark blue robe. She could see the wiry, dark brown hair at the open V at his chest.

"I'm so sorry to disturb you," he said earnestly, his brows slanted in concern.

"It's all right," she said breathlessly. "Is something wrong?"

"No . . . I mean, I hope not." He noticed her bewilderment. "I was getting ready for bed and my guilt over telling Mrs. Hanson to prepare this room for you overwhelmed me. I don't mean to be insensitive," he said, his mouth curving in wry apology, "but I often am, nevertheless. Or at least that's what Joanna, my ex, used to say. I'm overly practical. This is the most luxurious suite, containing many of your personal belongings, and I felt like an intruder in it knowing you were going to stay here as well. I obviously missed the subtler issues at hand. Anne was quite irritated with me. I'm sorry."

"Please don't worry about it. I'm fine," she assured, her hushed voice automatically matching his.

"You're sure?" She was touched by his obvious concern. "I haven't yet gotten into bed. We could still switch rooms easily enough."

She shook her head and attempted a smile. She felt cracked open by these unique circumstances, the very meat of her exposed to his concerned gaze. "No, really. I'm fine."

He nodded once. "If you're sure. I'll let you get some rest then." Her eyebrows went up when he hesitated. "You'd let me know? If there was anything I could do to help? Anything at all?"

Heat flooded her cheeks. She'd thought her performance had been quite good, but Gerard had obviously seen right through it.

"Of course. But like I said, I'm fine."

"Ian always said you were very strong," he said, his gaze drifting across her features.

"He always said that you were there for him," she returned. "I can see what he meant now."

He had a nice smile—easy and unaffected . . . appealing. "I'd hoped to make your acquaintance under more ideal circumstances. But I can't say that I'm sorry to have finally met you. You're everything Ian praised. Good night."

"Good night," she said quietly, shutting the door on his retreating back.

He studied every detail of her face as she succumbed to pleasure, enraptured by her expression of agonized ecstasy, aroused to the brink by her whimpers and sharp cries. He hastened to focus the view tighter on her eyes, and then replaced his hand on his aching, swollen cock. His fist pounded ruthlessly on the shaft, the rigid squeeze as he thrust upward over the swollen head making him shudder and groan harshly. He struggled not to blink as he ejaculated, semen shooting heedlessly onto his hand, wrist, and belly.

He didn't want to miss even a fraction of a second of Francesca's surrender.

She fell limp on the mattress, her knees curling up in a fetal position, panting, her damp fingers clutching at the sheet. It came upon her in a rush, as she knew it would. It always did following climax by her own hand, now that Ian was gone. Tonight her disgust at her weakness was sharper than usual, lying in his bed, replaying memories she knew she should let go. Her misery choked at her throat, seeming to rattle her heart in her chest, pierce the very core of her bones.

How could he do this to me? She hated him for it.

He'd awakened nerve, flesh, and soul, made her feel more alive than she'd ever been in her life, only to leave her alone, a human conflagration cursed to burn incessantly, without purpose . . . without any hope of peace.

Chapter Two

an shoved aside a chifforobe, the action causing a leg to fall off the ancient piece of furniture. It heaved to the floor at an awkward angle. The back panel fell off with a subsequent crash. He coughed as he inhaled the dust that flew up from the floor like a miniature mushroom cloud.

Bloody attic was a menace, he thought furiously, blinking dirt out of his eyes. *All* of the attics were. They were six that he'd counted so far in the gothic Aurore Manor, each at the top of various towers and turrets. This place was a veritable warren of hidey-holes, of dust and forgotten things, of workshops filled with Gaines's oddities and fascinating, patented inventions . . . of occasional perversities that screamed of Gaines's depravity.

A house filled with secrets. Trevor Gaines's lair. Gaines: wealthy aristocrat, brilliant inventor of quirky machines and timepieces, convicted rapist and serial reproductionist. A sick pervert who got his jollies out of having sex with and impregnating as many woman as he could, whether by manipulative seduction or rape.

Trevor Gaines, Ian's father.

He knew from his research into Gaines's history that the police had carted away relevant evidence during a search after Gaines had been arrested for the rape of a woman named Charity Holland some twenty years ago. That's when they'd found two videos Gaines had secretly made of himself raping two women, one of them being Holland. The police hadn't taken all the incriminating evidence, though. Ian was convinced they'd barely scratched the surface of the proof of Gaines's crimes. It had been cleverly hidden from eyes less determined than Ian's. Like the evidence he'd discovered yesterday, for instance.

In a hidden compartment in Gaines's antique rolltop desk, Ian had unearthed neatly maintained journal calendars. Inside the leather-bound calendars, in Gaines's neat, methodical handwriting, had been a list of women and dates that stretched from when Gaines was sixteen years of age to the last entry, when he was thirty-five. Hundreds of women's names had been listed in that journal over the decades. As time went on, the entries became more and more concise and detailed. At first, Ian had thought the dates referred to times he'd seen or possibly had sex with the various women. It took him longer to decipher the markings on the calendars with X's or circles. Eventually, he noticed the common rhythm and came to the sickening realization that Gaines was keeping track of each woman's menstrual and ovulation cycles. Ian had discovered Gaines's plan book for optimizing impregnation.

He hadn't been able to eat for the rest of the day after making that bitter realization.

What could possibly drive a man to such ends? Ian became consumed by the question.

His hopes for the attic today had been minimally fulfilled thus far. Perhaps the most significant thing he'd found were some letters sent from Louisa Aurore to her son at ages eight, nine, and sixteen years old, respectively—letters she'd sent to Trevor Gaines.

He'd only found those three letters—the sum total of missives that Trevor Gaines had either saved in memory from his mother, or the entire collection that Louisa had ever penned to her son. Ian tended to believe in the latter theory versus the former. From what he'd learned about his paternal grandmother thus far in his obsessive search, she was a cold, heartless bitch. She'd sent Trevor away to boarding school when he was seven after she'd married a new husband. Ian got the impression from a couple of letters Gaines had written to friends that he wasn't unhappy about being sent away. He hated his new stepfather, Alfred Aurore, it seemed, and was highly resentful of his garnering all his mother's attention. As far as Ian could determine, Louisa had ordered away her only child and promptly attempted to forget he existed for ten years. If Trevor had ever experienced any anguish over his mother's abandonment, he'd channeled all of it into his studies, becoming well-known as a gifted student of mathematics, physics, and engineering. He showed a particular proclivity for computerized mechanical objects, patenting his first invention—a clock component—at the age of eighteen. It only increased Ian's bitterness to acknowledge it, but apparently he owed some of his mathematical and business acumen, and almost all of his talent for programming and mechanical ability, to his godforsaken father.

He'd have gladly sacrificed all of it to have an even vaguely normal father. He'd have forsaken all of it to be clean of Trevor Gaines.

After Louisa's second husband died of a heart attack at age forty-nine, Louisa had inherited his entire estate. She was already the heir to the fortune of Ian's paternal grandfather, a man by the name of Elijah Gaines. Her second husband's death was what had precipitated that last and third letter when Trevor was sixteen. *If you have nothing better to do, you may see your way clear of spending Christmas at Aurore. We are in a state of deep mourning here, of course, but that brings little to bear. As you know, I've never given much thought or care to the holidays. You would undoubtedly be happier spending your Christmas as you usually do, in the company of your headmaster's family, fiddling with your silly sprockets and machines.*

Charming, cuddly woman, Ian thought, scowling as he aggressively kicked aside the moldering remains of the shattered chifforobe. Not that he was feeling sorry for Gaines. Not in a million years. Gaines's mother may have been partially responsible for creating a sick psychopathic rapist who clearly hated women as much as he was obsessed with them, but Gaines's crimes far extended past the feeble excuse of a selfish mother.

He scowled, noticing that the collapsing piece of furniture had broken a plank in the flooring. Kneeling, he shoved aside debris with vicious disregard, feeling much of it crumble beneath his harsh hand.

He reached beneath the shattered floorboard and wrenched up on it, the breaking wood sounding like a shot going off in the still attic. He spied something pale in the dim evening light streaming through the dusty windows, his searching fingers settling on elasticized material. From the compartment beneath the floor, he withdrew a holey brassiere, and then a handful of several crumpled pairs of moth-eaten women's panties. He started when a cockroach scurried out of one of the holes, tossing the rotting garments on top of the rubbish heap with a sound of disgust.

A loud, harsh laugh pierced his focus. Ian stood rapidly, taking a defensive stance without thought.

"He liked to take a piece of all of them—all of his ladies," the bearded, hulking man jeered.

"Get out of here, you tramp. How many times do I have to throw you out of this place? I bought this house. It's mine, now. You can't just wander in and out of here like you used to do," Ian said ferociously, charging across the creaky floorboards. He'd like nothing better than to sink his fist into flesh at that moment. It'd be a damn sight better outlet for all of his fury and depression than sorting through the filth Trevor Gaines had left behind from his worthless life. He grabbed the front of the man's dirty overcoat and shoved his large, solid body against the wall next to the staircase, causing air to whoosh out of the other man's lungs. He pressed the ridge of his forearm against the derelict's throat, bloodlust making his heart pound in his ears. Despite the harsh treatment, Reardon managed a rough laugh, his wild amusement sending Ian into a higher pitch of fury.

"Maybe, maybe," Reardon's eyes moved across Ian's contorted face. "Maybe this *is* your home. Maybe you *do* belong here. I know what you are."

Outside the realms of his fury, Ian felt surprise. They spoke English to one another instead of the local French, and while Reardon's voice was rough, his speech was quite refined. The townspeople thereabouts were wary of Ian, but a few newcomers to the area had told him the name of the local outcast who lived illegally somewhere in the Aurore Woods on the manor's property. Ian had chased Kam Reardon out of the country house on two other occasions. At first he'd thought the tramp was stealing from his food stores, but soon realized his supplies hadn't been touched. In time, he'd begun to suspect that Reardon was pilfering electronic equipment and materials from Trevor Gaines's workshop. Ian hadn't realized until now, however, that Reardon could string more than two curses and a grunt together.

"I know what you are, too," Ian grated out, jerking his forearm so that the other man gagged and his head clunked against the wall. "You're a thief and a poacher and a waste of space upon this earth."

"Aren't we all? Aren't we all his nasty leavings, no better than those rotten panties you just found? Just think," Reardon said in choked voice, his eyes gleaming with malicious merriment. "Some of those pretty little things might have been your mother's."

A white-hot fury pulsed through every fiber of Ian's being. He pulled back his fist to strike, but unintentionally met the vagrant's stare. Piercing light gray eyes speared through a slightly grimy, heavily bearded face. Lucien's eyes—

It was as if a pitcher of ice water had been thrown in his face.

He started back, horror seizing him. "Get the hell out of here," he rasped. "*Now*, before I bury you with all of this other trash and burn the heap around you."

Reardon's teeth flashed surprisingly white and straight in his swarthy countenance. "Fitting, wouldn't it be? *Brother*."

Ian winced, realizing he'd betrayed the truth of what he'd seen with his display of acute revulsion. Reardon straightened and brushed off his jacket, as regal and disdainful as an offended prince who wore the finest of coats instead of something that looked like it'd been salvaged from the trash. His mouth curling, eyes burning, he leaned forward. "You should watch out," Reardon breathed softly. "You look an awful lot like him, wandering around this place. People will start to swear that dear old daddy's ghost is haunting this garbage dump."

Ian closed his eyes at the sound of Reardon's heavy boots on the stairs, fighting down the bitter taste at the back of his throat.

Later that evening, he shoved aside an uneaten dinner that had mostly come from a can. He stood to remove the meal from the quarters where he'd been staying and noticed his reflection in the mirror. After a strained moment, he set down the plate and glass on the dusty bureau, his mission forgotten. He peered closer at his image.

When had his two- and then three-day overgrowth become a full-blown beard? When had he gotten that feral look in his eyes? When had he started to resemble Kam Reardon?

Resemble *worse* than Reardon?

You're starting to look like him. People will start to swear that dear old daddy's ghost is haunting this garbage dump.

He hissed, smashing his fist into the bureau and sending the china plate crashing to the wood floor, where it shattered jarringly.

Stupid fuck. Ian was nothing like Trevor Gaines. His entire reason for buying this godforsaken house, for sifting through every item in its rat-warren rooms, was to purge that criminal from his mind and body. It was an exorcism of sorts.

He's in your very blood, a nasty voice in his head reminded him. *You'll never be free of the taint of him.*

His other life—the once methodical, organized, sterile one that had recently been transformed by Francesca, blessed by light and laughter and love—was starting to feel like a dream to him, an elusive memory that he couldn't quite grasp with his clutching fingers. His world was starting to become a watered-down nightmare—not terrifying, necessarily, but dirty and gray, vague and pointless. A personalized version of hell.

"No," he said roughly out loud, his gaze growing fierce in the mirror. He *did* have a purpose . . . a goal. Once he understood who Trevor Gaines was, once he comprehended why his biological father had become so depraved, he could more easily separate himself from the man. There was a method to his madness.

Just be sure the madness doesn't get you before the method ever works.

He snarled at the sound of the sardonic, taunting voice—*his* voice, his own doubts about his mission breaking through the surface. He turned away from the vision of the disturbing image in the mirror.

Just a little longer.

He'd search just a little longer. Surely there was something in this old ruin that would help him pigeonhole Gaines, categorize him like a neat, labeled forensic specimen; something that would allow him to wrap his brain around the enigma of a man that had become like a spear piercing deep within him, its handle broken so that he couldn't get an adequate hold to extract it and allow the wound to heal cleanly.

He muttered a curse and threw himself on the dusty, sagging canopy bed, staring up at the ceiling. His fury had become his constant companion. It was the only thing that ever penetrated his numbness, coming upon him in frightening, savage waves.

No. There was one other thing that made him feel, even here in this gray wasteland: the sharp pain of desire. Against his will, Francesca's beautiful, anguished face rose in his mind's eye as he'd seen her last night on his computer screen, the image rising to torture him. He clamped his eyelids tightly, trying to banish the evocative, haunting image . . . and failing.

As usual.

He did this for her, he recalled with furious desperation. If he didn't exorcise his demons, how could he present himself to her with any honor? How could he offer himself to her with a stained spirit? She was lightness and warmth. Every casual glance she sent his way conveyed more love than he'd ever known, more than he'd ever even been capable of envisioning before she entered his life.

No . . . he wouldn't be set off balance by Kam Reardon, another one of Trevor Gaines's *leavings*. He wouldn't be knocked off his path by his mad half brother.

If you're not like your pervert father, how come you want to do what you want to do this very second?

He grimaced at the silent, sarcastic question. He should get up from this bed, perhaps go for a late-night run. He could delve into more of the research he'd collected about Trevor Gaines, try to connect the disparate clippings of information he'd gathered, looking for a meaningful outline . . . do *anything* to focus his mind away from the computer that sat on the desk.

For the next minute, he remained on the bed, stiff and unmoving, an invisible battle warring inside him. A sweat broke out on his temple at the effort he expended.

Still, no amount of rationalizations and silent bids for self-control could stop him from rising from the bed and grabbing his computer. He was what he was, and this, at least, he could not control or banish. With a sense of grim inevitability—not to mention a wild hunger combined with a healthy dose of self-disgust—he sat on the bed and opened the video.

It was the equivalent of masochistically flailing himself, but he did it anyway, knowing from experience it was impossible to resist the urge. Maybe Reardon was right. Maybe he was like his father.

Moments later, he stared, utterly transfixed by the image of Francesca's sublime face as ecstasy overcame her.

He continued to watch even after he'd climaxed. He received no real satisfaction from his masturbation, but it did make him feel. It was the equivalent of cutting his own skin, one of the few things that penetrated his numbness.

He only roused when his emissions cooled on his belly and he experienced vague discomfort. He glanced at his reflection in the bathroom mirror as he cleaned up, once again reminded of Kam Reardon's nasty insinuation.

Once again thinking of Kam Reardon, period.

Of course.

Reardon was another one of Gaines's biological children. Perhaps his mother had lived somewhere near here. One thing was certain, the people in the local village insinuated that Kam had lived illegally on the Aurore property for a while now. Reardon, out of all Gaines's ill-gotten children, would likely know more secrets and insights about Gaines then anyone. He was bound to give Ian some answers.

He tossed aside the towel and left the suite with a newfound sense of grim purpose.

The next morning, Francesca hurried down the hallway toward the penthouse entrance, eager to greet her visitor.

"Thank you so much for coming," she said when the elevator door opened before she even saw Lucien. "I really didn't want to interrupt, though, with Elise just returning home."

"I figured you might feel that way, so I brought her along," Lucien said, stepping off the elevator along with a stunning blond woman with large sapphire eyes.

"Elise," Francesca muttered, torn between discomfort at her sudden appearance after such a significant break in their friendship and the genuine happiness she felt at seeing her. Elise's warm, gamine grin was, as always, a striking contrast to her elegant beauty. It also went a long way in helping Francesca forget her embarrassment.

"Don't be mad at him. He couldn't shake me," Elise said, eyes sparkling as she glanced up at Lucien. "I latched onto him and wouldn't let him come without me."

"I'm so glad you did," Francesca said, a smile breaking free. The two women hugged. Francesca blinked several times when they broke their embrace and she looked at Elise's beaming face. "I understand you just came from your parents? You must be . . . exhausted."

Elise's lips trembled in amusement. She'd shared stories with Francesca in the past about her . . . *colorful*, trying parents. Louis and Madeline Martin had been a large part of what Elise had fled when she'd come to Chicago, looking for a way to make her life worthwhile. It wasn't always easy for a gorgeous heiress who had been handed every material luxury on a platter to make a meaningful existence, Francesca had learned. With Lucien's guidance and love, and Elise's determination and talent, she'd done just that, however.

"Exhausted is one way to put it. Louis and Madeline always extract their pound of flesh. But how are you?" Elise asked pointedly, her brows bunching as she studied Francesca.

"Fine. I'm fine," Francesca assured. "Just . . . very happy to see you. Both," she added, looking up at Lucien. She looked down, faltering at the sight of their compassionate gazes. "I'm so sorry for . . . you know . . . avoiding your calls. It had nothing to do with you. It was wrong of me. I know that, now that I've seen you two again . . ."

"None of that, now," Elise chastised softly, taking her hand, the naturalness and elegance of her gesture humbling Francesca further. "We're friends. Lucien and I know how much pain you've been in."

"Thank you," Francesca said earnestly, hoping Elise understood the depth of meaning behind the two inadequate words. "Come inside and sit down. I'll get us something to drink."

A half hour later, the three of them sat together in a salon, Francesca in a winged-back chair and Lucien and Elise on a couch across from her, their hands lightly clasped together in a prizing, comfortable gesture. Their commitment to each another was almost tangible to observe. She was glad to see them both so happy, but still . . . her chest ached dully at their steadfast, touching exhibition of love.

After Lucien had finished talking, she set down the club soda with lime she'd been sipping and leaned back with a sigh.

"I see. I understand now what you meant yesterday by advising caution. If Noble should default on even the smallest thing in the contract with the acquisition loan company, Ian's private shares could go into someone else's control." Her hands formed into fists as she thought about everything Lucien had just told her. "You're right, Lucien," she said after a pause. "Ian was assiduous about the idea of keeping one hundred percent of the shares in his company in private ownership. He wouldn't like taking the risk, if it could be avoided."

"Mind you, the chances of a default occurring are very small," Lucien said fairly. "But as opposed to a bank loan, if there was even a slight default, the acquisition loan company could legally take shares of Noble Enterprises as alternative payment. It's happened before . . . and sometimes in hostile takeovers. Not that I'm saying anyone has any underhanded or malicious intent in this situation—"

"No, of course not," Francesca murmured. "As you said, the method is used regularly for quick cash. It might be a viable means to make the Tyake acquisition, if it weren't for the fact that keeping Noble Enterprises exclusively private meant so much to Ian."

"Other companies might be willing to take the risk. The potential consequences are negligible."

"But not in the case of Noble Enterprises," Francesca finished, meeting Lucien's stare. "Not in Ian's case."

Lucien's slight nod of his head told her she'd got it exactly correct, in his opinion.

"We should start looking for the money elsewhere then. No reason to keep putting it off," she said, leaning forward, suddenly filled with a sense of purpose. "Will you come with me and talk to Gerard, James, and Anne? I'll listen to their rebuttal, of course, but now that I understand your caution, I don't think there's much they can say that will change my mind. They probably won't be pleased, after all the work Gerard has done on this. Anne and James dote on him almost as much as they do Ian. I get the impression he can do no wrong in their eyes."

"Of course," Lucien said, helping Elise to stand. "I wouldn't let you face this alone."

She'd been right. Gerard, James, and Anne were concerned about her expressed doubts in regard to the proposed plan and at first argued their points eloquently. But with Lucien's support and Francesca's own reports of past conversations she'd had with Ian about his desire to keep the company under his exclusive control at all costs, she eventually won their agreement. Even Gerard, who had put so much time and work into the proposal, eventually conceded that the decision was hers, and said that he'd follow and support her in whatever she chose. He methodically began to list alternative sources of capital and brainstorm with the rest of the board, his affability making her appreciate him even more.

"We have a lot of work ahead of us, and time is still of the essence," Anne said during a lull in their deliberations. She looked at James worriedly. "And here we are, with Christmas soon upon as and the Anniversary Ball to follow."

"Anniversary Ball?" Francesca asked, curious.

"Yes, it'll be James's and my fifty-fifth on Boxing Day." Anne beamed first at Francesca and then at James, her radiant expression reminding Francesca of a much younger woman. "We're having quite a do the night after Christmas. Belford Hall hasn't seen a party this big in decades. We usually were in London during the Christmas season," Anne added as an aside to Francesca, who understood her to mean they'd wanted to be close to their daughter, Helen, during the holiday.

"How wonderful. I hadn't realized. Congratulations," Francesca said.

Something seemed to occur to the older woman. "But you'll come! Of course. I wanted you to come all along, aside from all this business, you and—" She trailed off, realizing what she'd been about to say. She gathered herself. "But now, it will be a total necessity for you to be there. The five us should be together while we go through the process of liquidating assets and building capital, Lucien included. It will do you good, Francesca, to get a change of scenery. Belford Hall is a sight to behold this time of year. We'll spend a quiet Christmas Eve and Christmas Day, just family." Her eyes suddenly widened as if she'd been jolted by electricity. "I have it! The perfect plan."

James gave Francesca an amused glance. He was clearly used to Anne's occasional inspirations of genius and had long ago given up trying to stop her while she was on a roll.

"You said you had just finished a painting and didn't have a commission yet for the New Year. You'll do Belford Hall for your next commission," she said, as if it were obvious. "James and I have been considering hiring someone to do a painting ever since our fiftieth anniversary, but we've never gotten around to it. It must have been fate that we waited until now. No other painter James and I know combines the creative depths and knowledge of architecture that you do, Francesca. It's the perfect idea!"

James's amused expression faded to a thoughtful one. "You

know, she's right, Francesca. It's a very good idea. You'd be ideal to do the painting of Belford."

"We want the painting to show the splendor of Belford Hall in the springtime . . . the woods, the gardens. Not a grand painting, like you did for Ian for Noble Towers; an intimate one for our favorite room, where we'll gaze at it night after night," she said, glancing fondly at James. "You could begin with your preliminary sketches of the structure while you visit, and return when things are in full bloom," Anne said, seemingly making plans as she spoke.

"Well . . . maybe. I'll have to think about it," Francesca said, bewildered and set off balance by the turn of topic. She had to admit, a getaway might be just what she needed. She'd never been to Belford, although on several occasions she'd stayed with Ian at his grandparents' home in London while they visited Helen Noble at the hospital. "We did study Belford Hall while I was in school. It'd be amazing to see it, let alone paint it."

Anne took one of her hands. "I'm so looking forward to showing you my home."

Francesca grinned at her absolute certainty, finding it heartwarming to suddenly come face-to-face with an Anne she'd only glimpsed so far: the razor-sharp, unstoppable, warm, charming woman who managed to get the wealthiest—and sometimes stingiest—people in the world to open their checkbooks for her charitable causes.

"And you will come, too, Lucien," the countess insisted. "Not only because of the Noble Enterprises deal, but because James and I sincerely want to get to know Ian's brother better. You're part of our family."

"Thank you," Lucien said, seeming genuinely moved by Anne's request. "But this is Elise's and my first Christmas together. I doubt she'd approve," he added wryly, speaking for Elise, who was in the kitchen with Mrs. Hanson while the ad hoc board met. Elise was a chef, and liked observing and learning from the experienced housekeeper.

"Well she'll come, too. I'd consider us lucky to have that delight-ful, vibrant girl with us. I've met her before today, you know," Anne said as an aside to Lucien and Francesca, a teasing sparkle in her eyes. "Louis Martin's daughter is always a breath of fresh air to any stuffy function. Life of the party, guaranteed."

"If a breath of fresh air means a cyclone of gossip, you've hit the nail on the head as far as my wife," Lucien murmured, his lips twitching to break free in a smile.

Francesca caught Gerard's amused glance and laughed aloud for the first time in what felt like ages.

They all went over to Noble Enterprises that afternoon to meet with various Noble executives and members of the mergers and acquisitions team. They paused only for a brief, very enjoyable dinner together at Catch 35, where Gerard entertained them with family stories. Appar-ently, Gerard's father Cedric had been good friends with James since their early days at Cambridge, and it'd been James who introduced his friend to James's considerably younger sister, Simone. Gerard played raconteur, regaling them with stories about James and his father as young men. He painted a picture of Cedric Sinoit as sort of a cheerful clown, always contriving hilarious, inevitably failed attempts to outdo James. Francesca laughed with them all yet again, the shadows of her grief pushed aside for a few bright, vibrant moments.

The complexities of the acquisition continued to be trying for Francesca, who had to struggle to understand concepts that were second nature to people like Lucien and Gerard. They went back to work until late, putting together the skeleton of a plan that could be carried out methodically even if the board wasn't on-site in Chicago.

By the time she entered Ian's suite again it was past midnight and she was good and exhausted. After she'd forced herself into Ian's dressing room to hurriedly extract a nightgown and change of underwear from a drawer, she realized it was best to be worn out. If she was fatigued, there was less of a chance she would feel too deeply.

By the time she padded barefoot to bed after a shower and her bedtime ritual, she was dead on her feet. Despite her appreciation of her weariness, the sight of Ian's bed and the process of peeling back the luxurious bedding seem to send a jolt of unwelcome adrenaline through her.

She retrieved a book from her purse, determined to escape her ruminations about the business deal, not to mention her evocative memories that sprang up being in Ian's bed.

She reread the same paragraph four times, unable to absorb what the words meant. The sheets felt cool and sensual against her shower-heated skin. She vividly recalled how divine they felt when Ian had carried her from their private room on several different occasions after a round of challenging, intense lovemaking. She glanced at the closed paneled door at the left side of the room. Gerard had stayed in this suite. Had he tried to enter that locked refuge? she wondered uncomfortably. Did he suspect what was on the other side?

Once—even a year ago—she would have dismissed such thoughts as ridiculous. Why would a man suspect such intimate, sexual things when coming upon a locked door? Ian had broadened her horizons, however.

She remembered one evening last March when Ian had tried to explain things to her.

They were scheduled to meet Lin and a new man she was dating for dinner at Lucien's fashionable restaurant, Fusion. Ian had led her into the private room beforehand. She'd followed him with a familiar sense of mounting excitement spiced with just a hint of trepidation. He'd instructed her to strip naked, and then restrained her wrists to the straps that hung from hooks on the wall.

She'd waited in anxious excitement after he'd positioned her, standing with her back slightly bent forward, her knees straight, her spine arched slightly, her feet planted about a foot and a half apart, her bottom protruding, the wrist restraints stretched tight. He'd used a black leather flogger on her—not cruelly, never that— but using the leather straps to awaken and fire the nerves on the surface of her ass, hips and thighs, his dominance over her carefully controlled and deliberate, designed to arouse, not harm. His occasional gentle reminders to maintain her rather awkward position with her breasts thrust forward and her ass made conspicuous for the flogger had not offended, only aroused her.

As always, he'd frequently pause to rub her prickling, stinging skin soothingly with his open palm. Sometimes he'd use a finger vibrator on her clit or massage the tiny bundle of burning nerves with a bare finger in a bull's-eye fashion while he plunged another into her pussy. Closing her eyes in the present, she could still hear his low, raspy voice through her whimpers and cries, telling her how beautiful she was . . . how desirable.

That's right. You're never more beautiful than when you trust me and let go. Come again, lovely. Come against my hand.

Toward the end, after he'd allowed her to climax several times, he'd told her to straighten completely. He'd come beside her and she'd seen for the first time that his cock protruded from his open pants. She'd kept her eyes glued to it as he stroked his heavy, swollen erection and gently used the flogger on her breasts. She could still hear how rough his voice had gotten as he stimulated them, turning the pale globes a pale pink, pausing to occasionally caress and pinch the tips until they were almost painfully erect and sensitive. When she'd been unable to stop herself from coming from the precise nipple stimulation, his need had overtaken him. He'd taken her from behind, his scalding, forceful possession thrilling her.

She loved it when he finally lost control.

Afterward, he'd carried her out to the bed. She could recall how good the cool sheets had felt next to her overheated, sensitive body, so delicious sliding against the hot, prickly skin of her ass, hips, and breasts. It'd felt wonderful to sink into the mattress, even more so when he came down next to her on his side and took her into his arms.

He'd touched her heated cheeks with a fingertip.

"You need a moment to cool down before we get ready," he'd said with a small smile. "You still wear your passion."

"It will fade by the time I shower and dress," she'd murmured, stroking dense, swelling biceps.

"Not as easily as you might imagine. A woman always shows tell-tale signs of good sex. For you, it's far more blatant. You radiate like a beacon. I don't like strangers to see you this way," he'd said thought-fully, still brushing her cheek and brow. "The vision of you after love-making is mine, and mine alone."

She'd laughed softly, not fully understanding him.

"Don't be ridiculous. People aren't mind readers. They can't know what we were doing before we go out in public."

One raven-dark brow had risen. "You're mistaken. Men know. Many of them anyway."

She'd opened her mouth to argue, but sensed he wasn't engaging in his typical dry teasing. "How?" she'd asked, mesmerized by his touch on her face and his somber expression. "*How* do men know?"

"By the amplified color here and here and here," he said slowly, touching her chest, cheeks, and lips in turn. "Even after it fades, it still leaves a telltale glow. By your muscles, your overall level of relaxation, and seeming satisfaction with life. By some indefinable sense of comfort in your body, the way you move and carry your-self . . . your sensual awareness, I guess you'd call it. You show it most here," he said huskily, brushing a fingertip over her eyelid gent-ly. "Your eyes slay me always," he'd said, his mouth tilted in wry self-amusement at his poetic turn of phrase. "But during and after lovemaking, your soul shines out of them," he finished, his small smile fading.

She'd swallowed thickly, moved by his gruff, unrehearsed anthem.

"I can't believe men can really see all those subtleties. Are you sure it's not just you?"

His abrupt smile awakened her body with a jolt. "No. Most men can immediately spot a sexually satisfied woman, whether they put it in concrete, conscious terms or not. We're much more practical than women. We lack finesse as a whole, but in matters that are crucial, we're forced to learn early on the meanings of the subtle signs on the trail."

"The trail of sexual conquest, you mean," she said, rolling her eyes.

His mouth twitched. "Men's goals are simple and blatant enough when it comes to sex, even if the means of pursuing them isn't. Women, now," he mused thoughtfully, still stroking her. "Aren't always so aware of their goals. They're a mystery to themselves, so men have little hope in figuring them out. You're very inward. Secretive. A real conundrum."

She bit her lip to stifle a moan when he put his hand between her legs and gently probed between lubricated labia.

"We're pretty much just like our sexes, don't you think?" he asked, studying her face as he rubbed her slick, appreciative clit. "You're delicate and tucked away. Deep and soft," he muttered, pushing a thick finger into her pussy. "You're an enigma—only giving your secrets away to the worthy."

Her mouth had trembled in combined amusement and renewed arousal. "It's no wonder I can't keep any secrets from you then."

He'd touched his small smile to hers and brushed his groin against her thigh. Despite his recent explosive orgasm, his cock was growing firm and full once again. "We men live much more on the surface." He shifted his hips against her, making his re-arousal obvious. "No chance of hiding *that*, so why try? Can't hide the single-minded, savage intent," he said, his smile in his voice even though she couldn't see it as he kissed her ear seductively and shivers coursed down her spine.

"Hmmm, hard to disguise the beast, no matter the finery," she'd murmured with breathless humor as he kissed her cheeks and temple with increasing ardor. She squirmed beneath his hand, and as always, he firmly held her hips captive, stilling her. He slid another finger into her. She moaned and trembled as he took her mouth in a possessive kiss.

"You make disguising it a complete impossibility, Francesca," he'd said against her lips a moment later. He'd rolled her onto her back and speared her with his cock in a movement that was both graceful and every bit as savage as he'd just suggested.

When she pulled herself out of the poignant, erotic memory, the book was spilled on the mattress, forgotten, her nightgown was up above her breasts and her hand was beneath her panties. She made a sound of ragged impatience and shoved the panties down her thighs.

It was no good. She burned, but her touch wasn't adequate. It would make her come, but it wasn't enough.

It was never enough.

Frustrated to the point of distraction, she rose from the now mussed bed and rushed to the dressing room, her cheeks hot and her nipples sensitive, the crests feeling abraded even by the soft silk of her gown. At the back of one of the drawers that Ian had designated as hers, she found what she wanted: a small, powerful vibrator. She'd hidden it amongst some of her lingerie before she'd vacated Ian's residence.

Within a matter of seconds, she was back in bed, her thighs splayed wide, the vibrator humming as she pressed it to her clit.

Ian had used this very tool on her many times. Sometimes he used it on her while he spanked her over his knee, combining the sting of punishment with the pleasure of the vibrator to optimal effect. Oh God, she'd loved it when he bound her wrists and ordered her over his knee, how she was at his mercy as he caressed her naked body and swatted her ass until it burned. She could feel every nuance of the tension in his strong thighs and experience firsthand his arousal in that position—the leap of his cock when he landed a smack on the bottom curve of a buttock, the way he greedily squeezed her pinked ass and ground his erection against her.

And what he'd do to her when her punishment was finished and she was limp from wave after wave of orgasm . . .

He would make it clear she'd had more than her share of pleasure, and then it was time for his. He'd own her completely, fuck her until she had no choice but to explode again in the midst of his furious, white-hot possession.

It was too much to bear, this brutal, precise remembering, but she had to give in to it, just as she'd always eventually surrendered to him. She flipped the switch on the vibrator to a higher setting and felt the air licking at her wet pussy, her hips thrusting and circling greedily against the precise little instrument. She thrust a finger into her vagina and groaned wildly at the inadequacy of the penetration, wanting more, needing a thick, throbbing cock to fill her, agitate screaming nerves, force her soft flesh into total submission—

Needing Ian.

Damn him straight to hell.

She thrust another finger into the tight channel. Too long. It'd been too long since she'd been stretched and filled and possessed. She was so close . . . so close to relief. She withdrew her fingers to the tips and plunged back into the warm, clamping channel, rhythmically, imagining someone else pleasuring her.

You will come for me now, lovely.

So certain. So firm. She had no choice but to obey.

Knocking at the door shattered her fantasy.

She froze, gasping for air. Her pussy burned and throbbed with impending climax. Someone rapped firmly on the door to the suite once again. She arose from the bed rapidly, her legs feeling weak.

She tossed the vibrator that glistened with her juices beneath the sheets and scurried toward the door.

"Who is it?" she asked, trying to disguise her breathless state. She pressed her hand against her pussy through the cloth of her gown and winced. She'd been on the very edge of climax. She ached for release.

"It's Gerard. I'm sorry to bother you again. May I come in for a moment? I promise I won't take long."

She glanced down at her appearance in alarm.

"I'm sorry, I can't right now, Gerard. I was getting ready for bed. I'm not dressed."

"I can wait while you put something on," he called through the door. "Please, Francesca. It's important."

She opened her mouth, but could think of no other protest. He'd shoved aside the only excuse her lust-impaired brain could supply.

"All right," she said, flustered. "Give me a moment."

A minute later, she opened the door and managed a weak smile.

"Come in," she murmured, waving toward the seating area that took up half of the large main room of the suite.

"Thank you," Gerard said, giving her an apologetic glance before he stepped over the threshold. Francesca closed the door, pausing to cinch the robe she wore tighter. She'd washed with soap and very cold water and waited for her breathing to even, but her skin still felt prickly and her cheeks warm. Was Gerard going to make interrupting her masturbation a habit?

It's not his fault. It's yours for being so stupid and relenting to your memories . . . to your need so easily.

She cleared her throat, banishing the thought, and followed Gerard to the seating area. She sat on a chair across from where he'd settled on the couch. He was dressed similarly as he had been last night, except tonight his pajama bottoms were black and his robe a deep blood red. He scraped his thick hair off his forehead with his fingers in an anxious gesture and studied her closely.

"Gerard? What is it? Is something wrong?"

"I'm fine. How are you doing?" he asked intently.

"Very well, thank you," she said, laughing at his pressured, formal tone.

He smiled. "Considering the circumstances, I mean."

"Yes. I know what you meant," she conceded. Her polite, pointed glance told him she was ready to hear why he'd insisted upon talking to her.

"Again, forgive me for intruding. It's just that's it's hard to talk to you with the others always there. Privately, I mean." His gaze traveled over her face and ever so briefly lowered to the small patch of exposed skin at her chest above her closed robe.

Men know. Many of them anyway.

She shifted uneasily at the recollection of Ian's words and the knowledge of what she'd been doing before Gerard arrived.

"Why do you need to speak to me alone?" she asked.

"It's this proposed trip to Belford Hall, the painting commission—have you given Anne a certain answer about whether or not you agree to it?"

"Not entirely, no, even though she acts—"

"As if it's a decided deal," Gerard said with a dry smile. "Classic Anne, to operate as if her wishes were already reality. It works amazingly well for her. Usually." She noticed a lock of waving hair had fallen appealingly onto his forehead when he'd raked his hand through it. She returned his smile with effort.

"What's the trip have to do with why you wanted to speak with me?"

He leaned forward, his thighs parting slightly, his elbows on his knees. His sleeves fell back, revealing strong forearms sprinkled with dark hair.

"It's just . . . well, do you really think it's a good idea? To go to Ian's childhood home, with the state of things between you two being what they are?"

Her smile fell. She blinked past her shock at his words. "I honestly hadn't thought of that. I was thinking of it being a getaway . . . a change of scenery. But of course you're right. Belford Hall was Ian's home. It will be again, someday."

"Francesca," Gerard began hesitantly. His face suddenly tightened in frustration and he hissed something she couldn't quite catch beneath his breath. "What exactly *is* the state of things?" he asked in a pressured rush.

"The state of things?" she repeated stupidly.

"Between you and Ian," he clarified. She just stared. "Have you officially broken your engagement?"

"How could I possibly do that, when I haven't spoken to him in over six months?"

His head went back in sudden understanding. "So it's not officially off. *He* didn't . . . say anything?"

"Before he disappeared?" She heard the edge to her tone and inhaled, trying to calm herself. She felt very thin-skinned for some reason, exposed and vulnerable. Gerard didn't deserve her anger. He was just asking what Anne, James, and he had probably been burning to know all along. "No," she replied more calmly. "One day, Ian and I were happy and looking forward to our marriage. The next, Ian's mother was dying and everything changed."

Gerard nodded slowly. "It wasn't just Helen's death, though, was it? It was this business Lucien revealed to him, about being his brother," he said, his brow furrowed in concentration.

She just nodded, feeling uncomfortable at her lack of awareness of just how much Anne and James had told Gerard about Ian. It struck her that both of them were poking around in the dark for morsels of information.

"Lucien seems like a very smart, decent guy," Gerard said. "I'm a little confused as to why it was so upsetting to Ian to discover he was his half brother. I feel as if I'm missing something there. Is it something to do with their father?"

Francesca's expression remained impassive. So, Anne and James *hadn't* revealed the toxic truth about Trevor Gaines to Gerard.

"There is more to the story, but it's Ian's story to tell. I hope you can understand my not talking about it. I'm sorry, Gerard."

"Do you think I'm not used to being odd man out when it comes to my family?" he asked drolly, but then noticed her confusion. "Anne and James have said much the same to me in regard to Ian. I understand, but that doesn't mean I'm happy about it. I don't appreciate being left in the dark. Ian isn't only my cousin. My house is less than fifteen miles from Belford. I spent a great deal of time with Ian, when I was a young man and he was a boy. Both of us found ourselves parentless at approximately the same time. I feel like an older brother to him," he said, frowning. She could feel his mind working as he studied her face. "So you're still looking out for Ian? Protecting his secrets, even in these circumstances?"

She stiffened, her compassion for him fading. "It's a common courtesy, Gerard."

He made a conciliatory gesture with his hand, but she could tell his mind was already fastened on a different topic. "We're all worried about his state of mind. I'm sure you are as well. I'm concerned for Ian, of course, but I'm also very worried about James and Anne. It's like they're living the nightmare of Helen going missing all over again."

"Are you implying that you think that Ian is like Helen?" Francesca asked incredulously. "Gerard, Helen had schizophrenia. It's not the same—"

"I know that. But if he's not . . . entirely capable," Gerard said delicately, "we'd like to see to him, get him the care he needs. You have no clue whatsoever as to Ian's whereabouts? No hint or vague suspicion?"

"None. You know as well as I that Ian is comfortable walking every inch of this planet. He might be anywhere," she said starkly. *I am the Cat that walks by himself, and all places are alike to me.* Her heart seemed to contract at the poignant, remembered line from the Kipling poem that she had always associated with Ian, even before she had been introduced to him. Would Ian ever be able to discard that armor he wore of determined aloneness? She'd thought he could. Once. Now she doubted he could ever be free of his past.

"We never really talked in depth much when I followed him to London for a few days," she continued quietly after a moment. "His mother's condition occupied almost all our attention. After she died, Ian just disappeared off the map. In the beginning, I had neighbors check in at his other residences in several countries. Lin gave me the contact phone numbers. No one admitted to seeing him, though."

A shadow passed over Gerard's face. "Yes. We did much the same, in search for him. Upon James's request, I went to several of his residences and hotels where he frequently stays looking for him but . . . nothing."

She didn't respond. Of course they'd looked for Ian. She sighed, disappointed they hadn't learned of any crumb of information she hadn't discovered.

"In answer to your earlier question about whether or not we're still officially engaged, the answer is no," she said more calmly than she felt. She met Gerard's stare steadily. "I took off Ian's ring when I left here months ago. I'm not engaged to him anymore. Ian didn't need to say it out loud. His actions speak louder than words."

His tense, worried expression gave way. He stood, surprising her by taking her hands and drawing her up to a standing position.

"I'm sorry. More sorry than you know. I didn't mean to cause you further pain by bringing all this up."

"It's all right. I understand. I've recognized you and the others are walking on eggshells."

"Ian was wrong for treating you the way he did. What's more, he's a fool for letting you go. Not only are you brilliantly talented and sweet and fresh, you're so . . ." he paused, his mouth growing hard as he stared down at her, his gaze flickering lower over her covered breasts ever so briefly, making the already sensitized crests prickle with awareness. His hands were large and warm and encompassed her own. His body didn't touch hers, but standing just inches apart, she became abruptly aware of his male strength. She went still when he reached up and touched a tendril of her hair.

"Beautiful," he finished, his jaw rigid.

She inhaled his scent. She stepped away, breaking his hold on her hands and faced the fireplace mantel. She was confused by the turn of events. She wasn't ready to consider being with another man, let alone Ian's relative. Rationally, it seemed wrong to her, but there was something more elemental that had made her step away.

Gerard felt wrong. He *smelled* wrong.

She looked fixedly at the white marble mantel, her thoughts and feelings a confused, jumbled mess.

"I'm really tired, Gerard. You should go," she managed, her back still to him. She stiffened when she felt his hand on her shoulder.

"Francesca."

She turned and reluctantly met his stare.

"There's nothing wrong with needing someone," he said quietly, his nostrils flaring slightly. "There's nothing wrong with needing. Period."

The burn in her body had never entirely dissipated, but at this point, she knew it was foolish to think it would be truly vanquished by her own hand . . . or anyone else's, save one.

"I know that. But sometimes the timing *is* wrong," she said.

Something passed over his features. He nodded once and dropped his hand.

"I see," he said. She inhaled a breath of relief when he stepped away from her. "I really did just come here tonight to express my concern at the idea of you going to Belford Hall. I don't think you're ready for something like that."

"Really? And yet you thought I'd be ready for this?" she asked, glancing significantly at the space between them.

"No, but I'd hoped you were ready to take comfort."

Her smile was a mixture of amusement and bewilderment. "Is *that* what you offered when you came here tonight?"

His expression hardened. Suddenly she saw firsthand the razor-sharp edge that had made him such a formidable businessman.

"Yes. For a start," he said.

She remained unmoving by the fireplace, her incredulous smile a thing of the past, watching him leave the room.

Chapter Three

The next evening, Gerard and Francesca got on an elevator with Anne and James at Noble Enterprises. All of them were in a good mood, having put some satisfying work in with the mergers and acquisitions team that afternoon. The initial liquidation of assets and talks on the acquisition were going smoother than they'd expected or hoped. Of course, things could always pop up to hinder the deal, but more than likely Noble Enterprises would own Tyake soon after the New Year. Francesca was becoming so interested and self-invested in the deal, she occasionally even forgot she was doing it for Ian.

When several members of the M&A group had hesitantly mentioned going downstairs to the restaurant Fusion for the Noble Enterprises annual Christmas party, Anne had abruptly ended the meeting and shooed all of the employees down to the party.

"I hadn't realized. Shame on Lucien for not telling us," Anne said as the elevator sunk down to the lobby, referring to the fact that Lucien had worked with them for most of the day, but left in the early evening saying he had some business to which he needed to attend. Obviously, that "business" had been the preparation for the large corporate party at Fusion. The elevator stopped at the lobby of Noble Towers, and they got off together. A bright light went off in Francesca's eyes.

"Get out of here, damn it," Gerard bellowed. The man who'd snapped the photo scurried through the lobby and out the revolving door onto the street. Gerard looked furious. "Stupid photographers. Word about the Tyake acquisition has got out somehow."

"You don't think the press knows that Ian isn't at the helm, do you?" Francesca asked nervously. The fact that Ian hadn't been actively running Noble Enterprises had been a well-kept secret since he'd left. Ian was known for being the genius behind the company, after all. Public sentiment about Noble products could dip if it were known he was absent.

Gerard shook his head. "No, it's not that. It's just good for selling papers. Everyone was always curious about Ian's beautiful fiancée," he said, giving her a small smile. "But Ian always kept you under tight wraps. I suppose they feel it's their chance to splash your face across the papers."

"Lovely," Francesca muttered under her breath, wishing the conversation would end. She *wasn't* Ian's fiancée. She started to cross the lobby and the others followed.

"And look—the security desk is empty so the photographer had free rein. I suppose he's at the party. I can't believe it's December twentieth already," Anne murmured thoughtfully, casting a glance at Fusion's glass doors. "Ian always holds the party the Friday before Christmas. And here we were keeping those poor people late working."

"I'm sure they don't mind," Francesca said as they crossed the granite floor, her heels clicking briskly. She'd hesitantly accessed the vast wardrobe that Ian had bought her while they'd been together, not wanting to show up for a business meeting wearing her typical artist's costume of jeans and paint-spattered T-shirts. "It's a relief for them to get the bulk of this under their belt before the holiday, I'll bet." She peered toward the glass doors of Fusion. The large bar area of Lucien's restaurant appeared to be hopping with partiers. Something occurred to her and she paused.

"Do you mind if I meet you three at Everest?" Francesca asked, referring to the restaurant where they'd made reservations. The Nobles had insisted upon taking her to dinner to commemorate her last night in the penthouse. Now that most of the intensive work on the Tyake deal was under their belt, Francesca had announced she was returning home. Her wounds had festered far too much as it was, sleeping in Ian's bed. "I asked Lin to send some documents we might need as references before she left for the holiday, but I forgot to tell her to send them to Belford Hall."

Anne stopped dead in her tracks, an ecstatic expression overcoming her face. "So you *are* coming to us at Belford Hall for Christmas? You'll do the painting?"

She couldn't help but laugh at the break in Anne's utter confidence of her plans coming to fruition. Francesca had just made her final decision about Belford Hall that very morning. Davie had decided to visit a cousin's family in Michigan for Christmas. Although he'd tried to talk her into accompanying him, she knew she'd feel like a fifth wheel. Francesca had told him she'd decided to take Anne up on her offer. She'd once primarily considered the earl and countess as Ian's grandparents, but she'd begun to think of them as friends. Her parents were taking a cruise for the holiday, so she had no obligation in that direction. Besides, a change of scenery would do her good, not to mention the fact that she felt about a hundred times more comfortable and at ease with Anne and James than she did her own parents. Even Gerard had gone out of his way to make her feel like she belonged. All of them had done this despite her broken link with Ian, and she appreciated their efforts so much. True, she was having a niggling of doubt about Gerard being at Belford. But hadn't he been the one to suggest she not go to Ian's childhood home to begin with? He couldn't have any clear-cut designs on an English countryside seduction, given the fact that he'd warned her about going, could he? And besides, she was sure she could handle his unexpected, likely fleeting interest in her. Ian had definitely suggested he wasn't a man to be unduly shot down by one woman's disinterest. There were plenty of other willing fish in Gerard's pond.

"I booked a flight for Christmas Eve. Why do you act so surprised?" Francesca teased Anne. "You've behaved like it's all a done deal since you first mentioned it."

"Yes, but it's always nice to have even the most certain plans confirmed," Gerard said dryly. Anne gave an impish grin and they laughed.

"Eleanor will be so thrilled that she has someone else to spoil," Anne told James.

"Mrs. Hanson is coming?" Francesca asked.

"Oh yes. As I've told you, we haven't had a do like this Anniversary Ball in ages. When we did have them more regularly, however, Eleanor was indispensable. We've been running on a skeleton staff at Belford, so we've had to hire in temporary help for the holidays to pull everything off, and we'll need Eleanor to organize everyone. Lucien and Elise are coming as well. They arrive early on Boxing Day and have agreed to stay at Belford."

"It sounds exciting," Francesca said, Anne's enthusiasm spreading to her. "There is one thing: If my goal is to do preliminary sketches while I'm there, I'll need all my materials available when I arrive."

"Not a problem at all," James said, and Francesca was confident in the Nobles' ability to acquire what she needed for the project. Both were patrons of art museums and avid collectors.

"But I'd still like you to relax a little before you begin working," Anne said with a cautionary glance. "The New Year is soon enough to get started."

"And there is celebrating to be done," Gerard said, smiling. He casually placed his hand on Francesca's shoulder. "I'll go with you to speak to Lin. We'll meet you two at Everest in ten minutes or so," he said to Anne and James.

Francesca was glad her smile didn't waver at Gerard's suggestion. He'd been so kind to her today, so officious, and yet militantly polite and appropriate in their interactions. He was Ian's family—a part of a unit where she'd so wanted to belong. She'd almost forgotten her discomfort over the fact that he'd tried to seduce her last night.

Or maybe I just want *to forget,* she told herself as he led her to Fusion, his hand still casually resting on her back.

A sinking feeling dampened her short-lived good mood when Gerard opened the glass door to Fusion. Even though she'd been the one to bring up talking to Lin, she hesitated. She hadn't returned to Fusion since Ian had left. Not only had Ian and she frequently dined at Fusion, it was where they'd first met. It'd been a cocktail party in Francesca's honor for winning a highly reputable commission to paint the centerpiece mural for the newly built Noble Towers. It all came back to her in a split second—she, so gauche in her secondhand-store dress, so determined to hide her awkwardness; Ian, so arresting and intense as he pinned her with those dark-angel eyes as he'd told her that he, and he alone, would designate the view for the painting.

"I suggest you see the view in question before you take undue offense, Ms. Arno."

"Francesca," she snapped, made a little defensive by all the sophistication and formality of the reception in her honor, not to mention his arrogant assumptions.

She saw that flash in blue eyes that reminded her of a storm on the horizon. For a split second, she regretted the edge to her tone.

"Francesca it is," he said softly after a moment. "If you make it Ian."

Gerard touched her shoulder, jerking her out of the vivid memory. He pointed across the bar. She saw Lin looking as elegant and glamorous as usual, and talking to a tall woman. She nodded. He took her hand and led her through the loud, animated crowd of Noble partygoers. A gorgeous Christmas tree glistened behind scurrying waiters and chatting people. A jazz trio had been hired to entertain the Noble employees. Several couples had taken to the small dance floor. She caught a glimpse of Elise in the open kitchen in the distance, her beautiful face sober in concentration as she stirred a pot and sprinkled some ingredient into it. Soon, she would finish her training here at Fusion and be a fully qualified chef, ready to open her own restaurant. The vision of her friend heartened Francesca, sending a spark of warmth through a chest that had gone cold at the memories of Ian.

Lin greeted them warmly, nodding her head when Francesca stated her mission.

"Of course I'll send the documents to Belford Hall. Would you like me to arrange your flight for you?"

"No, of course not," she said, her cheeks heating. Lin was Ian's executive assistant, not one of his secretaries. Even if she had been a secretary, she cringed to think of Lin doing errands for her because of Francesca's past association with Ian. All of that was over and done. Ian had made that clear. "I have it all arranged, thank you, though. I fly out very early Christmas Eve."

Lin nodded, her gaze lowering fleetingly between Gerard and her. Francesca realized Gerard was still holding her hand. She gently extricated herself from his grip, trying to hide her discomfort.

"And you, Gerard? Where will you spend Christmas?" Lin asked smoothly.

"With Francesca at Belford," Gerard replied, smiling at Francesca. "I wouldn't miss James's and Anne's Anniversary Ball for the world."

Francesca tried to tamp down the sudden anxiety she felt when a quizzical, concerned glance flickered across Lin's features before she gave her usual warm smile, and wished them both a happy holiday.

When they'd started out jogging, the cool December air had been chilly. Now it felt wonderful against her heated skin.

"You were right," Davie said as he ran next to her down North Avenue. The usually busy thoroughfare was clogged with holiday traffic as people prepared for Christmas in three days. "This weather is perfect for a jog."

"Plus, it always makes you feel good to be on your feet when you see traffic like that," Francesca said, grinning.

Davie glanced at her face and did a double take. He smiled when Francesca gave him a quizzical look.

"It just took me by surprise. It's nice to see you smile again," Davie said.

"Thanks. I'm looking forward to Christmas, which comes as a bit of surprise. I was far from being able to say that two weeks ago."

Davie nodded as he searched her profile for a moment. "Do you think you're getting over Ian?" he asked quietly.

Her smile faded. The void in her chest cavity ached as she focused on it. She didn't speak for a moment as they approached a cross street, keeping her gaze averted from Davie's. "I don't know if I'll ever be 'over' Ian. I doubt I'll ever be able to . . . you know. *Feel* about anyone the way I did him," she said, purposefully avoiding the loaded word.

Love.

"Well, time is the key. You never know what the future will bring," Davie said briskly. "So . . . what's it been like for you working with Ger—"

The sound of screeching brakes cut Davie off. Both of them slowed and came to a halt several feet before the street, confused as to why the car had stopped so abruptly at a green light. Their bewilderment only mounted when the back door swung open and a man with sandy blond hair, a craggy face, and wide shoulders sprung out.

"What the hell?" Davie muttered.

Something about the man's expression as he stared fixedly at Francesca sent an alarm going off in her head. He charged them with a rapid single-mindedness that stunned her—like a walking tidal wave. Davie instinctively put out his hand and pushed back on Francesca.

"*Go . . . run,*" he said.

But the man was already upon them. He grabbed Francesca's arm in a brutal grip and tried to pull her back toward the street. The jolt of pain she experienced sliced through her confusion at the turn of events. Anger and panic rolled through her. She jerked her arm backward, but the man's grip was like steel.

"Let go of her!" Davie yelled, throwing his weight against the man's arms and attempting to come between them. But the man just snarled and batted sideways with his massive forearm and hand, like he was swatting at a fly. Davie was thrown back. The man now had both of Francesca's arms in a vicelike hold. He started to turn her roughly, as if to secure her in his arms from the back. Francesca took her chance while she still faced him and made a haphazard jab in his crotch area with her knee. By pure luck, she hit him bull's-eye. Air whooshed out of her assailant's lungs. His khaki-green eyes bulged.

She experienced a jolt of pure fear when she saw the hatred that entered his gaze. He lifted one of his hamlike hands and curled it into a fist. She twisted in his hold, desperate to escape what she suspected would be a painful blow. But then Davie reentered the fray, sinking a punch into the side of the man's belly. The man grunted. In his momentary weakness, Davie shoved him away from Francesca. The man reacted by angrily thrusting Francesca in the opposite direction. She landed hard on the sidewalk, scraping her hand as she stopped herself from going all the way down. She barely noticed. All of her attention was on the two men.

"No, Davie! *Don't,*" she shouted in panic when she looked up and saw Davie pursuing the thug as he ran toward the still-stationary car. Davie was trim and in good shape, but the man was a monster in size compared to him. Her friend hauled up short when the man clambered into the backseat and slammed the door hard. The driver punched the gas. The vehicle spun, brakes shrieking. Davie backed out of the road frantically, nearly falling in his haste.

The car shot off in the opposite direction of North Avenue and the traffic.

Davie turned and stared at her, face white and eyes wide with shock. "What the hell was *that*?"

Francesca just shook her head, too shocked by the abrupt storm of unexpected violence to speak.

Ian entered the dingy suite he occupied at the Aurore mansion and immediately stripped off his shirt. He'd combined his exercise with a search in the property's many lanes, meadows, and woods, but Kam Reardon's place of residence continued to elude him.

"You can't hide forever, *brother*," he muttered sarcastically under his breath, swiping at the glaze of perspiration on his ribs and abdomen. As he headed toward the bathroom to shower, he considered where he should search this afternoon. He came up short when he noticed the red light blinking on the answering machine. The device must have been twenty years old. Ian had hooked it up to the residential phone line and given the number to only one person.

He hit a button, sudden wariness making his sweat slickened skin roughen.

"Ian, it's me. I know you haven't been feeling up to returning calls, and you said you didn't want me to contact you on this line unless there was an emergency. But something's happened. . . . something I knew you'd want to know about right away . . ."

He listened, his backbone going stiff. After the beep signifying the end of the message, he listened to it again.

He went into the bathroom, where he rapidly extricated a pair of scissors from his grooming kit. He raised them to his neck and began to cut off his beard with a single-minded purpose.

*   *   *

They paused at a security gate, but the man on duty just waved them through. Francesca sat forward and looked out the window when the driver started down a long lane that ran through a forest.

"You'll get a view of Belford Hall once we round this bend up here," the Nobles' driver—a man named Peter—said, noticing her piqued interest through the rearview mirror. She'd met Peter before when she'd stayed with the Nobles in London.

"I'm very excited to see it. We studied it briefly while I was in school for architecture," she said breathlessly.

They took the curve. Her expression flattened in amazement at the view that unfolded. Peter must have noticed.

"Sight to behold, isn't it?" he asked quietly, pride in his voice.

"It's incredible," Francesca replied. A strange feeling crept over her as the black sedan glided toward the enormous, stately Jacobean-Tudor mansion set amongst elaborate gardens and woods that would be ablaze with color during the spring and summer. She'd seen grand homes many times in her studies as a student of art and architecture . . . but *this*.

For some reason, the entire experience struck her as surreal. The past year of her life, everything that had happened since she'd looked into Ian's eyes at Fusion over a year ago seemed to collapse into an insignificant minute. Suddenly, she was again the awkward, slightly defensive girl who had lived much of her life overweight and bullied by her peers.

What in the world was she doing *here*?

She'd known Ian's grandparents were titled and wealthy, of course. She'd known Ian grew up in the midst of splendor for a good part of his young life. But she was quickly realizing that she *hadn't* really gotten it. Not in the sense of true understanding. Could an American ever truly comprehend the elegant, rich history and tradition of a British nobleman? It struck her fully for the first time, coming like a disorienting blow, that just a half year ago, this fairy-tale house would have been one of her and Ian's future homes.

She glanced down at herself nervously as they neared the entrance and several people stepped out the front door onto the drive. Thank goodness she'd taken some items from the penthouse's dressing room before she'd returned to Davie's. She'd never been gladder that Ian had gone against her wishes in the beginning of their relationship and purchased her a wardrobe. She'd never been more thankful *he'd* specified the items he wanted her to have. It was almost as if he'd been there to advise her as she'd packed. As in all things, Ian's taste in clothing was exceptional, conveying a sense of effortless taste and understated class. The black skirt, silk blouse, leather boots, and cashmere coat she wore weren't showy by any means, but they were of the highest quality. At least she had nothing to be ashamed of in that arena. She must rely on prayer and good luck to prevent her from making a fool of herself in some other situation at Belford.

James opened her door before Peter could come around, he and Anne anxious to greet her. Their warm hugs went a long way to calm her anxiety. James's face was deeply lined with worry as he examined her closely after they embraced.

"We heard from Lin about what happened. Gerard couldn't believe his ears when I told him; he was livid. He's already at Belford, by the way, but ran over to Chatham—that's his house, just a stone's throw down the road—to take care of some business," James added as an aside. "He says to tell you he'll be back for dinner tonight."

"Did they catch the perpetrators?" Anne asked, also referring to the jarring assault on her and Davie that had occurred in Chicago several days ago.

"No, not that I'm aware of. We gave our descriptions to the police, of course, although neither of us got a good look at the driver. But I wasn't really expecting them to make an arrest, as random as the whole thing was. Davie tried to get the license plate, but it was obscured. Intentionally, probably."

"You did tell them about your connection to Ian, didn't you?" James asked pointedly.

Francesca froze. *There is no connection between Ian and me,* she wanted to scream, but checked herself when she saw James's lined, worried face. He only meant well, of course, and she understood what he was getting at. Ian and she shared a past connection, but a connection nonetheless.

"It never really came up, James. I'm afraid the whole incident was a typical, mundane one to the Chicago PD." She braced herself against a wind that whipped some escaped hair against her cheek.

"Come on, let's get you out of the cold," Anne urged.

"Welcome to Belford," James said as they escorted her inside the massive oak doors, Peter following with her luggage. Once again, Francesca heard that tone of pride. It rang even stronger in James's voice than it had in Peter's. And why shouldn't James be proud of his ancestral home? Francesca wondered as she stared openmouthed at the entrance hall: the richly carved oak-paneled walls, the grand staircase bedecked in fresh evergreen garland, the master paintings of various ancestors, the twenty-foot-tall lit Christmas tree, and the stunning domed stained-glass ceiling.

This is where Ian had grown up?

Somehow the idea of an energetic, scampering ten-year-old and this grandeur just didn't mix in her brain, she realized dazedly as her boots tapped on a meticulous design of marble tile. But then again, Ian had never been a carefree child. These surroundings *were* perfectly suited to his cool self-containment, his consummate confidence in almost every decision he made.

She stopped in the middle of the hall and spun around once on her feet, trying to soak it all in. She met James's sparkling, dark eyes.

"What do you think?" he asked, smiling.

"I'm awestruck, of course. It's magnificent. I feel like a bumbling American," she added under her breath.

"The only thing we want you to feel," Anne said, stepping forward and taking her hand and with a significant glance, "is at home."

Anne escorted her to her assigned suite on the second floor. While they chatted about the schedule for the next few days, a woman knocked and asked politely if she could unpack. At first, Francesca was confused by her request. The woman was young and pretty—in her twenties, probably about Francesca's age. She didn't wear the stereotypical clothing of a maid, but instead an attractive dark blue dress that belted at the waist, a tasteful silk scarf, and fashionable flats. She looked more like a chic young executive than a maid.

"Why don't you come back and do it while Francesca showers," Anne suggested warmly. "She's going to freshen up after her flight."

"Of course, my lady," Clarisse said, taking her leave.

After Francesca had showered, she walked into the suite only to find Clarisse stowing her unpacked suitcase in the massive walk-in closet.

"I have a glass of club soda and lime waiting for you. Her ladyship said it was your favorite drink. I hung up this dress for you to wear tonight for Christmas Eve dinner. I thought it might be the one you had in mind, but please let me know if you'd like another," Clarisse said kindly, waving at the dark red off-the-shoulder dress hanging on a hook just inside the open closet door. Francesca swallowed uncomfortably. It had been the nicest dress she'd packed, and she'd done so with the ball in mind, not Christmas Eve dinner.

"I . . . yes, of course. That was nice of you," she faltered, unwilling to put her ignorance on display.

"Not at all," Clarisse said brightly. "Is your dress for the ball going to be delivered? I only wanted to know because I can look out for it for you, air it out, and get it ready."

"Um, it's all still in the works. I'll let you know," she said, blushing. *Oh no.* The anniversary party must be a lot more formal then she'd realized . . . or had any experience to realize. And the "quiet Christmas Eve and Christmas, just with family" must be as well, Francesca thought with rising discomfort.

She felt too embarrassed to highlight her stupidity in front of a stranger. She'd just have to confess her ignorance and lack of preparation to Anne tonight. Perhaps there was a shop nearby where she could pick up something appropriate? Even as she thought it, she had a sinking feeling she was doomed to stand out like a red-faced fool at the ball. It was bad enough in regard to herself, but she hated the idea of embarrassing Anne and James on their special night.

She turned down Clarisse's amiable offer to do her hair for dinner, and the maid vacated the suite. Francesca turned to stare at the dark crimson dress, her fears about highlighting her gaucheness once again taking center stage. Funny, she thought she'd outgrown her insecurities. But then again, she'd really only become comfortable at high-profile events or formal dinners because Ian was there, his effortless, complete confidence spreading to her . . . always strengthening her.

She didn't have him to lean on now, though. She'd been kidding herself to think she could function and hold her head up in surroundings such as these.

At least the dress did good things for her complexion, she decided later as she examined herself from the front and back nervously in the full-length mirror. The skin of her shoulders and back gleamed. Ian had frequently told her that her shoulders and back were two of her best features, and often bought her dresses that highlighted them.

Stop thinking about what Ian thought, she snapped at herself as she reached for a pair of black suede leather heels that featured an ankle strap. She wore her long hair up, accessorizing with a favorite triple-strand pearl choker that Ian had given her and matching earrings.

It was the best she could do, she decided grimly as she looked from the mirror to the golden clock on the sofa table. Anne had said they'd meet in the sitting room—wherever that was—at seven for a drink before dinner.

Francesca couldn't be sure if Clarisse really just happened to be walking by when she went down the grand staircase, or if her presence there was by design. Everything seemed to happen so effortlessly in the Noble household, as if all had been choreographed by some god of graceful etiquette.

"Thank you," Francesca said to Clarisse when she led her to a white and crimson paneled door and opened it for her. Perhaps the maid noticed Francesca's anxiety, because she gave her a heartening smile.

The first face she saw upon entering the warm, cozy room was Gerard.

"Don't you look like a vision," he said, his gaze running over her with clear masculine appreciation. He looked very handsome and at ease in a tuxedo with black tie, his forearm resting on the mantel of the fireplace, highball glass in hand. Anne and James were there, calling their greetings as they stood from two plush, chocolate brown sofas that faced each another before a crackling fire.

"I have to wash off all the paint and present myself in a decent light at least a few times a year," Francesca said breathlessly to Gerard after she'd greeted them all. She turned her chin when Gerard leaned down to kiss her, so that his warm lips brushed her cheek. She glanced around, realizing that the room was quite large with several comfortable seating areas. "What a beautiful room, Anne. What a beautiful *tree*," she exclaimed, moving past Gerard to admire the eight-foot pine decorated with tiny white lights and handcrafted German ornaments, some of them clearly antiques. Her gaze lingered on the painted ornament of a miniature motorcycle. The Christmas tree in the Great Hall was all about grandeur, but this tree was clearly an intimate one for a private gathering place. "Is this where you and . . . Is this where you usually celebrated Christmas with the family?" she asked Anne, who had approached to stand next to her. She looked lovely in a winter white dress and diamonds.

"Yes, almost always," Anne said, handing her a glass of something steaming in a crystal cup. Francesca caught a whiff of the delightful brew.

"Is this Mrs. Hanson's Christmas punch?" she asked, pleasantly surprised. Anne nodded. The taste of the mulled apple cider, rum, and spices gladdened her like a familiar smile. It did, that is, until she recalled toasting Ian with it last Christmas Eve in the penthouse.

No. Had it really just been a year ago that she'd felt so steadfastly secure in her love?

"It was Helen's favorite room," James was saying from where he sat on the plush, dark brown sofa close to the fire. *And Ian's.* The thought automatically popped into her head as her gaze swept past the little wooden motorcycle to the fine art collection on display in the room and the rows upon rows of books in the built-in shelves. She knew his taste so well.

"And Ian's, of course," James added belatedly, confirming Francesca's suspicion. His eyebrows went up and he took a draw on his drink when Anne shot him a subtle, repressive look. Gerard gallantly changed the topic.

"And here is where Anne and James plan to showcase your painting," Gerard said, waving at the area above the large fireplace where currently a fine John Singer Sargent oil of a striking Edwardian-era woman in a blue dress hung. To think that they planned to replace a master's work with her own left her stunned.

"Since we spend so much time in here," James said, "we thought it was the ideal place to enjoy it."

"And be reminded of you," Anne said, taking her hand and almost immediately easing her anxiety.

Her fears about making a fool of herself were mostly groundless,

Francesca discovered. It wasn't that she suddenly became confident in handling herself in the midst of such style and grandeur, by any stretch of the imagination. It was the kindness and easiness of James, Anne, and Gerard—and even the house staff. Thanks to Mrs. Hanson's presence in Chicago, she was somewhat used to being served dinner. Ian's housekeeper had insisted upon the tradition every once in a while, and Ian was too tired—or wise—to fight with her every time she mentioned it. Francesca found herself relaxing for the first time since she'd landed in London as the meal came to an end, and the footman served fruit and cheese for the last course. Even with the stunning formal dining room and the service of the exquisitely prepared, festive dinner, it was James and Anne's warm kindness that set the mood. Gerard, too, went out of his way to charm her, his dark eyes gleaming with pleasure every time he coaxed a laugh out of her.

Francesca found herself hoping that the men would go to some gentlemanly retreat following dinner and that she would have Anne to herself—isn't that the sort of thing they did in books like *Brideshead Revisited*? She really needed to speak to Anne about this dress situation for the ball. Much to her disappointment, however, they all retired to the sitting room together for coffee.

"I'm shocked that it all was so blatant—right on a busy city street," Gerard was reflecting on the attempted robbery against her and Davie, once they'd settled near a crackling fire. "Is Chicago experiencing a crime wave?"

"Not any more of a wave than usual," Francesca said with a smile. Gerard was settled next to her on the couch, looking every bit as comfortable in his formalwear as most men would jeans and a T-shirt. He really was extremely handsome, she added to herself fairly.

"It must have been so frightening," Anne said from where she sat next to James across from them. "He certainly was a bold criminal."

"He must have been a very stupid one, as well," Francesca added with a small laugh. "Joggers don't usually carry many valuables."

"Assuming theft was their intent," Gerard said, his mouth grim.

"What a thing to say, Gerard," Anne scolded, repressing a shiver. "Let's talk about something else. It's Christmas Eve. Do you have everything you need for the ball, Francesca? We can run out on Boxing Day to the village, if you'd like to pick up anything. I have to check the donation boxes are set up at the church anyway."

Francesca glanced anxiously from James to Gerard. She didn't really have any choice but expose her ill prepared state in front of them. "Yes, I would like to go with you. In fact, I think I'm in trouble. Clarisse was asking about my gown for the ball. I brought this for it," she said, glancing down at the crimson velvet and feeling her cheeks begin to burn. "I'm sorry. I've never been to something this . . . special before. I'm afraid I'm not at all prepared."

"Well we'll just *get* you prepared," Anne said with unwavering confidence. "There's nothing to be concerned about. It's just a party, and it's just a dress."

"Wear that one again," James agreed, nodding at her velvet dress. "Very pretty. I like it."

"Hear, hear," Gerard said.

"Tell you what," Anne said matter-of-factly. "The stores are open on Boxing Day, and Stratham has two nice dress shops. If we find nothing, Clarisse will spruce that one up for you for the ball."

"I'm sorry to be a bother."

"Please don't let it worry you, dear," Anne insisted. "Your being here is what's important, not a silly dress. Be comfortable. We're rarely so fancy at Belford, but as I've told you, we've hired in extra staff for the holidays and the ball. Don't be fooled into thinking we're stuffy or pretentious, you just happen to be seeing us when we're especially decked out for the festivities. Now, let's play a game or do something *fun*, why don't we?"

They spent a pleasant, relaxing Christmas Eve together. Nevertheless, Francesca was aware of a sore spot in the vicinity of her heart, a raw, abraded place. It was more difficult than she'd realized, sitting there in Ian's favorite room, surrounded by Ian's relatives on such a special holiday . . . without Ian.

Her loneliness seemed to swell inside her chest as Gerard escorted her up the stairs at the end of the night. He caught her hand and steadied her when she faltered on the top stair.

"Too much of Mrs. Hanson's punch?" he asked, smiling.

"No, that's not it. I've just grown out of the habit of wearing heels."

"Not standard apparel for an artist, I expect."

"Hardly," she said, highly conscious of the fact that he kept her hand in his. The domed, high-ceilinged hallway was cloaked in shadow. Her heart started to beat uncomfortably fast as they neared her room.

"This is me," she said, nodding toward the door. Still, he didn't release her. He stepped closer. She kept her gaze trained on his crisp white dress shirt.

"Francesca?"

"Yes?"

"It's past midnight. Merry Christmas."

She looked up to return the greeting. He covered her mouth with his, coaxing her lips to part for his tongue. For a second, she allowed it. Perhaps she was curious. Maybe she was a sad, lonely woman who desperately wanted to feel connected to another human being in the once-in-a-lifetime way she'd connected to Ian.

His arms came around her and his kiss deepened.

A chill went through her when she realized she was thinking of him as the equivalent of a sex toy. He was a human being, not a convenient object to feed an insatiable, unquenchable desire.

She broke the kiss and pushed against his chest. He didn't immediately release her.

"What's wrong?" he rasped. His mouth moved along her neck persuasively, his hands tightening at her waist.

"Gerard, let go. It's not right. I don't want to," she said quietly.

He lifted his head and looked down at her in the dim light. "Francesca—I know you must think this is odd, what with my being Ian's cousin. I've thought about it, too."

"You have?" she asked uncertainly.

"Of course. Ian is like a brother to me. Do you worry he'd be upset with us? Feel betrayed?"

"Why should he feel betrayed?" she asked irritably, her teeth set on edge. "He's the one who left."

"I agree."

She blinked at his steadfast reply and was once again caught by his stare. Her cheeks flushed. "It'd just be wrong."

He studied her for an uncomfortable moment, seeming to read her face. Slowly, he released her.

"I disagree," he said gruffly. "I think it'd be amazing. I'm not going to tiptoe around the fact that I want you. I might in these circumstances, with a different woman . . . with a less intense attraction, but I won't with you. The other night, you said the timing wasn't right. I want you to know I'll be there when the timing *is* right."

She inhaled, feeling that scored area in her chest. "It never will be right. To be honest, I'm ashamed to say that the only reason I allowed that just now is because you remind me of him a little. You're part of his family." She shrugged helplessly. "Maybe I just wanted to feel like I belonged to all of that."

"You *do* belong. Any stranger could have seen that if they were watching the four of us tonight. Ian won't always stand between us," Gerard said firmly when she didn't respond. "He abandoned you, Francesca." He touched her cheek with skimming fingertips.

"Do you think I don't know that?" she asked bitterly, jerking her chin and halting his touch.

"I see he left quite a collar on you," he said, his fingertips lowering to her throat where he caressed both her skin and the pearl choker Ian had given her. "But I'm persistent. I'll break it."

"Good night, Gerard," she muttered in a strangled voice, turning away from his touch and opening her door. She refused to look up as she shut it, but she knew he was still standing there, his gaze boring into the door.

He watched her get into bed wearing not a stitch of clothes, pale limbs gleaming in the golden light of the lamp, full breasts heaving although her cheeks were dry. She was clearly upset, but forcing herself not to cry, tamping down her anguish. Her body had clearly been trained for pleasure. She struggled to exist without it, he realized as she reached for her pussy, her actions striking him as arousing despite the almost angry quality of her masturbation . . . maybe *because* of her focused fury. She hated this obsession, this absolute necessity to feel.

All the better for him.

He could tell by the way she almost immediately plunged her finger into her vagina that she needed to be filled. She craved, but when would she succumb to her hunger? He unfastened his trousers and reached for his cock, his eyes glued to his computer screen.

He paused with his hand wrapped around his throbbing erection when she frantically finger-fucked her pussy and used her thumb to stridently massage her clit. At the same time, she put one wrist above her head and fixed it to the pillow. Her back arched, the display of her plump, round breasts making his mouth go dry. Her face tightened in a poignant expression of thwarted desire and acute frustration.

Jesus. His breathing came raggedly as he pumped his cock harder. She was mimicking being restrained. He watched with a tight focus, his arm moving like a piston as he vividly imagined holding her down on the mattress and pounding his cock into that snug pink pussy.

He came before she did, his orgasm sharp and delicious. She was still writhing, clearly about to climax, when he shut off the video feed, no longer interested.

Things were progressing well, he told himself as he set aside his computer and dried the semen on his belly with a tissue. He'd set the ball in motion. It was no good hunting wounded prey if it remained invisible to his sights. Certainly he would be lured into the open now, with the threat he'd provided . . . the bait.

All Gerard had to do was wait and let the unfortunate drama unfold.

Christmas Day was spent very pleasantly. Anne gave her a tour of Belford Hall following a delicious brunch. Afterward, they exchanged gifts, and Francesca was glad to see that the ones to her from Anne and James were small, token-type gifts in the style she'd given them. They must have recognized she'd be uncomfortable with expensive presents. Gerard, on the other hand, stopped her next to the huge, sparkling tree in the Great Hall before she went to her suite to dress for dinner.

"What's this?" she asked, confused when he handed her a dark red, rectangular box.

"My gift to you, of course. Merry Christmas."

Francesca glanced around uncomfortably, but they were the only people in the hall. She opened the jewelry box, gasping softly when she saw the stunning diamond and platinum choker nestled in black velvet.

"Gerard, I can't take this."

"Don't you like it?"

"Of course I do. It's stunning," she assured, regretting his concerned look.

"Then it must be yours, because you're the very definition of stunning," he said, his fingertips touching her cheek fleetingly.

"No . . . I couldn't," she said, holding out the box, but he refused to accept it. He just gave her a wry glance and turned away. She stood there in rising frustration and doubt as she watched him walk up the stairs.

The next morning she was getting ready to drive into town with Anne when a rap came at her door. Clarisse breezed in carrying a garment bag, her face radiant with excitement.

"It's come," she said, her voice trembling, her enthusiasm so great that Francesca truly sensed her youth for the first time.

"What's come?" she asked, puzzled.

"Your dress." Clarisse shook her head, beaming. "It's amazing. You never said . . . you didn't even hint . . . and he designs for the royals and all!" she sputtered.

Francesca laughed in complete bewilderment. "What are you talking about—"

But Clarisse was too busy hanging and unzipping the garment bag to pay attention. Francesca just stood there, her mouth gaping open at the most exquisite white and pale silver gown she'd ever seen or imagined. It fastened at the throat and was both sleeveless and backless. The design on the fitted bodice was of delicate silver leaves inlaid on white. Even though the white background was sheer, the dress was lined for modesty. The skirt was straight versus full, the sheer white fabric falling over a silver undergarment giving the impression of flowing, shimmering water.

"You must let me do your hair tonight," Clarisse was saying breathlessly. "I know just the perfect style for this gown. You're going to look amazing. Oh . . . and a note was delivered with it."

Francesca took the small white envelope with numb fingers, pausing to assure it was indeed her name on the front. The note was typed on linen parchment.

Francesca,
Forgive me for being remiss and leaving you so unprepared.

She just stared at the note for an extended moment, holding her breath, a strange, tingling sensation settling in her limbs. No . . . it couldn't be.

Forgive me for being remiss. Wait . . . hadn't Gerard said that to her recently? And he knew she didn't have a dress.

Disappointment flooded her.

"Are you excited for tonight? The ballroom is going to look so amazing. Did her ladyship tell you that the decorations are all in silver and white? You'll look like a fairy princess in it with this dress," Clarisse enthused, running her hand along the skirt so that the exquisite fabric flowed over her forearm.

"No. Just a lucky chance, I guess," Francesca said dubiously.

"My gown is nothing to this, but I still can't wait," Clarisse said.

"You mean you'll be attending the ball?"

Clarisse nodded, her eyes shining. "Her lady and lordship invited the permanent staff. It's sort of a nod to the tradition of the servant balls they used to have on Boxing Day years ago. Since it's also their anniversary, Lady Stratham thought it'd be nice to combine the celebration into one grand ball. We're all very excited. Aren't you?"

"Oh, yes," Francesca assured. She shoved the note into her pocket, ashamed of herself for the flash of hope that had gone through her for a split second as she read those typed words.

As it turned out, she and Anne were unsuccessful shopping for a dress in town. Of course she'd been spoiled for another one. No other dress stood a chance next to that exquisite creation that had been delivered. It rankled at her a little, knowing that Gerard had recognized how much she'd love it.

Later that afternoon, she held up the brushed and freshened red dress next to the white and silver gown. Her heart sank. Of course she'd wear the delivered gown. She realized the diamond choker would look stunning with it. Was that why Gerard had chosen it?

But no. She would return that choker to Gerard. It was too much. Far too much. Her triple strand of pearls would look just as lovely with the dress, along with the diamond pins Ian had once given her to wear in her hair. She tried to convince herself that her choice to return the necklace had nothing to do with Gerard's comment on Christmas Eve about Ian leaving a choker on her as he'd touched the pearls. No, he hadn't meant anything by giving her a diamond choker, as if to replace Ian's pearls. It was all ridiculous anyway. Ian had certainly not left a hold on her of any kind.

"Exquis," Elise said wide-eyed later that afternoon when Francesca showed her the gown. She and Lucien had arrived just before an especially lavish afternoon tea—Anne had explained that a traditional dinner wouldn't be served at the ball since it officially began at nine p.m., but instead hors d'oeuvres and then a midnight supper buffet were planned. After the filling tea of sandwiches, fruit, and pudding, Elise had accompanied Francesca to her suite to chat before it was time to prepare for the ball. Elise seemed to notice her puzzlement at her exclamation. Francesca's French was not good. "That dress rocks," Elise translated succinctly. "And you say Gerard gave it to you?"

Francesca nodded, unable to disguise her disquietude.

"He *is* a handsome one," Elise conceded doubtfully, plopping down on the couch. "Seems nice enough as well. Course he's not Ian."

"Isn't that for the best?" Francesca said dryly, hanging up the gown.

"I guess that all depends on what you think. Francesca?" Elise added when she didn't immediately turn around, but busied herself adjusting the gown. "What *do* you think?"

Francesca was glad when Clarisse rapped at the door, asking to start her bath in preparation for the ball. It seemed like a good time to change the subject.

Her heart pounded uncomfortably at eight forty-five that evening as she stood in the reception line with Lucien and Elise behind her, waiting to offer her official well wishes to the earl and countess on their anniversary. Elise and Lucien looked like a vision—Elise in a gown of deep purple that optimally highlighted the rare color of her eyes, an exquisite platinum and sapphire necklace and her pavé diamond and sapphire wedding ring; Lucien strikingly handsome, as usual, in a formal tuxedo with white tie. The Great Hall was breathtaking, decorated with firelit crystal globes, magnificent silver candelabra, and fresh, aromatic garland, the Christmas tree ablaze.

She wasn't quite sure why her heart was beating so fast in anxious excitement, but thought perhaps it was due to all the fine people filling the hall: the rich, the titled, and the famous mixing with the house staff and several people from the village. They all milled around, sipping the champagne being passed by waiters, waiting for the ballroom doors to be thrown open. A string quartet played in muted tones, contributing to the festive mood of anticipation. Lucien and Elise's presence right behind her in the line gave her some of the reassurance she sorely required. She glimpsed Clarisse in the distance, looking pretty in a pale gold dress. The maid gave a little wave and Francesca waved back, returning her excited grin.

She saw the back of a tall, broad-shouldered man in the distance in the receiving line wearing a tuxedo, and realized she'd get a chance immediately to thank Gerard for the dress. He deserved her gratitude. She'd never felt so pretty. The dress fit her like it'd been made for her. Clarisse had styled her hair in a delicate weave, using the diamond pins to skillfully form it into a red-gold, loose sort of crown that struck Francesca as unpretentious yet supremely elegant.

They finally reached the anniversary couple.

"Francesca, dear," Anne said, her voice sounding unnaturally high as Francesca leaned down to kiss her cheek and offer her congratulations. Why did Anne look so undone—strangely radiant and worried at once? Francesca wondered blankly when she straightened and noticed the countess's expression.

"The dress looks lovely on you. I knew it would."

An electrical pulse seemed to start at the very base of Francesca's brain and course down her spine, setting off a chain reaction to every nerve in her body. She stood as if frozen. It hadn't been Gerard she'd seen standing in the reception line with Anne and James.

"I didn't have time to tell you," she distantly heard Anne mutter apologetically under her breath.

"He just came down as the first guests arrived," James said.

Ian's face looked like it'd been carved from cold alabaster, but his eyes seemed to burn right through her.

"Well," he said quietly, his familiar deep, slightly gruff, British-accented voice seeming to scrape gently over her prickling skin. "Aren't you going to say anything?"

She inhaled fully for the first time since seeing Anne's anguished expression.

"Yes," she replied. "Excuse me."

She turned and plunged into the mingling crowd, the brilliant gowns and flickering flame and abrupt laughter striking her stunned brain like an assault. The only thing that she could be sure of, the only thing that felt terrifyingly real, was that invisible tether that had always seemed to join her and Ian stretching tight. It tugged painfully deep in her chest as she fled, threatening to rip at something vital.

Chapter Four

The tap that came at her suite door was light and cautious . . . feminine. She gave her face one last glance in the bathroom mirror and went to open the door. Her limbs still felt numb from shock.

Ian is here.

Her mind kept repeating the sentence like a harsh mantra, as if her brain was stubbornly refusing to absorb the truth and it had to be pounded into her consciousness by force. Even though she'd suspected that the knock was feminine, she sighed in relief when she saw Elise standing on the other side of the door. She stepped back, granting her entrance, and closed the door.

"Sit down," Elise instructed. "You're white as a sheet." She handed Francesca a glass of water from the bathroom a moment later.

"I can't believe it," she muttered more to herself than to Elise.

"Yes. It came as a shock to everyone. He told Lucien before I followed you up that he just arrived a half hour before the reception began. He snuck upstairs to his suite to dress before anyone realized he was here."

She tried to focus on Elise's concerned face. "Did he say why he came?"

Elise shook her head helplessly. She could read a hundred questions in her friend's sapphire-blue eyes, but Elise expressed none of them. She must know Francesca didn't have the answers, either.

"I have to go back down," Francesca said, setting the glass on a side table. "I can't hide in here like a moody adolescent. It'd be so rude, when Anne and James asked me here for this event."

"They would understand, I'm sure. Given the circumstances," Elise said. "Her ladyship is the one who asked me to check on you. After she tried to stop Ian from following you, that is."

Her gaze flew to Elise's face. "Tried?"

Elise nodded hesitantly. "He's out in the hall right now. No one could stop him. He barely allowed me to come in first."

A powerful feeling of dread and sharp anticipation surged through her.

"Send him in," she said, her level tone surprising her. Apparently, she was too numb with shock for emotional displays.

Elise bit her lip. "Are you certain?"

Francesca nodded and stood, steadying herself.

"I have to face him sometime. It might as well be now."

Elise's doubtful expression remained, but she turned to open the door.

He entered and closed the door behind him with a hushed click, his gaze steady on her the whole time. Her chin went up and her spine stiffened when he walked toward her. He came to an abrupt halt, reading her body language. His face seemed leaner than when she'd last seen him. That and his glittering gaze gave him a fierce look, like he had some kind of invisible fire burning nonstop inside him, fueling him . . . perhaps destroying him as well. His short, dark hair always created a striking contrast to his skin, but he seemed even paler than usual, as if he'd been cloistered from the sun.

"Where have you been?" she asked without preamble, unable to stop herself from expressing the question that had burned inside her for half a year.

He didn't reply for a moment. As always, she felt pinned by his stare. They stood ten feet apart or so. Francesca couldn't decide if the distance felt too close or like a yawning, mile-wide chasm.

"France," he said in his characteristic hoarse voice. She tried to gird herself against the familiar sound of it.

"Why?"

Her one word query seemed to hang between them, its various meanings hovering like a toxic cloud. For the first time, she saw uncertainty flicker across his stoic features, but it was quickly gone.

"There are some things I have to take care of . . . look into."

She waited, the tension rising between them, but he said nothing else. "That's it?" she asked with a bark of incredulous laughter. "That's all you're going to say by way of explanation for disappearing without a trace for half a year?"

His mouth tightened. "Would it really matter what I said?"

"No," she said without pause. "It wouldn't."

His expression hardly altered, but knowing him as she did, she sensed his flash of anger at her words. Or was it frustration?

"So you really don't want an explanation," he clarified.

"I'm saying there isn't one that would suffice, so maybe you shouldn't bother."

His nostrils flared slightly. "I see you're not wearing the ring anymore," he said after a moment, his gaze lowering to her left hand, which hung at her side.

"Are you surprised?"

He looked into her eyes again. Suddenly, she wished he was gone, or that she was anywhere else. In that moment, she'd glimpsed his pain, and it had acted like a spark to her own. It flamed to life, hot and scoring, seeming to rob her of breath. She barely kept her composure.

"No. Not really," he said quietly.

She inhaled with effort. Well, there it was. He'd known he was ending their relationship by doing what he'd done, and yet he'd done it anyway. She nodded once and looked away.

"Well, that's it, I guess," she said with a note of finality. She started when another knock came at her door. "Come in," she called, glad for the distraction. She was barely holding herself together, and the last thing she wanted was for Ian to witness her discomposure.

Gerard stepped into the room. His concerned gaze moved from Francesca to Ian and back to Francesca again.

"Ian. This is quite a surprise." The two men shook hands and gave one another a half hug of greeting. "We're all extremely relieved to see you."

"Gerard," Ian greeted solemnly.

Gerard's gaze slid over to Francesca. "Are you all right?" Gerard asked, and it was clear he was asking her, not his cousin.

She nodded. "Yes. I'm ready to go back down."

Gerard seemed uncertain when neither she nor Ian moved. He must have sensed the palpable tension swirling in the air.

"We have a lot to discuss," Gerard told Ian. "We've all been worried sick."

Ian's eyes gleamed as he glanced between his cousin and Francesca, but he didn't reply.

"I'll wait for you in the hallway, Francesca," Gerard said.

"Thank you," she said.

That strangling silence settled again when Gerard walked into the hall, leaving the door open.

"Excuse me," Francesca muttered, knowing there was nothing left to say. She was foolish to wait for anything. He remained unmoving when she walked past him.

"Francesca."

She paused before she reached the door, her back remaining to him. Her breath burned in her lungs.

"You may not wear the ring, but you're here in my grandparents' home. You're wearing the dress I sent."

She turned in amazement. "What makes you think I knew who sent it?" she demanded, her cheeks flushing with anger. Or was it embarrassment?

"You knew. Or at least you thought you knew before you second-guessed yourself. You know I never liked to leave you unprepared for any event where you might question yourself."

She gave a shuddering gasp. He hadn't said it cockily. He'd just stated it as an established fact. Damn him. He'd always read her like a book. What he'd said was true, of course. She'd recognized his taste in the dress. Her thoughts had immediately leapt to him when she'd read the message. Some part of her had realized the perfection of the gift suggested an intimate knowledge of her body . . . her person. But it was more than that. It struck her heavily for the first time that her actions for the past few weeks were far from being that of a person who had given up on her lover. She *was* staying with his grandparents in his childhood home and she *had* spent a great deal of time and effort on following through on what she believed would be his wishes for Noble Enterprises. Hadn't she hungrily eaten up the sights of his youth during her tour of Belford Hall, imagined him as a child, that distrustful, withdrawn boy slowly coming out of his shell, pictured him as a man filling even the most grand of the rooms with his bold presence?

If the fact that she'd agreed to sleep in his bed at the penthouse didn't prove his point, she didn't know what did. She hadn't entirely given up hope.

God, she was a fool.

Unwilling—and unable—to see the fierce pain in his eyes anymore, she turned and fled the room.

*   *   *

She thought maybe she'd never smiled more, and certainly never so unnaturally, when she went down to the Anniversary Ball with Gerard. It somehow seemed like a personal mission to show that she could hold her own in these circumstances.

The party was in full swing by the time Gerard escorted her downstairs, a small orchestra filling the house with music. Even through her shock and disquietude, Francesca wasn't immune to the beauty of the transformed ballroom. James and Anne certainly knew how to throw a "do," as Anne had called it. The already beautiful, white, wood-paneled room with enormous fireplace had been transformed into an ice palace. Round tables that seated eight were set up around the periphery of the large space, each of them with a fantastic, lit "ice" chandelier hovering above it, all of them unique and exquisitely beautiful. An elaborate, crystal candlelit bar was at one end of the room, a buffet table on the opposite would serve a late dinner in a few hours. James and Anne were just finishing their solo anniversary dance to kick off the ball when she walked in on Gerard's arm. Other couples were starting to join them on the dance floor.

"Shall we?" Gerard asked, nodding toward the dance floor.

"I'd love to," she said a little too brightly. She could tell from his quirked brows that he was concerned by her brittle animation. When he tried to bring up the topic of Ian's return while they danced, she made an abrupt observation on the beauty of the room. He seemed to take her hint, and kept things light for the remainder of the dance.

At some point, she wondered if Ian had known precisely what he was doing by sending her this backless dress. She sensed his gaze on her bare skin as Gerard and she circled on the dance floor. She ignored the sensation, continuing her conversation with Gerard with a fierce determination that hardly matched their lighthearted topic.

She spotted Lucien and Elise sitting at a table when Gerard led her off the dance floor. Relieved to see Ian wasn't there, she went to join them while Gerard went to find a waiter for drinks. She swore she wasn't looking for Ian in the crowded ballroom, but her gaze immediately found his singular form on the dance floor, his grandmother in his arms.

"No one can make Anne beam the way Ian can," Gerard observed with a smile as he arrived at the table, two waiters on his heels, one waiter carrying a bucket, champagne, and four glasses, another a platter of hors d'oeuvres and iced caviar. Her brow furrowed. Had there been a note of bitter envy in his tone? She wasn't entirely surprised. Only Ian could be so rude as to leave his grandparents worried and anxious for half a year, only to return and have them thrown in an ecstasy of happiness at the sight of him. Besides, it wasn't as if what Gerard said wasn't completely true, Francesca thought as she gave a reluctant sideways glance at Ian's striking profile. The countess looked especially diminutive next to his tall form, both of them moving gracefully on the dance floor. She'd never seen Anne look so happy, so relieved, and she stared up at her grandson, sometimes solemn as they conversed, sometimes smiling and laughing. No, she understood Anne's relief, empathized with it. Anne had lost her only daughter this year. She was likely feeling light-headed with relief to know her only grandson was alive and healthy.

You're every bit as relieved. In fact, part of you is euphoric at the evidence of his well-being.

It was a strange combination, she realized. Light-headed relief and focused fury.

She plunged into conversation with the others. Lucien raised his eyebrows when she allowed Gerard to pour her a third glass of champagne, but she was immune to his concern. She wasn't sure what she was feeling at that moment, so how could anyone else accurately interpret her mood?

Someone touched her lightly on the shoulder. She turned to find James standing there, straight and handsome in his tuxedo.

"May I have this dance?" he asked her.

"I'd love to," Francesca said, standing.

"Holding steady?" James murmured quietly once they'd spun together on the dance floor for a moment.

"All things considered, I think I'm doing very well." She met his kind stare and smiled. "I didn't get to tell you congratulations, earlier. Your and Anne's dedication to each other is wonderful to see."

His gray eyebrows went up. "I'm sensing an underlying message there."

She laughed, but averted her gaze. "What? Like that without a true dedication to your partner, there can be no trust? No future?"

"That's true," James said. "But people show their dedication in different ways. Anne's and my commitment hasn't always looked like it does today. I'm sure she questioned my dedication to her when I was in my twenties and thirties, traveling as much as I did, attending to business. I'm sure there was a time in Anne's life she had trouble recognizing that as devotion on my part to our marriage, but that's how I always saw it."

"Now I'm sensing an underlying message," she said wryly.

James smiled. "Did you listen to Ian? Did he tell you where he's been?"

"No. And I mean no offense, James. I know he's your grandson, and you're bound to feel differently about it than his jilted fiancée. No," she interjected when James started to protest. "That's what I am. No reason to sugarcoat it." She paused as the music swelled making talking difficult. "My point is," she said as the music quieted, "I'm not sure I want to know what he found so important to do that he couldn't pick up a phone and relieve your worry. Anne's. Mine. It was incredibly selfish on his part."

"I'm not trying to change your understanding of the situation, Francesca. Just—"

"Broaden it a little?" she finished for him, giving him a small smile.

"You can't blame an old man for trying," he said as the music came to an end.

"I blame you for nothing but loving your grandson," she replied honestly. James leaned down to give her a kiss on the cheek as they came to a halt. As he released her hand, another one took it. She looked over her shoulder and saw Ian standing there, one arm still around Anne's waist.

"May I?" he asked quietly.

The split second it took her to decide seemed to drag on forever. Without verbally acquiescing, she just went into his arms, her posture stiff. She hardly heard the music over her pounding heart. For several seconds, neither of them spoke as she told herself not to focus on the sensation of being in his arms, and did nothing but.

"How long do you plan to stay?" she asked without looking at him and tried not to breathe too deeply, lest she inhale his scent.

"I haven't decided."

She dared to look into his face. His blue eyes drew her like a magnet. "Will you be going back to wherever you were before?"

"Eventually. I still have unfinished business there."

His hand moved ever so slightly at her waist, skimming the bare skin of her back.

"You look incredibly beautiful," he said.

"If you still have unfinished business," she said crisply, ignoring his compliment—or trying to, "I'm surprised you came at all."

"An emergency called me away."

Her pulse began to throb at her throat as she stared blankly at his chest. Had he just pulled her closer, or had she moved toward him? His body brushed only lightly against her, but it was difficult to pull her mind off the sensation, especially when the tips of her breasts were tickled by his lapel. How did he do it, awaken every nerve in her body so effortlessly?

"You consider your grandparents' anniversary an emergency?"

"I didn't come for the anniversary, although I'm very glad to be here for it. The emergency was you."

Her mouth trembled as she looked up at his steadfast reply, betraying her. She looked over his shoulder, seeing Gerard twirling an ecstatic-looking Clarisse just feet away but not really absorbing anything but the feeling of being in Ian's arms.

"Your breaking off things between us wasn't easy, Ian, but you need hardly consider me an emergency. I've been doing fine."

"I know that. And I didn't break things off between us."

"You disappeared for half a year without so much as a text message," she said with dripping sarcasm.

"I thought it'd be best. A clean break. While I tried to figure things out."

"Well it worked," she told him with fake airiness. "The clean break," she clarified, rising anger making it possible to meet his stare again. It was a mistake. His gaze blazed down at her face, the emotion in his eyes palpable, but also completely indecipherable, like trying to read the meaning in a raging inferno.

"I didn't want to hurt you. It wasn't my intention," he said.

"Intended or not, you did."

His mouth went hard. His nostrils flared. Why didn't he at least apologize? He owed her that, didn't he? He was the most infuriating man she'd ever known. His hand shifted on her waist so that his entire palm was on bare skin. His heat poured into her. He pressed, as if he wanted to detail the sensation of her backbone. For a moment, she forgot what they'd been discussing as her belly brushed his pelvis. Her core contracted, the immediate sharp ache shocking her.

"Francesca, I think you might be in danger."

She blinked, totally disoriented by what had just occurred. It was as if her body had a mind all its own, straining toward him, aching for him against her will.

"What?" she asked, sure she'd misunderstood him.

"Someone tried to kidnap you in Chicago."

She made an incredulous sound. "Kidnap? What are you talking about? You mean that man who tried to rob Davie and me?"

"I read the police report," he said coldly. "That wasn't an attempted robbery. Why everybody else seems to be ignoring the obvious is beyond me."

"You read . . ." She faded off, scolding herself for her initial surprise. Ian had stunned her many times with his ability to get almost any information he desired, even highly confidential information. This was yet another example of his power, not to mention something that bordered on paranoia.

"Have you been spying on me?" she accused.

"No. But I've been keeping tabs. Just to make sure you were all right."

"Well your concern was misguided," she said sharply. "Both in the case of that attempted robbery incident and in general." She stepped back as the music came to an end. He dropped his arms slowly to his sides. "I've been doing just fine without you, Ian."

"You're lying," she heard him say quietly.

"Why would you assume that?" she asked under her breath as chatting people started to move past them as they left the dance floor.

"You're the other half of me. I feel like something has been ripped out of my chest not being with you. I think it's the same for you."

Her mouth dropped open at his quiet audacity. Her eyes burned at his stark declaration of pain.

"Then maybe you shouldn't have been the one to rip it apart," she hissed, knowing her naked heart was fully exposed in that moment, but not caring.

She turned and headed for the doors.

He sat alone in the sitting room, slouching on the velvet couch, his collar unbuttoned, his tie hanging loose around his neck. The fire was dying. It must be five in the morning. The huge house was utterly quiet around him following the clamor of the ball, making him feel like he was in the belly of a sleeping beast. He knew he wouldn't rest, so he hadn't even bothered going to bed.

Surely Francesca was safe here . . . in his grandparents' home. He knew how secure his grandfather kept the house, with its ancient and priceless treasures. He was grateful she was there versus in Chicago, seeing as how she refused to stay at his penthouse, which was also extremely secure.

Then maybe you shouldn't have been the one to rip it apart.

His eyelids closed at the memory of her saying that as she looked up at him, her expression utterly shattered. He'd done that; forced her into feeling as much pain as he experienced. What else could he do, though, but travel this alternative road, and pray that their paths met again? He couldn't have stayed with her and pretended he didn't doubt his place at her side.

He still couldn't. But he couldn't stay away, either. Not in these circumstances. Not until he at least understood the direction of the threat.

He thought of his first vision of her tonight, of a beauty that seemed to both warm him like a friendly fire and strike like lightning to the very heart of him. Desire stabbed through him, lancing and precise, a result of knowing Francesca lay within walking distance from him, soft and pliable in sleep. He winced and put his hand on his cock through his trousers, a purely instinctive gesture to stanch the ache. When that gave him no relief, he took a large swig of the brandy he held in his hand.

He'd always dreaded the idea of hurting her, guessing he probably would. Not intentionally. Never that. Just as a result of who he was.

Who he wasn't.

But it was stupid to dwell on things he couldn't control now. He was worried about that incident in Chicago. He couldn't believe no one else was as alarmed. Clearly, no one else had bothered to read between the lines about what had occurred on that busy Chicago street. A sick feeling swept through him. What if he'd somehow made her a target by leaving her so much power in his company? He should have realized that it might make her vulnerable. He'd had his fair share of potential threats over the years, both toward his company and his person. Usually, it was just a matter of crackpots shooting off their mouth. But there had been a few cases in which if it hadn't been for his special attention to security, he might have run into some real trouble. He'd never told Francesca about those incidents, not wanting her to worry, so it was no real surprise to him that she was doubtful about a potential threat.

His concern about that attack made him want to immediately take back control of Noble Enterprises. But would that action diminish the threat to Francesca? Or possibly just mask it?

His research into Trevor Gaines's sordid past would just have to be put on hold for the time being. Francesca didn't want him near her, but he'd have to contrive a way to manage it until his fear was calmed.

Again, her image rose to taunt him, the remembered sensation of holding her slender body while they danced, of touching the silk of her skin, a torture he eagerly sought. She looked more beautiful to him than she ever had, but he didn't kid himself that she hadn't also shown the signs of suffering. Her muscles had felt rigid with tension beneath his hand while they danced. Her face looked drawn and there were pale purple shadows beneath her eyes. She hadn't been sleeping. He wasn't surprised, but seeing her pain firsthand was yet another festering wound.

A muted sound penetrated his thoughts and he opened his eyes.

Francesca walked toward him, her loose, long, rose-gold hair glowing subtly like dying embers against the ivory robe she wore. Had his desire been so sharp he'd called her to him? For a spellbound moment as she drew nearer, he didn't know if he slept or dreamed. Was he more intoxicated than he'd realized? She stopped in front of his bent knees, her face sublimely lovely, her expression inscrutable. He didn't move a muscle, frightened he'd shatter the spell. He caught a whiff of her scent, of her hair. Her body. *No, she's not a dream.*

"I see you couldn't sleep, either," she said.

"I never even tried."

His fingers unfurled when she put her hand on the snifter he held. She set it on the table.

"I'm not doing this because I forgive you," she said, her large doe eyes gleaming in the firelight, her voice a smoky caress against his roughened skin.

"I never expected forgiveness."

"Maybe that's why you haven't apologized."

He watched, enthralled as she shrugged off the robe and let it drop heedlessly to the floor. She was naked beneath it, her skin a pale gold in the firelight. For a moment, she just stood there, studying his face as he worshipped her beauty.

"Have you been with others? Since you left me?"

He looked up at her question, meeting her stare full on without reluctance.

"No."

For a moment, her gaze moved over his face. Then she straddled him and settled, her weight in his lap making his lungs burn. He inhaled sharply, realizing he'd been holding his breath, and her scent fully pervaded his awareness: the achingly familiar scent of her perfume, her skin . . . her arousal.

He closed his eyes when she encircled his neck with her arms, buried her face against his neck and shoulder, pressed her lips to his neck and ground her pussy against his cock, her actions single-minded . . . electrical. Need clawed at him from inside, the pain of it impossible to control. His hands absorbed the softness of her skin. For a second, he just sat there, rigid, an animal straining silently—furiously—at fraying bonds. She shifted. Desire ripped through flesh and bone, exploding to the surface. His fingers furrowed in the hair at her nape. He clutched and pulled, forcing her head back, exposing her white throat and lush, parted lips.

He kissed her. It was like going from cruel impoverishment to indecent wealth in five seconds flat.

For an indeterminable length of time, he ravished her, unable to get enough of her singular taste and soft moans, becoming fevered by the fire he felt rising beneath the surface of her skin and penetrating from her pussy to his cock. He molded her curving hips to his palms, the once familiar, erotic fit maddening him. He used his hold to ground her down in his lap, their harsh moans mingling in their fused mouths.

"No," she said harshly when he began to move her off his lap in order to lay her on the couch. He was consumed by the idea of taking her, fusing with her, perhaps afraid that if he waited too long, this unlikely moment would pass. He saw the glint of determination in her firelit, dewy eyes. "I will stay on top."

For a moment, he didn't move, absorbing her meaning. His nostrils flared as a flash of . . . not anger, precisely, but frustration went through him. They had made love countless times, but never with Francesca in the position of control. But still . . . he understood her point.

He had lost her trust. She would fight against surrendering control again. He must tread carefully, or she would flee.

"All right," he said quietly.

There was a trace of defiance in her expression as she held his stare and scooted back on his thighs. They both unfastened his pants, their movements increasingly frantic. Ian grew hastier when she left the mechanics to him and cupped her hand around his cock through the fabric of his pants, making jacking motions up and down the shaft.

He hissed at the sensation of her hand enclosing the naked skin a moment later. She rose over him. The sensation of her wet, clinging flesh gloving the tip of his cock was divine, the feeling of burrowing into her warm, tight body sacred. Once she sat in his lap, and he struggled to reaccustom himself to the nirvana of being buried in her, she cupped his head in her hands, her thumbs caressing his face.

"You still want me."

He blinked, shock penetrating his lust at her fiercely uttered words.

"Do you think I ever stopped?" he demanded through a clenched jaw incredulously. "Do you think I ever *could*?"

She shook her head and he saw a tear glistening on her cheek. "I don't know what I think, except I hate you for making me do this." He felt her shudder all the way at the core of her body where he was lodged. "I hate you for making me need you so much that I'd lower myself to this."

"You have never once lowered yourself," he rasped, grabbing her hips, his fingers sinking into firm buttocks, moving her. She gasped and clamped her eyes closed. "Look at me," he said harshly. She reluctantly opened her eyes. "You have only raised me. I know I don't deserve you, but that doesn't mean that I don't burn for you. That I didn't. Every minute of every day."

She moaned and placed her hands on his shoulders. Despite meeting his stare for a moment, she kept her eyes closed as she began to fuck him, the tight, fluid roll of her hips leaving him gasping. She hopped in his lap, breasts bouncing, clearly needing the frantic joining he also craved. Their flesh beat together quicker and quicker. He studied her face in the firelight, sensing her wild desperation.

He tightened his hold on her hips and stilled her in his lap. Her eyelids blinked open heavily. He held her stare as he put his hand between her thighs.

"No," she whispered, even though she bucked her hips forward, bumping her damp outer tissues against his knuckles as his finger burrowed between her labia.

"I don't like to see you suffering," he murmured. "You need to come. You need relief."

He placed one hand at the base of her spine, his other between her humid thighs. He flicked and pressed her clit with the ridge of his forefinger, slightly pressing her body against the pressure from the back in order to increase her pleasure. He watched with a tight focus as every muscle in her sleek body tightened. He saw the flush on her chest and cheeks deepen, felt her slight tremors as she crested.

Her cry as she succumbed struck him as poignant. Sad. So beautiful it hurt. He nursed her through her climax, his cock throbbing in her convulsing vagina. It was too much to bear, but he forced himself to exist in the flames, not wanting the moment to end.

He couldn't survive that way forever, though. No man could. He leaned forward slightly at the same moment he pushed her back, so that her upper body was bent back between his spread thighs at an upward angle, her hair falling behind her, her weight supported by his spread hands on her back. He began to fuck her in that position, using his pumping arms to control the motion. His gaze moved hungrily over her perspiration-glazed, naked torso, her beautiful breasts trembling every time he thrust high into her, a tiny cry popping out of her throat as they slammed together.

He slid one hand up her back to her shoulder, using his hold to support her better and to optimize the thrusts of her pussy down on his cock. His groans twined with the muted keening sound she made. The friction was intense. Optimal. His flexed biceps felt like they'd pop out of his skin, he abused them so hard, never letting up an ounce on the tension, but he didn't care. The pleasure far outstripped the discomfort.

Desire rode him like a slashing rider, but he grimaced when he saw she'd closed her eyes again, blocking herself from him. He realized too late that instinct had taken hold. He was controlling their lovemaking, fucking her ruthlessly.

"Do you want me to stop?" he asked, the fist of passion gripping at his throat, making him sound strangled. He *would* stop, though.

He would, if she said the word. "Do you want to finish it?" he asked even as he thrust her up and down again and again on his voracious cock.

She clamped her eyes tighter and shook her head. A moment later, he felt a rush of heat around him. She was coming. He plunged her down on him and flexed his hips, sinking his cock to the hilt.

He let heaven fall. It crashed down like knives, spikes of pleasure ripping through him.

He pulled her against him while he still ejaculated inside her, hugging her to him desperately, breathing the scent of her release, moving her sweet body over him in a sublime dance he dreaded coming to an end.

She kept her eyes closed as she panted with her face pressed against his neck, filling herself with his scent. She wondered dazedly if she was trying to blind herself to the vision of him, or if she was childishly shutting her eyes in an attempt to hide her own treachery from herself. His hands moved, stroking her sides and back, his touch somehow soothing her and making misery rise at once. When mounting confusion and shame reached her throat, she held down a groan. She lifted herself off him, wincing at the abrupt extraction of his still firm, warm flesh from her body.

She didn't know if she was glad or anxious that he didn't speak as she stood and hurried into her robe.

"I have promised to paint Belford Hall for Anne and James," she said in a thick voice as she tied her robe rapidly.

"Yes. Grandmother told me," he said.

She glanced at him and impatiently ripped through the unsecure knot she'd just made and refastened the robe. He hadn't moved since she'd crawled off him, she realized with rising discomfort. He just sat there, looking devastatingly beautiful with his dark hair mussed, his tuxedo pants down around his thighs and his glistening penis falling against the stark white of his dress shirt at a slanted angle. Her fingers shook as she jerked at the belt of her robe too tightly.

"I was planning on doing the sketches while I'm here. If you plan to stay, however, I'll come back another time," she said, determinedly meeting his stare. His blue eyes glittered in the flickering light of the dying fire.

"You won't leave Belford," he stated flatly. "Not now."

"Well one of us has got to," she said, anger edging her tone at his finality. Not anger at him, for once. At herself. She couldn't believe what she'd just done. He had made her a stranger to herself.

No, you did that with your insatiable need.

"I don't want you to change your plans because of me. I won't stay long," he said.

Her feet wavered.

"Is there something you want to say?" he asked quietly.

"Yes," she said, lifting her chin. "This . . ." she glanced at his beautiful, satiated cock and looked away anxiously. "Didn't happen."

For the first time since he'd returned, she saw a small smile tilt his mouth. She took a reflexive step back. She hadn't been expecting that potent weapon.

"It happened all right," he stated unequivocally. "Do you mean that you prefer not to make it obvious to everyone at Belford that it happened?"

She nodded, not meeting his stare because she wasn't sure exactly what she'd meant.

"All right," he said, jerking his underwear and pants over his thighs and hips. He settled back in the couch, but left his pants unfastened. "I can agree to that, if it's what you prefer. It'll give us time to figure out what it means, I suppose."

"What *what* means?" she mumbled uneasily.

"Everything. What we mean."

She gave an impatient shake of her head. "There is no 'we.' I'm going to bed."

"I assume since you found me in here tonight, you'd checked my quarters first?" he asked from behind her.

She paused and cautiously peered over her shoulder. "Yes," she admitted, seeing no way to deny it. "Your grandmother pointed out your rooms when she gave me the tour. When you weren't in them, I came here. Anne said this was your favorite room."

He held her stare. "Go now to your suite and rest. I think you'll sleep now. But tonight—I'll wait for you in my bedroom after everyone settles."

She opened her mouth to deny him—God, how she hated his quiet arrogance. He spoke before she could come up with the most scathing response possible.

"I'm not saying it for me—or at least not just for me. You're burning from the inside out, lovely," he said, his voice hollow. "I know it's my fault, but I see how tired you are. I won't have you suffer while I'm here. I don't want you to become sick. You'll come tonight. You'll come tonight if only because we have no choice. Not while we're here together in this house. Maybe you'll rest easier . . . and so will I for a precious period of time."

Heat flushed her cheeks. She thought of denying him, but didn't want to add lying to the sins she was compiling since Ian had returned. She said nothing, just turned and left the sitting room, silently praying all the while she'd find the strength to prove his arrogant assumptions wrong.

Ian watched her go, forcing muscles that wanted to spring into action and claim her into complete stillness. After the door had closed behind her, he glanced around the increasingly dim room. The fire was almost out. It was always darkest before the dawn.

He lowered his head and caught her lingering scent. He inhaled deeply, taking strength from the fragrance, and stood.

On the way to his quarters, he heard a click and a subtle, scurrying sound on the oak floors of the hallway. He glanced behind him and saw the maid, Clarisse, standing outside Gerard's closed door, looking down as she finished closing the side zipper on her gown. Her head came up and she saw him standing there. She started. The shadows were so heavy in the hallway, he sensed more than saw her shocked embarrassment.

Neither of them spoke. Clarisse turned and hurried away in the opposite direction.

She slept better than she had in ages, not rising until twelve thirty. For a moment, she lay in bed, recalling all the tumultuous events of the previous night.

After she'd left Ian standing on the dance floor the night before, she'd searched through the maze of Belford, desperate to find the kitchens. Twenty minutes and two startled waiters' instructions later, she'd found what she sought: Mrs. Hanson bustling around the gargantuan kitchen belowstairs, preparing some of the last touches on the lavish midnight buffet.

"Francesca!" Mrs. Hanson had called in mixed shock and pleasant surprise when she'd appeared. But then the sweet older woman had acted like it was the most natural thing in the world for her to stumble into the kitchens in all her finery.

Mrs. Hanson had given her a cup of hot tea and let her sit at the center island, just like Francesca had grown accustomed to doing while at Ian's penthouse. Francesca didn't tell the housekeeper why she'd sought her out in such odd circumstances, but Mrs. Hanson seemed to understand without words. She must have heard the rumor of Ian's return. She answered Francesca's random questions about mundane things, like the feast, occasionally interrupting their conversation to call out instructions to the catering staff.

Francesca had eventually gone back up, forcing herself to remain at the ball until past one in the morning, going through the motions of enjoying herself and fastidiously acting as though Ian wasn't across the room. Ignoring him stole every ounce of energy she possessed.

Trying to ignore him, because it hadn't worked in the slightest.

Once she'd gone to bed, however, she was surprised to realize she couldn't rest, despite her exhaustion. There was no one left to fool but herself, lying there alone in the darkness, and Ian's return had halted that brittle self-deception. Sleep had been an utter impossibility.

Until she'd finally risen in desperation and sought him out.

He'd been right.

It was strange to feel so awake on that bright December day, her nerves tingling with awareness . . . so *good*, and yet so terrible at once. Quenching her desire had been what she needed to rest, and he'd known that. Some part of her must have known it, too.

She closed her eyes as she stood before the bathroom mirror, overwhelmed by a potent paradoxical sense of shame and arousal at recalling what had occurred in the sitting room. Never in a million years would she have thought she could be so bold . . . so desperate. The memory of what she'd done under the cloak of night felt like the recollection from another person's brain had been magically inserted to her own, all the details excruciatingly vivid, but also foreign somehow.

He'd left her. He'd offered no explanation as to why (not that she'd allowed him to give a reason) and practically the moment he returned, she had sought him out and let her pussy rule the day.

No. You let his cock rule.

Yet another reason it was difficult to meet her own gaze in the mirror as she got ready. Shame, anger, and longing were an unbearable brew.

She showered and dressed in jeans, boots, and a warm sweater and smoothed her hair into a ponytail. She left the suite a moment later, carrying her sketchpad, pencils, her coat, hat, and gloves in her arms.

They all were in the sitting room when she arrived—Lucien, Elise, Anne, James, Gerard . . .

Ian.

The mood in the cozy sitting room was very casual and easy-going, everyone looking pleasantly lazy after the late-night festivities. She'd interrupted Elise in the process of animatedly describing a funny scene from a comedy that was currently popular. Her friend was curled up in the corner of the couch, her knees resting casually on Lucien's thighs. She envied Elise's ease in such splendid surroundings, a natural consequence of her upbringing, an innate confidence Francesca herself could never hope to achieve.

"Good morning," Francesca said to everyone. "I apologize for being down so late."

"Nonsense, we all slept in," Anne assured. "But you look rosy this morning. You must have slept well. I'm glad to see it."

She was determined not to meet Ian's stare at Anne's incendiary words, even though she felt his gaze on her heated cheeks. She couldn't help but notice from her peripheral vision that he was dressed much like her. Her heart used to do a leap on the rare occasions when she saw him in jeans, knowing it probably meant he wanted them to go motorcycle riding together. He really did become a different man on the open road. She loved seeing his wind-whipped hair, his relaxation palpable in comparison to his typical rigid control, his full-out smile . . . the vision of him laughing without restraint. Even though she lectured herself not to look, she couldn't seem to stop herself from glancing furtively at his long, muscular jean-clad thighs and narrow hips as James pulled up a chair for her and Anne went to pour her a cup of coffee from the service arranged on the sideboard.

"You weren't planning on starting work on the painting today, were you?" Anne asked as she approached, noticing the sketchbook and coat she'd placed on the floor next to her chair. "But I was hoping you'd relax before beginning on that, take a little vacation. Why don't you get started after the New Year? I'm having the canvas and your supplies delivered on the thirtieth. We're all determined to be lazy today, after last night. We're thinking about taking in a movie in town," Anne said, handing her a china cup filled with coffee and cream. Francesca took a sip of the hot brew.

For some reason, irritation was rising in her at the idea of them all being so casual and accepting of Ian's unexpected return . . .

. . . of his prolonged, unexplained absence.

He could do murder and his friends and family would rush to see to his every comfort.

You certainly were eager enough to see to his every comfort last night, you hypocrite.

"Vacation?" she asked, her light tone disguising not only her chaotic thoughts, but her anger. "Does that mean we're all off the hook then?"

"Off the hook?" Anne asked uncertainly as she returned to her seat next to James.

"Has Ian let us all off the hook?" she clarified, her anger making it possible to stare directly at Ian as she took another sip of coffee. "Are you planning on returning to run Noble Enterprises, now that you're back?"

She could tell by the stunned silence that no one else had yet dared to ask him the question. Ian returned her stare calmly before replying.

"I haven't decided yet. Lin has kept me generally apprised of what's been going on, and Lucien and Gerard filled me in on the details of the Tyake acquisition last night."

"I do hope you're pleased with our efforts," Francesca said.

He didn't blink at her quiet sarcasm. "I am. You've all arranged things almost as precisely as I would have. Everything is in place for the plan to move forward in the New Year. I was waiting until a moment when I could thank you all more formally, but Francesca's right. You all deserve my gratitude now . . . as well as my apologies for leaving you in such a fix. I can't thank you all enough, for all you've done on the Tyake acquisition," he said, glancing at each of them in turn. His quiet sincerity left her feeling even more agitated.

"That's what family is for," James replied for everyone.

She stood, taking her cup to the sideboard. She hadn't meant to say those things; she really needed to get ahold of herself. No one deserved her bitterness, save Ian.

Save herself.

"I hope you all have a good time at the movies," she said with a smile, picking up her coat, hat, and the fingerless gloves she wore for outdoor sketching in the winter. "I think I'll get started on some rough sketches before the canvas arrives. I could use a little work."

"She's right," Gerard said. He stood to retrieve her sketchpad and pencils while she put on her gloves. "Work always sets things on track, I always say. And I'm not going to the movies, so I'll take Francesca to the gardener's cottage. That's where you two were saying you wanted her to set up base while she draws, isn't that right?" he asked James and Anne.

"Gardener's cottage?" Francesca asked, hearing of this for the first time.

"Well, it's not really a gardener's cottage anymore," James explained. "It hasn't been anyone's cottage but an occasional guest's for the past twenty years. But it'd be a good post for you. It's right at the edge of the woods, and it's got an excellent straight-on view of Belford through a picture window. It won't do for the details, of course, but we figured that since it's so chilly out, it might save you a few days from the cold while you get the panoramic sketches. I had Mr. Sayers turn on the cottage furnace just yesterday, so it should be warm enough by now. If you think that'd be useful?"

"Very useful," Francesca assured. "Thank you for thinking of it. It'll save me having to go in and out to thaw out my fingers, for a few days, at least."

"I'll take her to it," Ian said, standing. Gerard shared Francesca's nonplussed expression.

"I said I'd show her to it. You should go and relax with the others," Gerard said.

"We'll both show her then," Ian said quietly, but his eyes flashed dangerously at Gerard before he picked up his coffee cup.

"It's not really necessary for you to come," Gerard prevaricated as Ian set his cup and saucer on the tray on the sideboard.

"It is, actually," Ian said. James shifted uncomfortably in his chair at the hard edge to Ian's tone. Ian's stare at Gerard was one that Francesca could only describe as a silent, simmering challenge. Concern mingled with her annoyance. His calm exterior was far more brittle than she'd ever seen it before. "Because the gardener is off today, and I have the only other set of keys to the cottage."

Gerard flushed. Clearly, Ian had preempted Gerard's actions and asked his grandfather for the keys in advance. There was something subtly, but distinctly proprietary underlying Ian's statement, as if he was reminding Gerard who the future master of Belford was. Or who the master of *Francesca* was. Resentment bubbled up into her chest. She noticed Elise giving Lucien an uncomfortable glance in the prickly silence that followed, and Anne and James did the same. Ian was acting like a caveman. It was all extremely awkward. She shot a fulminating look at Ian, which he didn't notice as he studied his cousin.

"Come on, Gerard," she said with false brightness. "I'll enjoy your company."

Gerard seemed a little angry, not to mention embarrassed, which made her even more irritated at Ian. At first, she thought he was going to stand down, but then he gave her a smile and nodded toward the door as if to say, *Let's proceed then.* With everyone watching them in the uncomfortable silence that followed, she felt she had no choice but to follow Ian out of the room, Gerard falling in step behind her.

Chapter Five

She, Ian, and Gerard walked to the cottage at the edge of the woods, their boots crunching on the frosty path leading through the gardens, the cold winter air seemingly doing nothing to cool either her irritation at Ian or the charged atmosphere swirling among the three of them.

The cottage itself was nice, she decided once Ian had unlocked the door and they'd entered, but chilly despite the furnace being activated. The interior was modest in comparison to the luxury of Belford itself. In fact, the little house looked like it hadn't been redecorated for several decades. She found the shabby elegance of it cozy.

"Stay here. Both of you," Ian said after he'd closed the front door. She gave Gerard a questioning glance, but Gerard was watching his cousin dubiously as well.

"What is *with* him?" Gerard mumbled for her ears only.

Francesca just shrugged, too irritated to reply.

They stood next to the cold hearth of the fireplace as Ian stepped into the kitchen and looked around, and then stalked down the hallway, his dark head just two feet away from the low ceiling. At first, she'd thought he was inspecting the place like someone might a rarely used property in order to make sure there were no leaks or property damage. By the time he returned to the small living room where she stood, however, another suspicion had struck her.

"Ian, you're not checking out this place for . . . I don't know, *bad guys* or something, are you?"

"What's this?" Gerard asked, both amused and confused.

"Just making sure everything is in order for you to work here today," Ian said evenly, stepping closer, blue eyes pinning her. His size struck her suddenly, his *presence*. He was really too large for these cramped quarters. She stepped back reflexively, and then felt foolish when he only knelt and started to build a fire.

"Were there any other unusual occurrences either before or after that man tried to take you in Chicago?" Ian asked in an offhand manner as he began to arrange logs and kindling.

"No one tried to *take* me," she insisted. She noticed Gerard's puzzled expression. For some reason, a sharp somatic memory of the assailant's brutal grip rose to her awareness. She rubbed her upper arms as if to erase the unpleasant recollection. Was there any possibility that Ian was right in his suspicion? "And in answer to your question, no. Nothing unusual at all has happened other than that."

"Gerard? Anything odd that you noticed while you were in Chicago?"

"Other than the fact that the waiters there whisked away my plate the second I took my last bite, everything was boringly normal," Gerard said dryly.

Ian just continued to build the fire in silence. She shook her head in disgust, knowing him well enough to recognize he wasn't going to argue, but that he hadn't changed his mind in the slightest. She left Gerard and looked around the little house, familiarizing herself with the location of the bathroom, which was in the hallway between the living room and bedroom. The small, tidy bedroom included a made double bed, upholstered chair, a desk and bureau. She'd be very comfortable working here, she decided. She found some tea bags in a kitchen cabinet and filled the kettle on the stove.

When she returned to the living room with a mug of tea in her hand, Ian had successfully started a fire. It felt warm enough for her to remove her coat.

"There's hot water for tea, if you'd like it," she said politely as she hung up her coat. Personally, she was hoping both men would vacate as quickly as possible. She'd never be able to focus with Ian there in the small confines of the cottage, sending her simmering, churning emotions up to a full boil.

"That sounds good," Gerard said, starting for the kitchen.

"I'm going to walk around and inspect the grounds a bit, maybe look in at the stables," Ian said pointedly to Gerard, who came to a halt. "Why don't you come with me? There are some things we need to discuss."

Francesca went still in the process of lifting her mug to her lips, her gaze bouncing from Ian to Gerard to Ian again. Surely Ian wasn't planning on confronting Gerard. *Surely* he wasn't considering talking to Gerard about *her*. The thought angered her—what right did he have to tell Gerard what to do when it came to her? At the same time, she'd be lying to herself if she said she didn't experience a little relief. She'd already determined she wasn't interested in Gerard's advances. With Ian here, Gerard's attraction to her just seemed to muddy the waters even more when all she needed was clarity.

"Francesca doesn't like people around when she works," Ian said quietly when Gerard opened his mouth—Francesca would have guessed to protest. "It makes it difficult for her to concentrate."

She took a sip of her tea to hide the pain that went through her at Ian saying out loud something she'd told him once in an intimate moment. It seemed too strange, the paradox of the closeness she felt with him combined with a glaring distance, given his actions. It suddenly felt unbearable. Strangling. She wanted nothing more than to be alone.

"It's true," she told Gerard apologetically. "I freeze up when people are around."

"We'll walk then," Gerard said, shrugging. "I have plenty of questions for you as well, Ian."

"Grandfather bid on an old boxer-engine World War Two motorcycle at Higsby's last month. Care to have a look at it?" she heard Ian say to Gerard as they headed toward the door.

"Is it in running condition?" Gerard asked, and Francesca was glad to hear the note of interest in his voice. Ian was trying, at least. He must feel guilty for his earlier heavy-handedness with his cousin. She'd always heard from Ian that Gerard and he were close. If they weren't getting along, it was most likely due to some misplaced jealousy on Ian's part.

"Needs some work." Ian opened the front door and cool air rushed into the room. "I'll be able to keep an eye on the cottage from the grounds, but lock this after we leave," he called back to Francesca.

Francesca rolled her eyes.

"Francesca?" he prompted in that hoarse, compelling voice of his. She met his stare reluctantly. "*Double* lock it. Please."

"Fine," she muttered, willing to say anything to get him out of there. It felt like she hadn't taken a full breath of air into her lungs since she'd entered the sitting room that morning. She finally did so after she'd slammed the door shut behind the two men and twisted the locks.

She couldn't take this for much longer. If Ian didn't leave Belford sometime very soon, she would have to be the one to go. It was a simple matter of survival.

But could she really do it? Could she really walk away from him after so many months of worrying, so many unbearable nights of feeling his absence like a gaping hole in her spirit?

If he could do it, you can.

Somehow, that incendiary thought didn't help any.

*   *   *

Ian and Gerard returned after their inspection of the grounds, but thankfully her focus on the sketch gave her some measure of defense.

Or so she'd thought.

Someone tapped lightly on the door, but then immediately used the key to enter. Ian. He knew she'd be lost in her own little world. She glanced around distractedly from where she sat on a chair in front of the cottage picture window and saw him walking toward the fireplace, looking rugged and very appealing with a load of logs in his arms and his short hair windblown. He met her gaze, but didn't speak as he put the logs in the firebox and kindled the fire. She resumed moving her hand over the sketchbook propped in her lap, distantly aware that Gerard stood for a moment at the threshold looking at her before walking out again, closing the door gently behind him.

The thought that she and Ian were alone in the cottage penetrated her awareness. She swallowed uneasily, her entire focus transferring from the view before her and the unfolding image on the page to the sounds of him moving behind her. What had Gerard and he talked about? Would he say anything to her now that they were alone?

She heard his boots scuffling on the marble hearth as he stood. He returned the poker to the holder, with a muted sound of metal on metal. She tried to locate him in the room by sound in the anxious silence that followed.

Her sketching hand went completely still a second later when she felt him touch her nape at her hairline, his fingertips cool . . . slightly abrasive. Shivers cascaded down her spine.

I'll wait for you in my bedroom tonight.

Her heart seemed to jump into her throat. He hadn't said the same words he'd uttered in the sitting room early this morning, and yet she'd heard them perfectly in her head. She sat looking out the picture window, frozen, every cell of her being focused on him standing just behind her. His fingers moved slightly, stroking her, creating a fresh wave of tingles down her spine . . . tightening her nipples.

"I'll lock the door from the outside. Start back to Belford before it gets dark. If you don't, I'll come and get you."

It could have been that he was alluding to the fact that she frequently lost track of time when she worked, and that she would be expected for dinner at Belford. It could have been that he was referring to her prickliness when it came to his presence, and he was letting her know point-blank if she stayed too long, she'd have to endure him.

Whatever the subtleties, he was making it clear that he'd claim her upon his whim.

Anger swelled in her breast at the thought, but that sensation was nothing in comparison to the other places in her body that his touch had enlivened.

Those places prickled with awareness long after he was gone.

That evening after she got out of a warm, relaxing bath, she found Clarisse in her suite hanging out a dark green dress for her to wear.

"I poured some club soda for you," Clarisse said, nodding at a glass on a tray sitting on the coffee table. "Her ladyship told me to tell you that they met up with some friends who are staying in town over the holiday, and they've been asked to dine at Belford tonight— a Mr. Gravish and his wife. Her ladyship is friends with Mr. Gravish's mother, and his wife was a school friend of Mr. Noble's."

"Ian you mean?" Francesca asked.

Clarisse nodded. "Yes, she knew him when Mr. Noble was still a boy, you know, in the local primary. Back when he first came to Belford Hall, I believe. One of the older maids told me he hadn't ever been properly schooled before he came to England, and so her ladyship enrolled him in the local school for a year and gave him a private tutor in order to get him up to snuff. Mr. Noble was sharp as a blade, though, even if he was rough around the edges. It only took that year before he was ready for private, but that's when he met Mrs. Gravish—I mean, she wasn't Mrs. Gravish back then, of course." Clarisse realized she'd been prattling on and gave Francesca an anxious glance. "Anyway, I'd started to stay that everyone is going to meet in the sitting room at seven before dinner," Clarisse said. She held up a pair of brown suede pumps. "These with the dress, miss?"

"Sure," Francesca said distractedly, thinking about what Clarisse had said about Ian as she removed the towel on her head and watched the young woman bustle around. "Did you have a good time at the ball last night, Clarisse?"

"Oh, yes. It was amazing." She said excitedly before something seemed to occur to her and she hesitated.

"What is it?" Francesca asked as she toweled her hair.

"It's only . . ." She bit her lower lip as she withdrew silk underwear from a drawer. "Mr. Noble returning . . . it must have upset you a lot." She fumbled, looking at Francesca worriedly. "I mean . . . we heard that you and his lordship's grandson were engaged to be married . . . before," she finished lamely.

"We were. Once. But that's over now," Francesca said, picking up a comb from the dresser.

"But you must still have feelings for him." Clarisse burst out.

Feelings for him. Against her will, Francesca felt his fingers brush against the tingling skin of her nape. She shivered and her sex tightened just from the memory. "I mean . . . Mr. Noble is the most handsome man I've ever seen," Clarisse added lamely.

"Handsome is as handsome does," Francesca said with a small smile. "I'm going to go and dry my hair. Oh . . . and Clarisse?"

"Yes?" Clarisse asked over her shoulders, holding a pair of sheer stockings in her hands.

"No offense or anything, but I'll pick out my own underwear. Call it an American thing."

Clarisse's blue eyes went huge before she saw Francesca's smile.

Laughing, she scooped the underthings she'd set on the bureau back into the drawer and closed it.

Francesca dried her hair, and then used a curling iron to make a loose fall of waves. Leaving the bathroom, she stared at the conservative wool dress Clarisse had set out for her for dinner. She thought about Ian's arrogant assumption that she would go to him tonight in his bedroom.

Maybe she would. Maybe she wouldn't.

Whatever she chose, she would be miserable. It was only a matter of when she'd feel it. He was the one responsible for all these opposing feelings, all this unbearable friction grinding away inside her. Her agitation caused a usually buried but all-too-familiar rebellious streak to flare to life inside her.

She hung the green dress back in the closet and withdrew a long-sleeved, ruched sheath dress in brilliant cobalt blue. Five minutes later, she studied herself in the full-length mirror. Her long hair spilled around her shoulders, the reddish-gold color a striking contrast to the brilliant hue of the dress. She wore drop pearl earrings and no necklace. The dress had a low-cut, square-neck collar that left her throat, chest, and the top curves of her breasts exposed. It clung to her body, but the ruched fabric added an element of modesty. Overall, the dress gave the impression of sophisticated, confident sexuality.

The last thing she wanted to do at that moment was to let the world suspect how she felt on the inside. This dress would handily disguise all that.

Or that was her plan anyway. She thought it might work until she walked into the subtly lit sitting room minutes later, chin held high, only to discover it was empty. Deflated, she paused just inside the room, checking the clock on one of the bookcases. No . . . it was seven o'clock sharp. Had Clarisse mentioned the wrong room?

A sudden prescience overtook her and she turned to the right. Ian stood at the far side of the room looking devastating in a tuxedo with black tie, a book in his hand, his eyes gleaming from the shadows as he watched her.

She wavered awkwardly in her heels for a moment before she recalled the confident, unconcerned role she was supposed to be playing for the evening. *Shit,* she thought as Ian calmly replaced the book he'd been perusing in the shelf and walked toward her. She'd never been much of a good actress.

"Where is everyone else?" she asked.

"I was about to ask you the same thing," he said. His gaze dropped over her, lingering on the exposed skin of her chest and breasts. Her nipples pinched tight. She gritted her teeth. "That's a pretty dress."

"You bought it for me," she said, as if it were an unimportant, throwaway fact. She started to glance around the empty room, but did a double take when she noticed his small smile.

"And are you *wearing* it for me?" he asked, his low voice causing her neck to roughen in awareness.

"I brought exactly four dresses to Belford. You'll likely see me wear most of them. Knowing you, you'll think I'm wearing all of them for you. I can't control what you think," she said coldly.

"No," he said, his gaze lowering over her once again. Hot. Possessive. His nostrils flared slightly. "It's hard enough to control our own thoughts. Isn't it?" She realized she'd been staring covetously at his chest and wide shoulders. He looked indecently handsome in his tux.

She inhaled sharply and looked around the room. "Should we go and look for the others?"

"No, the fire has been laid and a man was in earlier restocking the liquor. This is where we are meeting. Would you like anything from the bar?" he asked.

"A glass of white wine, please," she said, eager for an excuse to get some distance between them. She stayed where she was at the edge of the room, comforted by the shadows that clung there. He returned soon enough, however, a glass of chardonnay in one hand, a highball glass of bourbon and water in the other. She took the glass from him quickly when he offered it.

"Who told you we were meeting in here tonight?" she asked, fixating on the reason why they were alone instead of surrounded by the protection of chatting friends and family.

"Gerard mentioned it I think. He must have gotten the time wrong."

"Maybe he wanted to get back at you for earlier," she said, taking a sip of the chilled, dry wine.

"Get back at me?" he asked in polite confusion, black brows arching.

She rolled her eyes. Sometimes he was so *British* in what he chose to notice and what he decided to ignore.

"Earlier today. Here in the sitting room. The keys to the cottage?" she pressed when he remained impassive. "What *was* all that about between you two?" she demanded, finding a vent for her all of her unspoken, volatile questions.

"It was nothing," he said, shrugging. She gave him a sarcastic glance. He frowned and took a sip of his drink, seeming to consider. "Gerard and I are like brothers at times. As you probably guessed from working with him on the Tyake acquisition, he would do anything for me, and I would do the same for him if he were in a pinch. But the other side of that is a little . . ."

"Brotherly rivalry?" she said dryly. "You never told me about that part of your relationship with him before."

"I don't consider it relevant," Ian replied, leaving her with the definite impression that if there was an issue, it was on Gerard's side. "Maybe it's inevitable. His mother and my grandfather were exceptionally close, even though my aunt Simone was almost a generation younger than Grandfather. Gerard was always close to my grandfather as a result of that bond, and they only grew closer when Gerard's father and mother died years back. Gerard was only eighteen when they were killed in a car wreck. He stayed alone at Chatham, a force unto his own from that day forward. But he still sought out Grandfather. He needed him, I think. Craved a pillar of strength, despite his show of independence. My grandparents have been parental figures to both Gerard and me. It's only natural that there might be some friction once in a while."

"And then there's the whole issue of the title and the properties being divided up between you two," Francesca observed. "How does Gerard feel about that?" she wondered, knowing from personal experience that Ian was very insouciant about the fact that his grandfather's title would go to his nephew versus his direct descendent—Ian himself.

He flashed a glance at her, his eyes catching the firelight. "You seem awfully interested in Gerard."

"He's been very kind to me since all this business with Tyake started up," she said stiffly.

"I'll bet he has been," he muttered before taking a swift draw on his drink.

He was there for me a hell of a lot more than you were.

His eyes widened slightly. She felt scored by his stare. She hadn't said the furious thought out loud, had she? Maybe it didn't matter. Ian was a mind reader when it came to her. She tore her gaze away from his and lowered her head. Her anxiety mounted even higher when she glanced again at the empty room . . . the intimate lighting.

His presence and nearness seemed to set every cell of her being vibrating in acute awareness. If only she could shut off this immense attraction she had for him . . . this compelling *connection*. Ian had found the strength necessary to sever that connection by leaving her. Why was it so hard for her body and spirit to comprehend that rift?

She hesitated, wanting nothing more than to swallow the familiar question again, but the burn had become too great on her throat and tongue.

"What is it?" he asked quietly, obviously sensing her internal battle.

"Are you well?"

She closed her eyes briefly, mortified at how shaky . . . how *naked* her simple question had sounded in the silent room. "In good health, I mean," she hurried to say. When he didn't immediately reply, she met his stare. She struggled to explain. How could she tell him in these circumstances that she'd existed in hell, wondering if he was suffering or sick for all those months . . . alone. "It's just . . . you've lost weight," she added lamely.

"I'm healthy enough. The state of unhappiness doesn't qualify as an illness."

"I'm sure there are plenty of psychologists out there who would disagree."

"Do you think I need treatment?" he asked deadpan, his blue eyes spearing.

"What if I do?" she defended. "Most people who've been through what you've been through would benefit from some support."

"Don't worry, Francesca. Please."

The thread of entreaty in his tone, the way he said her name like a gentle caress with that rough voice, made emotion surge up on her unexpectedly. "Were you unhappy with me? Did I just not want to see the signs?" she asked before she could stop herself. She was a little horrorstruck by her boldness. Or was it her weakness that had made her ask? Would her allowing one question to escape set off a mass outbreak of wild, shameful curiosity?

She had never despised herself more, and yet still she waited, perched on a ledge of anticipation waiting for his reply. The question seemed to hang between them in the full silence. Her throat swelled when he stepped closer and she could make out the tiny, ambient dots of blue in his eyes. He touched her with the ridge of his forefinger just beneath her chin, and then gently stroked her throat. She shuddered at the caress.

"I have never been happier in my life than when I was with you. I didn't know what happiness was until you," he breathed out.

"Then *why*? Why did you leave?" she asked, unable to disguise her wretchedness. The words seemed to cut her as they came out, having grown sharp and crystallized from being kept inside for so long. Her heart seemed to stop when he brushed the corner of her mouth and cheek with the side of his hand. It felt so good, but she turned her chin away from him in hurt and confusion. He set down his drink on a nearby bookcase in an impatient gesture and stepped closer, using both hands to capture her face, a palm on each side of her jaw. He lowered his head until his mouth was just inches from hers.

"Because after my mother died, after I found out about Trevor Gaines, I had never felt more dark standing next to your brilliance, never so hollow beside your fullness," he said in a quiet, pressured voice. "My leaving had nothing to do with you, Francesca. Nothing. It was about me, trying to figure out who the hell I am. *What* the hell I am. I still don't know . . . and I don't deserve you until I do."

"You're Ian Noble, no different than you were before you found out about that foul man," she grated out. Her eyes burned, but she didn't want to blink lest she spill tears. "And that's not an answer, what you just gave me."

In the distance, she heard heels tapping on the Great Hall marble floor and a woman talking as though giving instructions.

"I'm sorry. It's the only answer I have," Ian said bleakly before he dropped his hands, grabbed his drink, and walked toward the fireplace. He set his glass on the mantel and faced the door just as Anne entered the room with a maid.

"Ian," Anne said in surprise. "You're down early."

"We were confused about the time," Ian said as Anne approached and he leaned down to kiss her cheek in greeting.

"We?" Anne asked, glancing around.

Francesca walked out of the shadows at the edge of the room. Anne's eyes went wide in pleasant surprise as Francesca greeted her.

She mentally damned the maid when she chose that moment to switch on a lamp. Anne's animated expression fell when she noticed the strained quality of Francesca's smile and her damp eyes.

Lisle Gravish was a nice-looking but fussy man of about thirty-five whose affected accent and pretentious jokes abraded Francesca's already raw nerves. His wife, Amy, defied all English stereotypes with her perfect beauty queen smile, exotic, curling jet-black hair, and the curves of an Italian film goddess. It looked as if a display case from Cartier had exploded on her, she glistened so greatly with diamonds. She combined all this glamour and beauty with talent. Apparently she was a gifted opera singer. Francesca wondered irritably as she watched Amy flirt outrageously with Ian during dinner if she'd begun to sprout those amazing breasts while they'd still been in primary together. Ian didn't necessarily reciprocate the flirtation, but he did occasionally smile. Ian's full-out smiles were so rare, and so brilliant, that in Francesca's opinion, they were the equivalent of another man's hotly whispered indecent proposal.

Perhaps that extra dash of jealousy added to her already chaotic mix of emotions was what made her careless in her interactions with Gerard, who sat next to her during dinner. She hadn't realized how distracted she'd been, failing to send up red flags as they talked quietly together. Things finally pierced her distraction when Gerard leaned close to her and spoke near her ear as they waited for the main course to be cleared.

"You have yet to wear the diamond choker I gave you."

"That's because I plan to return it. I told you it was too much," she murmured softly, keeping her face forward because Gerard's lips were barely an inch from the side of her head.

"Hold on to it for a bit. You might change your mind," he said silkily, his breath causing her hair to stir and tickle her ear. "Not that I'm complaining about your not wearing jewelry tonight. A wise woman knows that no decoration is necessary to complement absolute perfection."

She glanced across the table and saw Elise's wide-eyed, comical stare. Given Elise's amused look, she guessed Gerard was gazing down at her breasts. She grabbed her water glass, her jabbing elbow forcing Gerard to lean back in his chair. Elise suppressed a laugh and choked on her wine. Her suspicion about where Gerard had been gaping was confirmed when she noticed Ian's stone-cold stare.

Gerard took her hand as they left the dining room.

"May I have a word in private?" he asked her. "It won't take but a moment." Perhaps he noticed her hesitancy. "It's about Ian."

She glanced behind them anxiously, but no one immediately followed them out of the dining room. Anne, James. and Lisle had already gone ahead, while the rest of them lingered in the dining room. They were momentarily alone in the Great Hall. She nodded once hesitantly and Gerard pulled her toward a private alcove that was situated behind the massive grand staircase.

"What is it?" she asked in a hushed tone, made uneasy by his secrecy given his earlier flirtation. Especially when he stood so close and leaned down over her. She realized he was striving to keep quiet, and resisted stepping back.

"Have you spoken with Ian yet? About where he's been? About what he's been doing? I was speaking to Anne and James, and they're curious to know," Gerard whispered.

"No," she said, not thinking that Ian's general reply of "France" counted as much of an answer at all. "But he's given me the impression he's going back there. He said he has unfinished business . . ." She faded off at the sound of a door opening and conversation echoing in the all. She heard heels tapping and recognized Lucien and Elise's voices, then Amy Gravish's laughter.

"The sitting room, correct, Ian?" Lucien asked.

"Yes," came Ian's deep, quiet voice.

"Unfinished business? Is he leaving soon?" Gerard asked once the sitting room door closed and the hall was quiet once again.

"I don't know for sure," she whispered. "You mean he hasn't revealed any of this to you or his grandparents?"

Gerard shook his head. "Francesca," he began uneasily. "Is there a possibility that Ian has been . . . ill? Perhaps hospitalized."

The blood rushed from her head. "Why do you say that?" she asked, alarmed.

Gerard shrugged. "It's a pretty good explanation as to why he'd disappeared off the face of the earth for so long."

"No, he said he wasn't sick, and I believed him. I thought maybe he told you something about where he's been when you walked earlier . . ."

"No, that wasn't what he wanted to talk about with me," Gerard answered grimly, looking thoughtful. "I get the impression he'd been speaking to Lucien about what he's been doing, though. The two of them certainly clammed up quickly when I walked in on them in the billiards room earlier today."

An uneasy feeling went through her. She knew the intimate truth he shared with Lucien. They'd been talking together about their biological father, Trevor Gaines. What had Ian been doing all these months in regard to Gaines? And how in the world did he think it would help him discover who he was? She'd never hated anyone or anything more than she did that criminal. He was dead, but he was continuing to make Ian's life a misery.

Her own.

She blinked when Gerard wrapped his hand around her upper arm and pulled her closer.

"Have you *asked* him why he left?" he asked in her in a pressured whisper.

"No," she said, starting to become offended by his intensity.

"Don't you think that would be the easiest solution?" Gerard asked.

"Excuse me."

Francesca jumped at the unexpected hard voice. Ian stood there, his hands behind his back, staring at them coldly. Francesca stepped away from Gerard, realizing too late that her action made her look guilty. She lifted her chin and gave Ian an annoyed glance, feeling her pulse starting to throb at her throat. Gerard let his arms drop to his side and faced Ian rapidly, as if expecting a blow.

"Yes?" Gerard asked coolly.

"Grandfather is looking for you," Ian said, his stare on Gerard like twin nails made of ice.

Gerard seemed to hesitate for a moment, but then he nodded briskly. "Francesca?" he said, holding out his hand for her. She paused, reluctant, but then reached for it as a last-ditch effort to escape the incipient explosion hinted at in Ian's eyes. Ian halted her action by taking her hand in his before it ever reached Gerard.

"I need a word with Francesca," Ian said to Gerard with a note of finality.

Gerard's jaw tightened. "Very well," he said coolly when Francesca didn't protest. He turned and left them. Ian didn't look at her, just stared toward the Great Hall. It took her a moment to realize he was waiting for Gerard's footsteps to fade. She could hardly tell when they finally did disappear, because her heart had started to beat so loudly in her ears.

She knew what usually happened when Ian's eyes became fire and ice at once. He firmed his hold on her hand and pulled her behind him into the hall. She could have refused to go with him.

She could have, but she didn't.

Chapter Six

She followed him, struggling to keep up with his long-legged stride in her heels. He opened a paneled door that Francesca knew led to an area Anne had called the reception room when she'd given her the tour, a formal, gilded room that Anne said she rarely ever used anymore. She thought he'd pause in the empty room, but instead he continued walking purposefully straight through the room to another door.

"Ian," she called from behind him, her breath coming erratically. But he didn't turn, just opened the door and pulled her after him. They were in a short, dark corridor. She followed him down it. He opened another door and turned on a light, prompting Francesca to pass before him. This wasn't a room Anne had shown her, Francesca realized. She had a brief impression of a long, narrow mudroom with locked gun racks on the wall, dozens of coats hung on hooks, a giant Chinese urn filled with umbrellas, assorted Wellington and snow boots lining the wall, and an oversized washer and dryer. Two worn upholstered chairs that had probably once adorned a great room faced each other, placed there for convenience, Francesca supposed, for people to sit and put on or take off boots before walking or hunting on the grounds.

She spun around when she heard Ian shut the door with a thud. Blood roared in her ears when she heard the snick of the lock.

"What are you doing?" she asked when he came toward her.

"You asked me this morning if I'd been with another since we'd been apart and I told you no. Can you say the same to me?" he demanded coldly.

"I don't owe you any explanations for my behavior for the last six months, Ian," she grated out, infuriated by his manner, but inexplicably excited as well.

"Are you sleeping with my cousin?" he shot out, stepping closer. She backed up until her bottom ran into the edge of the washer.

"No. But even if I was, it wouldn't be any of your business."

"Do you *want* to fuck him?" he asked crudely. "Because he obviously wants it. Rumor has it he's a good lover. Do you figure he'd do the trick for you?"

She slapped his cheek. Hard. She'd never hit anybody before. It felt *fantastic* . . . and yet she'd never hated her loss of control more. Her flash of aggression barely seemed to penetrate Ian's consciousness.

He opened his hand along her jaw and tilted up her face. "Francesca?" His voice was quieter this time, but it was still an order for her to respond. He pressed nearer still, until their fronts were plastered together, her breasts heaving against his jacket-covered ribs, the fullness behind his fly becoming increasingly more obvious against her belly. It felt so good, so elementally right, that for a moment she couldn't focus on what he was asking her.

"Answer me."

"No I don't want to *fuck* Gerard, damn it," she spat, so angry that it was true, furious that she couldn't find some way to sever this throbbing cord of connection she felt to Ian. His gaze ran over her face hungrily. She found herself straining toward him, her teeth bared.

Her feelings were so confused in that volatile moment, she honestly couldn't say if she wanted to kiss him or bite at him like an animal and draw blood. His eyelids narrowed. He frightened her a little bit at that moment. She wasn't the only one about to lose control.

"Go on," he said.

She blinked at his low taunt and felt his erection swell against her. Her heartbeat roared in her ears.

"Take a bite, Francesca."

He barely got out her name before she put her hand on the back of his head and pushed him to her, her mouth molding his roughly, her teeth scraping his lower lip as she sucked the captive flesh, her tongue licking and plunging and seeking. It was an angry consumption more than a kiss, and one he didn't allow to be one-sided for long. Within seconds he leaned down over her, forcing her back to arch, the barrier of their clothing feeling both insubstantial against their mingling heat and pressing bodies, and also unbearably intrusive. God, she needed to feel his naked body against hers, needed to be filled by him . . . absolutely required him to prove he was there with her in that moment in the most primal way possible.

She lost all sense of time or place as he kissed her with a hunger that matched her own. His hand firmed on her jaw and he sealed the kiss, backing up a few inches when she craned toward him. She met his blazing stare.

"Do you want me to ask you permission to bend you over and fuck you hard, or do you just want me to do it?" he rasped. She whimpered when she realized he'd plunged his hand below her neckline and was extricating a breast from the confines of her demibra. He lifted it above the edge of the neckline. She felt his cock leap next to her belly as he stared down at the exposed flesh, the vulnerable, tender nipple. Before she could draw a full breath, he leaned down and sucked the nipple between his lips. She squealed at the abrupt, delicious sensation of him drawing on her greedily. Her hips thrashed against him, grinding against his erection. By the time her nipple popped out of his suctioning, hot mouth, it was hard and pebbled and reddened.

"I asked you a question," he said, white teeth flashing before he bit and nibbled at her mouth and she felt her core go liquid with heat. She struggled to recall what he meant. "Tell me whether you want to give me permission or you want me just to take you," he said roughly against her mouth, seeming to understand she required a reminder.

She closed her eyes in mortification even as she continued to shape his lips to hers. He'd never asked her permission before. If he was ready to take her, he just would, knowing very well she'd be prepared to meet his need. That's how she wanted it . . . how she needed it.

"Don't make me ask," she said raggedly, her eyes remaining sealed tight.

"Fine. Then I'll just fuck you," he said, his nostrils flaring. His hand lowered, lifting her dress. He found her unerringly, shoving long fingers into her panties.

"Ah, that's good. So sweet, so wet, so ready," he hissed next to her swollen lips. She quaked as he rubbed her well-lubricated clit with the ridge of his finger, his actions neither gentle nor rough, but Ian-like. Perfect. She gritted her teeth and pushed her hips against him. He grunted, and the next thing she knew, he turned her and he was sliding her dress up over her ass and hips, bunching the material at her waist in a fist. She felt him press firmly at her lower back and she responded instinctively, leaning her upper body against the washing machine. He began to lower her panties as he stood next to her, his pelvis pressed against her hip, his erection feeling full and extremely arousing next to her skin. He backed up slightly to get her under-wear between them and shoved them down her thighs. Her eyes sprang wide in painful anticipation in the ensuing seconds as he paused with her hip and buttock still pressed against his cock and ran his hand over her bare ass. She made a helpless sound in her throat as liquid warmth rushed through her, wetting her even more.

Then he was behind her and she was clutching her eyelids shut again in unbearable excitement at the sound of his zipper lowering. He put one opened hand on her inner thigh and she parted wider for him, her breath burning in her lungs. She bit her lip, the buildup killing her, as he widened her slit with his finger. She could just imagine him standing behind her, his cock in one hand, a determined, rigid look on his face as he looked down at her. He pushed the fleshy, tapered head of his cock into her, making the air fly out of her lungs.

"Hold steady," he said tensely.

He firmed his hold on her hips and thrust. She bit off a scream. He stretched her wide, his cock pulsing high and hard in her. It burned deliciously.

"Try to keep quiet. I brought you as far from them as I could, but there might be staff around," she heard him say through the roar in her ears before he started to fuck her with long, forceful strokes, popping her ass with his pelvis in a regular, driving rhythm. She stared blankly at the control mechanisms of the washer, her mouth hanging open, inundated—no, overwhelmed—by sensation. Her hips drove back on him instinctively, her arm muscles going rigid as she braced herself against his powerful possession. She knew she shouldn't be allowing this to happen, but one didn't rationalize about a hurricane or earthquake. What he did to her—what Ian *was*—was a force of nature, and all she could do was grit her teeth together and take the glory of him.

He grunted gutturally behind her, his pace never wavering, only growing stronger . . . faster. She didn't protest when he wrapped his forearm around her waist to steady her and lifted one of her legs, forcing one knee onto the edge of the washer, opening her even more for him. He drove into her, their bodies smacking together, and this time she couldn't prevent a small scream. He paused. Sweat popped on her upper lip at the sensation of him filling her while she was in such a vulnerable position, pried wide for him.

"Do you want something to muffle your screams?"

She nodded, panting. She was cresting at the sensation of him throbbing deep inside her, his balls pressed tightly against her wet, overly sensitized outer sex creating an indirect pressure on her clit. A towel fell before her face, and she realized he'd reached above her to a shelf. He immediately began to fuck her again, grunting as he slammed into her. Her eyes sprang wide. She'd never been penetrated more deeply, and he took her relentlessly. The washer began to move, rattling against the wall as he plunged into her. He cursed heatedly in response to the noise, but he didn't slow. She could barely keep herself in place for his possession. He cupped a buttock as he fucked her, prying it back, exposing her even further to his plundering cock and ruthless gaze.

She crammed the towel against her mouth, muffling her scream as orgasm ripped through her.

"That's right. God that feels good," she heard him say roughly as if through a long tunnel. He continued to fuck her without pause as she shook in release. Just when her spasms of climax began to wane, she felt him jerk his cock out of her. He groaned loudly, and she knew the sensation had been as unpleasant for her as it was him. She turned her head.

"Ian?" she asked, disoriented.

"Give me the towel."

She blinked at the sound of his terse command. She lowered her knee from the washer, feeling sluggish and dazed, and turned around. Her satiated fogginess vanished in an instant. The vision of him standing there scored her, his pants and underwear bunched around his strong thighs, pumping his fearsome, glistening erection with his fist.

"The towel," he prompted again between clenched teeth. His face convulsed. His body jerked. She hurried to hand him the towel, but was too late. He began to ejaculate, ropy white streams erupting from his cock and splattering on the tile floor. He looked so beautiful in that moment, so strong, and yet so helpless in the clutches of desire it caused her heart to squeeze unbearably. She hurried to him, cupping him in the towel from below and folding the edge over the head, so that the material absorbed his semen. She made soothing sounds as she gently pumped him in her towel-covered hand, using the fingers of her other hand to stroke the rigid, warm, convulsing shaft from above. His groan as he clutched her shoulders told her it felt wonderful, and for that stolen moment, it was all the knowledge she required.

His grip on her shoulders softened. His shudders waned. Slowly, she looked up to meet his face. The color in his cheeks made his eyes look even more blue than usual.

"I knew we'd have to return to the others," he said gruffly, his breath still coming erratically. "I didn't want that," he glanced at the semen-damp towel she still held between them, "to be making you uncomfortable."

A flash of heat went through her at the idea of his essence filling her while she mingled with the others, his come spilling into her panties, wetting her thighs . . . While she found it arousing in theory, she knew he was right. It would have been uncomfortable, not to mention potentially embarrassing.

"Thank you," she murmured. She moved the towel, folding it to dry him as best she could before she pulled it away and set it on the washer. She bent for her panties, pulling them up over her thigh-high hosiery and into place. The mundane mechanics of the aftermath of thundering passion brought it home to her, what had just happened. She lowered her dress. Acting on an impulse, she suddenly grabbed the offending towel and tossed it into the washer, setting the mechanism to its hottest temperature and turning the machine on. It was stupid, and immature, and she knew it—as if she *really* believed she could wash away what had just occurred.

She kept her head lowered, avoiding his stare. "Do we really have to go back to join the others?" she asked thinly. How long had they been absent? It probably couldn't have been much more than fifteen minutes, as focused and distilled as the twist of fury and desire they'd both been caught in had been.

He paused in the process of pulling up his pants.

"Francesca."

She looked around slowly.

"I'll take you straight to my bed now, if that's what you want. I said we'd go back to the others for your sake, not mine."

In a sweeping instant, it all came back to her. It didn't matter how tender she'd felt toward him as he shook in climax. It didn't matter that she wanted to give herself to him again and again. He'd left her. He couldn't promise her a future.

He *wouldn't*.

Where did you have to go that was so important that you left me without a word?

The question felt like it scalded the back of her throat, but she didn't ask it. He obviously was not burning to tell her the answer . . . to give excuses. Her pride wouldn't let her ask, especially when he clearly didn't want to offer up the explanation.

"I want to go back with the others. Anne will worry if we don't," she said, her voice sounding hollow.

His eyebrows arched as he hastily began to refasten his trousers. "She'll worry no matter what. But it's your decision."

She smoothed her dress and hair.

"I can go back in with the others first. I'll tell them you went to the ladies' room. You can go and freshen up before returning," Ian said. He let his hands fall and she saw he looked as immaculate and gorgeous as ever, possibly more so than earlier, with the added color in his face.

"All right," she said in a thick voice. It was difficult to say what she was feeling, given her impulsivity. Her rabid hunger.

"Francesca?" She met his gaze reluctantly. "You *will* still come to me tonight. I know what you need, and it wasn't this. Not entirely. This was for me. I needed to know you belonged to no one else."

"I belong to myself, Ian," she said starkly before she walked to the door and unlocked it.

But what sort of a comfort was that, really, when she couldn't trust herself? And wasn't there an element of truth to what he'd said? Who knew, better than Ian, what she needed?

And she *did* need. Crave, in fact. Not only Ian, but the beautiful, raw, sometimes shocking intimacy they'd once treasured. That they'd *just* shared.

How could she possibly both desire this connection she felt to him and yet despise it at once?

Her pulse began to thrum again at her throat as she sensed him behind her, silently following in the shadows.

Lucien and he stood at the corner of the large room near the bar, a fair distance between themselves and the rest of the chatting group. Anne had put on a classic jazz selection, which further muted their conversation.

"Don't tell me you're not interested in finding out more about Gaines," Ian said, scanning the room. Francesca was still in the ladies' room.

"You know that I am. I'm more interested in locating our siblings, though. The ones who already know about their biological father anyway. Like this man, Kam Reardon, that you told me about."

"They deserve to know. All of them. If no one in their life has told them, then we should."

He felt Lucien's stare on his profile. "Forgive me for saying so, Ian, but the knowledge doesn't seem to have sat well with you. If you're an example of what might happen, I think it's a terrible idea to spring the truth on innocents." Ian met his half brother's stare angrily, but Lucien didn't flinch. "Take it from someone who knows. There's no joy in telling someone that Trevor Gaines's sickness was one of the reasons they walk on this earth. Watching how you reacted makes me think we should bury his name along with his worthless corpse and never mention the likes of him again."

"You don't really believe that," Ian grated out. "You're curious. You certainly listened when I told you everything I've found out about him so far. There's more to discover. Reardon has answers, I'm sure of it. I just haven't been able to locate the bloody bastard and I had to leave before I could," Ian said, taking a drink. Francesca entered the room. He regretted the telltale glow of her cheeks and her hesitant smile as she joined the others, and yet he wouldn't have changed anything. He was *glad* her flushed cheeks and slight embarrassment following their absence was there for everyone to witness.

Savage that he was.

And yet . . . he had no real right to mark her as his, he thought as he ground his teeth in acute frustration.

"Do you plan on telling Francesca what you were doing in France?" he heard Lucien murmur and knew the other man was also watching Francesca's entrance.

"No. And please don't tell her, either," Ian said, sounding harsher than he intended. He met Lucien's stare. "She would try and talk me out of it."

"So would Elise, if I were on your mission," Lucien said. "Do you know why you haven't told Francesca what you've told me?"

He shrugged. "You understand what she can't."

"I *do* understand. I'll admit . . . I am curious about Gaines. How can I not be? And I want to be involved in contacting any of our brothers and sisters who are interested in making the connection. Maybe there *is* a chance of us finding some blessing among all the senselessness. I doubt it, but who knows?"

"We've become friends," Ian said, his gaze still stuck to Francesca.

"True. There's been one sliver lining. But my point is, the reason you aren't telling Francesca what you're doing isn't because she won't understand. I think you know she might understand perfectly well, but still try and talk you out of it. It's because she's the only one who has the power to change your mind that you're not telling her, and you know that. So you're stubbornly not telling her so you can continue with this obsession."

"Obsession?" Ian spat.

He blinked, realizing that Lucien looked uncomfortable. Concerned? He glanced over to the others and saw Anne, Elise, and James looking over at them worriedly, while Francesca seemed startled. He'd shouted, when he hadn't meant to. What the hell was wrong with him? He inhaled, trying to regain his splintering control. He clamped his mouth shut, waiting for their observers to look away. "Have you told Elise what I've told you?" he asked Lucien in a more level, quiet voice after a pause. "Have you told her you plan to visit Gaines's estate with me when the time is right?"

"No," Lucien admitted. "But the only reason I haven't is because she'd probably tell Francesca while we're here at Belford. Even though you didn't tell me you were dead set against Francesca knowing until just now, I'd already guessed it was true. I'll probably tell Elise when we're on the plane back to Chicago."

Ian scowled. "It's the same reason I haven't told my grandparents. They're crazy about Francesca. They'd probably tell her . . . beg her to save me or some foolishness like that."

For a moment, neither of them spoke as they watched the others talking near the leaping fire. Ian tensed when Gerard approached Francesca, but then she looked up and stared directly at him, her dark, shining eyes striking to the core of him, as always. She turned away when Elise said something to her.

"Are you sure you know what you're doing?" Lucien asked quietly from beside him, and he knew his half brother had seen Francesca's charged glance across the room. Or was Lucien literally asking him if he had control of himself—if he was in his right mind? Ian chose to believe the former, finding the latter question too disturbing to consider.

"No," Ian rasped, taking a drink. "But I can't stay away from her."

"I think you'd better decide who's in your blood more. I, for one, pray it's Francesca and not Gaines," Lucien said pointedly before he picked up his drink and went to join his wife.

Ian grimaced at the admonishment. As if it were a simple matter of his *choosing* Francesca over a disgusting pervert. He'd thought Lucien would understand—and in all fairness, maybe he did. Better than most could anyway. Lucien felt the taint of Trevor Gaines all right. But it wasn't a poison in his system like it was Ian's . . . something that needed to be purged at all costs. He must cleanse himself of the filth before he could claim peace.

Before he could ever hope to claim Francesca.

It took him a lot more effort these days to force his mind into the tight focus that used to come as easily as breathing. Especially tonight.

Would she come?

He sat at the desk in his suite, still wearing his tux pants and shirt, his tie loosened, scanning various documents Lin had sent him for his perusal. His interest in Noble Enterprises had increased ever since he'd returned to England, although it was still a shadow of his former focus on his company. Perhaps it was because he'd been thrown back into the midst of the details as he asked Lin question after question about Francesca's recent activities in Chicago, and subsequently was exposed to all of the details of the Tyake acquisition.

He paused, opening up a document that Lin had sent him in an e-mail with the subject heading: *Noble Enterprises purchase of Tyake goes public.* He hadn't opened it earlier because he'd already been aware that the story had broken, but he did so now to fill the time. Immediately a black-and-white photo of Francesca walking off an elevator at Noble Towers popped onto the screen, his grandfather at the periphery of the photograph. The headline mentioned something about the Noble family gathering for the Tyake acquisition, although it was mentioned in the first paragraph that Ian himself was notably absent. He took note of the date of the newspaper publication then fleetly typed a query to Lin.

If Francesca didn't come, would he have to resort to watching her image on his computer screen again? Lucien had accused him earlier of being obsessed by Trevor Gaines and his ugly history, but personally, Ian considered himself obsessed by the image of Francesca surrendering to ecstasy . . . of giving herself so trustingly. He craved the image especially now, when she shut herself off from him even while she desperately sought to find relief for the fire that burned her from the inside out. He was familiar with that particular brand of fire. It scored him daily since leaving her. He wouldn't watch her suffer unduly if he could offer her even a modicum of relief.

Knowing he was the one who had altered her expression from one of complete trust and love to one of anger and doubt made the vision of her former faith on the computer screen a hundred times worse. It also made the image that much more compelling, not to mention sadder.

His head jerked up at the furtive knock at his door. He quickly shut down his computer. She didn't say anything when he opened the door, just walked into the room. She'd changed out of her eveningwear. Instead of being dressed for bed, however, she wore jeans and a fitted T-shirt, her long, glorious reddish-gold hair still loose and waving down her back. It was the attire he most associated with Francesca— the garb of a free-spirited artist. He hadn't seen her dressed thus since his return, and seeing her now caused an amplification in the dull, familiar ache in his chest cavity. Her face looked pale when she turned to face him, her gaze fierce. He recognized her defiance as being that of a woman who had been wounded but not conquered.

He closed the door quietly and locked it. Still, she didn't speak as they stared at one another in the thundering silence.

"Well I'm here," she said stiffly. "I'd almost prefer it that you were triumphant instead of your acting like it was inevitable that I'd come."

He raised his eyebrows. "It would give you comfort to call me smug?"

"It would give me comfort to dislike you."

"You don't dislike me?" he asked, dropping his hand from the knob on the door and walking toward her.

Her large eyes moved over him warily. Her lips trembled. "You left me," she said hoarsely. "What woman doesn't hate her lover for that? Especially when she shows up at his door after the fact, begging."

"You're not begging," he stated firmly. "I offered to give you what you need."

"And nothing else," she smiled bitterly. "And what is it you suppose I need? To be punished for showing up here? I've half a mind to agree it's what I deserve."

"No," he said, hating to see her this way. Francesca was not born to be a cynic. He palmed her jaw and smoothed his thumb over her pale, smooth cheek as if he could erase her sadness . . . her desperation. "You're tearing at yourself, bloodying your spirit. You think you want to escape the bonds that hold you secure, but in reality, you need to be held tighter."

A muscle jumped beneath his stroking thumb. She stared up at him, a wild, angry longing in her dark eyes. "Why should I let you bind me tighter when you'll leave again soon, and I'll be alone, fighting against the bonds . . . bleeding once again?"

"Because I'll try my damnedest to come back."

"Promise me."

He blinked at her harsh demand. "I can't."

She made a muffled sound of misery in her throat, killing him a little. He touched his forehead to hers. "I want to be with you more than anything, Francesca. But I can't do that until I feel . . . whole. Please understand."

He took her into his arms and clasped her to him, tight, inhaling the scent of her hair. "There is no other woman for me. If I can never feel myself worthy of you, then I'll never want another. If I can't find a place at your side, it means I'll go through life alone. Please understand that. This isn't about me abandoning you. I'm the one who feels cast ashore alone while the rest of the world floats away."

He felt her shudder. She shook her head, her face rolling against his chest. Her arms slipped around his waist. "But I'm here. I'm *right* here."

"I know," he said, using his hand to tilt back her face. She stared up at him with shiny eyes. He brushed her lips softly with his own, absorbing the slight tremors that went through her body . . . cherishing them. "And you're suffering. Let me bring you relief."

She pressed closer to him, her light clothing allowing him to feel her firm, feminine body, her tension . . . her heat. Her eyelids closed. "Yes," she said. "I need help. I can't seem to . . ." Her voice broke, and he covered her mouth with his, hating to witness her misery. It hurt like a burning lash whipped against his insides to know he had done this to her—because of his need, he'd trained her to his touch, taught her to meet his needs, to exceed his desires. He'd told her once that there probably wasn't a handful of men on the planet who could dominate her sexually, and he'd meant it. She possessed such a strong, fierce spirit, she would only—*could* only—submit to a true mate. He'd recognized before that he was incredibly fortunate to be one of the few men to whom she could submit, but there, in that moment, he recognized how blessed he was . . .

. . . and how damned.

He kissed her deliberately while he began to undress her, gentling her when she grew frantic and strained against him, taming her when her hunger grew wild and she bit at him, tempting him. She made a rough sound of protest when he broke their kiss in order to pull her T-shirt over her head, but then his mouth was back on hers, drinking her sweetness, using his hands to unfasten her bra and massage her breasts, his fingers to coax her nipples into hard, delectable crests that made his mouth water.

He lifted his head and began to slide his tie off his neck. "Take off the rest of your clothes and come over here," he said, sitting on the edge of the bed.

He watched her while he waited, his gaze lingering on her flushed cheeks and lips, the pale globes of her bare breasts heaving as she panted. For a moment, he wondered if she'd balk at such a stark order, but she surprised him by quickly complying. She was hurting so badly. Both of them were writhing in a sea of agonized need.

His mouth went dry when she removed her shoes, and then jerked her jeans and panties down over her hips and ass at once. He'd forgotten how lovely she was. He recalled the first time he'd seen her naked—the willowy waist and curving hips, the pale, smooth erotic harbor of her stomach, the soft, reddish-gold hair between firm white thighs. He longed to press his face to her belly now, absorb her softness and heat, inhale the subtle perfume of her sex. She'd asked him once if he wanted her to shave her genitals as he did, and he'd answered with an absolute negative. He knew better than to alter perfection.

"Come here and turn around," he said.

She followed his instructions, walking toward him, naked. The ends of her hair swished next to her waist when she turned. Her ass was firm, but very feminine, curving deliciously. His hand itched to palm the plump buttocks, to slap them playfully . . . then not so playfully. He stroked her from waist to hip to buttock, amazed anew at the softness of her skin. He gently squeezed a taut cheek.

"Face me," he instructed when he realized he was becoming fixated on the delightful sensation of her flesh in his palm. She did so and he lifted the hand that held his bow tie. His already throbbing cock lurched against his pants when without prompting, she put her wrists together to be bound in front of her mons.

Oh God. She was so exquisite. So rare. So much more than he deserved.

He tied her wrists together, and then studied her face closely, looking for signs of her state of being, clues as to what she needed. Her chin was held high, but he saw the wildness in her eyes, calling to mind a gentle creature turned feral . . . a rabid doe.

He stood and went to the walk-in closet. When he returned to her, he carried a leather belt.

Francesca took care to keep her face impassive when she saw the black leather belt looped in Ian's right hand. He approached, pinning her with his stare, and began to roll back his sleeves. Her sex clenched tight and her nipples pinched at the vision of his strong, veined forearms sprinkled with dark hair. He always rolled back his sleeves before he punished her. She'd been conditioned to become aroused at the sight, but acute anxiety mixed with her lust tonight.

"I know I've never used a belt before," he said.

"You used to say it was too harsh."

"I don't have much to work with here," he said, and she knew he meant that he didn't have his room full of sexual equipment at his disposal. He opened his hand at the side of her neck and gently stroked her throat with his thumb in a soothing gesture, as if he'd known she was having difficulty drawing breath as desire and anxiety warred in her chest. "You can trust me to attenuate, Francesca. You know I'd never harm you." Her heart jumped. He closed his eyes briefly and she sensed his regret. "Not in this way, at least. Never. Do you believe that?"

"Yes," she said, holding his stare. That much, she did believe.

He nodded slowly, still studying her face so intently, she wondered what he read there. He'd said once that women were a mystery even to themselves. She couldn't have agreed more at that moment. She also knew he'd been given the gift of decoding her, though . . . and that's why she stood here, naked and bound before a man who had forsaken her.

"Then come over here," he said quietly, pointing at the bottom post on the grand bed. The four carved posts were seven feet tall. "Put your hands above your head and rest them on the post. No, don't bend over all the way," he instructed, using his hand to prompt her into the position he desired. When he'd settled her, she was mostly upright, but bent slightly at the waist, her weight braced by her bound hands. He put the looped belt strap between her thighs and gently flicked his wrist. She immediately parted her legs more at the silent prompt, liquid heat surging at her sex.

"That's right," he said gruffly. He swept her long hair around the shoulder furthest from him, fully exposing her backside. Her clit throbbed dully as he stroked her from flank to hip with his hand, pausing to squeeze a buttock in his palm. Then he did the same with the folded belt, running the sleek leather over her spine and caressing her ass and the back of her thighs. She moaned softly.

"I'll prepare you with my hand," she heard him say. She bit her lip when he spanked her bottom, that quick, expert slap achingly familiar. He spanked her again. It stung, but it aroused her almost unbearably. The flash of sensation as her nerves were awakened, the erotic sound of flesh against flesh, the sharp knowledge that she was allowing it . . . that she *wanted* it. He continued to enliven her flesh, spanking her by hand, escalating her arousal. At one point, she turned to look at him, hungry for the image of him standing there, his eyes hot and possessive as he watched his hand striking her ass with a tight focus. He glanced up and made a rough sound in his throat.

Francesca turned her head and closed her eyes, overwhelmed with a potent mixture of shame and desire.

Chapter Seven

He dropped his hand. Her bottom prickled and tingled, not unpleasantly. Her pussy felt hot and wet. She kept her eyes clamped closed, her ears pitched for signs of what he was doing in the silence. Then the folded leather strap touched her ass. He ran it over the smarting flesh in circles. Her clit pinched in anticipation. She clamped her teeth.

It was going to hurt. She dreaded it. She needed it.

"Hold steady," Ian said. He lifted the leather and struck gently several times. She knew from having done this with him before they were just test strokes as he got the feel for the instrument he used. He lifted the belt. Her muscles tensed. Then it came, that quick, bright flash of pain, more concentrated than what came from the paddle or the flogger. She whimpered. Her hips moved, but not to escape another blow. From arousal.

"*Shhh,*" he murmured, and his hand was there, soothing the stinging flesh, caressing her bottom. "Okay?" he asked after a moment of rubbing her.

"Yes," she said through gritted teeth. She waited, her anticipation so sharp it cut at her. *Whoosh.* He landed the belt again and she gasped. Immediately, his hand was there, easing the pain, mounting her need until all she craved was another strike of the belt. It was unbearable. It was exquisite . . . and just what she needed.

After five strikes, she was moaning uncontrollably in rabid arousal. He paused after landing a blow on the tender area of her buttocks just above her thighs. He palmed her from below tautly, and then abruptly released the stinging flesh, jiggling it, making her moan harder.

"Stand up straight," Ian said, his voice sounding strained. She backed away from the post. "Put your hands behind your head, elbows out, and face me."

She did what he said, her breathing erratic. When she turned toward him, the vision of him undid her. She shut her eyes defensively. He looked unbearably beautiful to her in his tuxedo pants with his dress shirt open at the collar, his sleeves rolled back displaying his strong forearms, his masculine hand gripping the belt. He stepped toward her and ran the folded strap of leather along her waist, her ribs, and the outer curve of a breast.

"Open your eyes, Francesca," he demanded quietly.

"No," she said shakily, determined to keep some tiny part of herself inviolate. Safe. She'd given all of herself once, and felt the consequence every second of her life. The caressing leather stilled on her breast, and then fell away. She sensed him crossing in front of her. He placed his hand on her shoulder.

"Bend over and spread your thighs. Present your bottom. Keep your hands on your head," he said sharply when she started to lower them as she bent. "I'll steady you with my hand."

The belt struck her ass. She whimpered. Her thighs quivered. She felt very exposed and vulnerable in this position.

"It's okay," she heard Ian say roughly, his hand rubbing her stinging ass. "Just two more strokes like that, and then you'll feel relief." His hand lowered between her thighs. She cried out in acute pleasure when he burrowed a thick finger between her labia and stimulated her clit. The burn didn't amplify slowly, it was suddenly full-blown at coming into contact with his rigid finger. She lurched forward at the unexpected, sharp sensation, but he caught her with his hand at her shoulder.

"That's right," she heard him say as he rubbed her clit, his voice that familiar rough-gentle paradox. "You're going to come for me and let it all go. Give all the responsibility to me."

"Oh," she moaned uncontrollably, the sting of her ass somehow amplifying the sizzle of her clit. It was delicious. Untenable. Then his hand was gone from her sex and the belt bit again at her ass. She cried out at the jolt of pain, the thrill of peaking ecstasy. He lowered the hand from her shoulder and used it to part her burning buttocks, further exposing her to him. She trembled when he ran the leather over her damp outer sex, and then along the cleft between the cheeks, teasing her asshole. The anticipation was killing her.

He once again put his hand on her shoulder. She heard the leather whooshing in the air. The belt struck her ass, cracking in her ears like a gunshot. She was keening uncontrollably, on the very edge of orgasm. She felt the leather fall past the back of her thighs to the floor and he was pulling her against him, the front of his pants pressing tightly against her, grinding her hip and buttock against his furious erection, his hand plunging between her thighs.

"Come . . . and keep it coming."

She ignited at his touch, exploding in orgasm. His harsh words echoed distantly in her ears as pleasure shook her in intense waves. *Come and keep it coming.* His hand moved between her thighs, the tension snapping back into her muscles each time after she shuddered in release. Why wasn't it stopping? Oh God, it'd never felt so good. So awful. So divine.

By the time her orgasm finally did begin to wane, he had to hold her tightly against his body, still supporting her at the shoulder in order to keep her from slithering to the floor. Her legs had gone weak; her flesh transformed to quivering mush. She panted for air as he encouraged her to straighten, then he was lifting her feet off the floor. The front of her body pressed against him, her belly heaving against his abdomen, her pussy quivering against his erection. His hand opened at the side of her face, cupping her cheek and jaw.

"I'm sorry. It was necessary. But I'm still sorry."

She blinked and brought his handsome face into focus. He looked rigid with need.

"I'm not. It was why I came," she rasped, her tongue and lips moving with extreme effort.

His jaw tightened; his gaze grew wild. "Come here," he said, even though he was carrying her and she really had no other choice to go wherever he took her.

He set her down before an upholstered, cushiony chair and immediately went to retrieve the sleek, padded armchair that sat before his desk. He placed it just behind her, so that she was between the two chairs. Francesca stood there panting, still a little dazed from her intense orgasm. The next thing she knew, Ian was sitting in the cushiony chair, long legs bent and thighs slightly spread, and reaching for her. He turned her before he pulled her into his lap, so that her bottom faced him.

"Put your knees in the cushion next to my legs and your hands on the seat of the desk chair in front of you," he said, his voice sounding rough. "I can't take it a second longer. I have to taste you."

His tense command penetrated her disorientation. She took the position he desired, guided by his touch. When she'd settled, she was on her hands and knees, her lower half on the cushioned chair where Ian sat, her hands bracing her upper body on the wooden chair. He put his hands on her ass, which was just inches from his face. She sensed his need when he immediately parted her cheeks, opening her molten sex to him.

"Send up your tailbone," he said gruffly, swatting a buttock.

She moaned, fresh arousal spiking through her, and arched her back, sending up her ass to give him better access to her pussy. She cried out when he slid his tongue between her labia and began to agitate her clit. He lapped at her from the top tip of her clit to her slit. She shook when he pushed his tongue into her pussy and fucked her with it for an electrical moment, massaging her buttocks in his hands while he ladled her juices into his mouth and groaned in harsh appreciation.

After he'd gotten his fill, he sent his tongue back between her labia, lashing at her clit until she bit off a scream. It was sublime. So intense, it was unbearable. She writhed and keened brokenly. His fingers bit into her sore bottom, holding her in place for his marauding mouth. He leaned forward, pushing closer, burying his lower face in her wet, aroused sex. His hold was absolute . . . unwavering. She had to take every bit of the massive pleasure he conferred as he drank his fill of her. When he sucked firmly while he twisted his head back and forth and whipped her clit with his tongue, she broke in orgasm. The pleasure was so intense, her elbows gave way and she grazed her forehead on the hard wood of the seat before she caught herself. He responded by grabbing her waist and ribs firmly and leaning back in the chair, pulling her back against him. She slid onto his thighs, so that her breasts pressed against his knees and her head fell over the edge of them. He continued to eat her relentlessly the whole time, pressing his mouth tightly to her climaxing pussy, squeezing her buttocks and occasionally slapping one, ramping up her orgasm.

His lashing tongue slowed with her shudders of release, but he continued to lick and suck her juices greedily even when she sagged into his lap, satiated and half-senseless.

"No one tastes like you. No one comes like you."

Her eyelids blinked open at his hoarse voice. He kissed her wet, overly sensitive outer sex once before he lifted his head.

"Can you stand up?" he asked, stroking the sensitive sides of her body.

"Yes," she said thickly. When she came off him, he stood and took her into his arms. She moaned softly when she saw how slick his lower face was with her juices. She tasted them on his kiss, closing her eyes in quiet bliss at their intermingled flavor.

He lifted her into his arms and carried her to the bed like he might a baby. She was glad. She wasn't sure if her legs would work properly. He sat her on the edge of the mattress, for a moment just staring down at her as she panted. He began stroking her with his hand, caressing her back and hip and thigh, soothing her. As she recovered, his touch turned demanding versus reassuring.

He cupped her breast, molding it to his palm. Her eyelids flickered open and she met his stare.

"Better?" he murmured, still massaging her breast.

She nodded.

"Then stand up," he said.

He helped her, since her wrists were bound. When she stood before him, he pulled her between his legs and clamped her hips between his strong thighs. He immediately began to play with her breasts, his manner deliberate, his blazing stare making her whimper in helpless arousal. She was bound and could go nowhere, do nothing but be the target of his need. Ian's desire was always monumentally focused and precise, but it seemed to have grown exponentially since they'd been apart. He gently squeezed her breasts, making the nipples protrude between his thumb and forefinger.

"I can't tell you how much I missed your lovely breasts," he said, plucking at her achy nipples, making them stiffer. He lifted the globes with both hands and let them fall, then lightly slapped at the outer curves, seeming to enjoy the shiver in firm flesh. Arousal stabbed at her clit—yes, even though she was half-insensate from her previous orgasms. She experienced a nearly overwhelming urge to shove her hands between her thighs to alleviate the pinch of lust. She sensed his hunger growing, saw the greedy gleam in his blue eyes. He gathered both breasts in his hands, pushing the flesh together.

She cried out raggedly when he leaned forward and tongued both nipples at once. She watched him with a tight focus, absorbing the image of his red tongue running over the beaded flesh, stimulating and sensitizing the nerves. Pleasure tore through her when he slipped one of her nipples between his lips and sucked strong enough to hollow out his cheeks.

"Oh . . . Ian," she moaned shakily after he'd sucked on her for a minute or so, her muscles tensing again with renewed arousal. He drew on her nipple, but she felt the tug in her womb. He continued to massage her breasts in his large hands, holding the flesh captive while he consumed her, sucking first one nipple, then the other, until the crests were unbearably sensitive, rosy, and glistening and Francesca was crying out once again in stark arousal.

He lifted his head and looked at her face, his nostrils flared. A flush had grown on his cheeks. He placed one hand on her inner thigh. She shuddered and clamped her eyes shut. She'd grown so wet her juices were wetting her thighs. The subtle evidence of her rampant need both shamed and aroused her, the mixed emotions creating a sharp friction inside her.

"Open your eyes," he demanded, his fingers still moving on her slick skin, amplifying the burn in her clit.

"No," she whispered.

"There's nothing to be ashamed of, lovely."

She twisted her chin, keeping her eyelids clamped shut. She disagreed.

His fingers paused and she restrained a moan.

"Very well," she heard him say, his voice rough with desire and frustration. "I can see you want this done and over with. Come onto the bed. I'll take my pleasure of you and put us both out of our misery."

Lust rushed through her at his words along with a fresh surge of shame. Damn him. No other man could say something so singularly selfish and make her so aroused. He knew she loved it when he finally let go and sought bliss in her flesh with a single-minded focus. He knew saying that would turn her on.

Standing, he released her from the grip of his thighs. She cracked open her eyelids cautiously. "Get on the bed, belly down, hands above your head. You won't have to look at me in that position," he said, his mouth pressed into a grim line.

"Fine," she replied, equally edgy with anger and arousal. Why should she protest? It was true. She didn't want to gawp at his savage beauty as he gave himself. It was all an illusion anyway, wasn't it? He wasn't giving anything. Not really.

He helped her onto the bed. She lay prone, her bound hands above her head. He gently extricated the pillows from under her forearms. She bit her lip to stifle a moan when he shoved them under her hips, elevating her ass. He parted her legs. She felt the air lick and kiss at her wet sex and thighs.

When he didn't immediately get on the bed with her, she twisted her face around to peer at him. She wished she hadn't. He was undressing. Completely. Forget about the fact that they'd been apart for a half a year, the vision of him naked was always compelling. Addictive. Ian usually only removed all of his clothes during the most intimate moments of lovemaking. She often wondered if he did that to make her crave the vision of his naked male glory all that much more.

If he did it for that reason, it worked. In spades.

She couldn't take her eyes off him as he unbuttoned the white dress shirt and pulled it off his shoulders with a flex of rigid muscle. She went completely still on the bed. It was true that he'd lost weight in the past half year, but he'd never looked more powerful. He must still be partaking of his rigorous exercise. His leanness only served to glove his physique more tightly. His stomach was slightly concave beneath his muscular chest, but the muscles there looked like a ridged, solid wall. His tuxedo pants fell low on his narrow hips. He unfastened them fleetly while he kicked off his shoes. He bent to take off his socks and noticed her staring through strands of her hair. He paused.

If she had any pride, given her previous protest, she would have looked away. As it was, she couldn't blink, let alone turn away.

He held her stare as he shoved his pants and underwear down his solid, strong thighs. She caught a covetous glimpse of his cock, heavy with arousal, flagrantly erect, the tapering head large, smooth, fleshy . . . mouthwatering. Then he was crawling on the bed behind her, and she could see him no more. She pressed her face into the mattress to muffle her whimper.

He didn't speak. There was no preamble. He just parted her buttocks firmly with his hand and arrowed his cock into her pussy.

Her lungs deflated in an instant. He began to fuck her powerfully. She gasped, but it was as if her lungs wouldn't fill . . . like there wasn't room for both him and air inside her. His cock pounded into her, the friction he created intense. For a few tense, breathless moments, she wanted him to stop. It hurt. No, it didn't hurt, it felt delicious.

She didn't know what it felt like. She only knew she was helpless to stop it. He was doing what he'd said he would, taking his pleasure of her. His pelvis smacked against her ass again and again, his cock pummeling her. He was fucking her single-mindedly, but he was doing something else to her as well. He was softening her with this erotic beating into her flesh, weakening her defenses, forcing her to give way, insisting she accept him. She tightened around him, every muscle in her body resisting even as her hips bobbed against him and they crashed together, two storm fronts colliding.

He leaned down over her, his fists pressing into the mattress near her head, still fucking her without pause. She would be sore tomorrow, but right now, it felt so good . . . so bad.

"Francesca," he grated out after a moment. "Open your eyes."

When she didn't respond, only kept her face in the mattress, her entire body a tightly coiled spring, he whisked the majority of her long hair onto one side of her head and shoulders, depriving her of the only cover she had. She made a hissing sound as he put his hand on her chin and gently turned her so that her cheek rested on the mattress. At the same moment, he thrust forcefully. A cry popped out of her lungs and her eyelids sprung open at the deep caress.

"Leave me alone," she said, wild with arousal, desperate, knowing he was breaking through her defenses.

"As if that's a possibility." He grunted savagely, but she couldn't tell if it was in lust or frustration when she turned and pressed her forehead to the soft sheets. His pushed his fists off the mattress. She sensed him straightening his upper body behind her. He squeezed her ass cheeks into his palms, plumping them together in order to amplify the pressure on his pounding cock, his manner lewd, single-minded. Her bottom still stung from her punishment. His rough handling of the tender flesh amplified the burn in her clit, exciting her. Then he lifted her ass off the pillows. She keened uncontrollably as he served her pussy to his cock, fast and furious, the frantic sound of their bodies smacking together blending with the pound of her heart in her ears.

Her eyes sprang wide. It was too much. She was going to come . . .

She squealed in protest when he halted abruptly, sheathed high and hard and throbbing deep inside her, and set her pelvis back on the pillows. He used his hand to twist her onto her side, one hip still pressed into the mattress. He fell down heavily behind her. The next thing her lust-impaired brain knew, he held her tightly against him, her back against his hard torso, his arms wrapped around her waist tightly, his face pressed against her neck. Her damned hair was spilled everywhere—probably in Ian's mouth—but he didn't seem to care or notice. The fronts of his strong, hair-sprinkled thighs pushed on the back of her legs, forcing her to bend, shaping her to him. He resumed fucking her, groaning deep and rough, his breath hot against her skin.

It was disorienting, to go from a relatively impersonal sexual position to one of such intense intimacy. She felt surrounded by him. She didn't have time to guard herself against the power of his embrace. He slid his hand over her hip to the back of her upper thigh, pushing it higher, giving him freer access to her pussy. He resumed his hold on her waist, gripping her so tightly against him she almost couldn't breathe. He was a solid wall of muscle behind her, resonating heat into her skin. She instinctively contracted around his cock with her vagina, lowering her bound hands to his hold at her waist, hugging him like she thought she could absorb him, wanting him . . . *needing* him to never leave.

"Jesus," he muttered thickly next to her neck. Their four hands rose and fell in unison as he used his hold on her to pump her back and forth on his cock, fucking her ruthlessly. She groaned in a fever of agonized delight. She needed him so much.

He would leave her.

"Tell me," he said harshly.

Her moan of misery came erratically, punctuated by the harsh staccato rhythm of him crashing into her. His cock swelled impossibly large. He was on the edge. So was she. He captured one of her breasts in his hand, his fingers pressing near her heart. She felt herself cresting. His head moved, his teeth scraping the tender skin of her neck. She knew there was no escape.

And had there ever really been a trap?

Always.

"I love you," she said fiercely, for what good was there in speaking the truth and whispering it?

He groaned gutturally and began to come. They were so entwined, she could feel it: the convulsions of his penis, the warmth of his semen shooting into her, the tightening of his facial muscles against her neck. His hand moved between her thighs and she quaked, her sharp cry mingling with his rough moan.

She joined him in bliss, and in that moment, it felt neither right nor wrong, just inevitable.

* * *

Minutes later, he rolled her onto her back. She watched him as he smoothed the hair out of her face and off her arms and chest. She looked sublimely beautiful, her face moist with perspiration and drying tears, the anger gone from her eyes, the tension erased from her features. The calm after the storm, he thought . . . and perhaps before another. It didn't dismay him. Nothing could have in that moment. She had said the words he craved, given him the balm that soothed his bruised spirit. She lifted her hips in compliance when he began to pull the pillows from beneath them. He felt her stare as he unbound her hands and tossed aside his tie.

He took her wrists and opened her arms wide, resting them on the mattress, drinking in her undefended beauty.

"*These arms*," he murmured tightly, kissing the tender flesh on the inside of her elbow. How could her *arms* be so inexplicably beautiful to him? But they were. He cherished every square inch of her. He could never convey to her how much. The round globes of her breasts heaved up and down as he lowered his head and pressed his face to the smooth, pale expanse of her belly. He kissed her, his tongue dipping into her navel, and looked up at her face.

"I worship you," he said.

He kissed her belly again, his eyes burning when he felt her shudder of emotion vibrate against his lips.

Francesca moved her hands, cradling his head as he kissed her belly, her fingers burrowing into his thick hair, relishing the sacred, full moment. He lifted his head, and she put out her arms. Her chest ached at the vision of him coming to her. He accepted her embrace, taking her into his. Their flesh seemed to melt together, fuse. As if it had been the sensation her body had been waiting for, an inescapable wave of warmth and heaviness went through her. She fell almost immediately into a deep, exhausted sleep.

She awoke with a start at the sound of a brisk rap on the door. She opened her eyelids and was blinded by the bright light of sunshine hitting the white sheets.

"Not now," Ian's sharp voice penetrated her sleepy disorientation.

She twisted her head around, her eyes widening at what she saw. Ian was behind her on his side, his elbow propping up his upper body. His short, near-black hair was mussed. Whiskers darkened his jaw. His naked glory was made obvious not only by the mere sheet draped low on his hips, but the fact that her ass was pressed snugly against his cock. She wondered what sort of expression she wore, because his mouth tilted into a god-awful-sexy smile.

"What's wrong?" he asked, his voice sleep-roughed. Delicious. "It was just someone bringing coffee. I sent them away."

She rubbed her eyes groggily, trying to gather herself. "I could have used it. I feel like I'm waking up after a weeklong sleep."

He removed a tendril of hair from her cheek, his fingertips lingering to caress. His body stirred against her. She went still in abrupt awareness.

"I know. You were dead to the world when I put the pillow under your head. I'm glad you slept so well," he murmured. "You needed the rest. I was worried about you."

Remembered images and sensations from the previous night pummeled her awareness, recollections of her submission to the punishment, of her multiple orgasms as he made love to her with such sweet, ruthless precision, of his total possession . . . of her admission. Deep, satisfied sleep had staved off uncertainty, but it slinked into her awareness now.

Her torso still twisted around, she looked into his gaze cautiously. The early morning light streaming through the sheer curtains seemed to make his cobalt-blue eyes glow. The vision of him filled her consciousness. She blinked.

"I don't know how you stood it, growing up with all these servants. Didn't you find it intrusive?" she asked, striving to change the topic from the incendiary one of how his volatile, intimate lovemaking hadn't only broken her defenses, but also made her sleep like a baby in his arms.

"I found it horribly intrusive when I first came to live here. There was actually more staff then than now. Most of the ones you see here now are temporary, hired for the holiday and visitors," he said idly, sliding his palm to her sheet-covered hip. He didn't push her tighter to him, but something about the possessive placement of his hand made her hyperaware of his cock pressing against her ass. More likely she was increasingly focused, however, because he was growing more erect by the second. It felt decadently arousing, lying there in a comfortable, mussed, sun-warmed bed plastered against Ian's swelling flesh. With a herculean effort, she scooted onto her back and came up on her other hip, facing him this time, their bodies separated by a few inches. She pulled the sheet up to cover her breasts.

"I can imagine," she said, ignoring his frown at her sudden movement. "You were so independent when you had to take care of your mother as a child. It must have been odd to all of the sudden have people everywhere ready to meet your every whim. Now that I'm here at Belford, I'm starting to appreciate how blatantly bizarre of an alteration it must have been for you."

His slight scowl remitted when she settled, the soft down pillow pressed between her arm and resting cheek. He must have thought she was going to get up and flee. For a second, she'd thought about it, but as always, the draw of him was too great. She'd always prized those moments in bed with him when he opened up to her, revealing his depths.

"I considered running away," he said starkly, bracing his head with hand, his bent elbow still on the mattress.

"Where would you have gone?" she murmured.

His expression flattened. "I fantasized about finding my mother's grave. I couldn't think about much beyond that."

Her heart went out to him. She knew that Anne and James had told him that his mother had died when he was a child, hoping to protect his already scarred soul from further witnessing her descent into madness. When Ian had finally discovered the truth about Helen being alive when he was a young man, he hadn't spoken to his grandparents for a year.

"I can understand how you eventually came around . . . came to love Belford," she said. "Despite all its grandeur, it's a beautiful home. Your grandparents have made it that way."

"Gerard helped," Ian said. He nodded toward the bedside table behind her. She twisted her chin to look. It was a round table with a lamp. Several silver-framed photos were placed on it. She saw one of a dark-haired, solemn boy standing next to a handsome young man wearing a half grin. Ian and Gerard. They looked to be in a garage and were standing in front of an antique roadster. In another, they both posed next to a motorcycle—the first one they'd rebuilt together, no doubt—and in that one, Ian's smile was every bit as wide and proud as Gerard's.

She sensed him studying her when she turned to face him again. "*Has* Gerard been coming on to you?" he asked.

She blinked, startled by his direct question. In a split second, a dozen different answers sprang into her head. She was well aware that if she told Ian the truth, it could permanently damage a relationship that by all reports, had been a very positive one for him. The last thing he needed at this point in his life was another reason for misery.

"Like I told you, Gerard's been very kind to me. Solicitous. In fact, between Anne, James, and him, I feel as if they've been treating me like I've just recovered from a terrible illness," she said with a small smile. She met his gaze levelly when he examined her closely. Ian scowled and she had the distinct impression he knew she'd sidestepped his question.

"It wouldn't be the first time we've been interested in the same woman," Ian said.

"Really?"

He shrugged negligently. "The women never mattered that much to me, so it never bothered me until now." Against her will, warmth flooded her at his words. He was admitting he was jealous because it was *her*. "Gerard was an orphan, too," Ian said quietly after a moment. She suppressed a sigh of relief that he hadn't further pursued the topic of Gerard's romantic interest in her. "He lost his mother and father when he was barely of age. Officially, Gerard chose to be independent, becoming master of his parents' home. He was at school most of the time, but when he was 'home,' he was usually here at Belford, not Chatham. I guess you could say we learned what it meant to be orphans together."

"And thanks to Anne and James's support and love, you both survived the trauma," she said, turning to face him again.

His dark eyebrows made a flicking motion in acknowledgement of her statement, but he seemed distracted. "What is it?" Francesca asked.

"Nothing. It's just . . . I was wondering. Were there any more incidents with photographers?"

She stared at him blankly.

"In Chicago. Lin sent me a photograph that was in the *Chicago Tribune* business section of you at Noble Towers getting off the elevator."

"Oh," she said, comprehension rising. "No, that was the only time. Security was a little lax—"

"Because of the Christmas party," Ian finished for her.

"Yes. Why do you ask?"

His eyelids narrowed. "I'm just wondering if that photo had something to do with the attack in Chicago."

Her eyebrows went up in surprise.

"Maybe some sicko caught sight of you and became obsessed. Or maybe it signaled to someone that you were in a position of power at Noble and they planned a kidnapping. I think it was the latter, given the fact there were at least two men—the man who attacked you and the driver. Two people rarely share a twisted obsession, but will easily team up over greed."

She came up slowly, bracing herself with her elbow.

"You've really been thinking a lot about this, haven't you?"

"Almost about nothing else," he admitted grimly.

"And so that really is the reason you came back. The only reason. Because you believed I was in danger."

He caught the edge to her tone. His expression went carefully blank. "I came back because I was worried about you, yes."

She just stared at him as her heartbeat began to pound in her ears. "The idea of me being harmed is the only thing that could penetrate your misery in regard to Trevor Gaines," she stated more than asked.

He didn't respond, but she saw the flash in his eyes—that one that always hinted at a storm on the horizon.

"What exactly have you been doing since you've been gone, Ian?"

There. She'd said it. She couldn't take it back now, not it or that underlying subtext that accompanied the question. *What is more important than me? Than us?*

"Ian? What were you doing in France?" she prompted when he didn't speak, just watched her with those dark-angel eyes.

"I told you," he said. "I've had business there."

A chill seemed to settle in her heart, but unfortunately, it didn't numb off the flash of pain she experienced. "I see," she said quietly.

"So you don't trust me enough—or care enough—to tell me, in other words."

"Francesca, it's not that—" he said sharply, but she interrupted him by flipping back the sheet.

"Excuse me," she murmured before she left the bed and hurried to the bathroom, walking past her discarded clothing on the floor. She'd find a towel to cover her nakedness before she retrieved them. The last thing she wanted to do at that moment was expose herself to Ian any more than she already had.

Chapter Eight

t was a cool, crisp, windless morning. She went for a long walk with Anne and Elise on the grounds after a light breakfast. She struggled to focus and take part in the conversation as they walked through fields, gardens, and woods, but could tell from the other women's concerned glances that her distracted, withdrawn state hadn't gone unnoticed. At Elise's request, they stopped in the ultra-modern stables on the return to the house.

"You're very quiet this morning," Anne said privately to Francesca as Elise stroked a russet-colored mare in the distance.

Francesca blinked, rising out of her ruminations. She gave Anne a smile. "I've been thinking a lot about the painting."

"You've been thinking a lot about Ian."

She started. She saw Anne's sad, knowing smile. "Is he coming around any?" the older lady asked hopefully.

Francesca ground her teeth together at the question. "No. He won't budge. He's determined to be miserable."

Anne sighed. "In my experience, people are seldom determined to be alone and depressed. It's more that they feel they can't escape it."

Regret sliced through her. "I know," she assured, frustration edging her tone. "But why is he so insistent that Trevor Gaines matters? Ian never even knew him! He's dead, thank God," she muttered bitterly under her breath.

Anne put her hand on her forearm. "I know it must be so difficult for you to understand, given your situation with Ian."

"You're right," Francesca said in a burst of honesty. "I'm furious with him for being so stubborn. And are you honestly saying you *do* understand him?"

"Yes. I don't agree with him, and I'm extremely worried about his state of mind, but I do understand," Anne said. She shook her head. "Ian had such a fractured childhood, caring for Helen as if he were an adult, worrying day in and day out he'd be put in an orphanage if the townspeople understood how mad she was, dreading the times when his own mother would cringe away from him in fear. I think that moment when Lucien showed him that photograph of Gaines, and it looked so much like Ian, might have been the worst minute of Ian's life, but one of the best, too."

"Best?" Francesca asked, stunned.

"Well not *best*, perhaps, but . . . *significant*. He could never make sense of his past. He always tried, but it's as if Helen's disorganization, her insanity, made it so hard for him to focus. The questions he used to ask us when he came here as a child: What makes a person go mad? Would he become like his mother? If his father wasn't schizophrenic, was there a chance he wouldn't be? Who was his father? Why hadn't he taken care of Helen?" Anne grimaced in memory. "The concept of an adult looking out for him was so foreign to him, he never even asked once why his father hadn't taken care of *him*."

Francesca closed her eyes to shield her pain.

"He always guessed his father had taken advantage of Helen's vulnerability," Francesca said after a moment. "He worried she'd been raped. I don't understand how finding out all his suspicions were valid—even *worse* than what he'd suspected—could have been remotely a *good* thing for him."

"Because you know how important clarity is to him," Anne said. "Ian has to be one of the most focused, methodical people I've ever known. He prizes seeing clearly above all else, partly I believe, because he was forced at a young age to deal with his mother's disorganization and irrational behavior. Do you realize how hard it would be, to understand who you are when your only guide is a woman ruled by madness? He coped by making their world as orderly, as controlled, as predictable as he possibly could. But still, so many questions remained for him. His early life—his very identity—still felt blurred to him."

"So finding out about Trevor Gaines was good for him because it made sense. It helped—"

"Focus the blur, yes," Anne said.

Francesca stared at Elise in the distance as she moved over to a big chestnut stallion's stall and began murmuring to the animal in French.

"You're saying that he would rather see the truth clearly, no matter how painful or ugly that truth is," Francesca said slowly. The anger she'd been feeling seemed to solidify in her chest cavity, making her heart feel like a winter-cold stone.

"Yes, that's what I'm saying," Anne said.

"It won't help him," Francesca said starkly. "There's no meaning to be found in a man like Trevor Gaines."

Anne sighed and turned to join her in watching Elise. "It's not the truth about Trevor Gaines he's trying to understand, not entirely anyway," Anne said bleakly. "He's trying desperately to understand himself."

After that conversation, Francesca was agitated, feeling like she wanted to jump out of her own skin. She made an excuse for wanting to examine some of the elaborate stonework on Belford Hall's façade, walking ahead of Anne and Elise. Although Anne looked a little concerned, she made light of her request for Elise's sake. By the time she'd used the passkey and security code Anne had supplied her with upon her arrival and activated the lock on the front door, entering Belford minutes later, she'd gained no peace. In fact, her edginess only grew when she saw Ian standing in the Great Hall talking quietly to Gerard. She had the distinct impression he'd been waiting for her return. He'd showered since she'd last seen him, his well-cut, crisp attire of black pants, white dress shirt, and light gray jacket in attractive contrast to the fact that he hadn't shaved this morning and sported a slight scruff on his jaw. The shadows on his face only served to make his eyes look more blue—and fierce—when he pinned her with his stare.

He said something to Gerard under his breath and walked over to greet her. The last thing she wanted to do was talk to Ian at that point, however. After last night and her talk with Anne, she was confused about how she felt. Her nerves felt stretched and raw.

She started to hurry past him as he approached, her eyes glued to the escape of the staircase.

"Francesca, wait."

She paused and glanced back at him warily.

"May I have a word?" he asked, nodding toward the sitting room.

"Not now," she blurted out. Distantly, outside the realm of Ian's stare, which seemed to make up her entire world for a breathless few seconds, she heard the door open and Anne and Elise enter.

His nostrils flared slightly and she sensed his barely contained, frothing emotions. He stepped toward her.

"It'll only take a moment."

"No," she said, feeling shaken . . . unsure. She didn't feel *angry* when she looked at him anymore, and she didn't know what to make of that. Her anger had been her strength. She turned to go, but Ian grasped her arm, halting her. In a split second, her volatility burst free. She jerked her arm, breaking his grasp.

"Let go of me," she exclaimed desperately. She turned and walked away.

"Francesca," Ian grated out, his frustration palpable. It alarmed her to hear that much emotion in the voice of someone who was typically so in control.

It pained her.

She kept walking toward the closest door, barely holding in an avalanche of emotion herself, blindly seeking an escape. She reached for a door randomly, but it opened before she touched it. Clarisse stepped out, her smile upon seeing Francesca sagging when she noticed her expression. Francesca said nothing, just plunged into the dining room and slammed the door abruptly behind her.

Ian started to charge after her, but paused at Anne's quiet warning.

"No, Ian. Let her be for now."

He made a rough sound of pure frustration and came to an abrupt halt at the sound of the dining room door slamming shut behind Francesca. Clarisse looked at him and jumped, giving a tiny squeak of alarm. From the periphery of his awareness, he noticed how pale the maid looked as she stared at him with huge eyes. What did she see, looking at him in that moment? He'd *frightened* Clarisse.

Gerard approached. Ian clenched his teeth. He really needed to get a handle on this fury he'd been experiencing toward Gerard. It was fueled by jealousy.

Wasn't it?

"Remind me never to get on Francesa's bad side," Gerard said in an attempt at levity.

"Shut up, Gerard," Ian ground out aggressively. He saw his cousin's eyes flash with anger, but he was too irritated to apologize. He strode across the Great Hall and opened the door to the sitting room. The abrupt manner in which he shut it undoubtedly conveyed that he wanted to be left alone.

* * *

"How long do you have?" Gerard murmured later as he pulled Clarisse into his suite and closed the door.

"Only an hour or so. I have to help with the lunch since Mina is sick."

"Long enough," Gerard said, placing his hand along the side of her throat and leaning down to kiss her. He immediately began to undress her, not in the mood for wooing. Not that wooing was required. Clarisse was young and biddable and more than willing to warm the future Earl of Stratham's bed. She arched against him as he unzipped her dress, pressing her breasts against his ribs, her hands moving over him, eager to please.

Very eager.

He removed her dress uniform and draped it in the crook of his arm. She plastered herself against him, her blue eyes springing wide when she worked her hand between their bodies and touched his erection. He was hard as a rock. He couldn't seem to get rid of his flagrant erection since last night no matter how many times he masturbated, which is why he'd subtly signaled to Clarisse earlier in the Great Hall, silently ordering her to his room for this unusual daytime tryst. His arousal was such that his hand would not suffice.

He needed to rid himself of this grinding sexual tension. He required concentration to discern the last part of the recorded sequence of Ian at his computer. At least he'd placed *that* camera eye in the perfect place in Ian's room.

"I suppose given *this*," Clarisse glanced down significantly at his cock, "you don't want a report on Francesca until afterward? I have some important information, you know."

"Like that she didn't spend the night in her room?"

She looked surprised. Gerard smiled grimly. "I have my ways of getting information, too, little one. I'm worried. Things between Ian and her are growing quite volatile. You saw how they were in the Great Hall earlier."

"Yes. Mr. Noble looked . . . scary. But do you really think he's dangerous?"

"He's unstable. I'm afraid he might have more in common with his mother than any of us like to admit. I can tell Anne and James are worried about it, but they don't like to say anything. It's too difficult of a topic for them, as much as they've suffered with watching Helen's descent into madness. Ian's state of mind is why I've had you looking out for Francesca. Sadly, it looks as if her feelings for him haven't been dampened by his volatility. It's not going to end up anywhere good between them," he stated grimly.

He ignored Clarisse's concerned expression and pulled her over to his bed without removing her lingerie, panties, and shoes. She had to half jog to keep up with him, her breasts bouncing in the push-up bra she wore.

"Bend over the bed," he said shortly. "You were right. I'm not in the mood to wait."

"Yes sir."

She did as she was told, and he smiled as he reached into the pocket of her dress still draped over his arm. He took out her Belford passkey. Clarisse had recently unwisely informed him that she frequently got in trouble from the maid supervisor for misplacing her key. Unfortunately for her, he'd learned that Clarisse had a history of getting herself into trouble, a fact that Gerard planned to use to his advantage. He opened a drawer on the bedside table and dropped the key inside before removing a bottle of lubricant and tossing aside the dress.

He didn't demand that she call him sir, it just slipped out every once in a while from habit. It didn't displease him. Not in the least. If fate hadn't been such a cruel bitch, Clarisse would have been his possession just like everything else at Belford.

He jerked down his pants and underwear and opened the bottle of lubricant. He approached her, rubbing the silky liquid onto his raging erection as he did so. She wouldn't be prepared for this quick of an entry, but he was, and that was all that counted.

He slid her panties over her ass and let them fall down her ankles. He squeezed a buttock, grunting in arousal. She was firm and taut, although not as fleshy as he'd like for what he had planned. Still, she'd do. He drove his cock into her, making her squeal.

Yes, she'd do very nicely.

He pushed his cock into her pussy, grabbed her slender hips, and began slamming into her with unapologetic greed. At first, her moans might have been from discomfort, but they quickly segued to the sounds of a woman who was enjoying being fucked. Her pussy was tight and muscular. Even if she hadn't agreed to pass information to him about private matters regarding Francesca, he might have chosen her for a regular bedmate during this particular stay at Belford. Clarisse would do almost anything he demanded of her sexually.

Which reminded him . . .

She was growing hot and juicy, moaning as he took her harder. He grabbed her buttocks and spanked one of them, watching his cock plunging in and out of her pussy all the while. She mewled at the spanking, so he landed several more, his cock jerking in excitement in her tight channel at the smacking sound and the rising color on the smooth cheeks.

He gritted his teeth in restraint and slowly drew his erection out of her, his cock falling and bobbing in the air before him. God, he was horny. If only he could get last night out of his head. It plagued him, those memories of what he'd seen . . . of what he *hadn't* seen, but only heard. Damn Ian for not cooperating and carrying on *all* of his antics with Francesca in places other than the bed, where one of two surveillance cameras was placed. True, his primary objective was to gather information, and he was close—so close—to decoding the movement of Ian's rapidly moving fingers as he punched in his private password to his computer. But that didn't mean that he didn't enjoy all the other things he'd witnessed in his cousin's room last night. Well, Gerard wasn't sure if *enjoyed* was the right word. It also enraged him, ate at him, haunted him to hear Francesca's cries and mewls of stark pleasure, to observe Ian dominating and possessing what Gerard could not make submit or own.

It would have been better for Francesca's health if she'd accepted Gerard. Much better. She was a fool to seek solace and protection from a man who was not destined to be on this earth for much longer.

That surveillance video certainly plagued his cock as well, Gerard thought, grimacing as he stroked his rigid erection. He was uncomfortable from sustained arousal, but also very pleased. He enjoyed discovering something that made him this stiff and virile.

He stepped out of his pants and underwear, pausing to remove his belt, looping it in one hand. Clarisse remained bent over the bed, but she looked anxiously over her shoulder. She made an arousing picture, her cheeks starting to flush from excitement, her bottom slightly pink, her outer sex visible between her spread thighs, the tissues slick and flushed. She saw the belt. His cock jumped in the air when her eyes widened in trepidation. Their sexual relationship had only begun the day before Francesca arrived at Belford, when he'd heard Clarisse would be the one to serve her. He'd never done anything like this to her before. He chuckled and smoothed the leather over her ass.

"Now I propose we make things between us a little more interesting," he said silkily. "I've recently come to recognize how thrilling the belt can be."

He didn't wait for her permission before he landed the leather strap and she fell forward, crying out sharply and catching herself with her hands.

Francesca recalled the labyrinth trail she'd taken on the night of the ball in order to find Mrs. Hanson. It seemed she'd gone a backward route. All she need have done was take the door off the dining room, which led to a staging area for serving, and then some stairs that went to the kitchens. Once she was sure Ian hadn't followed her, she paused on the stairs, gathering herself and drying a few tears while she listened to the sounds of pots clanging and sporadic conversation in the distance.

Mrs. Hanson gave her a warm greeting and gladly agreed to fulfill her request for a sandwich to go, after Francesca explained she was going out to the gardener's cottage to sketch. Work would help to focus her . . . ground her.

The housekeeper far surpassed her expectations, packing her a sack filled with an enormous chicken salad sandwich, fruit, two scones, a carton of milk, homemade oatmeal cookies, and a thermos of coffee and cream. Not wanting to run into Ian while she was feeling so frayed, she asked Mrs. Hanson to pass a message to Anne that she planned to work through lunch.

She kept repeating that conversation with Anne in her head as she sat at the picture window in the cottage and sketched later that morning. She realized she was willfully resisting what Ian's grandmother had said. If she accepted Anne's logic, she wouldn't only have to sacrifice her anger at Ian for leaving. She'd have to own her helplessness in dealing with his pain.

She'd have to admit there was nothing she could tangibly do to ease Ian's suffering but allow him to continue on this path.

That, she realized, was not an easy thing to allow.

Perhaps her anxious thoughts were the reason she was so dissatisfied with her preliminary sketches of Belford. What she outlined on the page shared little in common with the house she'd come to know, conveying a cold, austere, dead shell versus the warmth and proud tradition she was beginning to respect and love.

She ripped out the page from her sketchbook and crumpled it up in a fit of frustration. Impulsively, she grabbed her coat, then her sketchbook and pencils and headed out the front door of the cottage.

*   *   *

Ian stood on the threshold of the cottage entrance, tensing in wariness when he received no answer to his call. He scanned the room rapidly, taking in the dying fire and the crumpled sketch lying not far from the chair Francesca had scooted next to the window.

"Francesca?" he called again, his alarm rising. He sensed the cottage was empty, but perhaps she was just avoiding him, angry as she'd been earlier. He stalked through the kitchen and then down the hallway, peering into the empty bathroom. He'd prefer she was there, hiding from him. At least that would mean she was safe and unharmed.

The bedroom, too, was empty.

"Francesca?" he bellowed, his mind flying to dire possibilities, the very hint of which made his blood turn to ice water. He started at the sound of the front door slamming shut.

"Ian?"

His eyes sprang wide, relief coursing through him at the sound of her breathless voice. He began to walk out to meet her, but paused on the threshold of the bedroom when he saw her coming down the hallway.

"Where were you?" he demanded, backing into the room so that she could enter. The hall was dim, while the bedroom was sunlit. He peered at her face anxiously, searching for signs of distress. She carried her sketchbook under her arm and fisted a pencil in her gloved hand. Her nose and cheeks were pink from cold, but she appeared to be perfectly fine.

"I went into the woods a way to sketch Belford through the trees. I wasn't far. I could hear you shouting."

"You shouldn't have wandered off like that. I didn't know where you were."

"Obviously, the way you were yelling," she said. He was so relieved that she was all right—not abducted or wounded or worse—

that it took him a moment to notice her small smile. He blinked, sure he was mistaken at what he saw. He hadn't seen that particular, familiar expression of fond amusement for a long, long time.

He exhaled slowly. "Grandmother told me you sent word through Mrs. Hanson that you'd be out here. I'd prefer to know when you go out. In fact, I'd prefer that you weren't out in the grounds alone at all," he said, still studying her expression through narrowed lids, still wary of her mood.

She shrugged and went over to the desk to set down her sketch-pad and pencil. She approached him again, taking off the fingerless gloves and unbuttoning her coat. He caught a glimpse of a dark red T-shirt that fitted her narrow waist and full breasts tightly.

"Well? I'm not alone now," she said, her brows quirked upward in what he could only describe as a challenging expression.

"No . . . but for future reference," he said gruffly. He studied her for a moment, searching for more clues, but she just watched him calmly.

"I wanted to speak with you this morning about something in particular," he said uneasily.

"I'm sorry about the way I behaved."

He blinked at her simple apology. "I wasn't planning on harassing you about . . ." He paused uncomfortably, not wanting to put into words her upset over the reason he'd been determined to go to France. He cleared his throat. "What happened between us this morning," he sufficed. "I've been talking things over with Lucien, my grandparents and Gerard. They agree it would be a good idea for me to do a small press conference tomorrow afternoon here at Belford, just to announce our bid to buy Tyake and make it clear I was involved in the whole thing. I've contacted Lin, and she's arranging everything. I think it'd be a good idea if you didn't appear at the press conference, though. I'd rather keep you out of the public eye. Grandfather agrees."

She took a step toward him. "You plan on returning to work?"

"Yes, more than I'd been working before anyway." He met her stare. "I'm taking back control, Francesca."

"And what of this other important mission . . . this . . . this discovering of yourself," she said falteringly. He could tell she was guarding against sounding derisive at the concept, and he appreciated that. Still, he knew he needed to tread carefully with her.

"I'm not giving up on that. I'm sorry," he said when he saw the flash of disappointment shadow her hope. "I'll just have to divide my time more evenly. Everyone is very concerned about what happened to you in Chicago, and they agree it might be associated with the amount of control I gave you on the temporary board."

"I really don't know how you can assume that, Ian."

"I can because I've had threats against me before."

"What?" she asked, taken aback.

"It's not a big deal."

"What do you mean it's not a big deal? It's a big deal if it happens to me, but not to you?" she demanded.

"It comes with the territory. Usually, it's just a mentally ill person making ridiculous, unfounded threats," he said evenly.

"And when it's not usual?"

"That's why I have such good security," he said with a pointed glance. It was starting to get warm in here. He unbuttoned his overcoat. He glanced guiltily at Francesca's pale, set face when she didn't respond. "It hasn't happened enough in the past for me to worry you with it. Now, I'm feeling like an idiot for not considering it might happen to you in the position I put you in. For that," he said, meeting her stare, "I'm sorry."

For a second, she looked stunned. Then she blinked and shook her head. He held his breath when she laughed softly. "Believe it or not, I was happy to have helped out in the Tyake deal. It gave me something to focus on. I liked it more than I would have expected, considering."

"I've always said you have an excellent mind for business." She met his stare and comprehension settled. "Oh, I see. It wasn't *that* apology that you wanted."

"Or expected," she said quietly. For a second, the silence stretched between them, seeming to thicken. Take on weight. "I was happy to help you, Ian. Support you. I didn't realize it at the time, but I do now. It was the only opportunity you gave me to do anything for you. You wouldn't let me share in any other burden."

He heard her frustration and understood. "I was all right, Francesca—"

"You were split wide open," she interrupted him starkly.

He clamped his mouth shut. He felt the pain rise up in his chest, and tamped it down willfully. Anger filled the empty space. This is why he didn't like confrontations. It ripped the scab off old wounds. Made him *feel*, when that was the last thing he wanted to do.

"How would you have liked it," she asked in a quiet, trembling voice, "if I had been hurting as much as you were, and I ran away, depriving you of the opportunity to comfort me. How would you feel? *Ian?*" she pressed when he didn't respond, taking another step toward him.

His nostrils flared as he tried to expand his aching lungs while keeping his mouth sealed tight to prevent . . . what? He couldn't say. He wanted very much to walk away in that moment, but Francesca's eyes wouldn't let him.

She raised her eyebrows expectantly, waiting.

"Furious," he admitted finally. "Desperate."

"That's right," she said. She stepped closer still and reached up, putting her palms on either side of his face. Her eyes burned him like dark fire. The pain in his chest amplified despite his efforts to contain it. Grimacing, he grabbed her wrists and tried to push her away. She'd been ready for it, though. Her hands broke free of his halfhearted restraint. She threw her weight against him so that he caught her roughly to steady her, his hands at her waist beneath her coat. Cupping his jaw again, she tilted his face down toward her.

Christ. He hadn't been expecting this; hadn't read her unusual mood accurately. He wasn't prepared.

She sealed her front to his and went up on her toes. She kissed him. Sweet. Addictive. Insistent. Desire didn't hesitate, flooding into his blood, washing away his doubt . . . his anger . . . his pride. He should have walked away while he could, left to hunker down in solitude to silence that ache.

Once he tasted her, he knew he'd stay.

It was like keeping still in leaping flames, accepting what she gave him . . . knowing she saw his pain . . . letting her lick his wounds. He didn't really consciously agree to it. It was just that he couldn't move. He was paralyzed between pain and shame on one side, and rabid need on the other.

She moaned softly into his mouth, her taste permeating him. Arousal crumbled his last defense. He tightened his hold, spreading one hand on her lower back and the other on her hip and buttock. He bent down over her, forcing her back into a slight arch, grinding her against him.

She broke their kiss and pushed against him, straightening. He clutched her to him while she rained kisses on his jaw and neck. When she'd first pressed her lips to his, they'd been cool from the winter air. So quickly, she'd grown hot, feverish in her determination to give.

But he'd always struggled to take.

He felt her hands at the waist of his pants, unfastening them.

"Francesca," he began hoarsely.

"*Shhh,*" she soothed, her fleet fingers working the buttons through the holes of his shirt, the anticipation tearing at him so much that he moved to help her. She ripped the last button free and whipped back both sides of his shirt. She pressed her face to him. He held her head against him, staring out the sunlit window, seeing nothing as her mouth moved over him, kissing, licking, biting gently. His skin roughened in pleasure. He tried to take her into his arms and lift her to the bed when she sucked and nibbled at a taut nipple. She resisted him, however, whispering "no" against his damp skin. He looked down at her in helpless arousal as she laved the sensitive flesh with the tip of a dark pink tongue. He delved his fingers into her hair and hissed her name.

As if in answer, she began kissing his ribs, her hands massaging his back muscles, scraping her nails down his spine until he shuddered. He groaned in agonized anticipation when she dropped to her knees before him. Christ. It'd been so long for him, he didn't think he could stand the buildup to bliss. He couldn't understand in that moment how he'd ever lived without it.

She released his cock and jerked down his clothing beneath it. Her cool fingers gripping his swollen flesh made him wonder if steam would rise off him, he was so overheated. She held him naked in her hand, his underwear bunched around his balls, stroking his length firmly, no shyness or reluctance, her motions sure and firm, even a little rough . . . just like a man liked it.

Just like *he* liked it. Just like he'd taught her.

She bathed the head almost delicately with her tongue while she jacked the stalk vigorously. She looked up and met his stare as she arrowed him between her lips. He inhaled sharply as she sucked, and his cock slid along her warm tongue. He read the message in her eyes and it made him want to shout. Weep. Punish her for making him feel so much. Come in Francesca's sweet mouth and never stop. He furrowed his fingers into her hair and pulsed into the heaven of her, opting for the latter choice.

Sex was the way he'd learned best to demonstrate his feelings. He was just a man, after all. Still, wonder spiced his arousal. From where had this loving come on her part? This generosity? He couldn't understand it. All he could do was drown in it.

He never blinked as he looked down at her, eating up her image even as she consumed him. His girth stretched her lips wide. Her cheeks hollowed out as she treated him to that strong, singular suck that used to keep him awake at night in recollection. His cock popped out of her mouth when she leaned back extra forcefully. She slapped the bobbing stalk playfully, gave him an eye-crossing stroke from balls to tip with her fist, and then reinserted him into her mouth. She dragged her teeth back and forth over the sensitive head gently before she firmed her lips, ducked her head, and sucked him deep.

He groaned and tightened his fingers against her scalp, clamping his eyelids shut. The image of her was too arousing. He flexed his hips, his taut movements matching hers. Still, he was careful not to be too demanding. She hadn't done this in a while. Neither had he, and he wanted to stretch the exquisite moment . . . hang on.

He'd always known how free she was with her love, how unselfish, but today, at that moment, the truth cut at the heart of him. The pleasure sliced just as deep. What right did he have to always take what she offered so innocently, so wholly?

He stilled his flexing hips, restraining himself, but she grabbed a buttock with her free hand. She pushed, and he opened his eyes. She ducked her head, swallowing his cock, jerking slightly as the tip squeezed into her throat. Her nostrils flared. She moved her head back, pulling at him so strongly he gritted his teeth.

She pleaded with her eyes.

His groan felt like it ripped at his throat. He held her head in his hands, his thumbs bracketing the tops of her jaw, and thrust, taking what she offered so sweetly. If she gave, did that mean he deserved? He didn't know. He didn't care, he was being flayed alive by her mouth, by her love. Time stretched as he stared down at her, rapt, and she made love to him with fierce precision.

It was too fucking sweet.

He thrust deep and erupted, almost immediately jerking his body back in order to free her throat, ejaculating on her tongue. He held her to him, fucking her tight, wet mouth with his convulsing cock, giving her his seed and whatever else had been ripped loose from inside his spirit.

His body tightened in one last blast of searing pleasure.

He sagged, staggering slightly, and quickly righting himself, lest his cock impale her. He slid out of her mouth during his dazed fumbling. She grabbed his hips. A ragged laugh left his raw throat.

"What?" she asked, confusion and the beginning of a smile starting on her slick, swollen mouth. He'd left a white drop of semen on her bottom lip when he'd stumbled. Her beauty seemed to flash like a bright headlight on his already disoriented brain, stunning him.

"You actually act like you could steady me," he said, referring to their disparate size and weight.

She kissed the tip of his glistening cock. He groaned roughly at the erotic vision she made.

"I can steady you," she said, holding his stare. His smile faded. She rose before him, took his hand and led him over to the bed.

Chapter Nine

"We never even took off our coats," Ian said wryly under his breath as he helped her remove her T-shirt a moment later. He didn't know how she'd done it: given him the most intimate, heart-wrenching, balls-emptying experience of his life while they were almost both completely dressed and wearing winter coats. They sat at the edge of the mattress, Ian in only his unbuttoned pants, Francesca almost nude, their coats and discarded garments forming a pile at the bottom of the bed. He pulled the T-shirt over her head, and she seemed to notice his furrowed brows.

"What is it?" she asked

"Why?"

"Why what?" she wondered, pushing his shirt off his shoulders and pausing to sink her fingers into the muscle, rubbing until he closed his eyes in pleasure. It's one of the many things he loved about her. She was such an innate sensualist, always curious to experience, touch . . . taste. Yet another reason it was such a blessedly good thing that they both enjoyed it when she was restrained during sex. Her touch tended to erase all of his typical control.

"Why aren't you angry anymore?" he asked gruffly, taking the caressing hand in his own and kissing the palm.

She gave him a fleeting glance as he worked the shirt off his arms.

"I don't know," she said, grasping behind her on the bed. She stood and slipped the black cashmere overcoat that he'd once bought her over her nakedness. He didn't like it. Her naked body was a blessing to his eyes—curving, firm, exquisitely feminine, the very shape and form of his dreams. He looked forward to laying her on that bed and returning all the pleasure she'd just given him in spades. He caught her hand, scowling. She'd better not be planning on running off again—

"That's not an answer, Francesca."

She sighed, seeming to genuinely struggle to explain herself. "I meant it, I don't know why I feel different. For all I know, I will be angry at you again sometime soon for leaving the way you did. But something . . . happened."

"What happened?" he demanded, still holding her hand.

"I talked to your grandmother and she . . ."

"What?" he asked. He pulled her into his lap, disliking her distance. He opened the coat impatiently, exposing her naked breasts, belly, and thighs to his gaze, an admittedly cavemanlike gesture to demonstrate her availability to him . . . a probably useless but stark reminder of their intimacy. His love for her swelled when he saw her small smile. She really did understand him shockingly well. He opened his hand at the side of her jaw and tilted her face toward his in a silent prompt to continue.

"She seems to understand you better than I do," she said, perhaps a little regretfully, her fragrant breath softly fanning his face.

His eyebrows tilted up. "I think we both know it's not the same. She's my grandmother. Not my lover."

"Am I? Your lover?" she asked, her voice just above a whisper.

"Always," he said, brushing his lips against hers. "Whether you're in my arms or not."

He saw her swallow thickly and wondered if she fought back tears. Her voice was strong enough, however, when she continued.

"Anne reminded me of how you always need focus . . . have to have a clear picture . . . concise understanding. I don't agree with you in thinking that Trevor Gaines is somehow important, Ian. I think you give him far too much significance."

"I know you think that," he replied evenly, his thumb brushing her cheek.

"But I do understand how comprehending your past is so crucial to you."

Their stares held. Her dark brown eyes glistened. "I know you've been suffering, and I hate the idea, with everything I'm worth, of you doing it alone. I haven't stopped being furious at you for shutting me out."

"But?" he prompted quietly.

"But I'm tired of pretending that your actions are incomprehensible to me," burst out of her throat. "Because I love you doesn't give me the right to demand that you be different than what you are . . . who you are. Because I disagree with you, and because I believe you're dealing with your grief in a self-defeating way doesn't change the fact that I love you. And always will."

Neither of them spoke for a moment. Ian wasn't sure he breathed.

"If I were to be honest with myself," she continued in a more measured, hushed tone, "I would have to say that it didn't entirely shock me, your reaction over Trevor Gaines and your mother's death. I may not agree with how you dealt with your grief, but I understand it. I understand *you*. I can't go around pretending self-righteousness when your biggest crime was not grieving in the way I wanted you to grieve, in a way that was convenient for *me*."

He studied her flushed cheeks and slightly averted eyes. He wanted to thank her, but he found it hard for some reason. His voice box had stopped working. He stroked her face, and maybe she understood, because she turned and kissed his palm.

"That doesn't mean I think you should go off and obsess about Trevor Gaines," she added with a sharp glance.

"I'm not obsessing about him," he said, finding his voice. "I want to understand my origins, Francesca."

"Granted," she replied. "But I can't agree with you that it's a positive step, Ian. I think it's a futile, senseless search into the past, one that's compromising your future. I only have to look at you to know that it's hurting you, not helping."

"I disagree," he said, despising the necessity to differ with her in this moment when she was being so much more generous than he deserved.

She studied his face. He met her stare, determined not to flinch in this, but it took more effort than he liked.

"You're still not going to tell me what you were doing, precisely, are you?" she whispered.

"I can't. Not you, above all else," he said, unable to keep misery from entering his tone. What Lucien had said was true. He accepted that now. If he told Francesca about the dirty, ugly search in that hovel of a mansion, if he told her what he'd discovered thus far, she'd be furious . . . disgusted. She thought she understood him, but she wouldn't understand *that*. He knew she would beg him not to go back to Aurore alone. He knew he would listen to her above all else . . . and he just might concede to her wishes.

She shut her eyes, and he sensed her pain. He was dimming her glorious, light-infused spirit. *God*, he hated this. He pulled her against him, her head against his face, and inhaled the scent of her hair. It was on the tip of his tongue to say he would go. He'd monitor her well-being from a distance, perhaps hire a bodyguard to protect her. He didn't want to hurt her any more than he had, but he couldn't say what she needed to hear. Not yet he couldn't. But before he could utter a word, she struggled to get off his lap and stand.

"I don't want to talk about all that right now," she said with a breathless lightness that he didn't buy for a second. Had she guessed what he was about to say?

"What would you like to do then?" he asked gruffly, taking her hand to steady her as she stood.

"Lunch?" she asked. He blinked. Amusement pulled at her puffy lips. "Mrs. Hanson packed me enough for a platoon. I have it in the refrigerator. Then we can take a nap afterward?"

He couldn't resist her small smile . . . so hopeful, so unintentionally yet blatantly seductive. He couldn't resist her, period, and therein lay the crux of the problem. If he'd been able to resist her, he'd have been in contact with her since the first moment he fled to northern France to begin his search.

"Lunch sounds fantastic," he said, standing and taking her into his arms, pleasure rippling through him at the sensation of her naked breasts against his ribs. He leaned down to seize her mouth, and he hoped she read all of his gratitude as well as his desire in that kiss. "But if you think we're taking a nap afterward," he said wryly next to her lips a moment later, hitching her body up higher against his so she could feel his growing arousal. "You've got another think coming."

He saw her gaze flash up to meet his. Her laughter was like a warm, sunny day between bitter, lashing storms. There was no doubt. He was a selfish bastard. Of course he'd snatch at these stolen moments with her, greedy for every precious, golden second.

Much to her chagrin, he fastened his pants while he helped her put together their meal in the kitchen. When they returned to the bed, he insisted that she remove the coat she was using as a robe and eat her lunch naked.

"The vision of you is more sustenance than the food," he said gruffly, halting her when she tried to pull the sheet up over her breasts. He acceded to allowing her to leave the coverings on her legs for warmth, but insisted she leave her sex exposed. She'd found plates, utensils, cups, and napkins in the kitchen and split the enormous sandwich and fruit for their lunch. As she leaned against the fluffed pillows, however, and nibbled at her sandwich, she found she'd lost her appetite. Ian stared with focused intensity at her mons, even as he distractedly ate. Finally, he gave up the pretense of eating, took a swig of cold milk and set aside his plate. Her breath caught when he turned and firmly parted her thighs.

"Oh," she whimpered when he used his fingers to also part her labia. He leaned toward her, grabbed her plate in a seamless movement, and shoved it onto her bedside table.

"Have I ever told you that you have the prettiest pussy in existence?" he growled softly, nostrils flared, staring his fill at her pink, exposed flesh and clitoris.

"Once or ten thousand times," she managed, repeating her familiar response to his similar questions in the past. Everything beneath his intense gaze prickled and burned.

He pressed on her clit with the ridge of his finger, both of them watching. The vision of his thick, masculine finger embedded in her delicate flesh was mesmerizing. She gasped in pleasure at his quick, concise caress on the sensitive flesh. He slid easily in the well-lubricated valley. When he moved his hand, she bit her lip in disappointment. He trailed his fingers over her hip and belly, spreading a thin coat of the juices he'd found in her cleft along her skin. She looked into his face. His small smile told her how much her wetness pleased him. He glanced at her plate on the table.

"You didn't eat much. I was distracting you."

"You were," she said softly, blushing. "But that doesn't mean the distraction was unwelcome."

"Maybe." He reached for the small bunch of grapes left on her plate. "But you should eat more, nevertheless."

"I don't want any more," she said, reaching to caress the succulence of his bulging biceps, but he halted her gently, settling her hand on the mattress.

"You will eat more. I'm not the only one who has lost weight."

"You should eat, too, then," she countered with mock stubbornness.

He leaned back on the pillows with her and brought her into the circle of his arm. She smiled when he plucked a grape and pushed it against her lips. When she refused to part them, his smile widened at her playful challenge. He persisted in his mission, running the moist grape against her mouth, rubbing her with the fruit, tempting her . . .

He grunted in approval when she finally parted her lips enough and he pushed the fruit into her mouth, his finger lingering on her tongue. He lowered his head, watching his actions avidly. She closed her teeth around the intruder, scraping his skin erotically as he slowly removed his finger. She felt his cock swell next to her hip.

"Good girl," he teased, plucking another grape while she chewed and swallowed the sweet fruit, suddenly ravenous for more.

He pushed another grape into her mouth, pausing to let her suck on his finger. She drew hard and felt his cock jump.

"If you had any idea what I think about doing to that sweet mouth of yours—what I was thinking about doing earlier—you wouldn't tease me so much with it," he grated out as he retrieved another grape.

"I have a pretty good idea what you'd like to do," she said honestly, flavor bursting on her tongue as she chewed. "I want you to do it. You know that."

He stilled in the process of lifting another grape to her lips, his gaze narrowing. "Do *what,* precisely?"

A light blush spread on her cheeks. "You know," she murmured. His lifted his eyebrows expectantly. Was he *serious*? "Lose control more than just a little bit while you're in my mouth. Not . . . hold yourself back like you usually do."

"Most women wouldn't say I hold myself back in the slightest, Francesca. Just the opposite, in fact."

"Oh. I see," she said, her cheeks growing hotter yet. Was she depraved because she liked it when he lost himself in the moment and was focused entirely on finding pleasure in her flesh?

A laugh broke free of his throat. "It's a good thing one of us does," he murmured, pushing the grape between her lips. Despite his stated confusion, she felt his cock stiffen even further next to her hip. The conversation was arousing her, too, for some reason.

"It's just . . ." She hesitated as she chewed, meeting his stare. "I know you often hold yourself back until the end."

"With good reason," he said, frowning. "I would never want to hurt you."

"I know, and I don't want to be harmed," she assured, adding hesitantly. "But you could be freer with me. Once in a while. It wouldn't cause any lasting harm. I . . . it . . ."

"*What*, Francesca?" he asked tensely, the grapes forgotten.

"It turns me on when you use me for your pleasure."

For a moment, he just pinned her with his stare. Then his mouth shaped a curse. He whipped the blanket off her legs, exposing her full nudity.

"I know you're trying to tempt me into coming again in that sweet mouth, but it's not going to work, lovely. Not until I'm ready, it's not," he said grimly as he lowered on the bed and rolled over until he was between her spread thighs, belly down.

"I wasn't trying to tempt you into anything," she said, laughing breathlessly.

He gave her a half-amused, half-impatient glance. Her breath caught when he lowered his head to her spread pussy.

"Bend your knees and spread your thighs more," he ordered. She slid her feet along the sheet toward her shoulders, highly aware of his stare on her pussy.

"Ian?" she asked shakily when he plucked another grape. Her eyes widened when he pushed the dusky purple fruit between her labia and pressed it against her clit, up and down, around and around. He pressed hard. The grape's skin broke, cool juice running over her feverish flesh.

"You said it yourself. I need to eat, too," he said gruffly before he lowered his head between her thighs and began to feast with a suddenly ravenous appetite.

Chapter Ten

"Oh God," she muttered, her eyes rolling back in her head. Her fingers threaded into his thick dark hair, holding him against the very core of her while Ian worked his magic. He pushed at the back of her thighs and her feet came off the bed. She abandoned herself to pleasure, her consciousness drowning in it. His mouth and tongue were wet, firm, and delicious on her sex. The whiskers on his moving jaw agitated the tender flesh of her inner thighs, the low-grade burn amplifying her arousal. Despite her rapture, Ian's focus on making love to her was even more intense. When the pounding started at the cottage front door, it penetrated her awareness before it did Ian's.

"Ian, stop," she gasped. She scraped her nails against his scalp to get his attention. He rubbed her clit with a stiffened tongue and she moaned, pushing her to him despite what she'd said. The knocking resumed. She heard someone call Ian's name. "Ian, it's your grandfather. *Ian.*"

He opened his eyes and lifted his head. Her clit twanged in deprivation from pleasure and acute longing when she saw how beautiful he looked, his lower face slick with her juices, his eyelids heavy with arousal, the slits of his blue eyes burning with a barely banked flame. He blinked and for a moment he seemed to come back to reality. His nostrils flared and he inhaled, undoubtedly catching her scent. He gave her pussy a blazing glance and cursed before he rolled off the bed.

"I'll go and see what he wants," he said, grabbing his shirt and shoving his arms through the sleeves. He wiped off his face with the napkin near his plate. "You stay here. And don't you *dare* get dressed," he grated out with a hard glance before he walked out of the room, closing the door behind him.

Despite his pointed warning, she did get up and scurry into her clothing, James's voice resounding from the nearby living room leaving her feeling self-conscious. Besides, she could hear what he was telling Ian.

The front door slammed closed. A moment later, Ian walked into the bedroom. She sat at the edge of the bed, putting on her boots. His gaze ran over her clothed body. He frowned.

"You heard?" he asked.

She nodded.

"I'm sorry," he said, retrieving his socks and shoes and sitting on a chair to put them on. "I left my phone at the house because I didn't want to be disturbed coming out here. But you know how Lin gets when she's on a mission. There's been a couple glitches with the press conference tomorrow, and I need to get back and deal with them. She couldn't reach me, so she called the house phone and spoke to Grandfather. After I deal with those things, I really should work on a statement for tomorrow."

"It's okay. I understand," she said truthfully, tying the lace on her boots. She could just imagine the gargantuan task laid before Lin of coordinating a press conference on a day's notice from across the ocean.

"You'll come back with me?" he said, standing.

She gave him a knowing, wry glance. It wasn't really a question.

He didn't want her out here alone. She sighed, not feeling up to arguing with him after their intimate, stolen moments together.

"Okay. I can firm up the sketches I've done so far up at the house," she conceded, putting on her coat and standing to grab her things. He finished dressing and waited for her near the door. He remained unmoving when she approached. She stood before him and looked up at him solemnly.

He touched her cheek. "I hate it when we have to part."

She blinked, recognizing he was speaking about their interrupted lovemaking, but so much more.

"We don't have to be apart," she said softly, feeling his stare and stroking finger in places beyond the flesh. "Not in any permanent sense of the word. Not unless you choose it."

"I didn't choose any of this. Fate did. I'm just trying to deal with the fallout."

"You're wrong," she replied steadfastly. "You can choose, Ian. Your past? Or your future."

He dropped his hand. She sensed his rising frustration at their disagreement, but she didn't apologize. She started to move past him to the hallway, but he caught her arm.

He pulled her against him, his kiss possessive . . . hungry. She understood that he was reaffirming his right to touch her that way, and she reciprocated without hesitation. Her still-aroused sex throbbed. The time for pretending she didn't crave him—love him—with every ounce of her being had passed. She figured the realization had hit when she'd stood in the woods sketching earlier, wrestling with her warring emotions, and heard him calling for her, so desperate in his need.

Elise came to visit with her in her suite early that afternoon, bringing the sad news that Lucien and she planned to return to Chicago the day after tomorrow.

"Lucien hinted very vaguely that he and Ian might take a trip together sometime in the near future," Elise said as she looked over Francesca's shoulder at her completed sketches. "Do you have any idea where they are going?"

Francesca glanced back at Elise uneasily. "No. I don't know precisely what they might be doing or where they are going, but I can tell you, I don't think it's a good idea at all."

They'd agreed that the brothers were likely doing something associated with Trevor Gaines, and Elise didn't appear very pleased about the concept of the upcoming trip, either.

After Elise left to go riding, Francesca had gotten down to about an hour of some serious sketching, rising out of her trance at around three o'clock. She was restless. This was about the time Mrs. Hanson often took her tea, and Francesca had grown in the habit of sitting with her in Ian's kitchen while she'd spent so much time in the penthouse. It was a tradition she missed.

She was walking down the grand staircase, planning on going to the kitchen, when she saw Ian crossing the Great Hall toward the front doors with that familiar long-legged, purposeful stride. Her heart did its typical jump upon seeing him unexpectedly. She noticed he'd shaved and changed his shirt since they were out at the cottage. How he managed to look so distinct and sophisticated and elementally male at once never ceased to fascinate her.

He turned and paused when she called out to him.

"Where are you off to?" she asked, approaching.

His blue eyes flickered over her body, lingering on her breasts. She'd showered after her return from the cottage and changed clothing. His small smile was like a warm, sexual caress. Their differing backgrounds and styles of dressing had been a point of self-consciousness and awkwardness on Francesca's part since the beginning of their relationship. Ian, on the other hand, was typically sublimely nonchalant in regard to how she dressed, expecting everyone to treat her like a queen no matter how she was garbed.

I want you to know that I am far from being critical of your appearance.

Whether you're in pearls or your Cubs T-shirt, I find you to be extremely attractive. Perhaps you haven't noticed?

She shared his smile at the memory of him saying those words to her in that dry, sardonic tone of his.

"I don't have the type of clothing in storage here at Belford that I'd like for the press conference," he said. "I packed light for my stay. A haberdasher I know in Belford is going to set me up and deliver a suit in the morning. Speaking of clothing," he said, his gaze rising from the red *C* logo on the T-shirt she wore to her face. "I see you're wearing one of my favorite outfits."

She laughed and his smile widened. It felt so good, sharing a lover's inside joke with him.

"May I come along?" she asked impulsively.

He hesitated, glancing at the heavy, carved front door. She had the impression he'd rather keep her behind that locked entrance.

"It'll be a quick trip, and boring to boot," he warned.

"No it won't. I'll be with you."

His mouth tilted. His gaze was so warm on her. He was considering denying her, nevertheless; she could tell. She went up on her toes, brushing the front of her body against his solid form, and pressed her mouth to his, shameless in her attempt to convince him. That's all it took, and his arms were satisfyingly surrounding her as he took control, returning her kiss with blistering heat.

"You shouldn't take so much pride in being convincing," he said a moment later, his gaze scanning her face. Her toes had curled from his kiss. She forced them to relax now while she waited anxiously to see if he'd take her along.

Triumph zipped through her blood when he sighed, took her hand and led her to the front door.

The front door closed. Gerard walked out from behind the grand staircase and crossed the hall. He opened a paneled door and slipped into James's private office. It was empty. He walked over to James's large desk—an antique that had been passed from one Earl of Stratham to the next for the past five generations. It should have been one of Gerard's many belongings when James was gone. As things stood, although Gerard would be the next earl, James had decreed that this treasured desk along with everything else would be Ian's.

The Noble ancestors must be turning in their graves.

Screw James, Gerard thought as he slid open the right-hand drawer and lifted the lid of a red leather box. He smiled grimly upon seeing what was stored there.

He retrieved his cell phone from his pocket and dialed Brodsik's number.

"This is it. They're going into town. Francesca is with him," he merely said when a man answered the phone. He listened, frowning. "You idiot. I told you to stay close by to take advantage whenever the opportunity arose. Well it's not my fault you partnered with a fool. How do I know where Stern has disappeared to? He's your friend. No, *no*," Gerard interrupted bitterly. "I will not discuss your little blackmail scheme at the moment." He was outraged at the concept of a such a grubby, moronic criminal trying to manipulate him, but Brodsik would pay. In fact, Stern had already outlived his use, and Brodsik would very soon.

He paused, listening to Brodsik's defense for asking him for extra money beyond his fee. "Well I'd certainly call it a bribe, considering you're threatening me with exposure if I don't agree to your demands," Gerard replied wryly. "I've told you I'd have your money tomorrow. It takes more than a few hours to come up with that much cash. For now, do you still work for me, or not?" He paused, his mouth curled into a snarl. "Good. You know what to do right now. You'll have time to make it back to Stratham while they're at the tailor in town. Noble shouldn't be in there for more than an hour. The sun will still be up if you get your ass back here quick enough. Remember, I want Francesca to see you. What? Yes, we're still meeting tonight at the usual place in town. I'll have a Belford passkey for you. Were you able to purchase it?" He listened for a moment. "Good, because you'll need that gun tomorrow, won't you?"

He hung up and checked his watch. He had at least an hour, probably closer to two. Ian's paranoia was such that he locked the door to his suite even in his childhood home. Whatever he kept on his computer must be valuable, indeed. In his illicit observance thus far, Gerard saw little else being kept in the room that might warrant so much caution on Ian's part. Most of Gerard's allotted time would be spent using his inexpert knowledge of lock picking to get past the door. Still, the locks on the Belford suites were not complicated mechanisms, intended for privacy from servants more than actual security. He'd manage it, he thought grimly as he hurried up the stairs.

She enjoyed the short visit to the tailor, not at all agreeing with Ian's warning that she'd find it boring. What could be boring about watching a beautiful, sexy man be expertly fitted for a suit?

Mr. Rappaport, the owner of the haberdashery, seemed very eager indeed to provide a service to the Earl of Stratham's illustrious grandson. Francesca came to understand that he'd occasionally made suits for Ian when he was a child and young man. Mr. Rappaport pulled a chair up for Francesca in the luxurious working area outside the dressing rooms. He politely provided her with a magazine and a cup of tea, which held her interest, until Ian came out of the dressing area, that is, and stood in front of the triple mirrors. The magazine article was forgotten as she watched the gray-haired tailor—who was so petite, Ian looked like a giant in comparison to him—scuttle about, taking measurements and marking up the suit. Ian lifted his stark white shirt while the tailor took his waist measurement, and Francesca's attention redoubled. The pants hung on his frame loosely, emphasizing his lean, cut abdomen and the narrow trail of dark hair that ran from his taut belly button beneath the waistband of the pants.

Ian had been present on several occasions when he'd had dressmakers come and fit her for clothing, and had somehow found his quiet, focused observance of the ritual arousing. She'd never had the privilege of watching him endure the process, however.

She sensed Ian's eyes on her in the mirror as Mr. Rappaport began to measure his inseam.

"And you dress to the left, if I recall correctly?" the tailor asked briskly.

"Correct," Ian said, holding Francesca's stare. She frowned slightly, confused by the tailor's question. It took her a second to puzzle out that the tailor was asking which way Ian's cock rode in his pants, so as to allot for the volume in his measurements. Ian must have noticed her eyes widening as understanding struck, because she saw his lips tilt in amusement in the mirror.

After he'd finished, Mr. Rappaport scurried out of the dressing area when an assistant called to him. Francesca blinked in surprise at the vision of Ian stalking over to her, now wearing only the trousers and a partially buttoned shirt.

Her breath caught. She recognized that gleam in his blue eyes.

He leaned down, trapping her by placing his hands on the arms of the velvet chair. He swooped, capturing her mouth in a scalding kiss that soon had her forgetting where they were and everything but his possessive mouth and addictive taste.

"You're going to get it later, for getting me hard while I was in such a vulnerable situation," he muttered against her lips a moment later.

"I was just watching," she defended breathlessly.

He stood, his absence disorienting her.

"It was enough. Plenty," he added with a hard glance before he walked behind a door to change. Mr. Rappaport scurried back into the room a few seconds later, immune to her flushed cheeks and erratic breathing.

When Ian had finished at the haberdasher, they got some coffee to go at a quaint little tea shop and returned to the car. She relished in Ian's relatively relaxed mood. While Ian was never one to smile frequently, she was encouraged to see his small half grin with increasing regularity. Was he, perhaps, rising out of this pervasive depression that seemed to have weighted his spirit since his mother had died? It struck her that while they had danced around the incendiary topic of Trevor Gaines, they'd carefully avoided the sad topic of Helen's unexpected death last summer.

She studied him driving as they left the town of Stratham behind and headed for Belford on the narrow country road, the setting sun casting his profile in a reddish-gold glow.

"Ian, where are you keeping your mother's ashes?" she asked, referring to the fact that Helen had requested in one of her more lucid periods to be cremated.

He glanced at her swiftly, his blue eyes cool in his sunlit face.

"Grandmother has them. She's holding them for me. I didn't want to take them where I was going."

She absorbed his answer for a moment, blindly staring at the frozen-looking road before them.

"It wasn't your fault, you know."

The silence swelled. She glanced at him reluctantly. He stared fixedly out the windshield. Her throat felt tight. She could guess at how much guilt he carried for his decision to give permission for Helen to receive a medication that possibly had led to her liver failing, and ultimately death.

"You've given permission dozens of times over the years for medication changes and alterations in your mother's treatment. She was very ill. She wasn't eating. The medication was supposed to not only help with her depression and psychosis, but also increase her appetite. It was the doctor's recommendation, Ian," she said when she saw his Adam's apple bob as he swallowed thickly. "She would have died if she didn't start eating more."

"They could have kept her alive with a feeding tube," he said.

"Yes. They could have, I suppose. But the doctor recommended this course of action first, and I agreed with her recommendation. I know you did, too. You didn't want her kept alive on a feeding tube. You wanted to make a decision that respected her rights as a human being as much as you could. There's no way you could have known the reaction she'd have to that medication. The fact of the matter is, there's no clear-cut proof her decline was due to that medicine. You know how ill she was . . . how weak."

"The medicine did it," he said shortly, still staring fixedly at the road.

"You cared for her your whole life. You did a thousand times more than most sons. Whoever had been her primary caregiver would have faced a similar decision, and they'd have made the same choice you did, Ian. It was her time," she added softly. "She'd suffered enough."

His nostrils flared slightly, but she couldn't tell if he was angry at her choice of topic or moved by her words. His hands tightened on the wheel. It took her a moment to realize he was no longer focused on their conversation. He glanced in the rearview mirror, his brow furrowed. She looked over her shoulder and saw a car driving far too close to their bumper for safety. Ian sped up slightly, but the car followed, maintaining its close tail. Suddenly, the car leapt forward and hit them, making them lurch in the rigid restraints of their seatbelts.

"What's he *doing*?" Francesca asked in incredulous anger when the car behind them abruptly jerked the wheel into the oncoming lane. She yelped in alarm, sure he must have missed the corner of their bumper by inches or less.

"Francesca, get down," Ian ordered.

The vehicle—a dark green sedan—flew up next to them. Fear shot through her when she looked into the cab of the car and saw the familiar craggy features and furious stare.

"Ian, that's—"

Ian's hand pushed at the back of her head and rapidly flew back to grip the wheel. She bent below the window, finally doing what he'd demanded, lowering her face toward her thighs, straining against the seatbelt. She squeaked in alarm and grabbed the door handle when their car jerked violently. The man had intentionally rammed into them sideways. Their car careened onto the side of the road, gravel popping beneath the wheels. Fear shot through her veins like it'd been mainlined. They were going to lose control and wreck.

But somehow, Ian miraculously kept the car in control as he braked. She rose and peered over the dashboard cautiously. The dark green car had shot past them. Her heart racing, she wondered if the vehicle would double back. Instead, it just zoomed over a slight hill in the road and disappeared.

Shivers coursed over every inch of her flesh. She turned and met Ian's stare. His face looked rigid.

"Are you all right?" he asked tersely.

She just nodded. "That was the man."

His eyelids narrowed dangerously. "What man?"

"I saw him," she said, her tongue feeling numb. "That was the same man who attacked me in Chicago."

"Are you sure?" he demanded.

She nodded. "One hundred percent sure. It's not a face I'm likely to forget."

The two police detectives interviewed Ian and Francesca in the sitting room with Anne, James, Gerard, Lucien, and Elise all present.

"I'd like you to come down to the stationhouse tomorrow morning to work with someone to render a likeness of the man who has attacked you twice, Ms. Arno," Detective Markov said to Francesca as they stood in preparation to leave, putting away their notebooks.

"No," Ian said abruptly, standing as well. "The sketch artist can come here. I don't want Francesca going out until we get this situation under control. But Francesca is actually an artist herself. You can sketch this man's face, can't you?"

"Of course," she said.

Detective Markov looked at his partner, taken aback by Ian's decree. But then he shrugged, seeming to see Ian's point. "I suppose you're right. But we don't use a traditional sketch artist. We've acquired the technology to do everything on the computer. It's easier to send off the image to other police and crime officials that way. A few of us will be coming out to Belford Hall tomorrow for security during the press conference, as you requested, your lordship," Markov said, nodding respectfully to James, "so we'll just send the woman who specializes in the computerized renderings then. Will that suit you?" he asked Ian.

Ian nodded. "Yes, Francesca's not attending the press conference. I want her to stay away from the cameras. She can work with the artist during it. And you'll be sure and contact the authorities in Chicago about this man?"

"I'll report to you straightaway if they have any leads as to his identity."

"They don't at the present time," Ian said, his mouth slanted in irritation. How could he say that with such certainty? Francesca wondered. It struck her that he'd been in constant contact with the Chicago officials. "But they didn't bother to have Francesca work with a sketch artist or look at mug shots. They treated the case like a random attempted robbery and assault. It'd be best if you sent the sketch immediately to the Chicago police once it's made to see if they can make any connections. I know a man in the department who can help us. I'll pass on his contact information to you. I would have had him work with Francesca after this man attacked her in Chicago, but by the time I'd learned about things and got ahold of him, Francesca was already on her way to Belford. I thought she'd be safe here," he said, his forehead creasing. "Still, I don't understand why the man didn't stick around and finish things off while he had the chance. He did the same thing in Chicago. It makes no sense."

The detective shrugged. "I've learned in my line of work you shouldn't give these criminal types more intelligence or fortitude than they're due. When things grow a little tough, they'll more than likely run for it."

Ian looked far from convinced. Guilt wriggled in her belly at the sight of his rigid, anxious visage. She hadn't seen that expression on his face since the difficult months before his mother died, when he was consumed with worry. He hadn't wanted to take her off Belford's grounds, but she'd persuaded him. He'd been worried about her since he arrived, and now she had firsthand proof he hadn't just been paranoid.

Anne stood to see the detectives out. Elise patted Francesca's hand. "Are you doing okay?' she asked in a hushed tone.

"I'm fine. I was just more startled than anything," Francesca assured the others, including Ian, who was studying her.

"Do you think it's a good idea to hold the press conference tomorrow with this criminal hanging about?" Gerard asked.

"I've increased the security around Belford until we can find out more about this man's location. Hopefully he'll be apprehended soon," James said.

"Lin has checked out everyone coming. No one other than authorized visitors will be allowed onto the grounds," Ian said, sitting back down in his chair. "If we cancel now, it'll only fuel the rumors that are flying about in regard to Noble Enterprises being in choppy waters."

"I agree," Lucien said. "The business world needs to see Ian securely back at the helm."

James nodded, looking up when Anne returned to the sitting room.

"I've asked the staff to go ahead and serve dinner. We'll go in as we are," she said, referring to the fact that none of them were dressed for dinner. They'd all gathered upon hearing Ian and Francesca's alarming news, and hadn't left the room since the police had arrived to take their report.

It felt strange, but somehow comforting, to sit in the Belford formal dining room wearing her Cubs T-shirt and surrounded by so many concerned faces. It struck her later as she ate Mrs. Hanson's delicious raspberry tart for dessert, listening to the others talk, that she was surrounded by her true family. The familiar ache started in the vicinity of her chest as she watched Ian conversing somberly with James and Lucien that there was a good chance she'd never officially be part of that family.

Not if Ian couldn't come to terms with his demons.

Later that night, she said a quiet good night to Anne and kissed her on the cheek. Ian said her name as she was walking through the Great Hall alone toward the stairs. She turned to him.

"Were you planning on going up without saying good night?" he asked, approaching her.

"Of course not. I was going to say good night in your suite in a little while."

The almost indistinguishable lightening of his expression told her he'd liked her answer.

"I'll come with you if you want to get anything in your room, and then you're coming with me. I'm not in the mood for letting you out of my sight at the moment," he said, taking her hand and leading her toward the stairs.

"You'll have to at some point," she said, half-exasperated by his diligence and half-touched by it. "You don't want me at the press conference tomorrow, and I have to meet with the sketch artist, for instance."

"I've already arranged all that."

"Of course," Francesca said, giving him dry sideways glance. He seemed unaffected by her fond sarcasm as they ascended the stairs.

"Lucien has agreed to sit with you while I'm occupied. And after that, I've spoken to Lin. She's beginning a search for someone for you."

"Someone *for* me," Francesca said warily, her feet slowing as the neared her room in the arch-ceilinged hallway. "What's that supposed to mean?"

"Full-time security personnel," Ian said briskly, urging her with his hold on her hand to commence down the hallway. She pulled back. He dropped her hand, his expression going flat.

"Ian, I am not having someone follow me around twenty-four hours a day!" she exclaimed with heated restraint.

His eyes flashed back at her. "Just until we can get this situation under control. After that, if you only agreed to live at the penthouse, my worries would vanish. Well . . . decrease a good deal anyway."

She gave a bark of incredulous laughter. "I refuse to have you lock me up like a pet, Ian. Especially . . . given our circumstances," she added, leaving things vague on purpose. She was done hashing out his obsession with his past and what it meant to his present and future. For today, she was.

He came to an abrupt standstill. She faced him.

"You make it sound like I'm purposefully insulting you . . . demeaning you," he bit out.

"You *are* demeaning me by making all these decisions about me without even giving me the respect of talking to me about it. It's my life. Stop trying to take control of it. I have a right to my privacy, among other things."

"I'm very well aware it's your life," he replied ominously. "I'm just trying to make damn sure you go on living it in good health."

"Here's an idea," she replied heatedly, straining to keep her voice quiet in the resonant hallway, but not succeeding. "Ask me how I feel about it next time instead of just planning my life for me. It's not that hard, Ian!"

The sound of footsteps caught her attention. Her cheeks flushed when she glanced down the hallway and saw James, Gerard, and Elise rising up the stairs. They looked a little uncomfortable at accidently hearing Ian and her arguing, and kept their gazes averted before they disappeared from view down a corridor that led to their right.

She jerked the knob on her door. She plunged into the suite, leaving Ian standing in the hallway, not bothering to close the door. He'd come in anyway. She wasn't trying to send him away, no matter how sharp she'd just sounded or how arrogant he had. Francesca wanted to be with him that evening. She'd been affected by that harrowing experience on the road as much as him. His heavy-handedness, his single-mindedness in arranging her life just peeved her. Not that she was unused to it.

Not that he was unused to struggling with her over such things.

By the time she came out of her bathroom after washing up, wearing an ivory silk gown, robe, and slippers, much of her irritation had eased. He sat on the couch in her sitting area, flipping through her sketchbook.

"I like what you did today," he said quietly, nodding at the page. She knew he was striving for a neutral subject, and was thankful.

"Thank you," she said. She stepped toward him and looked down at her drawing. "Those are fruit trees at the edge of the forest, aren't they?"

He nodded. "Apple and cherry."

"They must look stunning when they bloom in the spring," she said.

"They do," he replied gruffly, still looking at the page and not her. "I wasn't satisfied with my earlier attempts. I'd rather paint Belford as if coming out of the woods, the viewpoint of someone returning after a journey, suddenly seeing not just a house or a landmark or an architectural prize, but a *home* and everything that implies," she said thoughtfully. "I'll have to run it by Anne and James, though. It would require me to put the woods closer to Belford Hall in order for me to get the house details. It would be inaccurate factually."

"Not really. Only recently," Ian said, puzzling her. He closed the sketchbook, set it aside and stood. "The gardens and yard area were only expanded in the past few decades. When I first came here as a boy, the forest was much closer to the house. I think my grandmother was worried about the woods being so close with a curious boy in residence. I also happen to know neither of my grandparents particularly cared for the clearing of the grounds. What you're describing is what generations of Nobles would have seen upon returning home from one of the forest paths."

He met her gaze soberly, and she knew he wasn't thinking about her painting. "We can discuss the issue about security more tomorrow, after the press conference. I don't want to fight with you right now," he said quietly.

"I don't want to fight with you, either. Not tonight," she replied honestly. He put out his hand and she took it, following him out of the room and closing the door softly behind her. They walked together to his suite through the shadowed hallway, the silence seeming to billow with rising anticipation.

They entered his suite and he locked the door. He removed his jacket and draped it on a valet stand. Then she was in his arms and he was pulling her against him. His mouth was feverish on her neck and ear, his intensity making her eyes spring wide. His body felt hot, too . . . and *hard,* she realized with a thrill. Yes, she'd felt the increasing electrical excitement building between them, but *this* . . .

He was liked a coiled spring. She'd sensed his palpable tension ever since the incident on the road earlier, but hadn't expected his anxiety to transform so quickly to arousal once he touched her.

She whimpered in stunned lust when he fisted a bunch of loose hair at her neck and pulled, so that her throat was exposed. His lips burned a trail on her neck before he seized her mouth in a kiss. It aroused her to no end, that scorching, desperate kiss, but tears burned her eyelids as well.

"Ian, I'm all right," she muttered raggedly a moment later against his mouth.

"No thanks to me. I shouldn't have taken you with me, today," he said grimly, backing away from her slightly, but keeping his groin pressed against her belly, the fullness there like a silent reminder of what was to come. She wanted it, too. Needed it. They'd both come very close to ending up in a fiery wreck earlier.

"I was the one who talked you into letting me go. Neither one of us would have guessed that man would come have come from Chicago to Britain."

"*I* guessed it," Ian said harshly. He untied her robe roughly and jerked the sides over her shoulders. Beneath the robe she wore a simple, thigh-high ivory silk gown. She gasped when Ian cupped a breast, shaping it to his palm. He hissed something she couldn't quite make out, then pressed his forearm to her back. When he leaned down over her, she instinctively arched against the brace of his arm. He sucked on the tip of her breast straight through the silk, his warm tongue rubbing the wet fabric erotically against the nipple, demanding that her flesh awaken to his call. Her sex tightened in answer. Francesca sensed the depth of his almost rabid need. He lifted his head a moment later when she moaned in rising pleasure. His eyes looked a little wild.

"I love you so much."

"I know," she replied. And she did. How could she deny it, when she saw the truth of what he said reflecting in his eyes like fiery words?

"I'm going to spank you and then I'm going to have you again and again, until we're both too exhausted to move." He opened his hand along her jaw. "I'm going to fill you up with me. I'm going to take my fill of you, Francesca. Not that it will work. It never does. I always want more," he said grimly, bending to take her mouth again in another kiss.

Chapter Eleven

eat rushed through her at his incendiary, erotic words. His voice still echoed in her head when he finally sealed their kiss.

"Are you going to spank me because I talked you into taking me into town with you?" she asked shakily.

"Maybe a little bit. But mostly I'm going to do it because I'll love it. And you will, too." She felt his cock swell next to her belly. He felt delicious and full and heavy.

"All right," she conceded, excitement starting to bubble inside her. Maybe it was the idea of danger hovering, maybe it was the knowledge—no matter how remote—that they could be separated at any moment. Ian might leave, true, but they were also only human. Life was cruel at times, and random . . . and so was death. But they were here together now, both of them teeming with life and lust and love. She would grab this moment with him, squeeze it for all it was worth.

"Come here," Ian said, taking her hand. She looked over at him in confusion when he led her to a stretch of blank wall between an antique chest and an elaborate oil painting of a man on a white horse in sixteenth-century garb. "I'll be right back," he said.

She watched him go into his closet, just as he had last night to get the belt. The skin on her bottom seemed to prickle in anticipation. Her clit did the same. When he came out of the closet, however, he wasn't carrying a belt, but instead a wooden paddle. Her eyes widened as he neared her.

"I thought you didn't have any things like that here," she said, eyes fixed on the paddle. At first glance, it looked like the paddles he had used on her in the past, but it wasn't. It was flat on one side and slightly convex on the other, an elevated ridge running down the middle of it. The paddle portion was about a foot long and three or four inches wide, not including the handle with a leather carrying loop attached on the end.

"I was thinking about how to improvise," Ian said with a small smile. Her breath stuck in her lungs when he removed a silver cuff link from his sleeve, slipped it into his pocket and began to roll back the sleeve on the arm that held the paddle. He flipped the paddle, holding it up for her inspection. "It's a miniature cricket bat. In fact, it's the first one Grandfather bought me when I came to Belford as a boy. I uncovered it in a cabinet in the billiards room earlier today. Well, in fact I was searching for it."

"With no intention of playing cricket whatsoever," she said, amusement mingling with her arousal.

"I played regularly in school," Ian told her with a smoky look as he transferred the paddle to his other hand and fleetly removed his other cuff link. She licked her lower lip distractedly at the vision of him rolling back the white shirtsleeve and revealing another strong, hair-sprinkled forearm. She could see the outline of his cock quite well in his trousers. It'd been trapped by his boxer briefs in an upward slanted position pointing toward his left pocket, the fat, tapered head delineated even through the fabric. Her mouth watered with a sudden acute desire to feel him plunging in her mouth. "I'm quite good at it, you know, handling the bat," he said, stepping toward her, the paddle now firmly in his right hand.

"I'm sure you are," she said, looking at him with mounting lust spiked with just a hint of wariness. She lowered her gaze to the paddle. He held it up.

"It's very light. They're made of willow," he said huskily. "Touch it."

She swallowed thickly and ran her fingers over the tool he intended for her punishment. It was lightweight.

"It will sting." She said her thought out loud, shakily.

"I believe it will, yes. I've never used it to this purpose. Be sure and keep me apprised of how it feels," he said, his small grin a little wicked, walking behind her. She gasped in excitement when he pressed the paddle to her ass and circled it against her buttocks through her gown and underwear. For an erotic moment, she just stood there while he ran the paddle over her prickling flesh softly.

"Drop the gown," he said thickly after a moment as he slid the paddle over the bottom curve of her cheeks and rubbed, now lasciviously.

She whisked the spaghetti straps of the gown over her shoulders and down over her breasts. The garment pooled around her waist. Ian continued to lewdly rub her ass with the paddle, but helped her, sending his fingers beneath the fabric from the back and pushing the gown over her hips. He lifted the paddle and the silk slipped down her legs, pooling at her ankles. He walked in front of her to the blank stretch of wall.

"Come over here," he demanded quietly.

She stepped out of the gown and the slippers she'd been wearing and approached him clad only in a pair of sheer lace panties. His gaze was on her breasts, belly, and mons, making her nipples stiffen and her clit swell and ache.

"Put your hands above your head and lean against the wall," he instructed, stepping aside to give her space, his arm bent, the rim of the paddle resting casually against his shoulder in what looked to be a familiar pose from his cricket days. A whole history of naughty references about Englishmen and spankings flashed through her brain, making her hide a smile. It aroused her, though, the idea of having her bottom smacked by the cricket bat . . . by the idea of having her ass spanked by the sexiest Englishman in existence.

That aroused her *very* much, she admitted, as she started to take the position, her head turned, gaze glued to Ian. He put his hand on the sensitive side of her ribs and she wondered if he felt the way her heart was pounding.

"No, lovely, don't bend over yet. Just lean against the wall. Put your feet behind the rest of your body. There. Perfect," he growled softly next to her ear. When she'd settled, her feet were about two feet away from the baseboard, her hands were above her head, her forearms bracing her weight, her breasts heaving six inches from the wall. She wasn't bent at the waist, but instead in sort of a vertical slant against the wall.

Ian moved behind her. She couldn't see him without straining around to look. She knew from experience he wouldn't like it if she gave in to her curiosity. He always said her eyes undid him. Instead, she stared fixedly at the blank wall and forced air into her lungs.

He slid his fingers beneath the waistband of her underwear and lowered them down over her ass to midthigh. She started to move in order to assist him in removing the garment, but he stopped her.

"No. Spread your thighs wider."

She did what he said, stopping when Ian said, "There." When she'd opened her thighs, the lace panties had stretched tight between them. She heard Ian grunt softly in male satisfaction and thought he must have appreciated the image of her lowered panties remaining on her thighs. *Lech,* she thought, smiling to herself. In fact, the thought of arousing him from such a small thing pleased her inordinately.

She sensed him standing just behind and beside her, her breath hitching when he pressed the cricket paddle to her bare bottom. At the same moment, his other hand caressed the side of her body, skimming her hip, waist, ribs, and breast. She shivered, the power of his stroking hand amplified by the threat of the paddle against her ass. Waiting for the first stroke was always almost unbearably exciting for her.

"We can talk more about your safety in the next several days, but in the meantime," he said, still caressing her, "promise me you'll be excessively careful."

"You were in the car, too. You promise *me* to be careful."

He pressed the paddle tighter into her ass cheeks.

"Yes, I promise," she said shakily.

"Then I promise, too," he said. He lifted the paddle. *Smack*. She moaned at the quick flash of pain followed by the familiar burn and prickles of arousal.

"Too much?" he asked, rubbing her ass with his left hand.

"No."

"It's a whippy little thing," Ian said. She bit her lip to cut off a whimper as he continued to soothe her bottom. She knew what he meant. The willow paddle *was* light and whippy, ideal for making the surface area of skin sting without causing any real harm.

He paddled her with it again. She whimpered at the burn. *Smack, Smack*. He paused to soothe her. "Yes, that's warming you up nicely," he said, palming a cheek and running his thick forefinger along her crack.

Liquid warmth trickled from her slit. She made a muffled sound of arousal in her throat when he suddenly inserted the paddle between her thighs and pressed it against her sex. Her eyes sprang wide.

"Oh!" she muttered in surprise.

"Good?" he murmured, subtly moving the paddle, stimulating her clit.

"*Yes,*" she hissed, curling her hands in fists against the wall. She ground her teeth together, her hips shifting, grinding her sex down, riding the bat.

"Hmmm," Ian growled next to her. She sensed his focus . . . his rising arousal. "I think I'll just have to take this with me when I go. The ridge in the middle of the back of the bat fits nicely between your lips, doesn't it?" he asked, referring to the slightly convex shape of the back of the paddle and how it burrowed ideally between her labia.

Her answer was an aroused moan. But then the paddle was gone and landing yet again, biting at the bottom curve of her ass cheeks, the sound of it striking flesh ringing sharply in her ears. He paused, letting her recover from the sting. This time instead of massaging her ass with his hand, he stroked her hip and belly, enlivening her nerves. She shut her eyes tight, her vagina contracting with a pang of lust, when he filled his hand with a breast. He stepped closer, bracketing her hip with his thighs, and pressed his cock against her. He placed the flat end of the paddle on her other hip and pressed, sandwiching her ass between it and his erection. She moaned in a rising fever as he gently pinched an aching nipple, turning it into a tight, hard, exquisitely sensitive point.

He lifted the paddle and spanked her with it several times. She felt his cock jump next to her hip every time he landed a blow.

"Do you remember the first time I paddled you?" he asked roughly, pressing the paddle into her ass cheeks. Her bottom was starting to burn in earnest. Her clit sizzled, plaguing her. She longed to stanch the ache with her hand.

"Yes," she replied thickly. How could she forget it? She'd been stunned by what he'd said he wanted to do to her . . . shocked that she'd allowed him to do it . . .

Incredibly aroused by the idea of submitting to him sexually.

He finessed her nipple with his fingers, making her grit her teeth in sharp arousal.

"I wanted so much to just to fuck you raw. I nearly did it, too, you were beyond beautiful. I'd never had unprotected sex before that moment, and I nearly gave in. You submitted so sweetly. I couldn't comprehend your trust in me. I still don't."

She clamped her eyes tighter, moved by his rough honesty.

"Some part of me understood you, even then, in the beginning," she said, her voice shaking with emotion. "You used to make me so nervous, and yet . . . you *didn't*. I knew I belonged with you. I knew *we* belonged. Being with you was like . . . finding home," she added brokenly.

"Yes," she heard him say after a pause. "And how I deserved it, I've never figured out."

"You don't have to figure it out, Ian. Just believe."

He grunted softly, backing away from her and removing the paddle. She whimpered at the loss of his solid heat, but remained in position, fighting her emotional upheaval, not to mention her curiosity as to what he was doing. She bit her lip at the sound of his zipper lowering, stifling a shaky moan of anticipation. A moment later, she felt his legs brush the back of her calves.

"Brace yourself against the wall and bend over. I didn't fuck you then, but I certainly will now. Because I can . . . and because you *are* mine, no matter what happens."

She swallowed to ease the congestion in her throat at the sound of his stark dominance mixing with the hollow sound of the acceptance of his fate. It seemed ridiculous to deny what he said. Even if he left her for good, part of her would always reside in him, and he would forever be in her heart. Her blood. Her spirit.

She repositioned herself, her hands pressed against the wall, bending at the waist, her panties still stretched tightly between her spread thighs. She felt the hard, tapered head of his penis probe between her thighs, finding her slit. He firmed his hold on her hips.

She cried out when he entered her completely, slapping his pelvis against her ass. He still wore his clothing, having just unfastened his pants and lifted his cock free. She could feel part of his exposed, round testicles along with the fabric of underwear pressing against her outer sex. He paused at the sound of her cry, fully sheathed in her, throbbing at her core.

"Are you all right?" he asked.

She gave a muffled assent. He transferred one hand to her clit, rubbing her firmly with the ridge of his forefinger. She glanced down between her legs and saw the cricket paddle suspended in the air. He'd looped the leather cord around his wrist. For some reason, the vision of the paddle swinging beneath her as Ian rubbed her clit sent a thrill of excitement through her. She mewled in pleasure and pulsed her hips.

"You're still sore from last night, aren't you?" he asked knowingly.

"A little," she admitted, although what he was doing to her felt so good, she was quickly forgetting the slight discomfort of harboring his large, erect cock so deep, so suddenly. He stayed completely still for the next moment. It was she who began to bob her ass against him, burning against his circling, pressing finger, fucking his cock several inches back and forth and getting the delicious pressure she required. He said nothing, either, but she felt his tension mounting behind her as he caressed her ass with one hand and set her on fire with his other, and she pumped on his cock, her moans and whimpers and the occasional smack of her ass against his pelvis on a forceful backstroke interrupting the silence. When it became clear as day that she was no longer uncomfortable, but very aroused, he gripped her hips, immobilizing her. The paddle tapped gently against her thigh where it fell. His hand moved between them, readjusting his underwear beneath his balls.

She bit her lip and keened deep in her throat when he began to fuck her on his terms with long, deep strokes. He flexed his hips up slightly every time he penetrated her completely, giving her a delicious jab of pressure on her clit. God, the man knew how to fuck, she thought distractedly as she pushed harder against the wall to keep from spilling over from his forceful possession. He smacked her ass with the paddle as he rode her, making her gasp. She was so hot . . . everything was burning—her ass, her clit, her pussy, her nipples, the soles of her feet . . .

She cried out brokenly when he withdrew his cock.

"*Shhh,*" he soothed, rubbing her hip as he moved beside her. She felt his cockhead brush against her hip, leaving a smear of wetness, and moaned. "I'm not trying to be cruel. I want to stretch things out a bit, that's all. Straighten up, lovely. Press closer to the wall again."

Panting, she tried to do what he directed, most of her brain focused on the terrible absence of his cock. He filled her so completely, fired such deep, secret flesh, that when he was gone, it was jarring. When she took a similar position to the one she'd been in before, he placed the paddle on her bottom.

"No, closer yet. Move your feet closer to the baseboard and brace yourself with your forearms. Press your cheek against the wall," he instructed, her voice sounding thick with lust. "Now press your pretty nipples there, too."

She moaned at the impact of his arousing words even before she did what he said. Her body quivered at the sensation of the cool, hard surface pressing against her fevered flesh. She turned her right cheek to the wall, glancing down at Ian. He'd unbuttoned the bottom buttons of his shirt. He still wore his clothing, but his cock poked out of the fastening of his pants between the plackets of his white shirt. She clamped her eyelids shut at the sharp pang of arousal that stabbed at her clit. He looked magnificently aroused, his cock deliciously full, heavy, and slick with her juices.

"No more of that," he murmured, stroking her hip and ass. "Open your eyes."

She followed his order, meeting his blazing stare. He began to paddle her ass, the smacking sounds filling her ears, the sharp burst of mild pain and prickling nerves crowding thought out of her brain, her consciousness drowning in the vision of Ian. He didn't strike her hard with the whippy paddle, and for Francesca, the sharp strikes only mounted her arousal. The experience was only exponentially more exciting because he stared at her point-blank. He usually preferred she turn her head when he spanked her.

Now she knew why. Looking into his eyes, seeing how rigid his facial muscles grew, how his stare grew hot enough to burn, she realized what a fragile thing his control was . . . How desperately he worked to restrain it.

He groaned harshly and she blinked, her gaze flying back to his face. She realized her stare had dropped to his flagrant erection and she'd been licking her lip hungrily. He gave her bottom a good pop and she jumped.

"Sorry," she said, unable to keep her amusement hidden.

"No, you're not," he muttered thickly, but she noticed his tiny smile. "Just for that, go up on your toes and turn your forehead to the wall. You can lower your hands and rest your head on them."

"What?" she asked, confused, even though she was already lowering her hands and resting her face in the cushion of them.

"You heard me," he murmured. "Go up on your tiptoes. It'll tighten all your muscles. You'll feel the paddle even more."

She flexed her calves, going up on her toes. He landed the paddle. Moisture surged at her core. She saw what he meant. The position tightened her leg muscles, but even more so, it was a somewhat awkward, vulnerable position. He paddled her bottom several more times, then paused to rub the stinging flesh.

"You're turning nice and pink," she heard him say.

"Ian," she pleaded in a strangled voice when he parted her cheeks and she felt his stare on her asshole. She held her breath in her straining lungs when he touched her—not penetrating her, just rubbing the sensitive area. In a flash, it all came back to her: her lying on the bed in the penthouse, her legs and arms trussed by rope, utterly vulnerable . . . completely open to him. She'd fleetingly wondered if she was wrong to give so much of herself to another human being, but love had silenced her doubts.

He'd left later that night.

She moaned in a mixture of misery and arousal.

"What is it?" he asked sharply. She realized he'd sensed her sudden uncertainty.

She swallowed in order to speak, but couldn't think of what to say. Her calves strained, the pain making it difficult to concentrate.

"Lower your heels," he said, stroking her buttocks and thighs soothingly. "Francesca?" he prompted when she kept her forehead pressed to her hands, her breathing coming erratically. "Do you not want me there tonight?"

She shut her eyes, knowing he referred to anal play. She could refuse him, and he wouldn't question her. It wasn't a matter of physical discomfort, though. In fact, his touch had electrified her with excitement. But she'd also experienced a powerful flashback relating to the trauma of giving herself . . .

. . . and being abandoned.

But hadn't she decided this afternoon that it was childish to withhold herself from him in order to punish him for her hurt, though? . . . To deprive him as if it was a crime for being himself.

"No," she said in a muffled voice against her hand. "I *do* want you there."

She felt his hand moving her hair. He swept it over her far shoulder and smoothed it from her forehead and cheeks.

"Look at me," he said.

She turned her chin reluctantly.

"You're afraid to give too much, aren't you?" he asked starkly, his blue-eyed gaze roving over her face, seeming to read her expression like the fingers of a blind man.

"I don't want to be left alone again," she said simply.

"I don't want you to be alone, either, nor do *I* want to be alone," he said, and she heard the note of desperation in his voice. "I'm trying, Francesca. Please know that. I'm trying so hard."

She closed her eyes. "I know it."

"I won't do anything you don't want, you know that. But I don't want to walk away from intimacy with you because I'm afraid, either. I'm trying to have faith, lovely," he added in a more subdued tone, his voice thick with emotion.

She opened her eyes slowly. "I have faith enough for both of us," she whispered. And when she said it, she felt the truth of her words. She believed he could find his way back to her. She knew he had what it took inside him to find his way out of his darkness.

He nodded once, holding her stare.

"Just a moment," he said, and she sensed him walking away. He was back in a moment, the paddle set aside, a bottle of lubricant in his hand. Her vagina tightened. She turned her face against the back of her hands. Should she feel ashamed for giving permission for this . . . for her need?

She wasn't sure. Suddenly, Ian was stroking her sore bottom tenderly and parting the cheeks. He penetrated her with his finger, and she sighed, her doubts lightening and flickering away like insubstantial moths. They were both silent for a taut moment while he slid his finger in and out of her ass, the caress intensely pleasurable, sacred because it was forbidden . . . and because it was Ian. Their silence continued while he prepared her to take his cock with his fingers— not just by penetrating her ass, but by using his other hand on her clit and pussy to mount her excitement.

"Ian, I'm going to come," she said breathlessly a minute later as he rubbed between juicy labia and thrust two fingers into her ass.

"Come then," he said hoarsely. "Let me feel your heat."

She crunched her facial muscles tight at the peaking pleasure, whimpering as she came against his hand.

"That's right," she heard him say as she shuddered. He inserted a long finger into her pussy while continuing to press against her clit and plunge into her ass. "Oh yeah, I can feel you coming perfectly," he rasped. He slid another finger into her ass and she cried out, a thread of pain ramping up her orgasm. *"Shhh,"* he soothed. "That's right. Your ass is on fire. You're so sweet," he said, milking her climax for all it was worth.

When she finally collapsed against the wall, sated, he withdrew his fingers from her pussy and ass. She let him guide her into position so that she was bent at the waist again, her bottom in the air. She blinked her hair out of her eyes, listening to the sound of his clothing rustling. He was removing his pants. Her ass clenched tight in renewed excitement, sending a sympathetic twinge to her clit. With her head down, she could see when he moved behind her. She exhaled some pent-up tension when she felt his touch at her hip, reassuring and warm.

"I'm going to go slow since I didn't have anything to prepare you," he said, referring to the fact that he usually got her ready for anal sex by penetrating her with a plug first.

She nodded, her long hair rustling around her like a stirred curtain. She stared blindly at the baseboard, every ounce of her awareness pinned to the feeling of Ian's cock pressing against her ass.

"You know what to do," he said, his voice sounding strained. "Press back against it."

She did, and there was that familiar stab of pain as the head of his cock slipped into her ass. As always, however, it was quickly gone. He remained still, waiting for her to recover. Then she pressed again, gasping, and he slid deeper, his stalk penetrating her. After they paused that time, and her pain had gone, he held her hips in his hands and began to gently pump. The lubrication eased things, but she could tell by his grunts of mixed arousal and concern that her ass muscles were clenching tightly around him, clamping his cock and resisting him.

Or was *she* resisting him?

Maybe even though she'd decided to give herself no matter what, part of her was still wary. Perhaps doubt still resided secretly in her mind and flesh. Anal sex had always been intensely arousing for her with Ian, the vulnerability required in the act amplifying the eroticism and excitement of sharing it with someone she trusted. She didn't want doubt and fear to steal the moment from her.

She exhaled, willing her muscles to relax.

Ian flexed his hips and slid further into her with a rough groan. "God that's good, Francesca," he muttered. He hadn't fully penetrated her yet, but he began to thrust, gently fucking her asshole. A jolt of arousal stabbed through her. She started to bob her bottom against his cock, but he gripped her tighter, his thumbs pressing into her buttocks.

"Hold still. I've got it," he rasped.

She stared at the baseboard, trying to keep still and panting, while he sawed his cock back and forth, back and forth, building a careful fire in her flesh. He had to bend his knees slightly, because of their disparate heights, and she wondered if he was uncomfortable. By the time he fully sheathed his cock inside her and pulled her ass against him, his full testicles pressing against her cheeks, she was on the verge of igniting. For a moment, he just held her.

"I can feel you perfectly. You're so hot," he said. She clamped her eyes closed at the sound of his barely leashed restraint.

"I can feel you, too. You're so . . . deep," she said in a strangled voice, her entire focus on his cock throbbing in such a vulnerable place.

"I have to move."

"Yes," she agreed.

Still holding her hips and buttocks tight, he took a step forward with his right foot, so that his hard thigh pressed against her hip, his other leg remaining between her thighs. It brought down his height sufficiently. He began to fuck her with long, firm strokes. A helpless, aroused whimper leaked out of her throat.

"All right?" he asked her, even though he didn't stop thrusting his hips, sinking his cock in and out of her.

"*Yes,*" she moaned emphatically. As always, it felt so good to give herself to him in this way, somehow both sublime and raunchy at once, riding the very edge of sharp eroticism. He began to fuck her harder, shifting his weight forward slightly on his front leg with each thrust, batting her bottom with his pelvis, the resulting whapping sound exciting her. His hips and ass found their rhythm, that stab and rolling motion he did so well that it made her eyes cross every time. She began to keen in pleasure, her ecstasy mounting as he began to ride her even harder, and the sounds of his satisfied grunts and groans struck her ears, twining with her cries.

"That's right," he growled. "Now you're giving yourself. I can feel it."

And she was. She was holding nothing back, opening herself to him, straining to give him pleasure, racing after her own.

God help her.

"Go up on your toes again," he ordered harshly, still plunging his cock into her faster and faster. "I'll keep you steady. *Do it*, Francesca," he said sharply when she didn't immediately respond, she was so lost in pounding pleasure. She did what he'd demanded, flexing her calves and raising her heels. She gasped when he thrust. How did he always divine the mechanics of sex so well? The position raised her ass, giving him a new angle of penetration. It tightened her muscles around him, made her feel him inside her body even more acutely. His guttural grunt told her he'd felt the fresh pressure, too, and that he liked it. A lot. He pulled his leg back, so that both of them were behind her, and drove into her with increased force, making a scream pop out of her throat. It hurt a little, he took her so hard, but it aroused her much, much more.

"Just a few more seconds," he grated out. "Stay up on your toes. It feels *so* fucking good. I'm going to come in you."

Her eyes sprang wide when he plunged deep and she felt him swell huge. His cock jumped inside her, making her stifle another shout. She felt the warmth of his semen as he began to ejaculate, heard how he trapped his desperate roar in his throat so that he made a wild, muffled, growling sound as he came. It was difficult to say why she loved it so much, having him take his pleasure even while she was slightly uncomfortable. He gave her so much bliss so often and so precisely. She relished the chance to give him an equally searing release.

After his last shudder of orgasm had shaken him, he continued to hold her tightly against him, breathing harshly.

"Put down your heels," he said eventually, his voice sounding both harsh and fond at once. She hadn't even realized she'd remained under his command, even after his moment had passed.

She did as he directed, sighing in relief at the release of tension. She'd wondered why it was so arousing for her to sacrifice a little in order to give him pleasure, but when he put his hand between her thighs, she no longer cared. It was enough that it was true. Her body knew what it wanted, what it loved. She was soaking, aroused to the breaking point. She could hear his fingers moving in her well-lubricated flesh and the sounds of his satisfied grunt at the flagrant proof of her arousal. Her clit sizzled beneath his expert touch. In a matter of seconds, she was coming against his hand while his cock twitched high inside her.

The entire experience hadn't only been an erotic and intimate one for Francesca, but also an intensely emotional one. She hadn't been aware of any tears falling, but they must have at some point. A few minutes later, while they showered together, Ian gently washed her cheeks clean of them. He looked into her eyes as the hot water rushed around their naked bodies.

"I know," he said quietly. "I *know* how hard this is for you. All of it. I'm sorry."

She swallowed thickly. There. He'd apologized. Was she petty to be gratified? She didn't think so. Wasn't it better that he felt he at least had the *power* to apologize for his actions? Before, it'd been as if he didn't apologize because it was like saying he was sorry for a tornado, hurricane, fate, or some other force of unpredictability.

Didn't saying he was sorry imply—even in a small way—that he realized he had some choice in how he responded to all of this?

His thumb moved, stroking her cheek as she looked up at him soberly. "I just want to know for certain that I deserve to be by your side," he said, his deep voice sounding hollow.

She shut her eyes upon seeing the pain he usually shielded so well. That dreaded feeling of helplessness hit her like a slamming wave. There was nothing she could say. He knew how she felt.

She went up on her toes again, ignoring the soreness of her calves, and took him into her arms, pressing their warm, wet bodies tightly together, using the only weapon she possessed to shield him from his misery.

Chapter Twelve

He'd said he'd take his fill of her that night, and he did just that after they returned to bed, making love to her with an almost wild desperation until they both collapsed and fell into exhausted sleep. The thought occurred to Francesca that he reminded her of a man feasting madly the night before he was forced into a barren imprisonment, but then she quickly shoved aside the thought, finding it unbearable to consider for long.

When they went down to breakfast the next morning together, she took his hand in hers when they reached the Great Hall. He turned, blinking at her gesture, his eyes widening slightly in surprise. She just gave him a small smile and didn't let go, even when they walked past several of the staff and into the dining room, where James and Gerard already sat reading their papers and breakfasting.

The house staff, a technician that Lin had hired, and Anne were all bustling around in preparation for the press conference. It was to be held in the reception room, since it was large enough to seat the thirty or so reporters that had been invited, but small enough for good acoustics.

Lucien and Elise hadn't come down yet, but Gerard, James,

Francesca, and Ian were sipping coffee and eating the breakfasts they'd served themselves from the sideboard, when Mrs. Hanson entered the dining room with a gray-haired, stern looking, thin woman. Francesca blinked and set down her fork when she saw Clarisse hovering behind the two older women, obviously uncomfortable.

"I'm sorry to disturb you during your breakfast, your lordship," Mrs. Hanson apologized.

"Don't be silly. Is something wrong, Eleanor?" James asked, looking politely puzzled.

"As you know, Ms. Everherd is the housekeeping supervisor. She came to me with a concern this morning, and I thought it best . . . well . . . with everything that's been going on," Mrs. Hanson said delicately, "that she report it to you straightaway."

"What's wrong, Ms. Everherd?" James asked.

"The staff has been informed about tightening up security around Belford Hall, your lordship, and we've all taken pains to be ever so careful. *Most* of us have, that is," Ms. Everherd said, glancing behind at Clarisse, her mouth set in a severe line. Clarisse looked very pale and younger than usual.

"Your lordship, I do apologize," she said quietly, her blue eyes shiny with anxiety. "I reported it to Mrs. Everherd as soon as I realized it was missing. It seems I've misplaced my passkey."

"Again," Ms. Everherd said severely.

Clarisse blushed and stared at the carpet. Francesca experienced a sharp pang of discomfort for the friendly young woman. She wished she could excuse herself and vacate the room, sure Clarisse didn't appreciate being called out like a child in front of an audience.

Gerard tossed his napkin on the table. "Really, Clarisse? When we've made it clear how important security is, especially with this press conference this morning."

"Do you know when you misplaced the key, Clarisse?" Ian asked her.

"No, sir," Clarisse said miserably. "It might have been anytime between yesterday afternoon and this morning." She blushed bright red. "I thought I used it to get into work this morning, but Catherine, the assistant cook, said I came in the back door with her."

"She's a featherhead," Ms. Everherd declared in a hard voice. "This isn't the first time Clarisse has lost her passkey."

"It'll be all right," Ian said calmly. "I can get her a new passkey when I finish up here and delete her old code."

"Clarisse, you really should be more careful," Gerard chastised mildly as he stirred cream into his coffee. "As if Ian doesn't have enough to be worried about with this press conference. Now our security has been breached."

"It's not all that bad. A lost key doesn't equate to catastrophe. It can be rectified easily enough," Ian said evenly. Francesca gave him a thankful glance for sparing Clarisse more shame. The maid looked miserable.

"It'll all be taken care of, no harm done. Thank you all," James said, including Clarisse in his glance, "for bringing the issue to our attention so it can be rectified."

Francesca felt extremely awkward when the three women filed out of the room. She considered Clarisse a friend, and hadn't enjoyed sitting at the table like one of her condemners.

Everyone continued eating in silence. Everyone but Ian, that is, Francesca realized. She slowed in chewing her toast when she saw the way Ian was sipping his coffee and studying Gerard through a narrow-eyed stare.

Later that afternoon, Gerard waited patiently in James's private office. He knew James would be near Ian's side for every second of the press conference, always ready to show absolute support for that apple of his eye, his tragic, perfect grandson. Gerard rolled his eyes at the thought. Gerard had used James's office in the past and was very familiar with the venerable room. When he'd mentioned he had important business to attend to and needed to miss the press conference, James had insisted he use his office, just as Gerard had known he would.

Gerard certainly had crucial business to attend to today.

Brodsik was late. The man was almost as scattered as Clarisse, and twice as thick. Add a healthy dose of greed to that combination, and it was the recipe for volatility. He hated when he had to put even a small amount of trust in men such as Brodsik and Stern. Stern, he'd already disposed of soon after the criminal partners arrived in England. Brodsik, he needed. Brodsik had been the one Francesca saw in Chicago, after all. His was the face that Ian and she equated to threat. Stern, on the other hand, was a walking, talking loose end with absolutely no purpose whatsoever to Gerard. He'd had to go early on.

Gerard had been forced against his better judgment to hire the two men after Francesca had blocked his plans to financially gain control of Noble Enterprises in a hostile takeover. Once that had occurred, he'd known he had to find a way to bring Ian out of hiding, and what would galvanize his *noble* cousin more than a potential threat to his abandoned lover? True, it'd been a risk. Ian had left his fiancée, after all. Perhaps he wouldn't care if Francesca were threatened? But no, Gerard had been correct. The moment Francesca had been in danger, he'd flown onto the scene, ready to play the role of tragic knight in shining armor.

He read Ian as effortlessly as a cheap novel.

It'd worked perfectly. The time to strike was now. He couldn't very well get Ian in his sights if he remained mysteriously invisible. Ian was vulnerable. No one would be utterly shocked when he finally went over the edge and took Francesca with him.

He checked his watch and scowled. In the distance, he could hear the muted sound of Ian speaking in the microphone. The press conference had begun. His cousin was busy rallying the troops, showing the world the face of a confident, brilliant leader.

But Gerard knew the truth. The password he'd deciphered from the surveillance video had worked. He'd copied Ian's files yesterday. All of them. He'd had the opportunity to begin to go through them last night—after he'd listened in on Ian and Francesca's rousing lovemaking, that is. Damn Ian for continually fucking in places Gerard couldn't determine beforehand, however. He'd repositioned one of the two cameras in Ian's suite, no longer needing the one aimed on the desk and computer. He'd positioned the surveillance camera in a spot where he'd thought Ian had sported with Francesca last night. But as in all things, Ian had refused to cooperate with Gerard's plans. He'd been forced to only listen as Francesca was paddled. Afterward, he'd masturbated as he'd eagerly listened to the sounds of her being sodomized. His climax had been so explosive after that, he hadn't bothered to spy on the couple's sexual activities any more. Instead, he'd plunged into Ian's computer files.

That's how he knew that Ian Noble was nowhere near to being the coolly aloof, in-control genius billionaire he pretended to be right now in front of those reporters' cameras. He was, in fact, a man on the edge of madness, teetering after his mother's death and the truth he'd discovered about the identity of his biological father.

Ian Noble, the son of a condemned rapist.

After Gerard had perused some of the volatile contents on Ian's computer, he'd calmly altered his plans.

The mark of *true* brilliance, after all, was the ability to glean a person's weakness and then add just the appropriate amount of pressure on that spot, so that the resulting break seemed inevitable in retrospect.

He'd learned that skill particularly well for the first time with his parents. He'd inadvertently learned that the make of car his parents drove had a weakness in the braking system. A school friend from Oxford who belonged to an influential family had let the industry secret out to another schoolmate, and Gerard had overheard. The news had not yet gone public. Once he'd had that information, all it had required was just a small mechanical nudge on Gerard's part—not difficult as he'd often tinkered and worked with cars and motorcycles since he was a boy—and voila. His parents were dead. Not only was their fortune and property his to do with as he pleased, but he'd been primed for a very lucrative lawsuit against the car company. It had been almost laughably easy, but Gerard knew that patience had been required in waiting for that perfect opportunity to arise.

Patience was his forte.

Apply just the right amount of pressure in just the right spot: that was his motto. Never overdo it. Certainly Francesca and Ian were the weak points in this scenario, but Francesca had proved to be too independent and meddlesome, thwarting his plans both for seduction and with the Tyake acquisition. She'd blocked his subtle efforts to finally gain control of Noble Enterprises along with that infuriatingly smug Lucien, one of many wild cards for which Gerard hadn't been able to entirely plan.

But again, Gerard was nothing if not flexible. One had to roll with the tide, not fight it. He felt like he'd been rewarded with a major boon, understanding just how vulnerable Ian was. Of course, he'd known his cousin had been weakened after his mother died and he'd disappeared. Gerard had moved quickly to take advantage of Ian's wounded and absent state. When the opportunity arose with Tyake, Gerard had been ready to strike at that rare weak spot that would have given him an inside hold on Ian's company. He needed Francesca's cooperation for that, however, and he'd quickly learned that with Lucien around to coach her, she wasn't quite as malleable as he'd hoped.

Now he had the ammunition he needed to set off an explosion, and if he was very lucky, he could include the annoying Lucien in that conflagration. Aurore Manor, the place where Ian had been holing up and surely descending into madness, would be the perfect location for him to die. When the story broke about what he'd been doing there, few would doubt that Ian Noble was a walking time bomb. They wouldn't be surprised at his self-destruction.

With his alternative plans, Gerard no longer wanted Ian at Belford, so it was now necessary to eliminate the apparent threat of Brodsik and clean up some ragged ends in the process.

He glanced up calmly at the sound of the door at the back of the room opening. He'd instructed Brodsik on how to enter, telling him to arrive early and stay concealed in the billiard room until Gerard could conveniently meet with him at a designated time.

"You're late," he said, remaining seated in the chair behind James's large desk.

"I had to be careful. This place is crawling with security," Brodsik said, walking toward him.

Gerard shrugged. "All due to the press conference. Ian is the god of the Western world of business, after all," he said sardonically. "Well? Are you ready to get down to business? I'll instruct you on how to get into Noble's suite from here. You'll remain hidden there until he arrives, then take him by surprise. I've already described how to get away cleanly afterward."

"Where's the money?" Brodsik asked roughly. Gerard threw a contemptuous glance at his hulking form. He pointed at a backpack that sat on the desk in front of him.

"It's all there. Your fee for the work, more than enough money to disappear and . . ."

"My incentive to keep quiet about my 'work,'" Brodsik said. He grinned, eyeing the backpack hungrily. Gerard had never seen him smile before. It wasn't a pretty sight. Something seemed to occur to Brodsik and his grin turned to a menacing scowl. "And if I should find out anything happened to Shell, I'm gonna hold you responsible. That'll mean more money," he said, referring to Shell Stern, his partner.

Gerard snarled, hatred and anger flaring in him fast and hot. "How dare you threaten me with more blackmail."

Brodsik looked a little taken aback by his sudden, intense fury. "*Something* happened to him. Shell's not the type to stay quiet for two minutes, let alone go missing for days. I'm not saying it was you who did something to him, but—"

"It certainly sounded that way to me," Gerard grated out.

Brodsik seemed to regret bringing up the topic as he continued to eye the backpack.

"Let's just get this show on the road," Brodsik mumbled, stepping toward the desk, his hand stretched toward the backpack.

Gerard made a halting gesture. "I'll open it for you in a moment. First, let me see the gun. I have a right to assure myself that you're prepared."

Brodsik looked like he was going to argue, his gaze glued covetously to the backpack. He eventually shrugged his linebackerlike shoulders and reached into a deep pocket of his parka, extracting an automatic firearm.

"It worked just like you said. The guy in London asked no questions," Brodsik said.

"So you needed to tell no lies," Gerard replied, his gaze running over the familiar gun with satisfaction. He'd used the very same weapon to kill Shell Stern less than a week ago. "Jago Teague is nothing if not discreet. He has to be, in his line of work . . . or *lines* of work, I should say. Well, let's get this over with, shall we? The sooner Noble is out of my life, the better. He's been in it for twenty years too long."

He unzipped the backpack. It contained no money whatsoever— he would never be bribed by anyone, let alone an idiot such as this— but did contain several of his work files. And something else.

He withdrew James's handgun and aimed it at Brodsik. Brodsik didn't have the opportunity to look surprised. Gerard fired point-blank at his head without blinking.

Brodsik's hulking body hit the floor with a jarring thud. Gerard calmly pulled back the right-hand drawer of James's desk. The red leather box where James always stored his private firearm was already open.

He gripped the gun tightly in his hand and schooled his face into an expression of blank shock.

Anne had referred them to the library for a place to do the computerized rendering without interruption. Francesca sat next to the computer artist, a woman named Violet, at a desk, both of them peering at the screen of Violet's laptop as the man's face took shape from Francesca's description. Francesca heard a distant sound like a firecracker going off. The sound itself didn't alarm her, but the way Lucien leapt up did. He'd been sitting in an armchair and perusing the business section of a French newspaper while Francesca worked with Violet. Now the newspaper lay on the Oriental carpet, forgotten.

"Lucien?" she asked in amazement when she saw his tense expression. A prickle of wariness went down her neck and coursed along her arms when he rapidly strode to the heavy doors and pressed his ear against them, listening.

"Come with me," he said, turning. "Both of you," he added, giving Violet a pointed glance. When Francesca stood, but Violet just stared at him in amazement, Lucien added, *"Now."*

Lucien pointed to a rear exit and nodded at Francesca, obviously expecting her to walk in front of him.

"Lucien, you don't think that sound was a gunshot, do you?" Francesca asked.

"I'm almost certain it was."

Her heart squeezed tight. "But . . . *Ian.*"

"Is not going to thank either one of us for running out there if there's a gunman on the loose. Please, Francesca," he said less harshly. "Do as I say. There are some policemen stationed at the back door in the kitchens. With their communication equipment, they'll know from the police at the press conference what happened up here quicker than we can find out ourselves. The security and police will need to secure the area anyway. They'll have enough on their mind."

It felt entirely against all that was natural to walk in the opposite direction of where Ian was when a gunshot had just been fired, but Francesca forced herself to do it. The rear door led to a dim corridor. She was starting to learn that many of the great rooms had a family entrance and a staff entrance, the staff entrance with access to the basements, kitchens, and servant's dining area. Lucien had been right. One officer was racing up a flight of stairs she'd never before used. They weren't the ones that led from the dining room.

"Get downstairs. Officer Inez is down there with the kitchen staff," the officer said.

"What's happened?" Lucien demanded.

"Someone's been shot. An intruder, we think. Things appear to be secure, but we're still not sure. Go on down with Inez, please."

He raced past them. The officer's terse, vague explanation seemed to leave more questions than answers, mounting Francesca's anxiety. Nevertheless, she mechanically followed Violet down the stairs, Lucien bringing up the rear, her calm actions belying a mind buzzing with fear.

Officer Inez had Francesca, Violet, Lucien, and the rest of the staff gathered in the dining room while they waited to hear if the house had been secured from the threat. There was only one entrance to the room, so it was easier for the policeman to guard, she supposed. Francesca was both nervous and thankful when she saw Officer Inez move into the outer corridor to stand guard with his weapon drawn.

She hadn't brought her cell phone with her into the library, and she'd never regretted a decision more. She sat next to Mrs. Hanson at the oak dining table, her hand in the older woman's. It was the worst time she'd ever spent, not knowing what was happening above them. Where was Ian? What was he doing? What about Elise, Anne, James, and Gerard? It was unbearable, wondering. She caught Lucien's stare, noticing how anxious and tense he appeared. He stared and took his cell phone out of his pocket, examining the screen. He exhaled in relief.

"Elise?" Francesca called to him, interpreting his expression.

"Yes," Lucien replied, tapping out a quick message on the phone. "She's fine."

Compassion for him went through her. He, too, had been waiting on pins and needles for news of Elise. She realized fully for the first time that he wouldn't be standing there at all if he hadn't given Ian his promise he'd look after her while Ian was at the press conference. If it weren't for that pledge to his brother, Francesca was certain Lucien would be upstairs despite police orders, searching for his wife.

Question after question churned around inside her, every one like a scraping knife. In the end, it was probably only a minute or two before they got news, but to Francesca it felt like an eternity. She squeezed Mrs. Hanson's hand extra hard, and Mrs. Hanson squeezed back, when Officer Inez's cell phone burbled just outside the room.

"Yes?" Inez answered, his deep voice echoing from the corridor just a few feet outside the dining room. Francesca didn't breathe in the pause that followed. "Yes, Ms. Arno is down here with us, along with Mr. Lenault. They're fine. Everyone is waiting in the staff dining room. It's all quiet down here." Another pause. "Yes. I'll tell them."

The balding officer stuck his head into the servant's dining room. "That was Markov. Mr. Noble wanted him to find out where you two were," Inez said, glancing from Francesca to Lucien. "And he wanted everyone to know that the family is safe. No one was injured. It's the intruder who was shot. He's dead, apparently."

"Who shot him?" Lucien asked from where he leaned against the sideboard, his casual pose belying a palpable tension in every line of his powerful body.

"It seems he came upon someone in the family when he broke in, and was taken by surprise. They didn't give me any more details, but Markov said they'd want you to go up there in a moment," Inez said, looking at Francesca. "They're still trying to get all the reporters and camera crew off the premises."

"They want me?" Francesca asked numbly.

"Yeah. They want you to identify the body, see if it's the same guy who tried to run you off the road yesterday."

A cold wave ran over her making her shudder. Mrs. Hanson put her arm around her and hugged her tight.

Francesca sprang up from her chair a while later when she heard Ian's rough voice in the corridor, identifying himself to Officer Inez. He crossed the threshold of the staff dining room a second later, his face rigid with tension, his eyes blazing when he saw Francesca racing toward him. Her legs felt weak with relief at seeing him alive and well, looking so tall and solid and wonderful to her in his dark suit and an ice-blue tie. Her arms flew around his neck. He held her tight against him, his hands moving over her back, rubbing her almost frantically, as if he wanted to make sure her flesh was real. She, too, needed that reassurance, gripping his shoulders, inhaling his clean, spicy scent deeply, as if she wanted to absorb it and store it for a lifetime.

"Thank God you're all right," he said, his breath hitting her neck in warm, pressured puffs of air.

"Thank God *you* are," she muttered feelingly. She backed up enough to look into his face, needing to see him. His dark brows were slanted as his blue-eyed gaze ran over her face. He seemed just as eager to soak in every detail of her. "When I heard that shot, all I could imagine was you in front of that crowd of people. I kept thinking—"

"*Shhh*, it's okay. Everything's going to be fine," Ian said quietly, brushing back her hair with his hand and palming her skull.

"Ian," Mrs. Hanson said weakly from just behind Francesca.

"Mrs. Hanson," Ian broke free sufficiently to give Mrs. Hanson a hug. "We're all okay," he assured the older lady. He glanced around at the rest of the gathered staff's pale, worried faces. "No one from the family or staff has been hurt. The police are evacuating the press and securing the area."

"*Lucien.*"

Ian, Francesca, and Mrs. Hanson started and looked around at the sound of Elise's anxious cry. Officer Inez was obviously not as familiar with Elise's appearance as he was Ian's. He was holding her in the corridor, and having more than a little difficulty doing so despite the fact that he had about hundred pounds on Elise.

"It's all right," Lucien said sharply, striding out of the room toward her. "That's my wife!"

Another wave of relief went through her at seeing Lucien lift Elise into his arms. Francesca caught a glimpse of her friend over Lucien's shoulder, her eyelids closed tight, an intense, grateful expression on her beautiful face. She knew precisely how Elise felt.

"Everyone is really all right?" Francesca whispered to Ian shakily, needing confirmation of Officer Inez's report "Anne? James? Gerard?"

"Yes, we're all fine," Ian assured. "None of the press were hurt, either. Only the intruder was shot. Detective Markov has the family waiting in the sitting room," Ian said, his mouth pressing into a hard line. "He wants you up there. He'd like you to identify the man's body."

"Okay," Francesca said, nodding. "Where . . . where is it . . . *Him*, I mean?" she muttered, flustered. It seemed surreal that she was talking about a dead man . . . a corpse. She'd never seen a dead person in her life.

"In Grandfather's office."

She nodded. Ian studied her intently.

"Francesca, I said that the police want you to do it, but . . . it's not a pretty sight. You're not obligated. I was able to identify him as the man who tried to run us off the road yesterday."

"But don't they want me to confirm if he was the man in Chicago, as well?"

"Yes," Ian said, a frown shaping his lips. "But you told me yesterday the man in the car was the same man in Chicago. Perhaps the coroner's photos would be sufficient for identification. I could speak to Markov about it."

She realized he was trying to protect her and caressed his jaw. "It'll be okay," she said softly. "Just . . . come with me?"

"Of course," he replied, as if there had never been any doubt of that.

Ian opened the dining room door to the Great Hall for her a moment later. Sunlight flooded into her eyes, temporarily blinding her and only adding to the surreal sensation plaguing her. She realized the sun streamed in from the open front door. Police personnel stood around the hall, a couple of them talking intently into their cell phones. Through the open door, she saw several cars parked in the circular driveway and heard the distant squawk and mechanical voices from police radios.

She started to walk toward the door where she thought James's office was, but Ian halted her with his hold on her hand. He pulled her over to the shadowed edge of the hall.

"Francesca, there's something you should know first if you do plan to go in there," he said.

"Yes?"

"Gerard shot him. The intruder came upon Gerard unexpectedly while he was working in Grandfather's office. The man drew a gun on Gerard. Grandfather keeps a gun in his desk, where Gerard was working. It's usually not loaded. According to Gerard, he thought to load it when the press conference got started. It seems he was spooked by what happened yesterday, and acted on impulse. Right-fully so, it seems. If he hadn't thought to load the gun, he'd be the one lying in there dead right now instead of the man. And who knows what would have happened if the intruder ever found you."

"Oh my God," Francesca mumbled, icy shivers clawing at her back and shoulders. "Are you sure Gerard is all right?"

"Physically, yes. But he's in a state of shock. The police are still questioning him." She saw doubt in his blue eyes as he studied her face. "Are you certain you want to go in there?"

She nodded, inhaling slowly to steady herself. "Yes. I'd like to get this ugliness over with and in the past."

He didn't look thrilled about her decision, but he led her to his grandfather's study nevertheless, staying close by her side.

Chapter Thirteen

Everybody stayed up late that night, the fading adrenaline in their blood making sleep difficult. Anne seemed especially concerned about Gerard, who was quiet and subdued by the time the police eventually concluded their investigation that evening, leaving two men behind to keep watch at Belford. For the second night in a row, they sat down to dinner without dressing, everyone rehashing the day's events. Ian was waiting for a call from Markov that might shed light on the intruder's identity and possible motive.

By the time they gathered in the sitting room after dinner, Anne seemed to be of the opinion that they'd discussed the alarming events of the day sufficiently. Francesca guessed from her worried glances at Gerard and her subtle altering of the topic of conversation that she worried her nephew had experienced quite enough for the time being. Francesca couldn't have agreed more. The image of that man's lifeless face covered in a shocking amount of blood kept flashing before her mind's eye. That was a *real* hole in his head and *real* blood. Her consciousness couldn't quite grasp it, even yet. She couldn't begin to imagine what Gerard was experiencing.

Something about the jarring events of the day seemed to melt away her reserve about the family knowing she and Ian were involved again. All afternoon and evening, he'd been by her side, her hand in his or his arm around her. It'd seemed entirely natural to Francesca, so much so that she didn't even think about it until that evening at around eleven when Ian's phone began to ring. She'd been sitting in the circle of his arm on one of the couches in the sitting room, her cheek resting on his chest, lulled by the comfort of his steady heart-beat and the warmth of the fire. He dug into his pocket and checked his phone.

"I'm going to take this," he said gruffly, kissing her on the temple before he stood. Everyone's gaze seemed to follow him out of the room as he stepped out into the Great Hall to take the call. A strained silence ensued while they waited for him to return, only broken by Anne asking if anyone wanted anything else to drink.

"That was Markov," Ian said, stating what they all had suspected. "They've discovered the identity of the man," he said, his gaze on Gerard. "His name is Anton Brodsik. He has a record with the Chicago area police that goes back almost thirty years—assault, minor drug convictions, robbery. He's suspected of having mob connections. He had a passport on him with a fake name."

"Is there any clue as to his motive?" Gerard asked, sitting forward in his chair.

"Not anything concrete. But for the past ten years or so, Brodsik has been associated in his crimes a lot with a man named Shell Stern. They were both arrested in a high-profile case three years ago—an attempted kidnapping of a sixteen-year-old boy in Winnetka, Illinois." Ian glanced at Francesca. "The police didn't have enough evidence to prosecute, though. No one was ever convicted for the crime. The boy was Sheridan Henes's son."

"Henes? The oil company heir?" James asked.

Ian nodded. "The FBI couldn't convincingly link the two to the case, but there was a strong suspicion against Stern and Brodsik. So they have been connected to kidnapping in the past. And they did try to take Francesca," Ian said, his eyes gleaming in the firelight as he looked at Francesca.

An involuntary shiver went through her. Anne inhaled raggedly.

"What of this other man, Stern?" James asked worriedly.

"They've found him. He's dead, too," Ian said.

"What?" Elise and Anne exclaimed at once.

Ian nodded. "Actually, the police recovered Stern's body from a creek several days ago. He'd been shot. His body had gone unclaimed, and they hadn't been able to identify him until now. Once Markov had Brodsik's passport, he was able to follow his trail into the country. Stern and he were on the same plane, both using aliases of course. After that, they were able to identify Brodsik's true name from fingerprints from the international crime files. They were able to identify Stern given Brodsik and Stern's history together."

"Who killed Stern?" Gerard asked.

"Markov suspects Brodsik did away with him. It wouldn't be the first time he's seen partners squabble over plans . . . or become unwilling to share when the ultimate prize grows closer. But they're still trying to confirm that with their investigation. As to why Brodsik might have murdered his own partner, I have no idea. I imagine they'll know more once they can determine where the two men were staying and trace their movements since they arrived late on Christmas Eve."

"They came to England on Christmas Eve?" Lucien asked.

"Yes," Ian said grimly. "The same day as Francesca."

"And no one else accompanied them?" Gerard asked.

"No. Just Stern and Brodsik," Ian replied.

"So that's it, isn't it?" Francesca asked. She swallowed thickly. Her mouth had gone very dry. "Both men are dead. The threat is done."

"It would seem so," James said slowly.

Ian frowned. "I wish I could be so convinced," he said before he sat and pulled Francesca back into his arms.

* * *

Neither of them attempted to disguise to the others that they were going up to bed together that night, leaving the sitting room hand in hand after saying their good-nights. Francesca was still feeling especially shaky and Ian seemed to sense it, holding her against him when they went to bed, neither of them speaking, just breathing each other's scent, prizing each other's presence. She awoke at dawn to the sensation of his lips firm and warm on her throat and breast, his hunger unshielded . . . raw. Their lovemaking was fierce and sweet, both of them desperate to jump into the bright blaze of passion and life, wild to escape the lingering menace of death and the shadows that always seemed to encroach on their happiness.

Francesca's eyes blinked open heavily as she had the incendiary thought as she lay in Ian's arms after they made love. Why were her thoughts so morbid and depressing? It took her a moment to understand her dark mood.

And so that really is the reason you came back. The only reason. Because you believed I was in danger.

I came back because I was worried about you, yes.

Fear gripped at her heart and throat. Once Ian was convinced that the threat against her had passed, would he leave again? She wanted to beg him for reassurance that he wouldn't depart again on his search, but pride stilled her voice. So did helplessness, as she recalled all too well that she didn't have the power to bring him peace when it came to his past. If he insisted upon putting himself back on that path, he'd have to travel alone.

They gathered in the hall later that morning to say good-bye to Lucien and Elise, waiting for Peter to come around with the car. Elise and Lucien's departure only seemed to amplify Ian's black mood, signifying the culmination of something he didn't want to end.

When he recognized his thoughts, he determinedly asked Lucien for a word before he left. He drew him into the alcove behind the stairs.

"Do you still plan to meet me at Aurore?" Ian asked his brother in a hushed tone.

Lucien's stoic expression barely stirred. "You still plan to go? Even after everything with Francesca?"

Ian realized Lucien was being delicate. He wasn't just referring to Brodsik and Stern's intent to harm or kidnap Francesca. He was talking about the fact that Francesca and he were clearly lovers again.

"Yes. I have to go back. I have to know as much about Trevor Gaines as I can."

Lucien didn't reply for a moment. Finally, he exhaled. "Yes. All right. I'm not sure it's for the best where you're concerned, but I won't leave you alone to deal with this. And it's not as if I'm not curious as well. Just contact me when you're ready, and I'll come."

Lucien started to depart.

"Wait. There's one other thing. It's about your mother," Ian said when Lucien paused. Lucien's eyes closed briefly.

"What is it?" Ian asked, noticing Lucien's reaction.

Lucien opened his eyes with a resigned air. "It's nothing. I was just waiting for you to ask ever since you arrived at Belford Hall. I was shocked when you didn't ask me straightaway."

Ian's pulse began to throb at his throat, although he remained outwardly calm. "I felt guilty about asking. I know you've just recently met Fatima," he said, referring to Lucien's mother. "I realize how discovering she's alive and forming a relationship must be very sacred for you."

Lucien met his stare. "You want to speak with her, don't you? Ask her about your mother? About Trevor Gaines?"

"Yes," Ian said honestly. "I do. I won't without your permission, though. You wouldn't have spoken to my mother about her past— about a vulnerable time in her life—without my permission, and I wouldn't speak to your mother without your agreement."

Lucien looked away. "What you have to understand," he said quietly. "Is that my mother's religion is highly prohibitive at the concept of a woman taking a lover outside of marriage, let alone having a child out of wedlock. Her family is a rarity for continuing to accept her even when she told them the truth about me. It wasn't an easy thing for her to open up and talk about my origins. Her shame is palpable. It's very difficult to witness her guilt."

Ian's heart paused in his chest. "You mean you've already spoken with her?" he rasped. "About Trevor Gaines? About my mother?"

Lucien looked at him with the gray eyes he'd inherited from Trevor Gaines, yet the degree of compassion he saw in his gaze was nothing that Gaines could have ever begun to pass on to his child.

"Yes," Lucien said.

"What did she say? Did Gaines force her into being with him?"

"No," Lucien replied starkly. "My mother is under the impression that everything Gaines did in regard to moving Helen and her to France was for her—Fatima. She was duped into believing he loved her while they were still in Britain. She'd caught his eye while he'd been visiting Helen, and then he *accidentally* ran into her while she was marketing in the town. He wooed her carefully. My mother was charmed by him—a handsome, accomplished, wealthy man. Their love affair was carried out clandestinely and lasted several months before he disappeared from her life."

Ian absorbed all of this, picturing the scene of seduction in the tiny town in Essex, Gaines wooing both women at once, the mad gentlewoman and her servant. But not just wooing. Gathering information about them of an intimate nature, their likes and dislikes, gauging their vulnerabilities, ascertaining their cycles. By now, Ian understood that Gaines's fascination with mechanical things, especially clockworks, bizarrely paralleled this obsession he had with women's reproductive cycles. He must have realized early on that the cycles of women who lived together often synchronized. Ian had a sick feeling it excited him, being in the know of such feminine intimacies, using that knowledge for his perverse aims.

"Did Fatima realize that Gaines was seeing my mother during the same time period?"

"No. As a matter of fact, Fatima had the distinct impression that Helen didn't care for Gaines. She assumed it was because of her increasing illness. Helen could be very withdrawn at times." Lucien's stare turned fierce. "And I don't *want* my mother to know until I have the chance to tell her. At this point, my mother is under the impression she was taken advantage of by a philanderer. If anyone has to reveal to her that Gaines was much, much worse than that, it will be me."

"Fine," Ian said distractedly, fixated as he was on what Lucien had said earlier. "But what did your mother say about my mother? Lucien?" he prompted roughly. Lucien still hesitated, but then seemed to come to a decision when he met Ian's gaze.

"My mother said that when they went to France, your mother decompensated considerably," he said quietly. "Helen used to be functional enough that my mother could leave her alone for an hour or two at a time. Your mother could see to her own basic needs, and she didn't pose a threat to herself. One morning, my mother returned from a shopping errand in the town where you grew up in France, only to find Helen missing. She searched, growing increasingly frantic. She eventually found your mother in the backyard in what sounds like a near-catatonic state, curled up in a ball, unresponsive. Helen was unable to speak, walk, or recognize familiar faces. My mother called the local doctor and the police. They undertook an investigation. It was determined Helen had recently had sexual intercourse, and there were some bruises on her body. But they were hesitant to call what had occurred rape. Helen was unable to testify as to what had happened, and she'd been occasionally witnessed in . . . erratic behavior by the townspeople since arriving. She might have gotten the bruises from falls, or even taken part in consensual rough sex—"

"How is a psychotic woman able to give informed consent?" Ian interrupted furiously.

"I'm just telling you the police's thinking," Lucien said, his gray eyes making Ian clamp his mouth shut. "No charge was ever officially made."

"She was raped," Ian grated out.

"My mother agrees," Lucien said regretfully. "Unlike the police officials, she was familiar with the cycles of Helen's schizophrenia. She'd never seen your mother decompensate to the level she fell to during that time period. It was clear to my mother she'd experienced a severe trauma. Helen didn't speak for nearly a month after the incident. My mother thought for sure when she discovered Helen was pregnant that she wouldn't be able to carry the child to term, she was so debilitated. All signs point to the conclusion that when Helen denied Gaines, he eventually resorted to rape. It's not as if there isn't clear-cut proof that he was familiar with those tactics," Lucien said bitterly.

Ian's grandmother laughed in the distance, the sound echoing off the walls of the Great Hall. It took Ian a few seconds to even recognize the familiar sound for what it was.

"And your mother gave birth nine months later," Lucien finished heavily.

"I can see why you wouldn't want your mother seeing me," Ian stated after a pause. He and Trevor Gaines looked appallingly alike, after all. If it weren't for the difference of their eyes, they might have been twins. Lucien's mother obviously remained ignorant of the fact that her seducer and Helen's rapist were one and the same man. If she were to meet Helen's son, however, the truth would be slammed home by the simple, blatant evidence of Ian's face.

"I *do* want you to meet my mother someday," Lucien said fiercely. "Of course I do. I'm just trying to convey to you the complexity of the whole thing."

"I would never let her anywhere near me, if I were you," Ian said, walking past Lucien to the Great Hall.

He suddenly wanted nothing more than for this whole conversation to be over. Lucien halted him with a hand on his upper arm. Ian looked at his brother, anger—that old, familiar companion—starting to bubble beneath the surface of his calm façade. Not anger at Lucien, but at some unknown, vague grayness that seemed to return in that moment to press down on him like a suffocating pall.

I can't escape it, no matter how hard I've been trying to for the past week, since the second you looked into Francesca's startled, glistening eyes as she stood in that reception line.

"You're my brother. She's my mother," Lucien hissed. "Of course I want my family to meet someday. *You're* not Trevor Gaines, Ian."

The fury reared in him, seeming to constrict his throat. He jerked Lucien's hold off him, a snarl shaping his mouth. He had that tight, hot feeling in his chest again that made breathing difficult. When he turned, he saw Francesca standing in the hallway, a startled expression on her face. He froze. Half of her face was radiant from sunshine, the other cast in a shadow from the grand staircase.

"Lucien? The car is here." Her gaze narrowed on Ian. She took a step toward him. "*Ian?* Are you all right? What is it?"

He didn't reply. Too much emotion had erupted in him too quickly. He walked ahead of both of them to the Great Hall and started up the stairs, taking two at a time. He'd already said his good-byes to Elise, and he couldn't force himself to take part in small talk at the moment. He did his best to ignore the sensation of Francesca's dubious, worried stare at his back.

It was technically too cold to ride a motorcycle, but Ian dressed for it, and the winter day was sunny and unseasonably mild, the temperature inching up to the high thirties. When he saw more than a half dozen press vans outside the main entrance security gate, he cursed bitterly under his breath and thought of turning around. His grandfather had told him that several news stations had called his secretary this morning about the shooting at Belford Hall yesterday, asking for interviews and a statement. James had denied requests for interviews, but he and Ian had come up with a basic statement, saying that all the visitors at the press conference and the family were safe, and deferring to the Stratham police for official news of the crime. The break-in and shooting had been made all that much more sensationalistic because it involved an earl, his heir to the title, and Ian himself, who had been making a reappearance on the business scene. In addition, the crime had happened during a well-publicized and well-attended press conference, the gunshot itself being picked up by press cameras. According to Anne, the press conference and chilling gunshot interruption were being replayed continually on national and local stations.

Screw it, Ian thought, waving a hand at Cromwell at the security gate, and turning onto the road a moment later. The press didn't know who was behind the black helmet with the face visor. Although certainly many of the people who lived locally knew that the earl's grandson was fond of motorcycles, he noticed that the majority of the vans were from London stations. If they chose to chase him, let them. He was edgy and restless enough to crave a challenge. Besides, he'd blow them away on the sleek MV Agusta he straddled.

He ripped past the vans parked on the side of the road at a lightning-fast pace, actually half hoping one or several would follow. He saw only a couple surprised, pale faces peer at him from the vehicle windows, none of them alight with the thrill of a chase, however.

The chill air rushing past him as he roared down the country roads was sufficient for clearing his head, though, seeming to blow out some of his anger and crystalize his thoughts.

He craved some numbing off.

By the time he returned to Belford, he felt frozen to the bone, but calmer, and more resolved. He used a back entrance to the grounds. Although relatively few people knew about the gravel road through the trees, Ian was gratified to see one of the security guards his grandfather had hired manning it. He returned the motorcycle he and Gerard had once mechanically enhanced to the chauffeur and mechanic, Peter. While he and Peter were talking about the Agusta's performance, he received a phone call. Seeing it was Detective Markov calling, he walked away to take it.

Twenty minutes later, he found James alone looking over some ledgers in the sitting room.

"I'm working in here instead of my office for the time being," James explained after they'd greeted one another. "Anne wants to send off the carpet in my office to have it cleaned . . ." He faded off reluctantly, and Ian knew he meant cleaned of Anton Brodsik's blood. "But I spoke to Detective Markov about it, and he said to hold off making any major changes or using the room until they've finalized their investigation."

"I just got off the phone with Markov."

"Did you?" James asked, immediately interested. "Any news?"

"Yes. Considerable," Ian said, sitting down in an upholstered chair near the desk where James worked. "They've done ballistics reports, and it seems that the gun Brodsik pulled on Gerard yesterday was definitely the same weapon that killed Shell Stern."

"So . . ." James said slowly. "Brodsik decided he didn't want to share any of the pie with his partner."

"Either that or they had a falling out over something else," Ian said.

"Does Markov have any indication whatsoever that another person was involved?"

"No. None."

James's astute gaze narrowed on his grandson. "But you don't believe him?"

Ian paused, thinking. "Given the pair's history of petty crimes, I just find it hard to believe that they'd engineer this whole thing themselves. I suppose it's possible, though."

"I'd hardly call the attempted kidnapping of the Henes heir a petty crime."

"Exactly my point," Ian murmured. "I doubt they were the main instigators of that one, either. Although considering the whole thing was botched, who knows?"

"Well, they're dead, so I suppose we'll never know the full truth. Ian?"

Ian blinked. He realized he'd been scowling, lost in thought at his grandfather's words.

"Are you still worried about Francesca's safety?" James asked, his forehead furrowed.

"Always," Ian admitted before exhaling. "But at least I've taken back control of the company, and hopefully she's been moved out of the limelight."

James nodded. "She's a very beautiful woman. Match her eye-catching looks with the thought of millions of dollars of ransom money, and there's bound to be some sickos out there who scheme up havoc like this. Brodsik and Stern must have seen that photo of her in the papers and conjured up the idea."

"That's what Markov and the police in Chicago are thinking," Ian said distractedly.

"Well I'm just glad to have it in the past. It's good news, what Markov told you. We should share it as soon as possible. Maybe I'll take everyone out for dinner tonight in town."

"I don't think the furor has died down sufficiently yet," Ian said dryly. "The entry road is swamped with media vans."

"I know, Cromwell has informed me," James said, referring to the security guard at the front entrance with a weary wave of his hand. "They'll give up and go home soon after they get bored enough."

"I plan to address the press again. Not about the investigation, per se," Ian added when he saw James's dubious expression. "That's the police's arena. I need to make a general statement, though, assuring that everything is steady with Noble Enterprises and that the threat is well contained. I'll do it in London. I was waiting for the results of Markov's investigation, but now that I have that, I can't put it off any longer," he said, feeling a bizarre mixture of determination and ambivalence. It was like his rational brain was telling him he needed to get on with his duty to his company and his mission in regard to Trevor Gaines, but his body was protesting, wanting to stay, longing to remain at Francesca's side. He inhaled when he noticed James's slanted brows, steadying himself . . . hardening his resolve. "Lin is insisting I need to move on another press conference, but I'd already realized the necessity. Here I was hoping to show my face to the public, quell any doubts about Noble's leadership and show the steadiness of the ship, and all hell breaks loose while I'm doing so."

"When will you go to London?" James asked, sitting forward in his chair.

"As soon as I can pack."

"Well," James said briskly, "if you leave as soon as possible, perhaps you'll be able to take care of business and return to us for the New Year."

"No," Ian said evenly.

The single syllable rung like a struck drum in the quiet room. He hated the flash of alarm that crossed his grandfather's features.

"What do you mean?" James laughed uncomfortably. "You'll be several days? A week?"

"I'll do the press conference later this evening. It won't take long. But I won't be returning to Belford Hall in the foreseeable future. I need to return to what I was doing, Grandfather. I must. Everything here—everything that's happened—doesn't change that."

He waited tensely. He hadn't told his Grandfather specifically what he'd been doing during his absence, merely saying he'd needed time to himself to regroup and examine his life after the death of his mother. He knew perfectly well that Anne and James knew it was more than that, although they weren't sure precisely what his motives were. Like Francesca, he knew his grandparents wouldn't approve, however, so he'd saved them the pain of worrying.

"But . . . Francesca," James said weakly. "Are you taking her with you?"

Expose Francesca to the dark, dirty, shameful house of a pervert? "No. I'd never want her to see where I'm going. Never."

"Ian—"

"You'll keep her here, won't you? Make sure she's safe?"

"I can't *keep* her here, Ian! She can make up her own mind where she wants to be," James said incredulously.

"I'll speak with her first. I'll ask her to stay, as a favor to me. She has to work on the painting anyway. Isn't the canvas being delivered today?" Ian asked smoothly.

James sighed. He knew Ian's tactics to avoid difficult topics all too well. "Yes, it's being delivered as we speak," he admitted, despite his scowl. "Anne is having them set it up in the reception room, since there's plenty of room there for Francesca to work, and we don't use it much. Francesca was insisting upon the canvas being delivered to the cottage—she can't get a view when she's inside her subject. I knew you wouldn't want her out there alone until everything is settled, though, so I contradicted her."

"Thank you," Ian said pointedly. "Because you and Grandmother care about her so much, I'm confident leaving her with you."

"I hardly think—"

"I'll speak with her. She'll agree to it," Ian interrupted. "The only thing I ask is that you encourage her to stay and continue to make her feel at home here."

James looked solemn. "Well you don't need to ask that as a special favor. As far as I'm concerned, Belford Hall *is* that girl's home."

"You'll contact me? At the first hint that anything is amiss?" James gave him a hard, arch look.

"I'm going to be available," Ian assured. He knew his grandfather was thinking of those months when Ian had cut himself off from the world. "It's not like before. I'll be in contact."

James's face was rigid with worry, but he exhaled with relief at this. "Well, that's something, I suppose. And Francesca? Will you remain in contact with her?"

Ian glanced away from James's worried gaze. "No," he said. "Where I plan to go, what I plan to do . . . I can't allow Francesca into that world."

Into that part of me.

"There's something else. I've hired a man, a retired American Army officer who used to act as a security guard for a top official in Afghanistan to watch over Francesca and things at Belford Hall. His name is Arthur Short. Lin found him for me. He arrives this afternoon. Do I have your permission to allow him to stay here at Belford?"

"Of course," James replied. "But I gathered from what I overheard last night in the hallway that Francesca was against your hiring security personnel for her."

Ian schooled his face into impassivity. "She's not keen on the idea, no. That's why I thought it'd be best if you invited Short here as a guest. Perhaps you can say that he's a member of your New York staff, here to discuss business? It will make things easier."

James gave an exasperated snort. "Francesca will be furious if she finds out."

"I know," Ian said, rising from his chair. "But I'd rather have her furious and safe than clueless and at risk. Do me a favor, though, and don't tell anyone else but Grandmother who Short really is? It'll make things easier for Short to maneuver. May I tell him you'll be expecting him?"

James agreed, albeit grudgingly. "Thank you," Ian said sincerely a moment later as he bid his grandfather good-bye, giving the elderly but still-vibrant man a hug. He wished he hadn't seen the stark concern tightening James's features before he left the room.

Ian packed and then asked a maid to request Francesca meet him in his quarters. He regretted packing first, as he had nothing to do afterward but wait for her knock on the door. With a sharp pang of remorse, he realized that every other time he'd awaited her knock, it'd been with a sharp sense of anticipation of what was to come. Now, he experienced dread that seemed to grow heavier by the moment.

He'd been using her vibrant, luminous spirit to stanch his wound, breathing her sweetness to chase away his shadows. It was just like he'd always feared. He would drain her, taint her . . . all because he was too weak to stay away from her. Over and over again while he'd been in France in Gaines's dark, rotting mansion, he'd told himself that he did all of this for Francesca. It was for her that he strived to understand his origins, to separate himself once and for all from the twisted character of his biological father.

Now that he'd learned he was, without a doubt, the progeny of rape, the need to comprehend his biological father's motives and cleave himself from his origins had only sharpened. He needed to compile what information he could and make some logical sense of Gaines before he could do that, however. It had been a dream to stay here at Belford in the warmth of family, to bask in Francesca's presence. But it was a dream he needed to awaken from if he ever wanted to find his rightful place in it.

Her light rap struck him like a death knell.

He opened the door. A strange, unpleasant tingling sensation coursed over his skin when he saw her standing in the hallway. She wore a pair of jeans and a light blue cotton button-down blouse that emphasized her narrow waist and full breasts. Her rose-gold hair spilled down around her shoulders and arms, but she'd pulled it back in the front, letting him plainly see the poignant expression of fear and resolve on her lovely face.

She knew.

His suspicion was confirmed when she stepped into the room and he closed the door. She said nothing when she saw his suitcase and briefcase sitting at the foot of the bed. For a moment, neither of them spoke while she stared at his packed bags. She finally looked at him. What he saw in her dark brown eyes cut at him from the inside out.

"This morning before he left, Lucien told me what he'd told you about his mother and yours," she said.

"So that's why you're not surprised that I'm going," he said.

"I suppose. That, and also James came into the reception room a while ago."

"Grandfather told you I was leaving Belford?" Ian asked, surprised. He thought his grandfather would give him a chance to speak to Francesca first and break the news himself.

"No. He didn't have to," she said quietly. "He said that Markov had called, and that all indications were that Stern and Brodsik were working alone. With them both gone, so is the threat. You didn't have a reason to be here anymore." Her chin went up. He was glad to see the flash of defiance and anger in her eyes. He'd much rather see that than her sadness. "You did tell me it was the only reason you returned to Belford, after all. Because you were concerned about my safety."

"I came because I love you," he said roughly. "I'd understand if you have trouble believing that, given the—"

"I believe it," she interrupted starkly. He saw her throat convulse as she swallowed. She studied the carpet for a moment, breathing through her nose, and he knew she was trying to steady herself. The desire to take her into his arms and soothe her was like a lance in his side, but he forced himself to ignore the instinct. The pain. It would just make things worse for her when he went. Worse for both of them.

And he *must* go. He must.

"After I spoke to Lucien," she said in a congested voice, "I did a little research online."

"About what?" Ian asked, wary. *She* hadn't started researching Trevor Gaines, had she?

"About children of rape."

Her simple reply made him blink.

"What about them?" he asked uncomfortably.

She crossed her arms beneath her breasts and looked away. "I know that to have substantial evidence that Helen was, in fact, raped must have been overwhelming for you."

"You and I both know I always suspected it, especially after learning about Gaines."

"Yes. But suspecting and knowing are two different things, aren't they?" she asked hollowly. He didn't reply. He was too busy experiencing the truth of her words. Confirmation that his mother had been raped had rattled him to the core—the description of how Fatima had discovered her, so vulnerable and hurt. "I don't know why I haven't tried to understand better," Francesca was saying. "Or I do understand, and just don't like to admit it."

"What are you talking about?" Ian asked her, bewildered.

"As I read some of those articles about other people who were the children of rape, some of their testimonials about what they'd endured as children and adults and how it had affected them, I realized that *I've* been the one who has been in denial." She met his stare. Her eyes glistened with tears, but her face remained defiant, seeming to blaze with something he didn't understand. "I wanted you to return to being the man I remembered, the lover I remembered. I didn't want to admit that the knowledge of Trevor Gaines had altered you. I didn't want to admit it, because to do so would mean that I was entirely helpless. To do so would mean I might have to turn you loose and let go forever."

"I don't want this to be forever," he grated out. "I want to find my way back to you."

"I know. I said I knew before—while we were in the cottage—but I really didn't," she said with a brittle laugh. Her arms tightened around her ribs as if she were trying to brace herself. "I think one of my problems is that you always seem so strong. So impenetrable. All those people I read about online—the ones who'd also been born of rape—talked about how it affected their self-esteem. They felt so ashamed, and worthless, even though logically they knew they hadn't done anything. So many of them wrote about what it was like when they realized—really *got* it—what it'd meant for their mother to bear them . . . raise them . . . the child of the man who had raped them."

Her shining eyes were like dark mirrors.

"It's hard to explain," he muttered after a moment. "Sometimes I used to think Lucien understood, but now I know even he . . ."

He faded off. Lucien, at least, was now secure in the knowledge that he wasn't a result of depraved, selfish violence. Yes, what Gaines had done to Lucien's mother was sick and unforgivable, of course, but this was . . . different. Ian knew most people would consider the child born of rape a monster, a vicious, cruel reminder to the victimized woman of what she'd endured.

Francesca nodded as if in understanding, even though he hadn't finished his thought. "And your mother couldn't come to terms with it like other women might." Ian closed his eyes and forced himself to inhale as Francesca put that horrible truth to words for him. His mother had had even less of a chance to psychologically cope with the rape and heal. When her psychosis was at its worst, she couldn't differentiate present day reality from horrific memory. She couldn't help it.

At times, Ian and Gaines had become one and the same for her.

He felt Francesca's hand on his upper arm and he resisted an urge to flinch. Her touch was almost unbearable, it was so sweet.

"When your mother was herself, though, Ian," she said in a quiet voice that vibrated with emotion, "when she wasn't being ruled by her illness, she *did* love you. So much. You have told me so many times how she loved and prized you. 'She was the sweetest, kindest, most loving mother in the world.' That's what you've told me. *That's* who she really was. That's who *you* really are, the person who deserved her love." Her hand tightened on his arm. "The man who deserves mine."

He inhaled, forcing the invisible clutches on his lungs to release. He opened his eyes.

"I have to go," he said.

"Let me come with you then."

"I can't. I can't stand to think of taking you with me, of you being there. Please understand, Francesca," he said stiffly.

She dropped her hand and took a step back. He clenched his teeth together at the loss of her touch, at the expression of defeat on her face. "It won't help you, Ian. I'm convinced of that. But even if I don't agree with what you're doing, I understand. Anne and James understand, too. Will you at least let us know you're all right this time?"

"Yes. I already told Grandfather I would. And I also told him I want you to stay here at Belford Hall," he said, finally meeting her stare.

Her eyebrows arched. "I can't promise for how long."

"I know," he admitted. "I can't ask you to put your life indefinitely on hold for me. But it would give me comfort for now, to know that you're here with my grandparents. Promise to at least stay for the next week or so."

She hesitated, her pink lips trembling. "All right," she said finally.

He nodded once, hoping she saw his gratitude. Realizing there was nothing more to say, he went to get his bags. He moved past her toward the door.

"Ian."

He had no choice but to look back at her and test his crumbling fortitude one more time.

"Find your way back to me," she whispered fiercely.

He turned, reaching blindly for the door handle, unable momentarily to breathe.

Chapter Fourteen

She stood before the canvas, her concentration such that she only became aware by degrees that people had entered the room and were speaking quietly to one another. She blinked, moving a tendril of hair off her forehead with the same hand that clutched a pencil.

"Hello," she called, her voice sounding dazed even to her own ears. She wasn't annoyed by the interruption for her work's sake, but she was disappointed. Since Ian had left yesterday, the only real peace she'd gotten was when she finally entered that coveted zone of creative focus.

"Mr. Sinoit was just saying that you seemed to be in a trance, and I was telling him that's how you always look when you work," Mrs. Hanson told her with a smile as she arranged a tea tray on a table between two chairs. The housekeeper's expression turned apologetic. "At least when your work is going well."

"It is going well," Francesca said.

"I'm sorry to have interrupted, but you worked through breakfast. It was just James, Short, and myself, and the pair of them talked about Brooklyn the whole time," Gerard said. Francesca smiled. She'd met the clean-cut, square-jawed Arthur Short, an American who worked for James, last night at dinner, and thought he was very nice. "I missed you and Anne," Gerard continued with a dry smile. "I thought some refreshment might be appreciated at this point. Anne's worried that your appetite is going off again since . . ."

Francesca forced a grin when Gerard avoided mentioning Ian and his departure. So . . . they were back to skirting the topic of Ian again. Not if she could help it.

"Since Ian left? Yes, I suppose I haven't been that hungry. But leave it to one of Mrs. Hanson's teas to get my appetite going again," she said, eyeing the scones, Danish, sweet cream, and fresh jam on the tiered porcelain serving dish.

"Shall I pour for you?" Mrs. Hanson asked.

"No, I'll do it," Francesca said, sitting across from Gerard. She opened her mouth to ask Mrs. Hanson to join them, but then closed it when she focused on Gerard. As much as it was the norm for her to take tea with the housekeeper, she doubted it was typical for Gerard.

"I'll just leave you to it then," Mrs. Hanson said warmly before departing.

"I'm glad to hear your sketching is going well," Gerard said. "May I have a look after we finish?"

"Please do," Francesca said as she poured from the china pot.

"I feel as if I haven't seen much of you lately," Gerard said.

She studied his face closely as she stirred cream into her tea. "Well, a lot has been going on, I guess. And I'm afraid I can become a bit withdrawn when I'm working on a project. How have you been?" she asked, her concern for his well-being after the shooting audible in her question. "I've never really had much of a chance to speak with you in private after what happened with Brodsik," she said. "It must have been awful for you . . . and still is."

"It was a shock, certainly," Gerard said, sipping his tea, his expression sober.

"I haven't thanked you, either." She set down the scone she'd picked up, her appetite suddenly fleeing. "If it hadn't been for you," she hesitated, not wanting to sound so melodramatic as to say, *I might be dead.* "Who knows what havoc Brodsik might have created?" she managed to say instead.

"As much as I would prefer that the circumstances were different, I am glad I was able to do what I could to stop him," Gerard said quietly.

"I would never wish the situation on anyone, but you responded very bravely."

He gave a small smile and set down his teacup.

"And you? Are you suffering again, with Ian's departure?"

She blinked at his question, given the fact he'd been avoiding saying Ian's name in her presence earlier.

"I'm doing all right," she said, keeping her voice even. "At least he's agreed to keep in contact this time. With Anne and James anyway. At least we're not fearful for his life or well-being."

"Yes, well that's something, of course." He paused. She sensed he was trying to broach a delicate subject.

"What is it, Gerard?"

"I'm well aware that you, Anne, and James know of some kind of secret about why Ian became so emotionally disturbed last summer and disappeared. And I understand," he said, holding up his hand in a placating manner when she opened her mouth to try and explain her silence yet again. "I value your discretion. I'm not trying to pry. It's just that . . . I came upon Lucien and Ian talking together in the sitting room a few days before he left Belford Hall. They were talking about a man called Trevor Gaines. Ian has apparently bought his house and has been conducting some sort of search in it. I only bring it up because I was very concerned by Ian's tone. He sounded quite . . . *intense.* I won't go so far as to say 'mad' but he certainly sounded obsessed with the topic."

Francesca swallowed thickly, shocked, absorbing the disturbing news while Gerard studied her. *Ian had bought Trevor Gaines's house?*

"I'm sorry if I've upset you. It's just . . . I assumed that Ian's secret that you've all been guarding is somehow related to this man Gaines. I wanted to assure myself that if you, Anne, and James were aware of whatever Ian is involved in, that you were also aware of how . . . unbalanced he sounds on the topic."

"Unbalanced?" Francesca asked warily. "I don't understand what you mean."

"Even Lucien was uncomfortable while they talked. I could tell. Who wouldn't be, with Ian ranting the way he was. He sounded very angry, but for the life of me, I couldn't comprehend at what his fury was aimed." His laugh sounded uneasy. "For a moment, I thought he sounded a little like . . ."

"What?" Francesca asked, her alarm mounting. The idea of Ian purchasing Trevor Gaines's home, searching in it. . . . Had he been *living* in that monster's residence this whole time? Ice water seemed to shoot through her veins at the thought. She shuddered, placing her hand on her chest when an uncomfortable spasm went through it.

"Gerard, what did you think Ian sounded like?" she asked, her voice growing high pitched.

Gerard winced. "Well he sounded a little like my cousin Helen," he admitted uneasily.

Francesca stared at him, shock making her flesh tingle. "Gerard, that's a horrible thing to say. Ian is as sane as anyone I know. He's been through a hell of a lot in a short period of time. He's had to deal with more than most could endure. More than you know."

"Francesca, please don't go," Gerard said when she abruptly set her napkin on the table and stood. "I realize that Ian doesn't often appear the way I observed. That's why I wanted to make sure I brought it up to someone who has an idea of whatever he's been experiencing for the past half year. I was aware that Lucien and he were discussing something secretive by their manner, but I'd never seen Ian behave in such a . . . an irrational way. Although," he added under his breath, "surely you've noticed he's been rather . . . *frayed* at times during this visit. Anne and James certainly have. Actually, I *have* seen him act oddly one other time in his life," he said, pausing in reflection. "When he first came to Belford as a child, he could be very moody and unpredictable. Sometimes he reminded me of one of those feral children, to be honest. Not to that degree, of course, but still . . . It was tragic to see it, imagining what he must have endured with only a madwoman for a companion for the first ten years of his life. For a moment when I saw him there in the sitting room, I was reminded of that child. I thought he was going to strike out at Lucien like a cornered animal."

"He would never do that," Francesca grated out, her chaotic thoughts suddenly landing on how wild Ian had looked the other day behind the stairs, how he'd flung Lucien's hand away from him. She didn't believe that Ian was mad for an instant, but what if he really had endured too much emotionally? She'd worried what he was doing during this soul search was unhealthy for him, but she hadn't imagined him doing something as extreme as buying Trevor Gaines's house and conducting some sort of obsessive search. And for what? What could he *possibly* hope to find?

A wave of powerful nausea went through her at the thought.

What if Gerard was right? She'd worried that Ian had been emotionally cut open with the news of Trevor Gaines and his mother's death, but what if he really was skating on the edge? What if he'd gone *over* the edge at times? He was always alluding to the fact that he had no choice in his mission, and she'd fought that concept tooth and nail.

But wasn't it true that the closer a person got to madness, the less and less choice they had? They felt compelled, ruled by powers other than their own.

I didn't choose any of this. Fate did.

She moaned softly, nausea rising to her throat at the memory of him saying those words.

"Francesca, please sit down," Gerard implored, standing and looking alarmed. "You look very pale."

"No. No, I'd just like to be alone," she managed, hardly aware of what she said when Gerard reached out to steady her. She removed his hand and somehow made it out of the room.

Francesca rushed into her suite, experiencing a strange sense of rising panic overlaid with a clear focus. She needed to go and find Ian. She needed to assure herself that he was safe and not descending into a place where she couldn't reach him. Never in a million years would she have allowed him to continue on this soul search if she'd thought his mission included spending time alone in Trevor Gaines's house, sifting through the remains of his sick life.

But was he alone? She wondered, pausing as she began to open her drawers. Hadn't Elise referred to the fact that Lucien might join him? When Elise had mentioned it before, she'd had some vague idea that perhaps both of them would go to Morocco together so that Ian could ask Fatima about his mother. She hadn't been happy about the idea, but it seemed downright healthy compared to what Ian had *actually* been doing and planned to continue to do. God, if Ian really was in Trevor Gaines's house, please let Lucien be with him. Lucien, at least, could steady him in this bizarre mission. She rushed to her purse and pulled out her cell phone.

"Elise?" she said a moment later, relief rushing through her at the sound of Elise's voice. "I'm so glad I caught you."

"Francesca? What is it? What's wrong?" Elise asked, making Francesca realize how panicked she sounded.

"Nothing, I hope. It's just . . . is Lucien with Ian?"

There was a short pause. "Yes. They're in France," Elise finally said.

"Elise, are they at Trevor Gaines's *house*?"

"Yes," Elise replied in a thin voice. "I'm not happy about it, but Lucien insisted he wanted to do it, especially for— Francesca, who told you where they were? Did Ian?"

"No, he told me he didn't want me to know above all else," Francesca said, frowning at the memory. He knew if she tried to talk him out of it, he might listen, so he'd preferred to leave her in the dark about the exact nature of what he planned. *Damn him.* "Gerard told me. He overheard Lucien and Ian talking. Why didn't *you* tell me what they were doing?" she accused.

"I just found out yesterday, before Lucien left. He told me that Ian didn't want you to know. I told Lucien I wasn't going to lie to you about it. In fact, I'd almost decided to call you one way or another. You just happened to call me first."

"It's *mad*," Francesca hissed. She blanched and grimaced when she recognized what she'd said. "Ian is already skating on the edge. How is wandering around that awful man's house going to help his state of mind any?"

"I agree," Elise said, sounding miserable. Francesca held the phone to her ear, listening as she dragged her suitcase out of the closet. She'd just pack some bare essentials and leave her nicer clothes and jewelry behind at Belford. She doubted she'd need eveningwear for this mission. "But they want to know if they can discover any other of Gaines's children, or at least I know Lucien wants that, very much. Apparently, there's a man who lives on the grounds even now who is . . . you know . . . one of Gaines's offspring," Elise finished uncomfortably.

A bitter taste rose at the back of Francesca's throat. It was such an ugly scenario. She hated, *despised* the idea of Ian submersing himself in it. She tossed her suitcase on the bed and opened it.

"I can't let him do it," she said, opening a drawer and grabbing handfuls of underwear and bras and tossing them into the suitcase. "It's absolutely *the* most unhealthy thing in the world for him."

"At least Lucien is there this time," Elise said hopefully. "I don't think it's a good idea, either, Francesca, but I understand the need to heal. For closure. And Ian . . ."

"What?" Francesca asked, pausing with some sweaters clutched in her hands.

"I think he wants to compile all he can learn. Try to make sense of Gaines's motivations, how he became the way he became. Lucien said something about Ian not being satisfied with the psychological profile a prison psychiatrist wrote about Gaines."

"And Ian thinks he can write it better?" Francesca asked incredulously. She shut her eyes, that feeling of nausea rising in her again. She remembered what Anne had said about her grandson's search for himself. *You know how important clarity is to him. He prizes seeing clearly above all else.*

"I don't think he wants to write a psychological profile, of course," Elise said uneasily. "I just got the impression from Lucien he's trying to fix in his mind who his biological father was, and that all available information from news articles and everything wasn't sufficient for him. He wants to sort it all out in some kind of organized fashion so he can make sense of it."

"Yes," Francesca said starkly. "And in doing so, prove to himself he's not Trevor Gaines." She tossed the sweaters in the suitcase and went in search of some jeans.

"You don't actually believe that Ian thinks he's even a *little* like that man?" Elise asked, sounding stunned.

"I think he's hurt and confused. And I think he's grasping for evidence of who he is in a place that will only give him lies for answers. This search is taking him down a dark path, one that could very well kill him," Francesca said grimly.

There was silence on the other end of the phone for a few seconds. "Francesca, do you really think things are that bad?"

"I don't know," she replied honestly. "Maybe."

They talked for a few minutes more while Francesca finished

packing. Elise grew more and more concerned as she listened to Francesca's worries, but Francesca assured her that she was actually greatly relieved that Lucien was there with Ian.

"But you're still going to Gaines's house?"

"Yes," she said. "As soon as I can get packed and hire a taxi to take me to the airport."

"Maybe I should meet you there," Elise said, sounding worried.

"No, it'll be all right, Elise. I'll call you if I think you need to intercede with Lucien."

"Call me either way once you get there," Elise begged.

"I will," Francesca assured grimly.

Gerard was waiting for her when she entered her one-bedroom flat early that evening. Clarisse started and gave a little scream when she turned on a bedside lamp and saw him sitting calmly in a living room chair.

"Oh my God, you gave me such a fright," the young woman squealed.

"Why are you so jumpy? Does it have to do with this?" Gerard asked. He turned his hand, the diamonds flashing in the light catching Clarisse's attention.

"Why do you have Francesca's necklace?" Clarisse asked, confused, staring at the diamond choker. She set down her purse and coat at the back of the couch and walked toward him.

"Shouldn't I be asking you that question?" Gerard asked.

She halted. "What do you mean?"

"Francesca came to me early this afternoon, in a panic because this very necklace had gone missing," Gerard lied smoothly. Francesca had told him no such thing. In fact, she'd sought him out, distracted and harried, and returned the necklace to him with apologies for being unable to accept his gift. He'd followed and watched her unobserved afterward, and saw her leave Belford Hall with a suitcase, her manner furtive as she got into a cab. "She was beside herself," he continued his story to Clarisse. "I told her not to worry—the necklace is insured, after all—and assured her that I would find it. And so I did."

Clarisse's mouth fell open. Her blue eyes grew wide in shock. "Wait . . . you can't mean you think *I* took it?"

"I found the necklace in your bedside table. You've been a very bad little maid, Clarisse," he purred.

For a few seconds, she just stared. She moved jerkily, suddenly lunging for the couch but stumbling. She caught herself on the arm of the sofa and fell into it.

"I never took that necklace!"

"I found it here," Gerard said simply, standing and walking toward her. He looked down at her, smiling.

"If you found it here, then you *put* it there," she muttered in rising disbelief.

"Don't be ridiculous. Why would I put a necklace that I already own in your apartment?" Her pink lips opened and shut several times as she stared at him in bewilderment. He was enjoying seeing her helpless. The trap had snapped shut with her securely in it. She would do whatever he said now. "Didn't Francesca tell you that I gave her this necklace for Christmas?" he continued. "She told me she planned to return it, though. We both know how obsessed she is with Ian. She must have felt guilty about receiving such an expensive piece of jewelry from another man. Misplaced loyalty. Even now, she's on a plane flying to confront the love of her life for having abandoned her once again." He shook his head sadly. "Those two are a keg of gunpowder set to explode, if you ask me."

Clarisse's wide eyes grew even larger. "Please don't do this. Don't tell Francesca I took that necklace. I need this job."

"I know," Gerard said earnestly. He nodded to several framed photos of her family set on the mantel. "You have a younger brother that's quite ill, isn't that true? Cystic fibrosis. Such a shame."

"How do you know about Scott?" she asked incredulously.

"I know all about you," Gerard assured, his voice rich with compassion. "Including the fact that you've been arrested before for stealing."

Every ounce of color drained from her face. "I was only sixteen when that happened. My friends dared me to steal some clothes from a shop, and I was stupid enough to do it."

He nodded. "A very expensive shop, no less. It seems you have a liking for luxurious things you can't afford," he said, rolling the sparkling choker over his fingers thoughtfully. "And you failed to mention that crime in your application as a maid at Belford, didn't you? Even though the question was asked, you lied."

"I was sixteen years old!" she repeated, her voice shaking. Tears filled her eyes. "Please don't tell Francesca I stole from her. I never took anything from her. I *wouldn't.*"

"*Shhh,*" Gerard soothed, taking her hands and lifting her from the couch. He palmed her jaw and caressed her cheek with his thumb, drying a few spilled tears. "I won't. There's nothing to worry about. No real harm has been done."

"You mean . . . you mean you're not going to tell Lady Anne or the police?"

"No, of course not," he said softly, stroking her. He was becoming aroused, feeling her young, supple body plastered against him . . . seeing how vulnerable she was. "As long as you do whatever I say."

She blinked, wariness freezing her expression. She started to back away, but he pulled her tighter against him, trapping her with his arms.

"What do you mean?" she asked. "What do I have to do?"

"If you don't want to be arrested for stealing a valuable piece of jewelry from a guest at Belford Hall, then anything I say."

"Like what?' she asked, horror creeping in to her delicate features.

"Don't look so alarmed," he laughed. "Hardly nothing." He made a mock-impatient sound when she continued to stare at him in rising fear. "All right, if you want some examples. I'm leaving Belford tonight, and I'd like it very much, if the occasion should ever arise," he said kindly, loosening his hold on her by degrees when she didn't attempt to flee. "If you said I was here with you all night, letting me fuck you just as you have been for the past week. That won't be too difficult, will it? And well worth it, to cover what you did."

"I never did anything!" she said, anger and helplessness straining her voice.

"Oh, but you did. Because I said you did. Who do you think people are going to be more likely to listen to, a maid with a history of theft, or the future Earl of Stratham?"

He pressed his thumb to her trembling lower lip and rubbed it. Her nostrils flared, but this time, she didn't try to back away. She knew she was caught, he thought. He shifted his growing erection against her belly.

"And as far as other things you might have to do for me to assure my silence, it won't involve anything you haven't been doing for me already. It hardly seemed like a trial for you to see to my needs previously. Why should it matter if you have to continue to do so whenever I request it? Like now, for instance. I have a small amount of time before I have to leave—a quarter of an hour or so—and I'd like to spend it pleasantly. Wouldn't you?" he asked, now palming both sides of her delicate face. Her trembling seemed to grow more violent. She refused to take part when he began to kiss her coaxingly, but he continued, undaunted.

He smiled against her lips when he felt a slight shudder go through her, and she began to participate.

Somehow, her kisses were even sweeter now than they had been from a willing mouth.

Francesca had debated how to tell James and Anne that she was leaving and had finally left a letter, apologizing profusely for her departure and explaining that it related to Ian, assuring them at the same time there was no cause for worry. She said she would return to finish her sketch as soon as she could. She felt guilty about hiring a ride and sneaking out so secretly, but was worried that Anne and James would try and talk her out of going. Ian had told his grandparents he wanted her to stay there, and she knew she wouldn't be able to disguise her concern for Ian if she spoke to them face-to-face. In conclusion, she promised them to be in touch very soon, and begged them again not to worry.

While she was at the airport, she researched the location of Trevor Gaines's home. She was able to find a local article about Gaines's arrest years back that mentioned his address. With the address in hand, she flew into a small airport in northern France and rented a car from there.

Aurore Manor was an hour and a half drive from the airport. She didn't reach the remote mansion until the sun was beginning to set. Even though Aurore and Belford Hall were both fine, aristocratic homes, the setting couldn't have been more different, Francesca realized as she drove down an untended, crumbling road through unkempt, wild-looking woods. Her gaze was caught by an odd vision within the shadowed trees where the sunset light penetrated. What appeared to be half of large a man—the upper portion only, the waist of his figure at ground level—moved. Then the shadow lowered and vanished completely. Francesca blinked in shock, her hand jerking on the wheel and she nearly lost control of the rental car. She shivered, unnerved by the impossible sight, strange associations to ghosts and fairy folk and mythical forest people popping into her brain.

Half a man melting into the ground? What in the world had she seen?

That impossible vision added to the oppressive quality of her surroundings—not to mention the knowledge of who had once owned the property—and only mounted her unease on arriving.

The house itself reminded her of some kind of dark, giant bird of prey hovering against the brilliant sunset, a patiently waiting vulture. She felt a little weak with relief at the vision of the two very normal-looking, luxury sedans parked in the weed-infested circular drive before the house. She was starting to feel like the only living thing in a landscape of death and ghosts. Her eyes widened when she realized a tall man wearing a dark coat stood in the arched stone portico leading to the front door, his body eerily still. He moved into the evening light when she pulled her economy rental car behind the sleek silver one.

Ian.

She watched him in rising amazement as she put the car into park. He stalked toward her, his dark, unfastened overcoat billowing out behind his tall, honed body. He wore a pair of jeans that fit his long legs and lean hips to perfection, brown work boots, a simple white T-shirt, and an unbuttoned overshirt. His jaw was darkened by whiskers. She was poignantly reminded of the lonely, noble savage she'd painted on a desolate Chicago city street years ago. His blue eyes blazed as he pinned her with his stare through the front windshield. He did *not* look pleased to see her.

He also looked as if he'd been expecting her. How had he known she'd arrive?

He opened her car door.

"What are you doing here?" he demanded without preamble.

She recoiled slightly at his rough question, but her chin went up defiantly. "I came looking for you, of course. How did you know I'd be here?"

"Short," he muttered, his mouth rigid. A cold breeze howled through the open door. She shivered, but Ian seemed unaffected.

"Arthur Short? James's employee? But how—"

He reached for her elbow. "Come inside."

"Let me get my bag," she said when he drew her out of the car and slammed the door shut.

"Leave it. You're not going to need it," he bit out.

"Ian, I'm *not* leaving," she said with conviction as he bustled her to the front entrance. He didn't reply, but his thundercloud expression was answer enough as to what he thought of her plans.

He opened the door and urged her forward. Francesca stumbled across the threshold, pulling up short when she saw Lucien enter the large, cavernous foyer where they all stood. Unlike Ian, he appeared as well-groomed and calm as always. The door slammed shut behind her, making her jump. She glanced back at Ian and then over at Lucien.

"How could James's business associate have told you I planned to come to France?" Francesca asked.

Lucien just raised his eyebrows in a wry expression and glanced at Ian.

"Because he's not Grandfather's business associate. He's the security guard I hired to watch over you," Ian said with barely subdued, blistering heat.

"Security guard? But I told you—"

"We said we'd discuss it," Ian interrupted. "But we never got the chance before I had to leave, so—"

"You just took it upon yourself to do whatever you wanted without bothering to consult me."

Ian scowled darkly. "It doesn't matter. You left so abruptly, Short barely had time to follow you. It took him by surprise. He followed you to the airport in London—"

"He followed me?" Francesca asked, spinning around to face Ian, appalled at the idea of being spied upon without her knowledge.

"For as long as he could," Ian said bitterly.

"He tailed you into the airport and heard where you planned to go when you bought your ticket," Lucien said from behind her. "He didn't have his passport with him, though, so he couldn't follow you. He wasn't expecting to have to leave the country so quickly, given what Ian had told him," Lucien explained when Francesca gave him a perplexed glance over her shoulder.

"Idiot," Ian said succinctly, looking extremely annoyed. He narrowed his stare on her, watching her from beneath a lowered brow. "Who told you I was here?"

"Gerard," she said.

His jaw stiffened. "Gerard? How did—"

"He said he overheard you two talking."

His lip curled every so slightly in an expression of . . . what, she couldn't quite say.

"Ian? What is it?"

"Nothing," Ian replied through a tight mouth. "Francesca, I don't want you here."

She dropped her arms and straightened her spine. "I'm not leaving. Not unless you come with me."

He looked mad enough to bite through a chain-link fence. She stood her ground, but something in his blue eyes made it difficult to do.

"You're here now. Come inside. It's freezing in this foyer," Lucien added from behind her, and she knew he was trying to give Ian time to cool down and see reason. Ian made a savage, furious sound in his throat and stalked out of the foyer ahead of them without another word.

"I had to come," she whispered to Lucien desperately. "It's crazy, him being here of all places. Is it true Ian has *bought* this place?"

"He owns it, yes," Lucien said succinctly, his tight mouth telling her he shared in her disquietude. "Are you going to come in? We were just sitting down to eat in the parlor. It's one of the only livable rooms in the house . . . one of the only warm ones as well," he added drolly.

"When did you get here?" she asked Lucien as they walked.

"Late last night, at around the same time as Ian."

She followed him into a firelit, shadowed room filled with heavy, ornate furniture covered in dingy, once-luxurious fabrics. An unpleasant odor of dampness and mold seemed to pervade the entire place. Ian sat on a deep couch facing the gigantic fireplace, eating a plate of food mechanically without acknowledging her arrival in the room.

"Are you hungry, Francesca?" Lucien asked politely. "It's just chicken, potatoes, and fruit, but we've got plenty of it."

"Yes, please," Francesca replied, realizing for the first time how hollow her stomach felt. She hadn't eaten all day. When Ian still refused to speak or look at her after Lucien left the room, she sighed and fell onto the couch next to him. The heat from the fire felt good. A wave of exhaustion hit her.

"Are you just going to ignore me?" she asked tiredly after a moment.

His whiskered jaw hardened. He swallowed and shoved his plate onto the coffee table before him. "How can I possibly ignore you when you've shown up here uninvited?" he said, anger simmering in his deep voice. "I don't want you staying here, Francesca. This place is . . . tainted. Poison. I don't believe in ghosts, but if I were ever to think a place was haunted, I'd think it was Aurore. It's not a place where I want you to be."

"Well it's not a place where I want *you* to be, either. Come with me, and we'll both be happy." Her flash of indignation faded almost as fast as it came. She peered around the shadowed room, making out the dark, depressing paintings of pale-skinned, hollow-eyed people and the massive, hulking furniture, some of which was covered in stained sheets. She could almost feel the dust and mold accumulating in her lungs as she breathed. "What an awful place."

Ian's irritated grunt seemed to say, *Didn't I tell you?* He leaned back on the couch, his profile rigid. Francesca wanted to demand that he tell her what specifically he was looking for on Trevor Gaines's property, but was worried he'd get up and refuse to speak to her further. Knowing him as well as she did, she understood that the majority of his anger at her presence came from helplessness. And perhaps shame at her seeing this dark part of his past.

As she was quickly learning, his shame wasn't logical. But that didn't mean he could shake it just because *she* wanted it.

Eager to change the topic that would sidestep his discomfort and fury, she landed on the disconcerting vision she'd seen as she drove onto the property.

"I can well believe you'd imagine this place is haunted. You won't believe what I saw just now in the woods," she said as Lucien walked into the room carrying a plate of food and a glass. "Thank you," she said gratefully as Lucien placed her dinner in front of her on the table.

"What?" Ian asked, turning toward her slightly, his brows knitted together.

"Half a man disappearing into the ground," Francesca replied matter-of-factly, picking up her plate and settling it in her lap. She took a bite. The chicken was moist and flavorful. "This is good. Did you get it in town?"

"Forget about the food," Ian said impatiently, peering at her. "What do you mean, *half a man*?" Lucien, too, was listening intently from where he sat in an armchair near the couch.

She paused to explain what she'd seen. When she finished, Ian shared a significant look with Lucien.

"It's him. Kam Reardon," Ian said to Lucien. "He must have some kind of hideout underground. It's what I suspected. I'm convinced there's a tunnel entrance into this house. He gets in, but I can't figure out how. If he's underground, that's why I haven't been able to find him when I search the grounds."

"Who's Kam Reardon?" Francesca asked. She quirked her eyebrows up in an expectant gesture when neither man spoke. "Well?"

"He's a wild man who lives on the estate," Ian answered flatly.

"He's our half brother," Lucien added.

Francesca froze in the process of chewing some potato. Ian stood abruptly, startling her. He was such a big man, but he moved with fast, razor precision at times. "I'm going to look for the underground entrance. I'm dead set to talk to Reardon. He's got to know plenty about Gaines, if he lived here his whole life. There's still a little light left to search," he told Lucien.

Lucien stood as well. "I'm coming with you. Reardon doesn't sound like the type to be too thrilled at the idea of anyone poking into his den."

Francesca set down her plate and got up. "I'm going, too." She ignored Ian's fiery, furious glance. "I'm the one who saw where the entrance was," she said. "It'll be tomorrow morning if you go looking for it by stomping up and down every square inch of land at the side of the road."

She headed toward the front door, praying Ian would cooperate for once in his life and follow her.

Chapter Fifteen

t took a little doing to find the spot. Darkness was falling, especially under the cover of the trees, even as skeletal as the limbs were with winter upon them. Thankfully, Ian had grabbed a powerful flashlight on the way out. Francesca led them to the general vicinity of where she thought she'd seen the "half man," recalling a singularly shaped stump of a tree that she'd almost run into in her shock upon seeing the unlikely vision.

There was barely any light left by the time Ian paused, pushing his foot down several times on the ground. Francesca heard a hollow, thumping noise.

"This is it," Ian said, his gruff voice in the cold, still air causing a shiver to course down her spine. She and Lucien drew near the flashlight and Ian's shadowed form. He knelt and moved his hand over the dead leaves, his gloved fingers seeming to stick on something.

"Back up a bit," he instructed. Lucien and she stepped back, and he lifted. The forest floor opened like a two-by-three-foot lid. Ian pointed the flashlight downward, revealing a dark hole and a wooden ladder. Francesca could barely make out his shadowed face as he peered downward, but she saw that he was scowling. He flashed a glance at her, and she knew he was deliberating on how best to proceed . . . undoubtedly wishing she wasn't there so he didn't have to worry about her.

"I'll go first, and call up to you if I think the coast is clear," he told Lucien.

"We're going with you, Ian. We're not going to stand up here in the freezing cold with no light," Francesca stated.

Ian gave her a repressive glance. Without another word, he shoved the flashlight in Lucien's direction and lowered into the hole.

"Holy Jesus," Lucien muttered in awe several minutes later. The three of them stood at the mouth of a large underground chamber that was lit by electrical lamps. The room had been at the end of a long tunnel, the floor earthen, the walls reinforced by wooden timbers. After only several seconds of being underground, they'd been able to see the light in the far distance and follow it unerringly.

"What *is* it all?" Francesca muttered dubiously, staring at table after table filled with odd, intricate mechanical devices, computers, and scattered tools. Many of the devices were moving, tiny metal cogs spinning, pendulums swinging. The sound of dozens of muted ticking noises resounded in the silence. Some of the mechanisms were large, but one table near them held tiny metal objects and delicate tools along with an electrical magnifying-type lens that reminded Francesca of something she'd seen in an eye doctor's office.

"They're all clockwork mechanisms, aren't they?" Lucien asked, approaching one of the tables and examining its contents in fascination.

"Different types of escapements," Ian said. Francesca looked at him in bewilderment. "The basic mechanism of a clock or watch. There are different kinds," Ian said, peering around the room. "Gaines was considered to be a mechanical genius. He patented several electronic and mechanical devices, many of them associated with clockworks. Reardon has stolen a lot of this from Gaines's workshop, I think. But I don't understand some of these things. It's like something I've never seen before—"

"I didn't steal anything!" Francesca jumped at the harsh male shout. "He left it to me. Left me that house you say belongs to you, too, only I didn't have the tax money and they took it from me," a deep, rough voice rang out from the shadows at the far end of the room. Francesca started at the vision of a tall, broad-shouldered figure coming at them with alarming speed. He was carrying a shotgun. Ian moved in front of Francesca, so that she had to look around his arm to see. She heard the innocuous, cheerful sound of eager paws and tinkling metal. She glanced down in amazement when a beautiful, well-groomed golden retriever approached her and Ian's legs and sniffed at them with friendly interest. There was a small, sophisticated-looking electronic device strapped on the dog's right leg. It looked, oddly enough, like a very expensive watch.

"Get back Angus," the man bellowed, startling Francesca. Kam Reardon's face was twisted in a fury. He paused when he noticed her peering around Ian, his frown fading. His light gray eyes ran over her face. Ian seemed to sense him studying her, because he put his hand back on her hip and pushed, urging her farther behind him.

Kam Reardon had Lucien's eyes. She leaned out again, her curiosity trumping her fear.

The man's frightening scowled returned. "Get the hell out of here," he growled.

"I'm sorry for trespassing," Ian said levelly. "We don't mean any harm, Kam. I came to talk to you. So did Lucien, here," he said, nodding at Lucien, who looked very wary eyeing Kam's pointed shotgun. "Lucien is our . . . brother as well," Ian said, seeming to hesitate at saying the word.

"And her?" Gaines said, nodding in the direction behind Ian. "Is she one of us?"

"No," Ian said harshly. Kam's gaze lowered to where Ian palmed the side of her hip.

"I said to get the hell out," Kam yelled suddenly, white teeth flashing in his dark beard. He cocked the gun.

"Go on," Ian said tersely, turning and pushing Francesca in front of him. Lucien followed. Ian handed her the flashlight. "Lead the way. Hurry," he ordered.

Francesca jogged down the dark tunnel, her heart pounding in her chest, highly aware that it wasn't just Lucien and Ian who were behind her. Kam Reardon was bringing up the rear. She could hear his footsteps grinding in the stony dirt, but imagined she could feel his simmering anger behind them as he followed, assuring himself they well and truly left his underground territory. The dog Angus frolicked next to them, an unlikely escort to such a tense eviction.

After they returned to the manor, Ian insisted upon searching for the suspected underground entrance where Reardon entered Aurore. Francesca went with them into the gloomy, musty basement that seemed to stretch forever in each direction. Ian and Lucien did, indeed, after much searching, discover a hidden door that led to a tunnel.

"It looks like it was built fairly recently, at least in comparison to the house," Lucien observed, running his hand over the wood timbers that enforced a different branch of the tunnel system than the one they'd been in earlier.

"I'm thinking it might have been constructed during World War II, during the German occupation. There was fighting in this vicinity. The owners might have wanted an escape route or a hideout if troops ever tried to occupy. Look at this," Ian said, running the flashlight along a plastic tube that contained multiple electrical wires. "Bloody bastard has me paying for his electricity," Ian said, his tone a strange mixture of annoyance, amusement, and respect.

Afterward, they all retired to the parlor. The fire was dying in the hearth, but still gave off sufficient heat to warm Francesca.

"How old do you think he is?" Lucien asked after they'd talked a while about the idiosyncratic Reardon.

"Hard to tell with that bloody beard and all the grime. Around our age, maybe younger," Ian said. "He's got a story to tell."

"He's clearly more than a wild tramp," Lucien said, standing and stretching. "He's organized and methodical . . . and brilliant, if I don't miss my guess."

"A chip off the old block," Ian muttered.

"Didn't the townspeople give you any idea of his background?" Lucien asked.

"I only got some of the newer residents to open up and talk," Ian said, the low flames of the fire flickering in his eyes as he stared. "They all seemed to be of the belief that he's a homeless, wild tramp."

"Why wouldn't the people who have lived here for longer talk to you?" Francesca asked.

She flinched inwardly when his gleaming eyes met hers. He'd hardly met her gaze at all since she'd arrived.

"Because I spook them," Ian said, his mouth slanting into a mirthless smile. "They think I'm Gaines's ghost." Her heart seemed to jump against her breastbone. She blinked when he stood abruptly from the couch.

"I'm going to bed," he said.

Lucien gave her a half-apologetic, half-compassionate glance when Ian stalked out of the room without another word.

Lucien indicated which room Ian slept in before he bid her good night, and opened a door at the other end of the long hallway.

She rapped on the designated door quietly before she entered, but Ian didn't reply. He stood unmoving next to an ancient four-poster bed with a drooping canopy of dusty, faded crimson velvet. She gave him a questioning, worried look when he just stared at the bed without looking around at her.

"I don't know where to put you to sleep," he said starkly, surprising her.

"I don't know what you mean," she said slowly, confused. Was he going to insist she sleep separately from him? Was he still *that* angry that she'd come?

"I mean I don't know where to put you. There's no place suitable," he waved at the sagging mattress on the old relic. "The beds are all like this."

She gave a soft bark of laughter when she recognized the direction of his concern. "Don't be ridiculous. I'll be fine. I've been camping before. It can't be much worse than . . ."

She faded off when he turned to her and she saw the utter bleakness of his expression.

"Ian," she whispered, her throat going tight. She rushed to him, hugging him tight, her cheek pressed against his chest. "I don't care where I sleep. I just want to be wherever you are. I just want to be with you, and know you're okay."

For a wretched few seconds, he didn't return her fervent embrace. Slowly, his arms encircled her waist. Then he was pulling her tight against him, his face pressing to the top of her head.

"You smell so good," he mumbled next to her hair. "If I kept my nose buried here, if I kept myself buried in you, I could forget this disgusting old house . . . all of it. You have no idea how much the idea appeals."

She whimpered softly, pressing her face closer to his solid heat. "I had to come. Please don't be mad at me. I know I said I understood about you trying to figure things out for yourself, but I didn't know . . ."

"I meant this?" he asked, cradling the back of her head with his palm and urging her to look up at him.

"I panicked when I thought of you being here," she admitted in a rush. "It just seemed so . . . awful."

"It *is* awful," he said dryly. "I told you it was. I told you I didn't want you here. It pains me to see it, Francesca."

She looked up at him through a veil of tears. "It pains *me*. If it's true that you think it will help you somehow, then tell me. Tell me *how*, Ian," she implored. A tear skipped down her cheek. "Make me understand, because I'm trying so hard to be on your side."

"That's just it," he said, profound frustration entering his bold features. He opened his hand at the side of her head, thumbing the skin of her cheek. "You can't understand this place. To you, it's just a dirty, moldy pile. But to me, it holds answers. Look at tonight," he added pointedly when she just looked at him, bewildered. "Kam Reardon. He'll be able to answer questions for me."

"If you can keep him from shooting you, first . . . maybe," Francesca said doubtfully.

"He's not going to shoot me. At least I don't think so. He apparently had the opportunity plenty of times before and never did," he said, still stroking her cheek, his expression thoughtful.

"That's not all that reassuring," she replied desperately.

"I'm sorry. If I can't explain it to you, then I don't know what to do," he said in a pressured tone. "I'm telling you there are answers here for me. About Trevor Gaines. About who he was. About how I got here on this earth."

"How is knowing all that going to make a difference to you?" she asked wildly.

He clamped his eyes together, his expression so frustrated it made it her want to weep. "I'm telling you that it makes a difference to me because it *does*. I'm *telling* you that it does, what else can I say to convince you? If I can figure things out, make sense of it in my mind—"

"But it's *mad*," she interrupted, growing frantic.

He opened his eyes slowly, spearing her with his stare. His brow furrowed slightly. Francesca froze when she saw his dawning comprehension.

"That's what you think? That I'm going mad?"

"I . . ." She shook her head, her mind spinning. *Did* she think he was losing his mental facilities? "No. No," she repeated, realizing it was true. He was emotionally overwrought, but he wasn't a madman. She met his stare, pleading for him to understand. "I'm just . . . scared. It terrified me, thinking of you digging around in that man's possessions, trying to understand him."

Her shaky admission seemed to hover in the air between them.

"I'm a little scared, too," he admitted after a moment. "But not of the same thing you are. Not of going mad. Not anymore anyway."

"What then?" she whispered, pulling closer to his heat.

"Of not being able to understand. If I can't wrap my head around who my biological father was, I can't . . ." He gritted his teeth and winced. "I can't get the poison of him out of me. I don't know how else to put it. If you'd just let me, I can *do* this, Francesca. I believe it now, more than ever. With Lucien here, with all the research I've already compiled, even catching a glimpse of Kam Reardon's life tonight, I'm starting to get a hold on who Trevor Gaines was." His eyes looked a little wild as he clutched tighter at her head. "If I can't do this, I can't feel right about being with you forever. I don't want to taint you—"

"You would never do that!"

"Damn it, Francesca," he shouted harshly. "This is *my* worry. This is my burden, and I'm trying to make it go away. I'm not doing this to be stubborn, or because I'm going mad. I'm not doing this because I want to alienate you! I'm doing this because I have to if I want to be with you. And that's all . . . I want . . . in the world," he grated succinctly out between white, clenched teeth.

She just stared at him, her heart pounding, unable to draw breath.

"Ian," she exhaled, a convulsion of emotion going through her. "Ian, I'm so sorry."

"Don't be. The last thing you should be doing is apologizing," he whispered harshly, grimacing, absorbing her shudders. "It pains me to see you in this place, but . . ." He shook his head and swallowed, loosening his hold on her and caressing her temple. "It strangely helps, too, I think. I don't know. It's strange. Tonight, I feel like it really is possible to maybe wrap my head around this whole nightmare. And I really don't think it's just because of Lucien being here, or discovering what an . . . *interesting* person Kam Reardon really is."

"I don't want you to feel alone," she said. "If I've made you feel that way, because you knew I wouldn't accept any of this, I'm sorry. That was selfish of me. I thought you were the one being selfish with all this, but I was wrong."

He leaned down, tilting her face up. He kissed her hard. Gentle. She didn't know which, and never did when it came to Ian. She felt his body stir and pressed closer, desirous of his heat and hardness.

"You are the most generous woman I know," he said against her lips a moment later. "The last thing you're being is selfish."

"You always think this poison you speak of is going to taint me, Ian," she murmured breathily. "But love is the strongest antidote to your fears . . . and yes . . . even against this supposed taint." She combed her fingers through his thick, short hair, scraping his scalp. He closed his eyes and groaned. "Let me make love to you here. Right here. In the middle of all your darkness," she said emphatically as she began to kiss his jaw, tenderly abrading her lips with his whiskers. She kissed his leaping pulse and he started.

"No," he said harshly, running his hands along her arms and captured her wrists. He held her and stepped away. His eyes shone with barely restrained emotion. "But you came, and I can't change that. And now that you're here, I have to have you. I suffered too much in this very room, your absence like a gaping hole inside me. I can't turn you away now. So *I* will make love to *you*. And then we'll both know if what you say is true, or if I am just using you to chase away the shadows."

He transferred her wrists to the small of her back and held them there with one hand. He bent down, forcing her back to arch, and began to devour her.

He became even more quickly intoxicated by her taste tonight, as greedy as he was for it. How he wanted to believe what she said was true, that her sweetness wasn't just a temporary escape from all this darkness, but a true home.

His rightful place.

He used his free hand to touch her, relishing restraining her supple body in the taut arch, knowing she was his to do with as he pleased, all because it was her pleasure as well. She was a decadence he couldn't believe he deserved, but he must, because her eagerness was inescapable. His cock swelled at the sensation of the taut lines of her back and ribs, the delicious round, firmness of her breasts beneath the fitted button-down shirt. He filled his hand with her, absorbed her soft moan into his mouth, felt her heat begin to resonate from her sex against his belly. His cock reared almost furiously.

He hissed and broke their kiss, releasing his hold on her wrists. Taking a step back with a goal in mind, he paused abruptly at the vision she made. Her lips were dark pink, damp and parted, her cheeks flushed. Her dark gold, red-tinted hair fell in loose waves down her back and arms. Her dark eyes shone with lust and love, her gaze like a steamy blessing.

He strode rapidly to the edge of the room, where there was a wooden bench. Ian thought it once might have served the purpose of being a location for placing shoes and slippers, but the lowness of the seat was what he wanted for his purpose. He lifted it and rapidly carried it to where Francesca stood, watching him silently. He set it down, his gaze once again glued to her luminous face and pink, lush lips.

She really was here.

"Sit," he rasped. The bench was much lower than a normal chair, so when she sat she was at kneeling level.

"I don't like to think of you kneeling on that disgusting carpet," he muttered, holding her stare as he fleetly unfastened his button fly. Her nostrils flared slightly as her gaze lowered over his abdomen to his crotch. He grimaced as he pulled his heavy erection free of his underwear and pants.

"No," he said when she immediately reached for him, her small hand tempting him, making his voice harsher than he intended. "I'm going to restrain you."

He hadn't unpacked, preferring for some reason to live out of his suitcase while he was at Aurore than to put his clothing in the closet and drawers, like a regular resident would. He found the tie he'd worn to the press conference and went behind Francesca. His cock jerked in the air when she immediately put her wrists behind her back. He knelt behind her, letting the tie fall to his knee, and moved her rose-gold hair aside to kiss her fragrant neck.

"You're so sweet," he murmured thickly as he began to unbutton her blouse, referring to her readiness to be bound, her insistence upon being there with him . . . everything. "I used to think I was taking advantage of you because you always gave yourself so freely, but you truly want to, don't you?" he asked, his lips moving on her tender skin. He opened the placket of her shirt, his hands immediately seeking out her warm, satiny-smooth skin. He groaned at the sensation.

"Yes," she whispered harshly. His fingers slipped over the front of her bra, and he grunted in satisfaction when he felt the front clasp. He opened the garment, spreading the cups back over her breasts.

"*Yes,*" she added emphatically when he filled his hands with the bounty of her bare breasts, shaping them to his palm, massaging them, pinching the plump nipples, glorying in her flesh. He watched over her shoulder, spellbound by the sight of his large hands on her full, soft breasts.

"Arch your back again," he ordered softly near her ear. He salivated when she did as she was told, her spine curving, the mounds of her breasts rising. He pulled her shirt and bra down over her upper arms and left them. She was bound by the garments, but it pleased him to restrain her wrists as well, so he did so quickly with the silk tie.

Her hair was scattered on her shoulders when he walked around to the front of her, her bare breasts heaving. She kept her back arched, displaying herself without a trace of the embarrassment she might have shown in the same act even a year ago. Her eyes glittered with excitement when her stare lowered to his cock protruding from his fly.

His hands itching to touch such a flagrant display of erotic beauty, he leaned down and stroked the sides of her ribs, feeling her shiver. He squeezed her breasts into his hands, knowing just what she liked—a little rough, a little sweet, greedy, and even lewd. He slapped the side of one breast lightly, watching as she bit her lush lower lip to stifle a moan.

"You're mine," he said.

"Yes."

He bent and ravished her mouth with his, continuing to stimulate her breasts, squeezing them together and finessing the nipples until she moaned feverishly against his stabbing tongue.

"Your mouth is so hot," he muttered, straightening. "This is going to feel so good." Without another word, he arrowed the fat, tapered head of his cock between her lips. She clamped around him immediately, sucking him deeper. He grimaced in pleasure, pulsing his hips, enjoying the sight of his cock stretching her pink lips and her dark eyes gazing up at him, so radiant . . . so giving . . . so helpless.

She had always been willing to accept her helplessness when it came to this thing between them. Why hadn't he?

He growled in pleasure at the sensation of her pulling at him, tempting him deeper. He'd first taught her how to perform fellatio when she was bound, and he continued to have a preference for it thus, even now. She knew the only way she could control the act was with the movement of her head and her strong suck, and now he took away the former, gripping the hair at the back of her head so that she couldn't drive him mad with her bobbing. It left only her suck, and she used what resource she had to perfection, making him snarl, his eyes rolling back in his head.

"There. Is that what you want?" he said roughly as he began to pulse his hips, fucking her mouth shallowly, sparing her throat. She almost imperceptibly nodded, her gaze never wavering from his face as he looked down at her. He continued to hold her immobile, using her for his pleasure, plunging his cock between her rigid lips. She sucked determinedly, her nostrils flaring. He gasped at the delicious sensation of the soft side of her cheeks brushing his stabbing cock.

They maintained eye contact as he carefully breached her throat. She shuddered, but quickly stilled herself. God, it felt divine.

He grunted gutturally and slid his cock out of her. She said nothing when he turned and hurried to the bathroom, coming back with a towel and a bottle of lubricant. He'd washed the towels when he arrived, so he knew they were clean. He'd washed the sheets, too, but the bedding itself was dusty and moth-eaten; it was only a matter of time before the sheets grew befouled. Francesca shouldn't come into contact with that bedding.

He shoved back the heavy velvet coverlet. A puff of dust rose when the bedspread landed. He quickly lay down two clean towels and returned for Francesca, helping her to rise. She just stared up at him as he reached around her and unbound her wrists, then begun to undress her.

"Do you remember the evening . . . before I left?" he asked hoarsely, removing her shirt and bra and unfastening her jeans. She didn't try to help him, but stood there compliantly while he undressed her.

"I'll never forget it," she said.

He glanced up at her face, pausing in the process of working her jeans and underwear over her hips and ass, her smoky voice capturing his attention.

"I must have watched the tape of your face a thousand times," he said starkly. He blinked, rising out of the spell of her eyes, and bent to remove her boots and socks. "I used to watch it here. In this filthy room. You think I've been obsessed by Trevor Gaines, but I was obsessed by the image of you giving yourself to me."

He stood, having removed all her clothes. He cupped her jaw. "I'm going to make love to you now like I did that night, like I've thought about doing in this room too many times to count. It was the image of you that kept me going when I was so alone here in this cursed place. Now you're here."

"Yes. I'm here with you," she said in a low, quavering voice.

He moved her toward the bed and the spread towels. He urged her sit at the edge, where he again bound her hands, this time in front of her.

"Now lie back and place your hands above your head. That's right," he muttered thickly, adjusting her slightly so that when she lay back, her bottom was at the very edge of the bed. "Now bend your knees toward your chest."

He stared down at her positioned body as he began to undress.

She trembled with excitement and love as she watched him remove his clothing, twisting her head on the mattress to see what she could between her bent knees of his muscular thighs, large, erect cock, narrow hips, tight-as-a-drum abdomen, and powerful chest. She licked her lower lip, almost tasting her anticipation as he poured some of the silky lubricant onto his fingers and placed the bottle next to her on the bed. He stepped between her thighs, so big and powerful. The thrill of submission that went through her at that moment, perhaps the strongest she'd ever experienced—pure and concentrated, true and complete. He grasped her knees and rolled them back, exposing her sex and ass to him. He slipped his middle finger into her anus, and she moaned.

Neither of them looked away from the other's face as he finger-fucked her ass, his arm moving faster and more stringently as time passed, their breathing coming more erratically. After he'd prepared her sufficiently, he lubricated himself and pushed the thick head of his cock against the resisting hole.

"Press against it, lovely," he rasped.

She pushed with her hips, moaning at the pain as he slipped into her ass. He opened both hands on her hips, holding her secure, and began to pulse in and out of her.

"Sweetest ass in the world," he said, his blue-eyed gaze boring down on her face. "Sweetest everything." He appeared to be utterly rapt as he deepened his strokes, impaling the snug flesh, his manner not harsh, but firm. Demanding.

His pelvis bumped against her ass cheeks.

"Look at you," he said, pausing, his chest heaving, perspiration gilding his muscular torso. "God, it can't be possible, but you're giving even more of yourself tonight." The realization seemed to enflame him. She saw the flash of lust in his blue eyes. He thrust, their skin smacking together. "Aren't you?" he asked more harshly as he began to pump, fucking her in earnest.

"Yes," she moaned, overwhelmed by the sensation of being filled by him, inundated by forbidden, delicious pressure. Her head twisted on the mattress. "Use me," she pleaded. "I'm here, Ian. Use me for whatever you need."

He growled viciously and accepted her invitation. She watched him as he abandoned himself to his own dark, primal nature, pushing down on her calves so that her knees pressed tightly against her breasts, fucking her with long, forceful, thorough strokes. Her clit throbbed and burned at the vision, but she strangely didn't wish he'd see to her pleasure. It was a thrill enough to see him lose himself. He'd always expressed amazement that she could give herself so trustingly to him, but at that moment, he trusted himself enough to give completely to her.

"Yes. Just like that," she chanted between swollen lips. "Fuck me so hard."

The ancient bed began to rattle on the wood floor from his forceful possession. She stared dazedly at the trembling canopy above her, utterly consumed.

"Look at me," he ordered roughly.

She stared at him, panting for breath, as he flexed his hips powerfully. She whimpered as he drove into her. He jerked and swelled inside her. He released one calf, reaching between her legs, his thumb finding her clit.

"Ooh," she mewled, her eyes springing wide as he rubbed the burning piece of flesh. Her ass tightened around him and he snarled.

"Tell me," he said.

"I love you," she gasped, shuddering in orgasm. He grunted and his cock convulsed as he began to climax.

"Always," he grated out, jerking his hips, fucking her even as he came.

Chapter Sixteen

F rancesca laughed softly after they showered together, incredulous and touched at the fact that Ian was truly worried about her sleeping in the bed.

"Ian, it'll be fine," she insisted, capturing his hand in the motion of spreading more towels and even some of his clean shirts on the mattress.

He scowled. "This place is disgusting. I really don't want to think about what might live in that mattress."

"You lived here all the time you were gone, right?" she asked, crawling onto the large bed. When she settled, her cheek pressed against one of Ian's casual shirts on the pillow. She inhaled the familiar scent of freshly laundered cotton. It was nice, even nicer when he crawled into bed next to her and flipped the sheet over them.

"Yeah," he replied, laying down on his side and facing her.

"You never got bit by anything, did you?" she asked, smiling as her gaze ran over his face. Her heart seemed to swell in her breast. He was so beautiful to her.

"I might have. To be honest, I was so numb, I wouldn't have noticed."

"Are you going to grow a beard?" she asked, running her finger-tips over his jaw.

"I don't know." He noticed her quirked eyebrows. "I never really think about things like grooming or bedbugs while I'm here."

"You just thought about understanding Trevor Gaines better."

She swallowed thickly when his gaze flashed up to meet hers. She sensed his caution.

"What will you do with all the information you gather about him?" Francesca asked.

"I don't know," he mumbled, catching her stroking hand and planting a kiss in the center of her palm. She wasn't put off. She placed her hand back on his jaw. He glanced up at her, seeing the question remain in her eyes.

"I thought I could write it all down in some kind of organized way. Try to make sense of it all."

"You mean, like write a book?"

"Not really. Just a compilation of facts," he said, flipping onto his back and staring up at the canopy. She suspected she was making him uncomfortable, but sensed he wasn't fully retreating from her. She waited patiently. "Not anything to be published. Just for me. And for . . ." He shrugged.

"What?"

"For anyone else who wanted to read it," he rasped after a moment.

Her neck prickled with awareness. She propped herself up on her elbow, looking down at his face. "You mean like Trevor Gaines's other children?" she asked quietly.

His gaze flickered over her. "Yes. Like Kam and Lucien, or whoever might turn up. It might help us all. To understand . . . even if the picture is ugly. It would be complete. As complete as it can be anyway."

For a moment, neither of them spoke. A full feeling grew in her chest.

"I think it's a good idea," she said after a moment.

"You do?" He looked surprised.

She nodded, holding his stare. "Will you promise me one thing?"

"I'll try."

"That you'll do other things besides this? Work and spend time with your family and *live*."

His nostrils flared slightly. "Yes. All right."

She heaved a sigh of relief and placed her cheek on his chest. His arm curled around her and he ran his fingers through her hair.

"And I'm going to help you," she said, growing drowsy.

"Who says?"

"Me," she whispered, turning her face and kissing his chest. "This isn't just about you seeing Trevor Gaines more clearly so you can get him out of your system. It's about throwing some light into the darkness, taking away some of the power of the ugly things that hide out in there. Finding out what you can and writing it all down will help you to do that. I see that now. And I'm going to help you."

He grunted, but he didn't argue. He just continued to move his fingers in her hair until she fell into a deep, contented sleep.

She awoke some time later to the sound of the bedroom door opening, the sound secretive. Eerie. The room was pitch-black. Ian had turned out the bedside lamp after she'd fallen asleep. She had the impression she'd been asleep for hours.

"Ian," she whispered, running her hand over his chest, her neck prickling with anxiety. He stirred next to her, and panic took the place of her drowsy unease. Ian was definitely in bed next to her. So who had entered the room?

Suddenly the room was flooded with light from the overhead fixture. Francesca blinked in shock at what she saw. Gerard stood just inside the door wearing a dark overcoat and gloves. There was a leather briefcase hanging from his shoulder.

There was a gun in his hand.

"So sorry to interrupt your sleep," he said, smiling. He came closer to the bed, the weapon trained on Ian.

Chapter Seventeen

an rose slowly in the bed, his arms bracing his upper body.

"Ah ah," Gerard said, waving the gun in his direction. "Stay completely still, please. I'm afraid Mr. Lenault has sustained a serious head injury and is out cold. No one will help you if you try anything. I'm not afraid to use this on you, Ian. In fact," he paused, his smile widening. "It would be my pleasure."

"Gerard, what are you doing?" Francesca asked, still stunned at the vision of him in the bedroom at Aurore, and completely unable to compute the fact that he held a gun and had it pointed at Ian's head.

Gerard gave her a sympathetic glance. When his gaze traveled down over her bare shoulders and the tops of her breasts, however, she shrank back, gathering the sheet at her throat and turning her body in the direction of Ian.

"I actually came for you, Francesca. There was something I discovered completely by accident recently. It alarmed me, especially after what I told you this morning about my concerns for Ian's sanity," he said, setting the briefcase on a chair side table. He kept the gun pointed at Ian even as he withdrew a slim computer from the case and flipped open the lid.

"What are you talking about?" Ian growled. Francesca slowly realized that he was drawn tight as a drumhead next to her. She glanced into his face as he stared at Gerard, tracking his movement. More shivers than she'd ever experienced in her life cascaded down her entire body, making her shudder. Ian was looking at Gerard with the type of loathing reserved only for mortal enemies.

"Just this," Gerard said, tapping his finger on the keyboard, his gaze flickering back and forth rapidly between his task and monitoring Ian. "There's something Francesca should see. Something you deserve to see," he said pointedly to her.

"Gerard, are you crazy?" she asked. "Why do you have that gun?"

"He wants to kill us," Ian said levelly.

Another rush of shivers ran the length of her body.

"You don't know what I want, Ian," Gerard said, his mouth slanting, his voice going harsh. "I suppose you thought it was easy, to think of me like James probably does, to consider me like my father—the cheerful buffoon."

"I never even knew your father," Ian said. "But I can tell you firsthand, James never thought of you or your father as buffoons."

Gerard gave a sarcastic bark of laugher. "He certainly thought little enough of me, once you came along, that is. But James never knew me. You never knew what I wanted. Nobody does. That's the way I work."

"I suspected enough," Ian replied, his entire focus on Gerard as he approached the foot of the bed. "Maybe not always, but recently I have."

"You're lying," Gerard said dismissively. "Nobody plays a part better than me."

"I may have been hopeful that I was wrong about you, and I admittedly didn't predict *this*, but I knew something was amiss. I may have been worried that jealousy was clouding my judgment, but I recognize the stench of something foul around you."

For a moment, Gerard blanched at Ian's calm certainty, but then his face contorted with anger. His fury seemed to fortify him. "Always so smug. Always so sure of yourself, even when you were a freaky kid. If you're so damn smart, how come you couldn't figure me out years ago? You were as blind as Anne and James," Gerard spat. "James never even guessed the truth about his precious sister's death."

"Are you saying you had a part in your parents' death?" Ian asked.

Gerard just gave him a bland glance.

"If we were blind, it was because we loved you. I regret it," Ian said. Her heart squeezed in anguish at Ian's simple statement of fact.

"Oh please. Don't turn sentimental on me now," Gerard said scathingly. "You were duped, and have been forever. Might as well just admit it. But I'm not the only one doing the fooling, Ian. I knew I couldn't rest easy, thinking of Francesca being fooled by *you*. She may have concerns for your sanity, but I wasn't shocked that her misplaced feelings for you overruled her judgment when she took off in such a rush to meet you here. As soon as I discovered what you'd done to her, I knew I had to come and prove to her what you really are."

"What I'd *done* to her?" Ian asked, scowling.

"Your surveillance of her. I've heard her say how much she prizes her privacy. I knew you wouldn't like it," he said, turning his attention briefly to Francesca as he hit a button on the computer and turned it, so that Francesca could see the screen, "When you discovered how Ian has been videotaping you."

Her breast was pressed against Ian's arm, so she felt the muscle bunch and strain as an image leapt onto the screen. *It was her*. She watched numbly, half not believing what she was seeing. She lay naked on Ian's bed in the penthouse, her hand between her thighs, every muscle straining for relief. She looked wretched even in pleasure. A moment later she shook in release.

"No," Francesca murmured, the reality of what she was watching crashing down on her. Her horror only grew worse when her re-corded image turned on her side and crunched into a ball, her body shuddering as she wept. In a flash, she remembered the moment . . . how vulnerable she felt, how miserable and empty and hopeless about a present without Ian . . . the bleakness of a future without him. The idea of somebody watching her at such a moment was too much for her to bear. "*Stop it*," she told Gerard desperately. She sat up slightly in the bed, her glance sliding across Ian's profile.

He wasn't looking at the mortifying image of her on the screen. His eyes blazed as he stared at Gerard.

"I'll kill you for this," Ian said.

Gerard snarled and tapped a finger. Another image leapt onto the screen, this one of her masturbating while tears wet her cheeks, one hand filled with a breast, the other between her thighs, her face tight with anguish. Another, this one not at Ian's penthouse, but in her suite at Belford Hall.

Another . . . *no*, it couldn't be.

She saw the image of her face transformed by surrender and bliss as she told Ian she loved him. *Always.* It was the video he'd taken of her on the night before he'd discovered he was Trevor Gaines's child . . . on the night before he'd left her.

"*No,*" she ground out between clenched teeth, lunging toward the computer, her only thought to extinguish the image of herself at such a vulnerable moment. Ian sprung after her, halting her with a hand on her shoulder when Gerard started at her sudden movement. He shoved aside the computer, letting the lid drop, the illicit sounds of their recorded lovemaking continuing. Gerard stepped closer to where they now sat on the bed, the gun extended threateningly.

"I didn't want to show you, Francesca. But you had to see. I knew you'd want to know he's not that different from his father—that criminal, Trevor Gaines."

"How do you know about Gaines's past?" Francesca asked incredulously.

"He thinks he knows everything," Ian said quietly. "But he's wrong."

"I'm not wrong," Gerard bit out, his glassy eyes flashing in fury.

"I didn't take those videos of you, Francesca. Not most of them," Ian said, not looking at her, but at Gerard. "The one I did, but you knew that. I would never do that to you," he said steadily through a tense jaw.

"I know that."

The gun jerked slightly in the air at Francesca's words.

"What?" Gerard asked, stunned. "Don't tell me you believe him, just like that?"

"Of course I do," Francesca whispered, examining Gerard in rising horror. "Ian would never do that to me. He'd never record me without my permission. And Ian would never want to see me that miserable."

Ian glanced over at her rapidly. She saw the gratitude and relief in his blue eyes. Sadness and compassion flashed through her. He'd worried she'd believe Gerard.

"He was watching you masturbate, you fool. He was getting off on it, spying on you," Gerard bellowed.

"No. You were," Francesca spat. She couldn't stop the shivers of revulsion and horror from rippling through her body at the idea.

Gerard's face grew red and mottled. Her point-blank refusal to believe Ian was a pervert who was spying on her without her permission and using the footage for sexual titillation seemed to exponentially amplify his rage.

"God you're a fool. You deserve him," he said, his mouth twisting. He suddenly shrugged. "I was going to have to kill you anyway, so what does it matter?"

"Then why did you even show it to me?" Francesca asked bitterly.

"Because it would have been all that much sweeter for him to see you betrayed by me before he killed us both. He couldn't let you live. He knows I've left you everything if I die."

"You did?" Francesca asked numbly. Everything seemed surreal. *Is this how it felt when you realized you were about to die?* She thought she'd be more panicked.

Ian nodded. "With Grandfather as the follow-up. But that works just fine for Gerard, because he's Grandfather's heir after my grandmother, if I die. All he has to do is wait, and he's proven he can be patient. What did you do to Lucien?" Ian switched topics seamlessly. "Is he dead?"

"No, but he will be. I hit him hard enough on the back of the head to fell a horse. When the fire starts later, he'll never wake up in time to get out."

Francesca made a choked sound. Why was Ian behaving so calmly? It was eerie to see, in these circumstances.

"You plan to . . . what, make it look as if I finally went over the edge, and shot Francesca and then myself before bringing this place down." He glanced coldly at the dusty, ancient canopy. His calm manner completely bewildered her, adding a touch of the surreal to unfolding events. "Not a bad idea. I thought of burning the place down a half a dozen times. It'll go up like a matchstick."

"My thoughts exactly," Gerard said levelly. "I brought along some fuel. It's precisely the type of thing a madman would plan."

"True," Ian said. "And I suppose you engineered some kind of alibi, just in case suspicion fell on you?"

"Of course," Gerard replied. "But it won't. Everyone at Belford has expressed concern for your mental stability. Even she," he waved the gun at Francesca. "Had her doubts."

"There's only one problem," Ian said.

Gerard looked both amused and insulted. "There's no problem," Gerard assured.

"There is, unfortunately. His name is Edward Shallon. He's the man I hired to tail your every move. He called me earlier when you flew into Paris, where he followed you."

Gerard's expression sagged. "You're lying," he said numbly.

"I'm not. Unfortunately, he lost you in traffic. I didn't realize you knew about Aurore or Trevor Gaines, or I would have expected you here. As things were, I assumed you were in Paris on business." He glanced at the computer at the foot of the bed. "Obviously, your surveillance equipment was in my room at Belford as well. You figured out my password on my computer. That's how you got the information about Gaines. I had file upon file of information I'd compiled so far saved on it. And the video of Francesca, which you added to your surveillance tapes in order to convince her I was as sick as Gaines. Or you, as the truth would have it."

Francesca glanced nervously at Ian when he said the last, hearing the cold fury in his tone.

"But Shallon definitely trailed you to Paris. He'll be able to testify to that. Do you have an alibi in Paris?" Ian persisted. "It's my understanding you left Clarisse in Stratham."

"Clarisse?" Francesca mumbled, confused by the reference.

The color drained from Gerard's face. He swallowed thickly, his expression nowhere near as confident as it'd been. Hope flickered through Francesca, but then his face darkened again with rage. She'd always thought him handsome, but he looked truly revolting in that moment. A wild thought struck her that his hatred for Ian had been brewing for a long, long time. How had he possibly disguised it so well?

"It doesn't matter," Gerard said. "I'll figure something out. It's too late to turn back now. I'd continue at this point, only for the pleasure of finally getting rid of you. Bloody nuisance." He raised the gun. Francesca started at what she saw behind Gerard, but Ian tightened his hold on her shoulder, sending a desperate, silent command for silence. It felt like her own heart was going to choke her, it seemed to swell to take up her entire chest cavity.

"One other thing," Ian said as Gerard took aim at Ian's head, and Francesca's lungs burned in gripping terror.

"What?" Gerard asked derisively, clearly done talking.

"You may have disabled Lucien, but I have more than one brother."

Gerard's vaguely puzzled glance turned to wide-eyed shock when Kam Reardon jerked his head back in a chokehold at the same moment that he wrenched the arm that held the gun, pointing it away from Ian and Francesca. Ian leapt from the bed so fast it was like he'd been ejected from a coiled spring. She followed him instinctively, unwilling to just sit there in bed, stunned. Ian rushed the struggling pair, but Gerard wasn't defeated yet. He jabbed his elbow into Kam's solar plexus hard and threw his head back viciously. The two men were close in height, Kam being a few inches taller. The back of Gerard's head smashed into his face, jarring him. Kam grunted and stumbled back, dazed, losing his hold, crimson blood shooting from his nose. Ian plowed into Gerard, reaching for Gerard's gun arm to restrain it. But Gerard had already been lifting it to an upward angle. They grunted as they vied for control.

The gun went off. Ian and Gerard stood as if frozen in some kind of bizarre dance. She stood there next to them, horrified. She gave a muffled scream when the gun fell from Gerard's hand and he fell to his knees. Ian backed away slightly and she saw the small circle of blood on Gerard's white shirt in the area of his abdomen. He wore a blank expression, his brown eyes wide. Ian ducked to retrieve the weapon, but Gerard was closer to it.

She saw it as if in slow motion. Fortified by years of hatred and a desire for revenge, Gerard must have had one last surge of adrenaline in him. Gerard whipped the gun away before Ian could grab it, grunting in pain. He jerked the weapon wildly in Ian's direction, but he paused for what must have been the smallest fraction of a second. A malicious glint fired in Gerard's face as he met Ian's stare.

Gerard swung the gun in Francesca's direction.

The sound of the gun going off seemed to rattle the entire room. She hit the floor so hard, her breath was knocked out of her. She didn't know what had happened. She was lying on the floor, the gunshot still ringing in her ears. Her lungs wouldn't expand. Her brain vibrated in shock. Was she shot? Was that why she felt so weighted down and unable to move?

She lifted her head, completely disoriented. Ian lay on top of her. She inhaled raggedly, her body starved for oxygen. He'd thrown himself in front of her. It'd been him that forced her down onto the floor. She was covered by his body. He lay facedown, his head next to hers, his face in the crook of her neck and shoulder.

"Ian?" she shouted. She ran her hands over him frantically. He lifted his head. She heard scuffling where Gerard had been and lifted her head as well, tensing in panic. She saw Kam leaning over Gerard's motionless body. Relief swept through her.

"Ian? Are you okay?" she asked in a shaky voice.

He met her stare calmly, only his head moving, and nodded.

"Is he dead?" Ian asked Kam.

"No. Not yet anyway," Kam added indifferently.

Kam stepped over Gerard. Using the bottom of his long coat, he flipped the lock on the gun and pried it out of Gerard's loosening grip. Over Ian's shoulder, she saw him set the weapon on the dresser, far from Gerard's reach. She gasped for air, her lungs still having trouble expanding.

"Ian . . . I can't breathe. Can you . . . can you . . ."

He rolled off her. With his weight off her, she inhaled with effort. Her relief and getting her lungs full of air lasted for as long as it took her to notice the blood on her right hand.

She sat up and stared in rising horror at Ian, who lay on his back, blinking as he stared up at the ceiling.

"He's been shot," Francesca said shrilly, scrambling up on her hands and knees and kneeling next to his body. "Call someone," she said to Kam, pointing at Ian's cell phone, which sat on a dresser not far from the gun. "Call emergency services."

Kam lunged toward the dresser and snagged the phone. He walked over to her and handed her the phone. "You call. Dial 1-1-2," he said roughly. He knelt on the other side of Ian. "I'm going to have to roll you on your side to have a look," he said to Ian.

"Do you have a doctor's license?" Ian asked sardonically, wincing slightly when Kam rolled him onto his left side. Francesca grimaced sympathetically as she dialed the phone.

"No," Kam rasped. "But I graduated from medical school. Unfortunately for you, I never finished my residency."

Ian gave a dry bark of laughter. Francesca had the strangest feeling Kam was serious, but she was too numb with shock to be surprised. Kam bent, examining the wound. The phone began ringing.

"What are you doing?" she asked anxiously when Kam stood and walked to the bathroom. He returned a second later with several folded towels. "Applying pressure to the wound." He knelt again behind Ian, who was still conscious. Her eyes widened in panic when a woman answered the phone in French. She'd never mastered the language. Kam's sharp gaze flickered to Francesca's face. He grabbed the phone. He began to speak in rapid French, holding the towel tightly against Ian's shoulder all the while.

A moment later, she jerked her gaze from Ian's when Kam brushed her arm with a towel. She looked up. She realized he was off the phone.

"They're coming," Kam said. She glanced at the towel he was handing her in confusion, and for the first time in several moments realized she was nude. Her cheeks heated with embarrassment as she whipped the towel Kam offered around her, covering herself. She noticed Ian's slightly raised brows and amused expression when she looked up again. Kam Reardon was clearly much, much more than the local wild man.

"Kam?" Ian muttered. "Maybe you should go and check on Lucien. He's just down the hall, third door on the left."

Kam nodded. He looked at Francesca. "You'll have to apply the pressure," he said, looking down at the towel pressed to Ian's shoulder.

She nodded willingly, replacing Kam's hand with hers. He rose and left the room.

"Francesca," Ian said intently. "Listen to me. Erase the video from the computer and put the computer back in Gerard's briefcase. *Now.*"

"What?" she asked, confused.

"Use something to cover your fingerprints and erase the files of Gerard's surveillance on the computer."

"But . . . won't the police protest about me altering evidence at a crime scene? What about if Gerard lives? What if he goes on trial for attempted murder?"

His nostrils flared and his eyes flashed. "I don't *care* what the hell the police think. Do you want other people seeing that video? A courtroom? It would kill you, and so it would kill me in turn. If the truth comes out that the tapes were erased, *I'll* take the blame."

A shudder went through her as the full impact of what he was saying hit. She nodded dazedly. "But I'm supposed to press on the wound."

"I'll do it while you're gone," he muttered, moving his left hand on top of hers, wincing at the movement. "Go on."

She returned a minute later, having followed his instructions as best she could. They'd just have to deal with it if Gerard had other copies of the video somewhere and they came to light in the investigation.

"Now get dressed," he said, his rigid jaw making her think he was in increasing pain.

She lowered next to him after she'd hastily dressed, taking over pressing on the wound and using the towel she'd discarded to cover him. She was glad to see the circle of blood on the towel on his shoulder hadn't grown much in her absence. "It's going to be okay. You're going to be all right."

"I know," he said.

She stifled a bark of hysterical laughter. Arrogant even now. "*How* do you know?"

"Because I didn't go through all this, only to die now," he said dryly. "It's just the shoulder," he said, wincing as he moved slightly. "It burns like hell."

"Keep still," she scolded. She lowered her head, kissing his lips softly. Fervently. She raised her head until their faces were only inches apart.

"Do you want to know who you are, Ian?" she said, her voice vibrating with emotion. "This is who you are. *This.*"

His eyes glittered as their gazes locked. He didn't speak, but she knew he'd understood. It might have been his last act on this earth, for all he'd known, covering her body with his to protect her, an act of selflessness.

Of love.

Francesca swam in a woozy dream world, aware of several people talking. Her exhaustion was such that she had to struggle for all she was worth to surface into consciousness.

It's important. Wake up.

She blinked open her eyes at her own voice in her head. It took her a second to recall where she was—in the hospital in Cabourg where the ambulances had taken Ian, Lucien, and Gerard after they'd arrived on the scene. The images and horror of what had occurred—the blood seeping from Ian's wound, the arrival of the emergency personnel, being questioned by police at the hospital while she was so distracted, worrying about Ian and Lucien. Ian had lost consciousness while they'd been in the ambulance on the way to the hospital, amplifying her anxiety and fear. She'd worried he was wounded more severely than his manner led her to believe just following the shooting. He stabilized quickly once at the hospital, however, and was soon declared ready for surgery to extract the bullet in his shoulder.

It was now the second morning after the whole bizarre nightmare.

Ian was recovering well following surgery. Lucien was fine, and was discharged from the hospital last evening soon after Elise had arrived. Gerard, on the other hand, had not yet regained consciousness. The doctors had been struggling to stabilize him before attempting surgery, but his condition was severe. The bullet had entered his abdomen, causing a great deal of internal organ damage and bleeding, but the trajectory had been upward, hitting one of his lungs as well.

The nurse last night had taken pity on Francesca when she saw her slumped in an upright chair near Ian's bed. She'd refused to leave his side, despite Anne and James's arrival and insistence she should check in to a hotel and get a few hours sleep. The nurse had encouraged Francesca to sleep in the extra bed in Ian's room at around three-thirty in the morning. Once Ian had awakened following his surgery and conversed with her a little, she'd been better prepared to rest. She'd staggered over to the empty bed and fallen into an exhausted, dreamless sleep.

"No, of course I understand," she heard Ian saying as she pushed herself off the mattress. She was heartened to hear that his voice sounded strong and rested, if concerned. "You needn't have asked my permission. Of course you should go."

"You're sure?" Anne asked quietly.

"Because we won't, if you don't want it. After what Gerard did, I'd understand completely," James said. Sadness swept through Francesca at hearing the weight in James's voice. He'd been hurt the most by Gerard's blatant treachery.

"I'm not the judge of whether or not Gerard should die alone," Ian said. "Go. Sit with him. He's family."

"My sister's son—" James broke off. Someone made a choking sound. Francesca walked around the curtain and saw James with his face in his hand, obviously undone. Her heart seized in anguish at the sight. Anne gave her a helpless glance. Francesca couldn't think of what to say. Anne took her husband's hand and led him from the room.

Francesca walked next to Ian's bed. He looked at her bleakly from where he lay propped up in the hospital bed in order to take pressure off the surgical site. She touched his hairline and dropped a kiss on his temple, inhaling his scent greedily for reassurance. She was relieved to see his coloring was better than it'd been last night, when he was still groggy from the anesthesia.

"Gerard isn't expected to last much longer," he said. "My grand-parents were asking permission to sit with him until the end."

She closed her eyes. It'd been what she expected to hear, but she hated to think of James and Anne's suffering. They'd already dealt with so much in their lives. The betrayal of Gerard, whom they considered as almost a son, seemed too cruel to consider.

"Are you feeling all right?" Ian asked her, his gaze moving over her face.

She smoothed her hair and nodded. "Yes. I was out cold for a few hours. How about you? How does the shoulder feel?"

"Okay. They're giving me something for the pain," he said, taking her hand. "Sit down," he directed. She came down at the edge of the bed, her hip brushing against his. She studied every detail of his features hungrily . . . worriedly. His lips tilted in amusement.

"You don't have to look at me like I'm a tragic poster child, Francesca. I'll be fine," Ian told her pointedly.

"I know. I know you'll be fine physically," she assured both him and herself. "I'm just worried about the effect of what Gerard did."

"On my fragile psyche, you mean?" he asked, his small grin widening slightly.

She gave him a repressive look. "You have to admit, you've been through an awful lot lately. Is it a surprise I'm worried about your finding out someone you loved—a part of your family—betrayed you?"

She brushed her fingertips across his mouth when it hardened, lowering her caress to his whiskered jaw. "I suppose not," he murmured. "But you shouldn't worry. It's different than my mother and the discovery of Trevor Gaines."

"How?"

He shook his head. "It's hard to explain. It doesn't feel as . . . personal. It was a shock, and I'm stunned that he hated me so much and I never realized. Gerard's desire for revenge seems sadder than anything," he muttered under his breath. "I'd feel bad for him if he hadn't pissed me off to no end for what he did to you, recording you that way."

"Surely his bigger crime was trying to kill us," Francesca pointed out.

"I have a feeling we were just the tip of the iceberg," Ian said, frowning. "I was always vaguely aware of the fact that he held back some resentment for my showing up and stealing his spotlight with Grandmother and Grandfather—both in the emotional and financial sense. I was also aware, though, that he contained his envy. I assumed it was because he knew that logically it was misplaced. He spent time with me, showed me affection, helped to bring me out of my shell. I thought it was his way of dealing with the altered circumstances my arrival brought. I appreciated him all the more for it. I never felt the same feelings of jealousy toward him, so I never guessed the depth of his hatred—or *why* he was trying to control his fury."

Francesca nodded, stroking his forearm. "You were also so blasé at the idea of Gerard carrying on the title. He obviously didn't have the same equanimity about your receiving James's inheritance."

"Obviously," Ian said dryly. "I was a grubby little orphan. Why would I feel resentment about not receiving a title? I didn't even understand what a title *was*." His expression darkened. "It'll die now, with Grandfather."

She started. "What will?"

"The title of Earl of Stratham."

"Poor James," Francesca whispered.

He squeezed her hand. Her gaze flickered to his face and was caught by his gleaming blue eyes.

"Will you marry me, Francesca?"

For a few seconds, she just stared, his deep, rough voice uttering the unexpected question echoing in her head.

"Before you answer, I should tell you that I mean right now. Here, in the hospital," he continued. "We'll be able to get all the blood tests done here, and I've already spoken to the chaplain while you were sleeping."

"Why *now*?" she asked, shock ringing in her voice, and she thought he understood she didn't just mean why was he asking her to marry him while he lay there in the hospital, wounded, but what had changed his mind about being with her . . . about him feeling worthy of marriage.

He shrugged, wincing slightly, forgetting his injury. "I guess I don't have any better answer except to say that after that night at Aurore, I feel different. I might have lost you."

Her throat tightened. "And I might have lost you."

"Life is fragile. But it's more than that," he said, his eyes shining as he looked at her face. "For the first time, I feel that I can beat this. I still want to understand my beginnings better. I still want to understand as much as I can, period. But there's light in all the darkness Trevor Gaines wrought. There's Lucien and Kam and who knows how many others, all of us struggling to make a life for ourselves, a good life."

She nodded, emotion filling her chest. "And there's you."

He kissed her hand slowly. Deliberately. "The last thing I wanted was for you to come to Aurore. But once you were there, I realized it was exactly what I needed. I thought the darkness could take you as well as me," he said, his voice gruff with emotion. "I should have known nothing could dim your brilliance."

"Ian," she whispered, through a throat that felt like she'd swallowed gravel. Her heart squeezed tight when she saw the trace of anxiety flicker in his eyes and she realized he waited. "The answer is the same as it was before and will always be. *Yes.*"

Epilogue

an, Francesca, Anne, and James stood in a half arc, watching expectantly as two of the Belford staff hung the painting above the fireplace.

"Straight?" one of the young men asked.

"Perfect," Anne said, her smile radiant. The two men lowered from their prospective ladders and gathered up their equipment.

"Thank you," James said, and the two painting-hangers turned to vacate the sitting room.

For a moment, the four of them just looked silently at the painting of Belford. Francesca glanced sideways at James's and Anne's beaming faces and a wave of happiness went through her. She was particularly proud of the finished product, but she was so thankful James and Anne loved it. Ian noticed how she looked at his grandparents and took her hand in his. She brought his hand in front of her, running her free hand over his knuckles with her fingers. When she brushed his platinum wedding band, a tiny smile flickered across his mouth at her silent gesture.

Her eyes burned with tears. She'd grown extremely emotional lately.

"It's perfect," Ian said, his eyes warm, as if he'd understood the strong feeling of love and joy that had swept through her at that moment.

"Absolutely," James concurred.

"It's so much better than I'd ever hoped for," Anne sighed. "You were so right to paint it as if coming out of the blossoming woods. Belford looks like . . ."

"The warm, beautiful home that it is," Francesca murmured.

"*Your* home," Anne said, her glance bouncing between Ian and her. Francesca and Ian's gazes met again briefly. Now that they were married, they'd agreed to spend their future summers at Belford Hall. This year, however, Francesca had spent the entire spring at Belford, painting the beautiful old home every day without fail. She'd fallen completely in love with the place, seeing it bedecked in all its spring glory. She hated being apart from Ian, even if they did see each other for long weekends and spoke on the phone or video-conferenced several times a day. They'd decided the arrangement was best, however. Francesca wanted to get the painting done and return to Chicago with Ian for good. Ian didn't want them to be parted at all period, but given that her reasoning for them being apart temporarily was for his grandparents, and only for the duration of six weeks, he'd reluctantly agreed to the plan. He came every Thursday and left on Sunday nights. She was glad they'd done it. James appeared to be the most affected of all of them by Gerard's betrayal and death six months ago. He seemed frailer as of late. Francesca knew the time with Anne and James at Belford this spring was precious, something to be treasured.

Ian had just arrived this evening for the hanging of the finished painting. He'd been gone for an extra day this time, having spent some time at Aurore with Lucien visiting Kam before he'd arrived at Belford. She'd missed him like sin. Their parting last week had been especially painful, given the unique circumstances. She couldn't seem to get her fill of looking at him, and he hadn't stopped touching some part of her since the first moment he arrived.

"Let's have a drink to toast the painting that piece of wall has been waiting for forever!" James said, his jovial manner elevating Francesca's good mood even further. He almost seemed like his old self tonight.

The French doors in the sitting room had been thrown open to a mild spring night. It was very pleasant, sitting and chatting with Anne and James with her side pressed tightly against Ian, his arm around her, sipping a lemonade while the sweet smell of honeysuckle wafted in from the garden on the light breeze.

"I can't believe how bright that young man is," James said pointedly to Ian after Ian had described some of his visit with Kam at Aurore.

"Absolutely," Anne concurred. "As brilliant as Lucien and you, in his own right. Does Kam still live in that underground . . . *place*?" Anne asked delicately, obviously unsure what to call Kam's subterranean workshop/residence. Anne and James had met Kam while Ian had been in the hospital in France after Gerard had shot him. Kam had looked distinctly uncomfortable when the elderly couple showered him with their gratitude for saving Ian and Francesca's life. Later, when Ian and Francesca had been married with Anne, James, Lucien, and Elise gathered around them, Kam had mumbled that there wasn't enough room for him, and insisted upon watching the simple ceremony from the doorway. Francesca had grown quite a fond spot for the terse, brilliant man, and she knew Ian felt the same way.

"No. He's moved into Aurore. Francesca and I have given it to him."

James blinked. "That's generous."

"Not really," Ian said mildly. "Trevor Gaines left it to him originally."

"It's so odd that Gaines showed any favor to one of the children he sired, isn't it? When he had no interest in any of the others?" Anne asked, frowning in disapproval as she considered Gaines.

Ian shrugged. "His interest in Kam appears to have been totally practical, although it might have grown into a fondness. Kam disagrees with me on that, but if you ask me, his actions toward Kam are one of the few indications he was a human being versus a monster. Kam lived on the property from the day he was born—his mother was a laundress and maid. When Gaines understood how brilliant Kam was, he hired him on as a kind of helper in his workshop. He eventually formed some sort of attachment to him, although Kam is very pragmatic, and scorns the idea of it being anything remotely similar to fatherly love. Kam was a bright kid, though, in more ways than one. He knew how to get what he wanted out of Gaines. He got Gaines to agree to send him to school in exchange for working for him. And Gaines did, surprisingly enough, even sending him both to college and then to medical school. Kam never finished his cardiology residency, though, and returned to Aurore when his mother became ill."

"What a fascinating story Kam has," Anne said, shaking her head in amazement. "I've never met anyone like him, and I've met my fair share of singular men," she added with a droll glance at Ian and James.

"Given his medical background and experience with Gaines, it's no wonder he's come up with all the brilliant technology he has," Francesca said. "Did Ian tell you he's sold his biotech patents for millions of dollars to a pharmaceutical company? They're going to make these revolutionary medical watches with his invention. The watches do everything from sending off a warning for an impending heart attack to tell a woman when the prime time is to get pregnant, and dozens of other valuable things besides. It's a biofeedback mechanism, so the wearer will constantly be educated as to their responses to the external world."

"Kam took what Trevor Gaines had started with his perverse obsessions and twisted greed and turned it into something that can really make a positive difference," Ian said, referring to not only Gaines's mechanical genius, but the fact that he had been obsessed with the "clockwork" type cycles of a woman's body in order to impregnate his victims. Kam had told Ian and Francesca that Gaines was interested in finding ways to measure and predict human biology, and had started to experiment casually. But it was Kam who had seen the far-reaching potential and furthered the work in a meaningful, groundbreaking way.

Ian glanced sideways at Francesca when she placed her hand on his thigh. A deep, profound sense of gratitude went through her at the growing peace in his voice when he spoke of his biological father. He was still appalled by who Gaines was as a man, but he understood him better objectively. Ian had been right all along, Francesca now admitted freely. Something about gathering information on Gaines, understanding his past and his surroundings and his work habits and his obsession—it had helped Ian get the distance he needed from his biological father. After speaking with Kam in detail about his shared past with Gaines, in addition to discovering some journals that had belonged both to Gaines's mother and Trevor himself, Ian had begun to suspect that Gaines had been abused as a young man by his new stepfather, Alfred Aurore. Gaines had despised Aurore, but the true target of his hatred was his mother, who had put him in harm's way and then done nothing to protect him. This, despite the fact that Gaines insinuated in his journals she knew the truth of what her new husband was doing to her son. That had, perhaps, been at the core of Gaines's hatred of women and his desire to force himself both into their bodies and their very existences, with a child. No woman's life could fail to be altered by a child, even if Trevor's mother had endeavored to deny that truth with her own son.

Ian freely admitted he'd probably never see the full, complex picture of Gaines, but even the more substantial outline of the man's motivations and life seemed to calm him.

She thought the bulk of Gaines's poisonous legacy had been miraculously extracted that night when she'd arrived at Aurore, and Ian had risked death for her. Some things were bigger even than a sociopathic parent, and that night had taught Ian what was really at the core of him. Ian had agreed to further his healing, meeting with a support group occasionally made up of other children of rape, trying to understand his shame and come to terms with it.

A small smile flickered across Ian's mouth as he studied Francesca presently, as if he had sensed her thankfulness as she looked up at him.

"I would never have thought anything good could come from the legacy of a man like Trevor Gaines, but it seems I learn about new things every day. Thanks to you," he continued more quietly, speaking to Francesca. "I can see and appreciate that now."

"If it weren't for your searching, you would have never been able to find the treasures that you have," she replied softly.

She became so lost in his eyes, it took her a moment to absorb Anne's brisk voice.

"Well, it's off to bed for me," Anne said brightly, giving James a significant look. James immediately set down his brandy glass.

"Oh no. I . . . We didn't mean to run you off," Francesca said contritely, realizing she'd been staring at Ian, entranced, making the couple feel awkward, no doubt. She felt an almost magical connection with her husband in those moments, a bond forged by the trials they'd faced in order to be together and the rich promise of the future. She couldn't wait to spend time with him alone, but there were still several important things they needed to talk to Anne and James about at the moment.

"Ian wants to speak with you both about what the police in London and Detective Markov told him about Gerard," Francesca reminded them.

She regretted bringing up such a heavy topic when she saw Anne's and James's expressions grow solemn, but at the same time, it was important news. Ian had already told her everything on the phone before he'd arrived, and they'd processed it together. She was glad he was the one who was going to first break the news to Anne and James, not the police. It was the elderly couple who had been most devastated by learning of Gerard's true nature and his subsequent death in the hospital the day after he'd been shot, after all.

In the hospital, Ian and she had agreed not to tell Anne and James about the fact that Gerard had hinted he'd had a hand in his mother and father's death. They had no solid proof, and the suspicions would just pain James even more than the clear-cut knowledge of his nephew's true nature. He'd adored his sister, and Gerard's father had been a lifetime friend.

"What have you found out?" James asked Ian.

"The Metropolitan police recently had a huge shakedown amongst their ranks. There were dozens of detectives and policemen who were charged with colluding in drugs and arms trafficking."

"I read about it in the paper," James said.

"One of the detectives arrested was a man by the name of Jago Teague," Ian explained. He scowled slightly. "Teague sounds like a real piece of work. He's dealt in the underground drug trade and sold arms illegally for years now. In his other life, he was a decorated detective and upholder of the law."

"What's Teague got to do with Gerard?" Anne asked.

"Teague agreed to give names of various people he's given illegal services to over the years in exchange for a lighter sentence. One of the names he gave as being a high-profile customer was Gerard's. After they'd taken down his confession, someone at the Metropolitan Police called Detective Markov here in Stratham and filled him in."

Francesca studied Anne's and James's faces anxiously in the heavy silence that followed. "Teague confessed to selling an unmarked gun to Gerard six months ago and buying the gun back from him two nights later. Upon Gerard's specific instructions, he then sold the gun again to a man that fit the description of Anton Brodsik. Gerard sent Brodsik to Teague," Ian said grimly. "It was a set up. He put the gun that killed Shell Stern into Brodsik's hands. He set up Brodsik to look like Stern's murderer, and then killed Brodsik with Grandfather's gun."

"I don't understand," said Anne, shaking her head. "Why did Gerard orchestrate all these things with Brodsik and Stern if he planned to kill you and Francesca himself and make it look like a murder-suicide?"

"I'm guessing he had no choice but to hire Brodsik and Stern in Chicago. Once he had, he needed to get rid of them. They knew too much, and could either blackmail him or implicate him if suspicion was ever cast on Gerard."

"Then why hire them in the first place?" James asked.

"To bring Ian out of hiding," Francesca said quietly. "Ian thinks Gerard tried to acquire Ian's company in a hostile takeover with his original plan for the Tyake acquisition. Ian has discovered that Gerard is the anonymous primary owner of the acquisition loan company he proposed that we use. *He* would have become the primary holder of Noble Enterprise shares if Noble defaulted on payment in even the smallest way—something Gerard could have easily manipulated to happen if he was left in any position of power on the board."

James's expression went flat. "But . . . Anne and I have used that loan company before."

"I know," Ian said. "And fortunately, Gerard never used his influence in your case unduly. I get the impression he was very methodical and very patient in the way he set up his chess game, getting all the circumstances and players just right. And it was never you he wanted revenge upon, Grandfather. It was me."

"All because of James's properties and money?" Anne asked, looking both stunned and outraged at once. "I can't believe it. And to think, we had no idea he was so affected by your arrival when you were a child, Ian."

"It changed the outline of his life, my showing up here one day out of nowhere. It's disappointing, and it's very upsetting, what Gerard did," Ian said quietly. "But it's not outside the realm of believability."

James sighed, and again Francesca's heart ached for him. "We've never mentioned it, but Gerard did frequently wonder about your mental stability in our presence. I suppose it was all part of his manipulation to make us think it was possible you could take your own and Francesca's life. We were concerned for you, but we never doubted your sanity, Ian. We knew your torment was of the emotional variety."

Ian stroked the back of Francesca's hand. She turned over her palm and squeezed him for comfort. "It was a hard time for me. And I suppose people really have gone over the edge from less. There were times in the months when I was at Aurore, before I returned to Belford, that I could almost agree with Gerard's insinuations. I'm not surprised you were worried," he told his Grandfather sincerely before he exhaled. "At any rate, once Gerard learned what I was doing in my absence, and understood who Trevor Gaines was, he must have been ecstatic to be provided with such an ideal setting for my downfall. I was at the desolate country manor of a condemned criminal and obsessed madman. The perfect place for Trevor Gaines's son from rape to finally tip over the edge."

"I can't believe these thoughts ever went through his mind," Anne said numbly. "I can't believe *that*, let alone that he'd *act* on them. He shot that man Brodsik in cold blood, right in this house?"

Ian nodded. "I suspect he invited him here, although we'll probably never know the exact circumstances."

"It's positively diabolical," James said. His face looked gray. Francesca looked at Ian anxiously.

"It's over," Ian said firmly. "It's all over, and we're safe. I only wanted to tell you because Markov also wanted to pass the news on to you. The murder occurred in your home, after all, and he owes you an explanation about the resolution of the investigation. I told him I would break the news first."

James inhaled slowly. "And I appreciate it, son."

"Are you all right?" Francesca asked James softly after a moment.

James seemed to try and rally, but she saw his struggle to do so. He grabbed Anne's hand. "I'll be better, to be honest, after a good night's sleep," he said with false cheerfulness. "I'd like nothing better than to leave all this in the past."

"I agree," Anne said. "Especially on such a beautiful night when we've just put up Francesca's painting and have so much to be thankful for."

"We *do* have so much to be thankful for."

Anne blinked, her gaze sharpening on Francesca when she spoke so fervently. Francesca smiled, knowing her secret was undisguised in her eyes, and that Anne, who was no fool, was reading it. An uncanny expression flickered across Anne's face. Francesca exchanged a meaningful look with Ian. It'd felt like a miracle, to be able to share such a precious gift with him, but to share it with Anne and James felt wonderful as well.

"We have more news," Ian said. "Much, much nicer news."

"No . . ." Anne whispered. "*Yes?*" she asked hopefully when Francesca just continued to beam at her.

"What? What's going on?" James asked dubiously.

"Ian and Francesca are going to have a baby?" Anne asked tremulously, hope and incredulity twining in her voice.

Ian pulled Francesca close and she hugged him in turn, pressing her cheek to his chest while still looking at Anne and James.

"Yes, we're going to have a baby," Ian said, his deep voice gruff.

"Francesca is always telling me I need to think about the future, not the past. Now it's all I think of."

James gave a bark of exultant laughter, all of his weariness over the talk of Gerard vanishing, twenty years seeming to melt off his visage in an instant. Anne gave an adorable little whoop of joy and took an unladylike gulp of her brandy, her eyes shining with happiness as she hugged her husband.

Francesca put her hand on Ian's chest, silently absorbing his warmth and the steady, strong beat of his heart, and basked in the moment.

Anne and James celebrated with them for a while and asked all the usual questions: How far along was she? Eight weeks. How long had she known she was pregnant? Since last weekend; Ian and she had gone together to a doctor in Belford. Where would the baby be born? At Belford, if it was all right with Anne and James. (It was beyond all right of course. The couple was ecstatic at the idea.) Ian and she had liked the doctor at the hospital in Belford very much, but they'd also guessed at Anne and James's reaction to the plan. They'd agreed they wanted to give their grandparents that gift.

After their joyous impromptu celebration, Anne and James said good night and gave them one last congratulatory hug before leaving them alone in the sitting room.

"Happy?" Ian asked her quietly, his gaze running over her face.

"What do you think?" she asked, grinning.

"I think you look like a thousand suns in my eyes. I've never seen you so radiant."

Her smiled faded. No matter how many times she experienced his sudden, sober intensity, it never ceased to leave her breathless.

"When I was looking at your painting," he said thoughtfully, "I realized how nice it would have been to have been married here, in the springtime. Do you think I was selfish, insisting we marry while

I was still in the hospital? It wasn't the most romantic of settings. I only know that suddenly, I couldn't wait."

"I know," she, touching his chest, holding his solemn gaze. "That's what made it so special . . . your having the faith to take a leap into the future. I wouldn't have had it any other way. But if it would make you happy, we can renew our vows here anytime. Every spring, if you like," she said, smiling.

He stood, her hand still in his. "Come with me," he said.

They walked together out through the screen doors onto the small stone terrace. It was a resplendent June night. The distant forest seemed to clamor with fertile life—tree frogs croaked, grasshoppers chirped, and a breeze rustled the tops of lush trees, making a soft sound like a sigh. She breathed the scent of freshly mown, dew-wet grass and honeysuckle as she followed Ian off the terrace into the yard. They walked without speaking. Ian paused after a moment. There was enough moon and starlight for her to make out a sitting area, one she hadn't discovered as of yet, hidden behind a thicket of rosebushes. When Ian sat in one of the wooden recliners, she made for the one next to it, but he pulled her toward him.

"Come here," he said. "You can't think I'd let you sit over there when I haven't seen you in days."

"Of course not," she said drolly, laughing. She started to sit in his lap, her back to his front, but he stopped her.

"No, face me," he murmured. "And lift your dress."

Her laughter faded and her sex clenched at his taut demand. She'd heard the need ringing in his voice and it ignited her own. She lifted the hem of her sundress to her waist, saying nothing when he put one hand on her hip and the other on her bare belly. They both watched him touch her in the moonlight, his masculine hands looking dark next to her pale skin. He moved, caressing and stroking, his hands seeming to spin a sensual spell over her. She felt her sex dampen and the familiar, sweet ache swell inside her.

"I still can't believe it," he murmured, caressing her belly.

"I expect it'll take both of us some time to get accustomed to the idea that a baby is growing in there."

"I don't mean the baby. I mean . . . I do. But I didn't mean *just* that. I meant I still can't believe you're mine. Most of the day I do, but at moments like this it seems so . . . incredible." She saw the gleam in his eyes when he looked up at her. She palmed his jaw tenderly. Their gazes held as he lowered her panties. His fingers moved deftly in her outer sex. He grunted softly when he found her damp. "Thank you for not giving up on me. Not in the beginning, when I didn't understand what was happening between us because I had no yardstick to compare it to. Not when I left you. Not even when I came back, and still felt I couldn't offer you what you deserve."

She sighed as he stimulated her clit and pushed a finger into her slit. It felt sublime. "You didn't give up on me, either. I thought you had, but you hadn't. You knew better than me what was required to make you feel whole."

"What I need is you," he said, a steely thread of urgency entering his tone. He removed his hand and she saw the glimmer of his belt buckle as he unfastened his pants. In a matter of seconds, she was sitting in his lap facing him, his cock embedded in her flesh. For several moments, they just sat motionless in the moonlight, touching each other's face and neck and arms, fused.

"It seems impossible," Ian said in a strained voice, "that I lived all those months without you. Even when I'm away from you for days, I start to feel like I can't breathe. I honestly don't know how I did it before."

"Some part of you knew it was required for you to heal," she said. "You did it because it was necessary, and you couldn't think much beyond that." His hands moved on her bottom, palming her buttocks. She quickened, tightening her vaginal muscles around him.

"It was like living in hell."

She blinked at his stark, raw confession. He'd never described it so blatantly before. He groaned in agonized pleasure and moved her on his cock. A muscle twitched in his tense cheek. "Tell me I never have to go back, and I'll believe you," he said between a tight jaw.

"Never," she whispered fiercely. "You walked through that hell for us, but now it's over. We're together. For always." She lifted herself and then sunk him deep, squeezing him tight. "Believe it, Ian. We're *exactly* where we belong."

Keep reading for an excerpt
from the next novel by Beth Kery

SINCE I SAW YOU

Available May 2014 from Berkley Books

Part of the Because You Are Mine series
Because You Are Mine
When I'm With You
Because We Belong

in Soong hurried down the sidewalk, her face coated in a thin layer of perspiration overlaid with an autumn mist. Damn this fog. There hadn't been an available taxi for blocks, and she'd finally ended up just walking the three quarters of a mile from Noble Towers to the restaurant. Her feet were killing her after a long day's work and rushing in high heels. To make matters worse, her hair would be a disaster from the humidity. She imagined herself at ten or eleven years old and her grandmother standing over her wielding a comb and a hair straightener like a warrior's weapons.

"You got this hair from your mother," Grandmamma would say, her mouth grim as she dove into her straightening task. Lin had been left in little doubt as to what her grandmother thought of the potential threat of her mother's rebellious streak surfacing in Lin herself. According to Grandmamma, hair was like everything else in a person's character: something to be conquered and refined by smoothing and polish.

Lin plunged through the revolving doors of the restaurant and paused in the empty foyer, straining to calm her breathing and her throbbing heart. She despised feeling flustered, and this situation called for even more than her usual aplomb.

By the time she entered the crowded, elegant restaurant, she'd repinned her waving, curling hair and used a tissue to dry her damp face. She immediately spotted him sitting at the bar. He was impossible to miss. For a stretched few seconds, she just stared. A strange mixture of anxiety and excitement bubbled in her belly.

Why hadn't Ian mentioned that his half brother looked so much like him?

She soaked in the image of him. He was very good looking, even if that frown was a little off-putting. He wore a dark blue shirt; the rich brown of the rugged suede jacket brought out the russet highlights in his hair. Kam Reardon didn't know it—and she'd never tell him—but she herself had picked out the clothing he wore. It'd been part of the mission Ian had assigned her to make his half brother presentable for a potentially lucrative business deal here in Chicago. Ian had suggested a new wardrobe for his trip to the States. Kam had grudgingly agreed after some skillful nudging on Ian's part, but insisted upon paying. It'd been Lin who had actually chosen the items, however, and sent the articles to Aurore Manor in France. It warmed her to see him wearing the garments, firsthand evidence that he'd considered the clothing suitable to his taste.

Her clothing selection hadn't done much to help Kam blend in, however. He was too large for the delicate chairs lined up at the super sleek, minimalist bar. He stuck out like a sore thumb in the trendy establishment, all bold, masculine lines and unrelenting angles.

No . . . not like a sore thumb, Lin amended. More like a lion that found itself in the midst of a herd of antelope. His utter stillness and watchful alertness seemed slightly ominous amidst the sea of idly chatting, well-heeled patrons.

Suddenly, she realized his gaze had locked on her from across the crowded dining area.

"Hello, beautiful. We have your table waiting," someone said.

Lin blinked and pulled her gaze off the man who was a stranger to her, and yet wasn't; her boss's infamous half brother—the wild man she'd been sent to tame.

She focused instead on Richard St. Claire's smiling face. Richard was a neighbor, friend, and the manager of the restaurant, Savaur. He owned the world-renowned establishment with his partner, chef Emile Savaur. Lin was a regular here.

She returned Richard's greeting warmly as they hugged and he kissed her on the cheek. "Can you hold the table for just a moment, Richard? My dinner companion is waiting at the bar. I'd like to go and introduce myself," Lin said, turning as he began to remove her coat.

"Mr. Tall, Dark, and Scowling?" Richard muttered under his breath as he draped her coat elegantly over his forearm, looking amused. He noticed her surprised glance as she faced him again. How did Richard know her dinner companion was the man at the bar? "You mentioned you were having dinner with Noble's half brother on the phone when you made the reservations. I noticed the resemblance. I can't wait to hear the story behind this little scenario," Richard said with a mischievous glance in Kam's direction. "He's like Ian Noble posing as a Brazilian street fighter."

Lin stifled a laugh at the apt description. "He's actually cleaned up quite nicely. Not six months ago, the people from the village near where he lived thought him homeless and mad. And he's not Brazilian, he's French," she said very quietly, dipping her head to hide her moving mouth. She smoothed her expression, acutely aware of Kam's sharp gaze still cast in her direction.

"I know—the accent. Not that he said much. He's been sitting at the bar looking like he's been chewing nails for the past ten minutes. Victor doesn't know if he's scared to death of the man or in love with him," Richard murmured, referring to the bartender serving Kam. Indeed, Victor was surreptitiously studying the tower of whiskered, glowering brawn seated at the bar with a mixture of wariness and stark admiration as he dried a glass.

Lin threw her friend an amused glance and walked over to meet Ian's brother. Kam was one of the few people seated at the teak bar, a half-full glass of beer in front of him.

"I'm so sorry for being late. Work was crazy, and there wasn't a single available cab to be found when I finally did get away. You must be Kam. I'd have recognized you anywhere," she said when she approached him, smiling in greeting. "Ian never told me how much you two resembled one another."

He turned slightly in his chair, giving her an unhurried once-over. She remained completely still beneath his perusal, her expression calm and impassive. Inwardly, she squirmed. Ian had also failed to warn her of the fact that Kam Reardon oozed raw sex appeal.

Although it couldn't have been any more than a second that he studied her, it felt like minutes before he finally met her stare. She recognized the sharp edge of male appreciation in his eye. A strange sensation rippled down her spine. Was it excitement? Or that uncommon brand of lust that strikes like lightning during a rare, uncommon rush of attraction. His face and form were similar to Ian's, although up close, there were notable differences: the nose was slightly larger, the skin swarthier, the mouth fuller, the hair not quite as dark, with hints of russet in the thick waves. Ian would certainly never go into public with a day-and-a-half growth of dark stubble on his jaw. Although Kam's clothing was suitable for the restaurant, it was far more casual than Ian's typical Savile Row suits. It was like seeing Ian in some kind of magical mirror—a shadowy, savage version of her debonair boss. Kam's silvery gray eyes with the defining black ring around the iris were certainly strikingly unique. Or at least the effect they had on Lin was.

"Ian probably never noticed our similarity. He's never seen me without a full beard," he replied. Another stark difference. Much like her grandmamma, who had learned English in Hong Kong,

Ian's accent was all crisp, cool control. This man's French-accented, rough voice struck her like a gentle, arousing abrasion along the skin of her neck and ear.

She put out her hand. "I'm Lin Soong. As you probably already know, I work for Ian. I can't tell you what a pleasure it is to finally meet you."

He took her hand but didn't shake it, merely grasped it and held on. His hand was large and warm, encompassing her own. The pad of his forefinger pressed lightly against her inner wrist.

"Does my brother make a habit of overworking minors?" he asked.

She flushed, the temporary trance inspired by his voice and touch fracturing. She knew she looked younger than her age, especially with her makeup faded from the mist and her hair curling around her face like a dark cloud. Besides, she *was* young for the position she held at Noble Enterprises as Ian's right-hand woman.

"I'm hardly a minor. Ian seems to find me capable enough for all my duties," she said smoothly, arching her brows in a mild, amused remonstrance.

"No doubt." His finger moved on her wrist and she suddenly pulled her hand away, afraid he'd notice the leap in her pulse.

"Actually, I'm twenty-eight," she said.

"Isn't that young for the position you hold at Noble Enterprises? Ian can't seem to function without you," he said, studying her narrowly.

"You might say I was groomed for the role. My grandmother was the vice president of finance for Noble. She'd get me summer internships during college and graduate school."

"And one day you ended up in Ian's lap?" he asked, silvery-gray eyes gleaming with what appeared to be a mixture of humor and interest. "Does your grandmother still work for Ian?"

"No. She passed two years ago this Christmas."

Her breath stuck when he reached around her waist. Was he going to *touch* her? She jumped slightly when a chair leg made a scraping sound on the wood floor. She exhaled when she realized he was pulling back on the chair next to him so that she could sit.

"Our table is actually ready," she explained.

"I'd rather eat at the bar."

"Of course," she said, refusing to be flustered. She set down her briefcase in the seat next to her and reached for her chair. A frown creased his brow and he stood. "Thank you," she murmured, surprised when she realized he'd grudgingly stood to seat her. Maybe he wasn't so rough around the edges after all.

"You're a cool one," he said as he sat back down next to her, his jeans-covered knees brushing her hip and thigh.

"What do you mean?"

He shrugged slightly, his gaze glittering on her face. "I thought you'd take offense to sitting at the bar."

"Don't you mean you'd hoped I would?" she challenged quietly. She transferred her gaze to Victor when the bartender approached, speaking before Kam had a chance to refute her. "Victor often serves me at the bar when I stumble in after a long day's work. He takes good care of me," she said.

"It's always a pleasure. The usual, Ms. Soong?" Victor asked.

"Yes, thank you. And will you please let Richard know he can give our table to someone else?"

Victor nodded, giving Kam a nervous, covetous glance before he walked away.

"Goodness, what did you do to that poor man?" Lin asked in a hushed tone, leaning her elbows against the bar and meeting Kam's gaze with amusement.

"Nothing. I asked him to give me a beer."

"That's all?" Lin asked doubtfully.

He shrugged unconcernedly. "Maybe not. Might have said something like, 'Forget all that crap and just give me a damn beer.'" He noticed her upraised eyebrows. "He was trying to get me to buy some fancy drinks and two bites of food and a sprinkle on a plate."

"Imagine him suggesting you eat and drink in a restaurant."

Much to her surprise, he grinned full out, white teeth flashing against his dark features. "The guy's got balls, doesn't he?"

Lin forced herself to look away from the magnetic sight of Kam Reardon's smile. It was a tad devilish, no doubt, and full-out sexy, but there was also just a hint of shyness to him in that moment, as if his interest was unexpectedly piqued by meeting her. And like her, he hadn't been prepared for it. It was potent stuff, to be sure. Perhaps she could forgive Ian for not giving her warning about his half brother, but surely his new wife, Francesca—as a fellow female—should have hinted at something that might prepare her for the impact of Kam.

"Most people who belly up to the bar expect a friendly chat with the bartender," she chided lightly.

"I'm not most people," he said, watching her as he also placed his elbows on the bar and leaned forward, matching her pose.

"Yes, I think we've established that," she murmured humorously over her shoulder. They sat close. Much closer than they would have if they'd been seated at a table. Their elbows touched lightly, their poses intimate. Too much so for having just met. She instinctively glanced downward, taking in his crotch and strong, jeans-covered thighs.

Heat flooded her cheeks. She fixed her gaze blindly on the glassware hanging behind the bar.

She silenced the voice in her head telling her to lean back and gain perspective. Lin Soong didn't hunch down over bars flirting with rugged, sexy men. His face fascinated her, though. She wanted to turn again and study it, the desire an almost magnetic pull on her attention. And . . . she could smell him. His scent was simple; soap and freshly showered male skin. No, it *should* have been simple, but was somehow light-headedly complex. Delicious.

"I wasn't trying to insult you by saying I'd rather eat at the bar," he said, referring to her earlier subtle jibe that he'd intended to offend her. "I'm more comfortable here. I don't like fancy places like this," he said, glancing around without moving his head.

"I'm sorry," she said, meaning it. "I wasn't trying to be pretentious by asking you to meet here. Even though Savaur might seem upscale, I consider it the opposite. It's almost like a second home for me. I'm good friends with the owners—they're neighbors of mine, in fact."

"Was that one of them who you were laughing with—presumably over me—when you walked in?"

She stared at him, aghast. "We weren't *laughing* at you."

He arched his brows and gave her a bland look, as if to say it was all the same to him if they were or they weren't. Lin had the distinct impression his impervious manner wasn't for show. He really must have built up a thick skin living like an outcast for all those years. She couldn't help but admire his nonchalance about what other people thought of him. It wasn't a thing she encountered much in this day and age. His concise observance mixed with his cool indifference and flagrant good looks left her unsure of what to say.

"I'm sorry if I gave the impression I was laughing. I was—*am*, I mean—very eager to meet you." She cleared her throat. It suddenly struck her that they were speaking in hushed, intimate tones. She was glad to see Victor appear with the menus. "May I order for you?" she asked Kam politely. She saw his flashing glance and knew she'd made another misstep.

"Which do you think? That I don't know how to place an order myself, or that I can't read?"

"Neither, of course. I was thinking of what you insinuated earlier about tiny servings. I promise you, I won't order two bites and a sprinkle on a plate. Emile Savaur knows how to feed a hungry Frenchman. He and Richard are often hungry Frenchmen themselves, after all."

She took his silence and slight shrug as agreement and ordered them both the steak au poivre.

"So Ian sent you to make me feel more comfortable for this experiment of his?" he asked once Victor had walked away, his low, vibrating voice amplifying the tickling sensation on her bare neck. Again, she experienced that warm, heavy feeling in her lower belly and sex.

She blinked. What was wrong with her? This whole experience was bizarre. It was his similarity to Ian that was setting her off-balance. She'd trained herself long ago to remain cool and professional with Ian Noble . . . even if in her deepest, secret self, her feelings for Ian were far from aloof. Only she herself knew that particular truth, however, although a couple friends seemed to have guessed at it, much to her discomfort. She struggled to focus her errant thoughts. She would have defended herself better if she'd known how potentially volatile this situation would be.

"Is that what you call it? An experiment?" she asked crisply.

"I could come up with a more accurate description, but I'm not sure you'd like it."

She laughed softly, glancing around when Victor set a glass of claret on the bar in front of her, along with some ice water. She thanked Victor and took a sip of wine, glancing sideways at Kam as she set down her glass. "I hope you don't mind Ian suggesting that we meet. Work together."

His gaze dropped slowly over her face, neck, and lower. "Now that I see you, I'm having less of a problem with the idea."

She chuckled and shook her head, trying to shake off the spell again. Flirtation, she was used to. But who would have thought the alleged "wild" man's subtle sexual advances would be so appealing? The way Francesca and Ian had described Kam, she'd thought he'd be some kind of social misfit. True, he was raw and primal, but he was hardly illiterate.

And those eyes packed a precise, powerful sexual wallop.

Of course there had never been any doubt that Kam was a genius. What he'd pulled off in that makeshift, underground lab in northern France was nothing short of revolutionary. The question at hand was whether Kam would do middling well with his brilliant invention or create an empire. Ian believed he had the potential to do the latter. Ian's concern was that Kam would alienate every potential opportunity for capital and expansion on his climb up the ladder.

"Ian explained to me that you were doubtful about the idea of selling your biofeedback timepiece to the luxury watch industry. He thought I might be of some help in . . ."

"Making this whole ridiculous thing more palatable?" he murmured when she hesitated. She'd been trying to carefully choose her words. The truth was, Ian had taken her into his confidence, explaining that he hoped Lin could alleviate his brother's doubts about the advisability of selling his revolutionary medical timepiece to the high-end watch industry. Kam had already sold his patent to one of the pharmaceutical giants for millions of dollars, his contract calling for an exclusivity clause that prevented him from selling to other pharmaceutical companies. But there was no prohibition from selling to unrelated industries. Ian thought that one of the sophisticated, groundbreaking mechanisms Kam had invented—a biofeedback timepiece that could do everything from tell time to send warnings for an impending heart attack to signaling to a woman when she was ovulating—would also be a smash hit in the luxury watch business. Lin happened to agree. The problem was, Kam's attitude was condescending about the industry.

To say the least.

Pair Kam's scorn about cutting a deal with one of the luxury watch companies with his rough manners, and it was a recipe for a business disaster. Thus the reason Ian had called in Lin to smooth over Kam's jagged edges and present him in the best light possible to the interested buyers gathering in Chicago for a series of business dinners, presentations, and meetings.

Problem was, according to Ian, Kam would likely be insulted if he knew Ian had sent Lin to polish up a man who had once been considered an intimidating, homeless vagrant.

"Why do you find the idea of selling your invention to a high-end watch company ridiculous?" she asked.

"Look at me. I'm not interested in that world. I don't cater to fashion or rich bastards," he responded, holding her stare. "It's a waste. At least in my dealings with the pharmaceutical companies, I shared the commonality of science. Medicine."

She considered him somberly before she responded.

"Yes. I understand you hold degrees in both biology and engineering from Imperial College, and that you received an esteemed scholarship to medical school there, as well. I can understand how the world of luxury fashion might seem beneath your scholarly interests, but—"

She paused when he gave a bark of harsh laughter. "I'm no academic, either. I never finished my residency. I'm not being highbrow by saying I don't want to work with the fashion industry." He took a swig of his beer and set the glass back on the counter with a thud. "I just think the whole business is a waste of time, no pun intended. No offense intended, either," he tagged on sheepishly with a flashing glance in her direction.

"None taken," Lin replied evenly. "Of course you have to feel comfortable with such a large business venture. I think you might be underestimating the business savvy and brilliance of some of the leaders of these companies. Watchmaking is an ancient art that has also been a forerunner in miraculous advances in technology."

"There isn't a damn thing those suits can teach me about watch-making."

She absorbed his disdainful yet supremely confident manner. From what she'd learned from Ian, he wasn't bluffing. When it came to both mechanical devices and the biological rhythms of the human body, Kam Reardon was a veritable Da Vinci.

"This could be a very lucrative venture for you," she reasoned.

He gave her a gleaming sideways glance, his eyes going warm as they wandered over her face. "How lucrative?"

"Twenty, possibly a hundred times more than the deal you cut with the pharmaceutical company for your device. Ian believes your invention deserves all the acknowledgments it can get. He wants you to have as much security as possible."

Kam rolled his eyes and exhaled with a hiss. "He's known we're related for less than a year and already he's pulling a big brother act on me."

Lin smiled. "I hadn't realized he was the elder of the two of you."

"By a year and a half. Lucien is the oldest of us all. Six weeks ahead of Ian," Kam said, referring to a third half brother, Lucien Lenault. She noticed him studying her face with a narrow-eyed gaze. Instinctively, she knew he wondered if Ian had told her about the background of their common heritage.

"Ian has explained to me about Trevor Gaines being his, Lucien's, and your biological father," she said without flinching.

"Did he also tell you that dear daddy was a fucked-up son of a bitch?" he asked with harsh flippancy before he took a swallow of beer. *Too* flippant. She sensed the edge of anger beneath his unconcern this time. His description of Trevor Gaines was apt. The French aristocrat had been a sick SOB who got his thrills from impregnating as many women as he possibly could, whether by seduction, rape, or other unsavory means. Using those means, he'd gotten Lucien's, Ian's, and Kam's mothers pregnant in a close span of time. There had been other victims, too. The newly discovered knowledge had nearly sent Ian over the edge when he'd learned of it last year. This much she knew: Kam came by his bitterness toward his father honestly.

"He told me," she replied simply.

His tense expression relaxed somewhat when she offered no false platitudes in regard to the unthinkable crimes of the man who had created him.

"I haven't got much use for all the money I received from the pharmaceutical deal," he said, turning the subject. "What am I supposed to do with a hundred times that amount?"

"Ian and Lucien both seem to think the capital will help you to build more advanced laboratories and equipment. You could potentially create a lasting company that could revolutionize the watchmaking and medical biofeedback industries and provide thousands of jobs. Ian has a lot of faith in your brilliance, Kam. But in the end, if *you* can't think of anything you'd do with the capital from another sale, then this entire conversation is pointless."

His nostrils flared slightly as they faced off in the silence. Just beneath his obstinacy and wariness, she sensed he was listening.

"I've arranged meetings with three watch companies," Lin said, sitting back slightly so that Emile could arrange bowls of his steaming, fragrant onion soup before them. "I can tell you firsthand that every one of my contacts is far from thinking it's a *waste of time*, as you put it. They're extremely interested in your product. Fascinated, in fact, although I get the feeling they're withholding judgment until they see it firsthand."

"And meet me," Kam muttered.

She met his stare calmly. "And meet you, yes. Thank you, Victor," she said when the bartender handed her a black napkin. He knew the white ones left lint on her black skirts. She was in the process of smoothing the napkin over her thighs when she glanced sideways.

Kam's gaze was on her lap. As if he'd noticed her sudden stillness, his stare flicked up to her face. The heat she saw in his eyes seemed to set a spark to her flesh. Excitement bubbled in her, the strength of her reaction surprising her. She couldn't deny it, this unexpected rush of lust. It was powerful stuff.

It *was* because he looked so much like Ian that she was having this reaction. It must be that. The forbidden held the power to tantalize. God knew there was nothing more taboo than her boss. Ian

Noble was the one thing she couldn't have . . . could *never* have. Even if he was the only man she'd ever loved, he was off-limits to her, now more than ever since Francesca Arno had entered his life.

But his newly discovered brother wasn't off-limits, Lin acknowledged as his hot, gray-eyed stare lowered to her mouth and she felt her nipples tighten. No, Kam Reardon appeared to be about as available as she wanted him to be.

About the Author

Beth Kery lives in Chicago where she juggles the demands of her career, her love of the city and the arts, and a busy family life. Her writing today reflects her passion for all of the above. She is the *New York Times* and *USA Today* bestselling author of *Because You Are Mine*. Find out more about Beth and her books at BethKery .com or Facebook.com/Beth.Kery.